BIRDS OF THE AIR

Birds of the Air

A NOVEL BY

Ray Salisbury

ANDRE DEUTSCH

First published 1988 by
André Deutsch Limited
105-106 Great Russell Street, London WC1B 3LJ

British Library Cataloguing in Publication Data

Salisbury, Ray
  Birds of the air.
  I. Title
  823'.914[F]   PR6069.A474/

  ISBN 0 233 98187 X

Phototypeset by Falcon Graphic Art Ltd
Wallington, Surrey
Printed in Great Britain by
Ebenezer Baylis & Son Limited, Worcester

In memory of Fanny Gardener

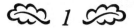

*T*hey'd called me for tea but they couldn't find me. I'd never been able to climb the laurel trees before because there were no branches low down and I couldn't scramble my legs up through my arms. I'd got up today by working my feet against one stem and my body against another and now I had a nice place to sit with my feet resting over a flat branch and my head just sticking out of the top of the hedge so that I could see where the crisp curls of last year's lilac had fallen and been trapped in the lacy patterns of the spiders' webs.

'C'mon, my duck. Tea's ready.' That was Nan again. Mum had called me first but I'd thought it was a trick because she'd been whispering to Michael down on the bricks below me and then he'd made a great splashing noise while he and my other cousins washed their hands in Grandad's old enamel bowl by the back door.

'Oh well, we'll just have to get on without you, Simon.' She didn't sound angry so it might still be a trick. The back door closed. P'raps they were watching for me to find out where I was hiding.

I settled myself against the stem but I couldn't see down to the back door without making the branches rustle. The sun made bluey flashes off the silver webs and I closed my eyes and let the warmth settle on my eyelids. It was always fine for Nan and Grandad's birthday in April and they had one big party and one big cake and Nan always made Grandad sit next to her and put his best suit on. At first there had only been me and the grown-ups but then my cousin Michael had grown up a bit and now he'd got his brother Jonathan and my other cousin, Stephen, was old enough to play but his sister was just a baby. They'd spelt Stephen's name with a 'ph' so that we didn't confuse it with Uncle Steven who'd got shot down in the war but people still seemed to stop and

1

think about it when they said it. I hadn't seen much of him until he was about five. At Christmas and birthdays we played ghosties around the laurel bushes and the gooseberry patch and down the side path, if it wasn't raining, but Jon got scared if I jumped out on him with my coat over my head so I'd started to hide and they had to find me. P'raps they *had* gone in for tea.

I eased myself forward and looked down but the bricks at the back were empty and there was nobody in the back garden or round by the sawing horse. Grandad's shed door was hanging open. The door had never fitted properly since Dad and Grandad'd first built it when Dad gót home from the POW camp and he'd said it was too much like building bloomin' railways. I could look right down at the pile of logs stacked inside. The pile was higher than me when I was standing next to it but now it looked flat to the ground. I could see right over the roofs of the barns in Brindle's field behind Grandad's hedge to our bungalow and the thin dark line of trees where Town Lane cut across the fields to the Westerton Road. Back behind me the roof of our village school poked up above the bushes in Nurse McLaine's garden and now Easter was over I wished it would be the summer holidays so that I could be ten and move up out of Mr Wade's class. I'd never been up this high in the bushes before and the black ribbon of Common Woods spreading out beyond the church looked even further away than when I used to walk up there with Grandad before Dad came home. The higher up you went – I looked down towards the back door but there was nobody about – the smaller things looked. The whole of our village was like the place Gulliver went to when Grandad took me to the top of the belfry and they said there was going to be a pylon at the Festival of Britain that would be the tallest building in London but Mr Wade didn't know if you were allowed up there and he certainly wasn't having me swarming about all over it and getting into mischief.

'Simon!' A match struck. That'd be Grandad out for a smoke. 'Come on, else you'll be for it.'

'Grandad?'

'Where are you?'

'Up here, Grandad.'

'Ah.' He moved in through the opening in the laurels where I'd had my camp when I lived here with him and Nan and I picked his face out through the twigs looking up at me. 'How'd you get up there, Simon?'

'Climbed, Grandad. They couldn't find me.'

'I'm not surprised. Didn't break any branches off, did you?'

'No, Grandad.'

He stood back and I could see him blowing dust off his shirt sleeves. 'Well, come on down and be careful you don't get green all over you. They're on the trifle now and there'll be hell to pay if you're not there when they come to blow those bloomin' candles out.'

Nan's house always smelt of oil cloth and lavender now they'd stopped using the oil lamps and she'd found that the smell of moth-balls set off her tickly cough. Grandad had grown a lavender bush at work over at Mrs Evans's garden especially for her and he used to bring the flowers home for her in his pockets when they went to seed and do them up in a little khaki canvas bag in the shed and stitch across the top with the big needle from his survival kit he'd kept over from when he was in Mespot in the first war. He said there were lots of things in there he wouldn't want to be without and that's why he kept them safe out in the shed. I'd only found a few buttons and a couple of medals and a ten packet of Turf with five in and some bits of cloth and some cottonwool and an empty tin when I went through it. Maybe it had a secret flap. And he had a cigar box with a—

'Well, sit down, m'duck.'

I squeezed between the sideboard and the back of Michael's chair. Grandad and Uncle Edward and Uncle Roger were sitting on the old sofa and they had to stretch to reach the table and forward so that they were out of the way of the cuckoo clock's striking chain. Nan and Old Gran were on either side of the range because they couldn't stand the heat on their backs and Mum sat between them with a tea towel over the back of her chair to stop the varnish blistering.

3

Aunty Sarah and Aunty Doreen were always up by the window because they were careful not to knock the flowers off Nan's cactus and Dad sat by me in case I got into mischief. There wasn't really room for Stephen and Jonathan so they squeezed up in the corner and ate their tea off the tray of the high-chair and they'd put Rachel upstairs with the coats in her carry-cot.

'And where in heaven's name have you been, Simon?'

'Shift up a bit, Michael.'

Dad heard me and Uncle Edward stopped talking.

'Are you listening to me, Simon? Didn't you hear me calling you?'

'Thanks, Nan.' I took my cup of tea carefully without spilling any in the saucer. 'No, Mum . . . well I did, but I thought it was a trick to find out where I was.'

'Well, Michael and Stephen understood and even little Jonathan.' Mum had her pretty green frock on that was tight at the top and came in at the waist and her red hair was a mass of waves like a tall fur hat.

'Oh leave it, Ina. He goes as deaf as a post when it suits him.' Dad poured salt on the side of his plate and jabbed a stick of celery into it. 'This isn't a patch on home grown, Dad.'

'Didn't get mucky out there with Simon, did you, lovey?'

'No, Mummy.' Michael lifted the tablecloth so that Aunty Sarah could see his knees.

Uncle Edward wiped the corners of his mouth with his pocket handkerchief and started to talk to Dad and Grandad and Uncle Roger again and Nan and Mum and Aunty Sarah and Aunty Doreen passed bowls-full of trifle about in all directions working out who wanted it with custard and fruit but no sponge or no custard but with cream on top and then they all stopped when they couldn't remember which was Grandad's because he didn't mind the skin off the custard and Mum'd put it on upside down. When they got them sorted out they found there was one over.

'Should've thought you'd've learnt to reckon by now, Fran, with all those years up at the post office.'

'Hush, Mum.' Nan was counting up the people against the

number of bowls but she stopped and looked at Old Gran, and said, 'Blessed silly!' and then she went round the table again. 'It's Simon.' .

'Ha—ugh!' I swallowed cold toast sideways and coughed.

'Not across the table, Simon.' Mum leant over and dusted the toast crumbs off the back of Uncle Edward's hand.

'It's Simon. I counted him twice.'

'See what a performance you've caused, Simon. Oh dear, oh dear.'

'That was clever, Fran.' Grandad sat back and twiddled the twisty end of his moustache.

'Especially as he wasn't here at all.' Old Gran was bending forward cutting the stone out of a cherry.

'Well, I counted him in and then I counted his empty chair. Must've done.' Nan dumped the bowl down in front of me and I held my breath to stop coughing. 'And whatever are you all ganging up on me for. And on my birthday as well and . . .'

There was a white crease running down the tablecloth and it disappeared under the red glass chutney jar and I could hear Dad picking at his thumb. When I looked up and forced my eyebrows down at the same time it was like looking out of a cave. Michael was doing it as well.

'We weren't ganging up on you, Fran.'

'Lot of silly nonsense.'

'S'sh, Mum,' Grandad said between his teeth to Old Gran and Dad whispered 'Why the devil didn't you go and get him, Ina?'

Nan calmed down after Grandad kissed her and said he prayed they'd have many more happy christ—birthdays together and Aunty Sarah said Mrs Flynn down the road from her was thrilled with the little matinée coat Nan'd knitted Jonathan and he'd grown out of and I said 'yes please' I'd like another helping of trifle.

'Right then. Shall I set fire to that there cake?' Uncle Edward flicked his silver lighter and flashed the flame from candle to candle until it got so hot that he had to wave it around to cool and suck the knuckle of his thumb.

Grandad pulled a lighted candle out of the cake and lit the

rest off it. 'That's the way to do it.' He said it like Mr Punch and Nan told him to sit down and stop getting candle grease all over the tablecloth.

'That looks nasty, Edward. You sure you don't want me to put some boracic on it?'

'No thank you, Sarah.' Uncle Edward was looking at me and I wondered if he was angry with me for laughing and slurping my trifle when Grandad talked like Mr Punch.

'Well, are we going to blow 'em out or sing first?' Uncle Roger was feeling in the pocket of his brown sports jacket for his cigarettes: he and Grandad usually bolted for the back door straight after tea.

'Silly Roger. You have to blow them out after.' Aunty Doreen nudged him and made a giggling sound.

Old Gran made out she was searching for cherry stones in her trifle but I could see she was looking up. 'Well, you'll have to put a spurt on. They're melting.'

'Oh my giddy aunt, so they are!' Nan shot up out of her wicker chair.

I nodded at Michael and took a good blow at the four in the corner that had been lit first and were smoking and Michael puffed as well and the rest of them sang 'Happy birthday to you' jumping from word to word like spots of water dancing on a hot plate.

Nan sank back and covered her eyes and said 'Thank you' and then she made Grandad open the window to let the smoke out while Mum and Aunty Sarah cut slices off the birthday cake and handed them round.

We all had to sit still for ten minutes to let our tea settle while the ladies cleared away and washed up and the men went into the front room. We sat back as far as we could into the old sofa and played measuring legs. Jon's feet only reached as far as my knees and Michael's and Stephen's legs were about six inches shorter than mine. Then we played trapping each other's legs until Nan told me to sit still or I'd burst the springs through the settee.

Aunty Sarah washed and Mum and Aunty Doreen wiped up and Nan put away because she knew where everything went. Old Gran had found the apron with the frayed edge she'd been wanting to darn behind the woodbox and she was trying to get Nan to remember what'd happened to her needlework bag.

'And somebody's picked up my handkerchief as well. Can't leave a blessed thing lying a—'

'Have you looked in your hair net?' Nan's voice came up from under the table where she was bent double putting the plates away.

Michael and Stephen started to laugh but I'd seen Old Gran's face change as she felt under the elastic of her net. She'd put her pension money up there once and got upset when she thought she'd burnt it with some old letters and she'd been even more unhappy when she found it and we'd gone out into the garden together and she'd told me what a fearful thing it was to get old and useless.

'Well, Mum?' Nan stood up slowly as if bits of her back were slotting into each other.

Old Gran sat down in Grandad's big armchair and opened the Sunday newspaper across her knees. Outside the light was fading so that it looked all brown like an old-fashioned photograph and the church bell donged for the half past six service.

'I expect you'll be having a special service here for Easter, Ina?'

'Oh, I shouldn't be surprised, Sarah. But I don't suppose we'll go. They insist on parading all out round by the fields and Pop will keep chanting the prayers and he's got no singing voice at all.'

'I'd quite like to go if I could find something decent to fit me.' Nan pulled her pinny round so that the band at the top came above her tummy. 'But then again I don't suppose I could stand all those people staring at me.'

'Well, it's not you they're giving thanks for.' Old Gran's lips hardly moved but she touched her fingers to her hair net.

'You should try having my nerves, Mum. It's not so very pleasant, I can tell you.'

'What about you then, Gran?' Aunty Doreen had pinched the last two saucers so that she could stand back and wipe them and keep an ear open for Rachel at the same time. 'Will you be going? You'd be nearly the oldest there.'

Old Gran's eyes lifted from the newspaper and I felt she

7

was looking back at things the others couldn't see. 'I would be the oldest. Old Mrs Wilkins can't get about much now. But it wouldn't be like the old days, Doreen. I remember the Harvest Festivals we used to have when—'

'We're talking about Easter, Mum.'

Old Gran stared back at the newspaper. 'I remember the Harvest Festivals when the Reverend Stuart was here. They did the state room out up at Greatwood House and we all met at different places along the way and got collected by pony and trap and—'

'Not at Easter, you didn't.'

'And the old duke used to dance with us all and they had proper music in those days – not some blessed band all vying with each other to see who can make the most noise.'

'They do make a pretty unholy racket, I grant you.' Nan took the last two saucers from Aunty Doreen but she gave one back to Aunty Sarah because it had a smudge of cream left on it. 'But I don't know as the duke made more fuss of you than he did of us when we were girls. And that was at Har—'

'Blessed flighty girls nowadays.' Old Gran crumpled the pages of the Sunday paper as she turned over from the fashion page. 'I'd take a strap to 'em. Anyway, my six months here'll be up by then and I'll get packed off up to Petersfield again.'

'Well, Rene's your daughter as well as me.' Nan's jaw was sticking out at Old Gran.

'Dear, oh dear!' Mum tutted and flicked her hair away from her eyes.

'Shall I tip this washing-up water out by the laurels, Mum?'

Nan relaxed back and folded the tea towel. 'Yes, please, Sarah. And then we can all go in the front room.'

They only used the front room for special occasions and Mum had come up yesterday to help Nan take the dust sheets off and fold them away and lay the fire. There seemed to be more of us every year. Uncle Edward was standing with his back to the fireplace and Dad and Uncle Roger were sitting in the easy chairs with the floral pattern covers by the side of the cupboard where Nan kept her wine glasses. Grandad usually sat in the big armchair in the hollow place at the side of the chimney where the stuffed sparrow-hawks stood on a mossy branch in their glass case. But he was kneeling down now blowing at the fire.

'You'll get great bags in the knees of those trousers kneeling about like that, Art.' Nan plumped a cushion up on the chair next to Grandad's. 'Whatever do you want to go—'

'I don't *want* to. I'm trying to get this ruddy fire to catch.'

'All right. No need to swear. Anyway, Ina and I laid it out all nicely so you only had to— Ooh, cor!' Nan had been sitting back into her chair but she started forward and then went stiff.

'Whatever's the matter, Mum?' Mum and Aunty Doreen and Aunty Sarah were wedged in on the sofa and they seemed to come up together like somebody picking up dominoes off a polished table.

'Cor. Something gave me the most fearful stabbing pain.' Nan held her bottom up off the seat and Mum darted forward and felt about under her and drew out a little cloth bag with flowers and suns embroidered on it.

'So that's where it went to.' Old Gran's crinkly, yellow arm reached out to Mum for her needlework bag.

'Cor, 's this what you sat on?' Mum held up Old Gran's silver bodkin and it glinted in the electric light like a fish hook.

'You'd better not've bent it, Fran.'

'Well, I'll go to . . .'

I could see Uncle Roger hiding his face behind his hand and Uncle Edward had been blowing and rubbing at his nose with his handkerchief and Dad was biting the inside of his lip. We'd been trying to get Miss Anderson to sit on a drawing pin at school for ages but she always saw it or it fell off or one of her pets moved it first.

'And you needn't think I can't see you sitting there smirking, Art.'

'I wasn't . . . argh!' Grandad coughed the way he did when he had bronchitis. 'Cor, blimey O'Riley! Bloomin' old wood. It doesn't seem to be drawing.'

9

'Ah well, Dad.' Uncle Edward gave his nose a last rub and arranged his hanky in his top pocket. 'You'll be needing a cowl. They had just the same trouble up at Truscott's. He's the new assistant golf pro at Greatwood, you know, Mum.'

'Oh really.'

'Yes. Smoke going all ways except up the chimney when they called me in. I had to go round and see him about one or two things anyway.'

'Never a moment's peace nowadays.'

Uncle Edward smiled down at Aunty Sarah. 'Yes . . . had to go there about one or two things anyway. But I got a couple of the men round first thing Monday morning and they soon got to the bottom of it.'

Uncle Roger started to say something about bottoms but Dad nudged him.

'Put a cowl on it and it was right as ninepence.'

Grandad was still on his knees but his face wasn't so red now.

'What's a cowl, Daddy?' Michael never seemed to worry about not knowing things. P'raps you didn't get moaned at for things like that at his private school.

'Little love.' Nan leant over and patted his knee.

'Hur-hrm!' Uncle Edward pursed his lips up at Nan and made a coughing noise so that Michael looked back at him. 'A cowl, Michael, is a square metal thing that goes on the top of the chimney and lets the smoke out without letting the wind rush down inside and blow it back into the room.'

'Be something if we could get some smoke out of this fire let alone up the chimney. Ruddy awful wood.'

'Art!'

'Sorry.'

'And when the wind blows' – Uncle Edward stepped a bit to one side so that Grandad had more room – 'the cowl swings round and makes air go up the chimney which draws the fire up and makes it burn. See Michael.'

Michael said he saw and Nan said it sounded just what they needed and Grandad said if the devil got his fuel from Cabby McAndrew's the fires of hell'd freeze over, and then he laughed and said maybe he'd leave it and try again later.

10

Jon was asleep now and he was dribbling. I wanted to go out to play but it was dark and the wind was blowing Grandad's apple trees about so that the branches went in all directions at once. Grandad'd told me once, when I was going to work with him, that we often got high winds in April and it blew the blossom off but sometimes it didn't and that's when we got a good crop of apples. Funny how the wind could blow all ways at once and if it was blowing against itself which way would the smoke go?

'Why didn't it smoke before then?' I hadn't thought I'd said it out loud until I saw they were all looking at me.

'What?'

'What's up, Mum?'

'It was you, Simon. You dreaming?'

'Dunno, Mum.'

'What were you saying, Simon?' Old Gran threaded her needle into her sewing bag and put her glasses down from her forehead on to her nose so that I could see she was looking at me.

'Well, Gran. It burned all right before and we never had anything on top.'

'So it did. P'raps it just needs cleaning.'

'Nonsense, Mum. We've only just got over having Mr Harmer in with sheets and brushes all over the place.'

'Good drop'a soot that, Edward. I'll let you have some for your celery.' Grandad tossed a sweet paper on to the sticks on the fire.

'And why doesn't the wind get sucked down as well as up?'

'Dear'o dear, Simon.' Mum was twisting her wedding ring round. 'I really don't know where he gets it from, Edward. I hope you're as inquisitive at school, Simon.'

'I expect it's the hot air, isn't it, Edward? Hot air rising?'

'That's the general principle, George.' Uncle Edward flexed his shoulders back and pulled a bit more of his shirt cuffs down to show his silver cuff links.

'And we'd be ever so grateful if you'd get it seen to.' Nan slid a cushion further up her back. 'Wouldn't we, Art?'

'Oh, yes. Spec so.'

'Well, you might sound a bit more enthusiastic.'

Grandad leant back on his knees the way he did when he

was resting from trimming the graves. 'I was just wondering why it's started smoking all of a sudden.'

The wind gusted up under the eaves and a loose tile on Mrs Simms's next door started to flap and they talked about how sad it would be if we had another rotten summer for the Festival of Britain. I watched a piece of wood smouldering for a long time and when it burst into flame it made a whoofing sort of bang that made Uncle Edward start forward and Uncle Roger reckoned it looked as if he'd got on the wrong end of Old Gran's bodkin. Grandad said Cabby'd slipped the odd bit of chestnut in with the wood and that's why it took so long to catch and popped about all over the place. The sparks exploded in different patterns and I could change the shapes of the patterns by closing my eyes tight and then opening them fast and I wondered if they'd still have the stoves going in our classrooms at school.

❧ 2 ❧

I hadn't got a clock in my bedroom and I didn't need one, especially on school mornings. There was a crack in the curtains where they met in the middle and when I could see the sun getting level with the ridge of Jimmy Phillips's bungalow roof I knew it was half past seven and getting on for summer and time to get up. Our rooster started crowing long before that and he woke the neighbours up so Dad had hung a sack of chicken meal from the roof where he stood so that when he flung his head back to crow he banged it and stopped. We'd crept up the garden to watch the first morning to see if it worked and when it did Dad said there were more ways of skinning a cat than choking him to death with strawberries. He wondered why I wasn't glad too and I said I was but really I didn't like him talking about killing cats because the Arnolds' cat next to Nan's had got an infection round her tail where her fur got clogged and they said she was dirty and took her to the vet and had her put down. She'd always been poking about in Nan's garden when I lived up there and she used to wait for me on my way to school and sometimes I gave her a bit of cheese and when I couldn't find the boys to play with she was always under Grandad's mock-orange blossom tree and I stroked her back and then she'd roll and I could tickle her tummy and she mewed as if she was talking to me.

'How's the enemy, my Ine?' The bed springs pinged in Mum and Dad's room.

'Nearly half past.'

'Better be seein' about it then.'

'S'pose so. Cuppa tea?'

'M'm. Please.'

Wonder if they'd buried her? Old Gran put flowers on great Grandad Grainger's grave when she was down here

13

and Grandad had a lot of graves he looked after for people and there were always wreaths and sprays round the stone with Uncle Steven's name on in the church. I'd've put orange blossom on her grave, if they'd let me, and birds' feathers because she liked birds. Funny she hadn't had a name. I could have called her Midnight or Charley if I'd thought about it. Too late now.

'Wake up, Simon. Oh you are awake.' Mum put my cup of tea with two biscuits in the saucer on the chair by my bed. 'Got to get you smart for school this morning.' She was rooting about in my drawers. 'Want to make a good impression on your first day of a new term, don't you?'

'Why, Mum?'

'Why? Well, because you do of course.' She folded my trousers on my bed and stood looking down at me. 'You want to do well with Mr Wade this term, don't you?'

'Will we have him for a whole year, Mum?'

'Yes, I suppose so.' She laid my socks and pants down by my trousers and bent the crooked collar of my shirt back. 'Don't you like Mr Wade?'

'No, Mum.'

'Why not, for heaven's sake?'

'Cos he shouts and bangs people on the head with his ruler and he never gives me a chance and—'

'All right, Simon. That's enough. It can't possibly be as bad as all that and you're going to have to buckle down to it anyway if you're not going to disappoint Nan and Grandad. Up you get now and wash and dress and hurry up for breakfast.'

We had lots of eggs now since we'd got three more pullets from Mr Jeyes' chicken farm. We'd gone up past the school and the Wobble fields by the village hall and I'd thought we were going to Cabby McAndrew's yard until Dad crossed over at Hanover Corner and went towards the lane to Hanover Park. There was a wide, boarded-up archway in the wall with double doors. I'd often seen it when I went with the boys to the park to look for jackdaws' nests in the old hollow chestnut trees. But there was a latch with a ring handle I hadn't noticed before in the doors and we'd gone through that. It was like stepping into a picture. I'd never thought about what was behind the wall. Woods, I'd supposed. But it was all laid out as a field that had been mown long by a thing on the back of a tractor. There were dozens of black chicken houses that looked like a photograph I'd seen in one of Grandad's magazines of an army camp taken from a plane and I wondered if Uncle Steven'd ever watched his bombs dropping down under him on to Germany.

'What the devil you dreamin' about now, Nip? Egg'll be cold.'

'What, Dad?'

'You 'eard. Wake up.'

'Can we go up the park an' look for jackies, Dad?'

'Dunno, Nip.' He dipped egg yolk in the salt at the side of his plate. 'Bit early yet I should think.'

'Bit early for what?' Mum'd made more toast.

'Oh, he's after a jackdaw. And look at all that toast, Ina. We'll never get through that lot in a month of Sundays.'

'Well, you might like it with some of that nice marmalade Mrs Norbitt made us. It ought to be eaten up.'

'Can we, Dad?'

'Oh surely not, Simon. They always come to a sticky end.'

'Dad?'

'Cor, blimey O'Riley, Nip.' Dad spread marmalade on a half slice of toast. 'I suppose so. But not yet.'

'When then, Dad?'

'Soon, Nip. Later on. Now eat that toast up and don't put so much butter on and get off to school.'

'And don't forget to try your best, Simon.'

'Yes, Mum.'

I stood outside the back door and zipped up my windcheater. I usually met Jimmy Phillips and Jerry Henry at the top of the Close on the way to school but they'd probably be talking about the holidays and that would make going back to school worse so I went down the back garden path towards the hedge to the field.

Dad had made a path around the chicken house with some flat white slabs that Grandad'd called wragstone when he was seeing what kind of a job Dad'd made of it when they

15

came down for Sunday tea, but they looked more like the marble they used in the churchyard and I knelt down and rubbed my hands over them to see if they were as cold as the gravestones.

Farmer Vine used to turn his cows out to graze in the back field but some men had separated it with a single strand of wire that gave us a shock when we touched it and it kept the cows up in the higher part towards the dell. The grass had grown long now and there were deep green circles that looked like the fairy rings in my book *One Magic Night* that Mum'd used to read to me when I went to see her at work at the Admiral's before Dad came back from the war. I'd always thought they were fairy rings but Geoff Gibbs'd laughed at me one day when we were playing wheelbarrow races and said they were nothing of the sort unless it was the fairies that made the pancakes and not the cows. I leant against the new fence post and pulled a strip of bark off it. The barbed-wire was gleaming blue steel and Grandad'd told me it got invented in the First World War. It was as tight as a bow string and I wondered why they'd put it up if the cows weren't coming down here any more. P'raps it was to make it more private. There was nobody about down by the entrance to the farm so I got between the strands and walked up the hedgerow at the bottom of the bungalow gardens.

Aunty Win was hanging her washing out and Mrs Latter-al next door was saying something about being out when the rent man called and I ducked down lower so that they wouldn't see me and think I was bird's-nesting. Mr Latter-al'd had a load of wood and he'd put some flat pieces over Flick Fenner's fence. Flick Fenner'd got married and sold his motorbike and Mum said I had to call him *Mr* Fenner now he'd settled down. He was building a shed: the four corner posts had been driven into the ground and an old door, with flaking green paint, hung between the doorposts and the cross bits had been nailed on. I bent my head down sideways. They didn't look straight and I wondered what he'd done with his white silk scarf he used to wear on his motorbike.

'What you up to, Simon?'

16

'Just going to school, Mrs Latteral.'

'Well, run along then, or you'll catch cold.'

My feet sloshed in my shoes and my trouser bottoms were soggy. A bramble from the hedge hooked in my shoe bag and I reached up to dislodge it so that it didn't pull a thread. The bramble sprang back and a cold pain shot through my thumb. The thorn had broken off black under the skin and the end was showing so I pulled at it with my teeth and spat it out. It felt like an injection and then it bled. I sucked the place and bit my teeth in against the ache. It tasted of iron and left my mouth gluey so I stroked my thumb in the wet grass and sucked the water.

'Started suckin' yer thumb then, Nipper?'

I tried to look up but the sun was in my eyes. 'No, course I haven't.' I bent to climb through the fence but my shoe bag slewed round and the barbed-wire caught on the back of my coat. 'Unhook us, can ya?'

Geoff Gibbs just stood there with his hands in his pockets chewing gum at me.

'Come on, Gibbser. Don't muck about.'

He pulled at the wire and it pinged free.

'Be careful. You'd better not've ripped it.'

'Shard-up! Else you'll be back through that fence again.' He was stocky, Grandad said, and he'd started putting Brylcreem stuff on his hair that smelt of lavender and cod-liver oil.

'What you doing up 'ere anyway?'

'Jus' bin up me uncle's with the club money. What you comin' up the back way for?'

'I dunno.' Water was oozing out of my lace holes. 'Just fancied a change.'

'Bleedin' mad you are and yer feet'er soakin'. C'mon, I'll race ya down to Gander's.' He set off before I was ready, looked back and then ran faster. I chased after him and my shoes made a noise like Mum unblocking our sink with her rubber plunger and my trouser bottoms thudded against my ankles as if they were fringed with lead. When I caught him up, he had his hands in his pockets again.

'D'you reckon he's gone yet?'

'Dunno.' Geoff stepped over the low box hedge and went

across Colin Gander's grass and peered in through his front-room window. 'Hang on. I'll go and see if he's in.'

I leant against the telephone box and let the back of my head rest against the glass. Up the road, past the Men's Club and Grandad's front garden, I could see the children filing in through the school gate. Most of the RAF kids from Tangmere who walked to school were there already but some who came on their bikes were still going by. They rode with their heads down so they didn't see me. Dave and John Harris passed with their sister in the middle but I didn't call out to them.

Geoff and Colin strolled out and went straight past me. 'Hey, we're late, you two.'

'Oh yeah. Better hurry up then,' and they ran off up the road together.

My feet fell flat on the pavement and the backs of my ankles hurt. It smelt dry and dusty as I passed the thick fir hedge around the cottage where the Smiths lived: old George and Bert looked small and bent – like the pictures in our history book about feudal times – when they went off to work on the farm, but they were spruce and scrubbed like dwarves in their tweed jackets – with the feathers in their darts sticking out of their top pockets – when they went to the Men's Club on a Friday night; and their sisters, Gert and Queenie, were sharp-faced and blue in their cardigans washing clothes in a tub by the back door and moaning at us for making a noise when we played here in the evenings. I crept by the dusty cobwebs around their gate that was grown over like a tunnel and stepped into the sunlight that flooded the pavement beyond their hedge. Mrs Ryall's gate was closed and the 'Beware of the Dog' sign had been painted again. The forecourt to the Men's Club had been cleaned from last night: the blobs of mud from the men's boots had brush marks on them where they'd stuck to the paving slabs when Mrs Norbitt had swept them. One of the thin metal strips on the iron fence at the bottom of Grandad's garden had come out of its socket. It was loose and I stood on it and bounced up and down and it bent. I looked up the garden half

18

expecting to see his head pop up from weeding behind some bushes and ask me what I was doing, but nothing moved. Up the side path the mock-orange tree was budding and a pair of goldfinches sat up in the top singing as if they were waiting for the leaves to come so that they could build their nest. They nested there every year and the Arnolds' cat used to sit under it and watch them with me. The tree was too thin to climb but once Grandad'd put his ladder up in the plum tree next to it so that I could see into the nest. The inside was woven out of moss and spiders' webs so that it looked like a bit of Old Gran's darning and Grandad'd said there were more wonderful things on earth than all the tea in China.

I walked on along the pavement to a place where there was a gap between the fruit trees up the long garden. Nan used to look out for me and wave when I first started school but the boys said it was sissy. She didn't do it now. P'raps she'd been waving at Mum. I hurried on past Nurse McLaine's thatched cottage to where some men from the Council were painting the school railings black and there was a new notice-board by the gate that said something about it being taken over by the Council, but they still called it 'Church of England'. Miss Anderson was on her step waving the infants in as if she was a policewoman moving the traffic on at the Greatwood Races. She was standing sideways on to me and her nose looked like a radish that'd grown half out of the ground against a stone and got bent.

'Hurry up to your classroom, Wilson. You're late.'

'Yes, Miss.'

'And don't give me any of your lip.'

I ran round to the side of her classroom and said 'huh' like Grandad did when Nan told him off for smoking. One of the old ladies from the alms houses was hanging her washing out. She tried to put a peg in without looking and missed and nearly fell over.

'What'd you say, Simon?'

'Nothing, Miss Turner.'

'Oh. Thought you did.'

*

We'd been mixed up like tiddlers in a jam jar, Grandad said. First we'd had Miss Anderson and then Mr Wade and then Mr Irvine, because a lot of new children from the camp had started and Mr Wade'd been in the army and knew how to cope with them and now that they'd got the age groups sorted out we were back with Wadey.

I stood in the cloakroom picking chips of paint off the door post for a few minutes and then I went in.

'You're late, Wilson.'

'Yes, sir.'

The camp kids had pinched all the seats at the back and Gibbser and Gander were on the far side by the window with most of the other boys from the village.

'Sit down then.'

Wadey stretched back the newspaper he'd been reading and threw it forward to the crease down the middle and folded it and sat on it. I pushed Gerald Mortlake over and slid in next to him. 'Right. Now we're all here . . . let's see what we've got.' He'd got some new glasses with thin silver rims soon after Denis Matthews'd knocked him out boxing and he was polishing them on his pullover. 'Not a lot.' He'd put his glasses on and was peering out at us like a blind bull. 'Pretty much the same as before in fact. Trouble-makers at the back.' Micky Leary and Paul Craven smirked at each other. 'Young ladies at the front' – giggles and stiff-necked looking to the front – 'layabouts on my left' – Geoff Gibbs's face relaxed from thinking he'd been left out of the trouble-makers – 'and the rest on my right. C'mon let's break you up.'

Some of us got up and shuffled about and one or two changed places but we finished up in more or less the same places.

Wadey looked along the two rows of girls at the front and muttered something about oil and water and flattened out a buff folder he'd had bulging from his coat pocket.

'I'm supposed to stream you.' He huffed on his glasses and rubbed them and put them back. 'But Lord knows how. If I do it on ability range your age'll be all over the place and if I do it on age half of you'll be bored and the other half lost.' He tapped his pencil on his teeth. 'You done fractions, Craven?'

'Yes, sir.'

'Wanna do 'em again?'

'No, sir.'

'What about you, Geer?'

'What, sir?' Maurice Geer'd been pushing a pen nib into a crack in the desk top and pinging it so that the shaft quivered.

'Fractions. You done fractions?'

'Oh . . . yeah. A bit.'

'Good. What about you, Henry?'

'No, sir.' Jerry half stood up as he answered.

'What, not at all?'

'No, sir.'

'H'm.' Wadey bit at his nail and then scratched his head. 'What about you, Mole. Oh no. Forget it.'

We giggled and Dicky Mole went red and his sister, who we called Granny, swung round and bared her teeth at Jimmy Phillips who she'd caught laughing.

'Got to get you past adding up first.' Wadey sighed. 'Hands up all those who've done decimals.'

We went on like this through fractions, long division, multiplication, who could read and who couldn't, who could read well and only a bit and who was under nine, over nine and under ten and over ten. Kenny Lane was dreaming and forgot to put his hand up at all and Mr Wade asked him if he was in the right class.

'I give up.' Wadey folded his glasses as if he had gloves on and put in his top pocket. 'I'm going to start you all off together and the fast ones can help the slow ones catch up and we'll have a test at half term and hope for the best—' Groans of 'not division again!' from the back and 'how'd you do fractions?' from the middle. '. . . and we'll all pull together,' Wadey yelled over the murmuring as if he was flattening out icing on a cake. 'Now I've got your books here.' He held up a tattered handful of exercise books. 'The horrors of which I'll go through with you individually while you write me a story about the most exciting thing that happened to you in the Easter holidays until playtime.'

I sat with the side of my head in the palm of my hand resting my elbow on the desk until my arm got stiff and then

21

I changed over. Scuds of sunshine filtered through the clouds across the desktops and we could hear Miss Anderson, in the next classroom, talking to the little ones. Whispering started at the back and spread. Wadey muttered 'quieten down' and it fell back, then started again louder. Paul Craven and David Harris were talking about a new kind of football boot that David's brother John was getting and then Gibbser told Kenny Lane to 'get out of it'.

Wadey slammed his pencil down and yelled at us. Then he went back to marking Michael Evenden's book and the whispering stayed at the level of a low hum. It was always the same. Just before playtime he'd get really wild and throw a lump of chalk at somebody but today we'd run out of things to talk about by playtime and had settled down to playing noughts and crosses and hangman and one or two even scratched about trying to remember what they'd done during the holidays.

I stood by the boys toilets at playtime and watched Cyril Tanner blowing into a pin prick in the silver top of a bottle of milk and shaking it and making it squirt up the backs of the girls' frocks and then Geoff Gibbs and Colin Gander wandered by with Kenny Lane and Derek Brown and Jimmy and Jerry behind them.

'What's up with Wadey, Mush?'

'Dunno.' Colin kicked at a loose flint.

'Looks a right fairy in those specs . . .'

I trailed off away from them across the small playground towards the air-raid shelter against Brindle's field where it backed on to Grandad's garden to look at the school rabbits. A couple of thrushes burst out of the bushes and I saw the prop of Nan's washing line push up over the top of the hedge. The line sagged where it showed through a gap between the honeysuckle and a fir tree and I picked out Nan's feet through the primula leaves. She had her fluffy blue slippers on and when she'd finished putting the washing out she'd go in and make a cup of Ovaltine and eat two digestive biscuits out of the tin with the geisha girl on it and then put the potatoes on low ready for Grandad coming home at twelve o'clock. If I'd still been living there I'd have sat and had a cup of tea with him in the woodshed after dinner and gone to work with him over at Mrs Evans's garden or walked down to the gate with him and stayed there playing until the children came out, wishing I was old enough to go to school.

I broke off a stem of dead nettle and poked it through the wire of the rabbits' cage. One of the grey rabbits came and nibbled it and then sat straight up and bounded back into his sleeping quarters.

'What'cha doin', Nipper?'

'Nothin'.'

'They ain't yours, ya know.' Maurice Geer'd been put in charge of the rabbits because his brother knew about breeding.

'Ain't your'n neither.'

'They are. More'n they're yours.'

I dropped my stick and edged along the muddy track between the fence and the back of the shelter and leant against the wall facing the big playground. 'I had a cat once.'

'Well, that's not a rabbit, is it?'

'S'pose not.'

Toby Little was standing on the compost heap over the far side of the school gardens and the little ones from Miss Anderson's class were trying to push him off. Jerry Henry and Jimmy Phillips were playing piggy-back by the roller and Gibbser and Gander were bunking Kenny Lane up a tree. The camp kids were playing football and the girls were practising netball. I tipped a worm cast over with the toe of my shoe and tried to pick it up but it was slimy and the bubbles of mud sank between my fingers. I wiped my hands in the grass.

'. . . and I think we'll have your boys on gardening one afternoon a week.'

I stayed bending down while Mr Miller and Wadey went by.

'. . . and think about some new arithmetic books as well.'

'Yes, Headmaster.'

Wadey's head only came up to Milly's shoulder and he looked even shorter as he bent forward to show how hard he was listening. Milly always wore heavy brown shoes that he

23

said he used for walking in Yorkshire, and grey trousers and a browny-green jacket. He had a different tie on every day and a coloured handkerchief to match in his top pocket. They were turning round so I slipped back down behind the shelter.

Somebody else was playing with the rabbits. She had a long grey mac on and ankle socks. She looked fat under her mac but her face was sharp like the queen's on a threepenny stamp.

'You new?'

'Yes.' She gradually fed a long blade of grass in until the rabbit's lips were touching her fingers and then she pulled them back. 'Tame, aren't they?'

'Yes. We haven't had them long.'

'We've got a rabbit at home.'

'Who's "we"?'

'Me and my brother.'

'Whose class he in?'

'Mr Irvine's. We both are.'

'Lucky blighters. He's the best teacher in the school. He let's us call him "The Guv". How old'er you then?'

'Nine.'

'So'm I. You ought'a be down with us in Wadey's class.'

'Who's—'

'S'sh.' I peeped round the shelter but Milly and Wadey were well past us. 'He is. The fat one.'

'He's not fat.' She stood up straighter.

'He is. I don't like him.'

She pulled another stem of grass and rested it through the wire. The rabbit's lips wibbled up it like a flame creeping up a spill of newspaper.

'Where'd you live?' She'd turned as she spoke and the sun coloured her cheeks and glinted off her hair like polished copper. 'In the village?'

'Yes. Eight, the Close.'

'Where's that?'

'Just down the road. Do you wanna come and see my ducks? My Dad's building a pond for them.'

She looked at the ground and the slope of her eyes and nose and cheeks made her look like Mary Magdalene

24

praying. 'I don't know,' she said softly. 'I'd better ask my mum.'

An ache like being hungry opened up in my stomach and I could see her mum saying 'of course not' or 'don't you dare, my girl.'

'I'll tell you tomorrow.'

'What?'

'Tomorrow.' She was closer to me now and she smelt like rain on Mum's lipstick. 'I'll tell you tomorrow.'

'Oh.' A button was coming loose on my jacket and I picked at the cotton. 'Yes. All right.'

'Bye then.'

She was gone, like a ball on the sea with the tide going out. I started after her to ask her where I'd see her and when, but she was too far away and if I ran after her Gibbser'd see and if she came to my house tomorrow she'd be disappointed because we hadn't got any ducks yet, although Dad was always talking about getting some because their eggs were bigger than chicken eggs, and he hadn't built the pond.

The rabbits had all gone in and the wind was making ripples in the puddles in the muddy path. I traced the toe of my shoe around her heelmark where she'd stood and squared my heel up against it. It was a lot smaller. Grandad said if you were skinny when you were small you'd probably be tall and if you were fat you'd be short but if you had small hands and feet you'd probably be thin. P'raps it wasn't her heel print at all. If it was she'd be short and thin. Whatever she was Gibbser'd be sure to poke fun at her if he thought I liked her.

Geoff Gibbs and Colin Gander were always together. Colin was taller and quieter than Geoff but he usually agreed with everything Geoff said and Geoff had hard knuckles and bony elbows. They always sat together and the other boys from the village hung around them and played with them and did what they wanted to do. I sat watching them and trying to think what to write about my Easter holiday. They looked bored. Wadey'd finished marking our books and he'd collected the dinner money and taken it up to Milly and they'd stood Dicky Mole up on a desk to watch for him coming back. Maurice Geer and Micky Leary and Drip Williams were reading comics and swapping them and the other camp kids were mucking about quietly and the girls were in a huddle up at the front talking about a new Tyrone Power film that Marie Maynard's big sister had seen and Geoff was trying to pick a fight with Laurence Elliot whose Dad had been caught pinching petrol from the camp and had to go away. I sat back behind Gerald Mortlake so that they couldn't see me.

'When's 'e comin' back then, Elliot?'

Laurie kept on writing.

'Elliot, I'm talkin' to you.'

An inky pellet plopped on to Laurie's book and one of the girls giggled.

'You deaf, Elliot?'

'No.'

'Neither'm I, Gibbs. So shut up.' Maurice turned the last page of his *Beano*.

'No business of yours, Geer.' Geoff sat back closer to Colin.

'I'm making it my business.'

'Sod off,' Geoff said under his breath and I looked away quickly but I knew he'd seen me. I bent lower over my book and tried to think of something to write but I had to look up when the girls started giggling again and somebody said 'go on.'

Swish! Flop! I ducked back as an ink pellet sped past my nose and slopped on the wall.

Geoff sat still with his ruler quivering and the wet pellet slid down the whitewashed wall leaving a blue-black trail. It stopped where one of the bricks stuck out further than the rest.

'That was your fault, Nipper.'

'It wasn't.'

'It was. You ducked. Clean it off.'

I dipped my pen in the ink and underlined the day's date twice.

'Clean it off.' Geoff stood up but he sat down again when Maurice Geer sighed and looked up as he folded his comic and swapped it for one of Drip Williams's. 'Go on, Nipper. Clean it off.'

'No.'

'I'll do it.' Margaret Mole spat on a piece of toilet paper she kept for when Dicky's nose ran.

'You sit down, Granny. Nobody pulled your chain.'

'You be quiet, Geoffrey Gibbs.' Margaret rubbed at the wall. 'And don't you call me that.'

'Granny, granny. Got a big—'

'*Shut up*, Gibbs.' Maurice passed his ruler to Micky Leary without looking up and Micky brought it down sideways on Geoff's head. 'Can't hear yourself think with you yakking away.'

Geoff rubbed his head and showed his finger to Colin. 'If that's bleedin' you're for it, Nipper,' and he went on grumbling to Colin and every time I looked up he was staring at me.

There was no sound except for Margaret rubbing at the wall and the occasional rustle of pages being turned over at the back and when Wadey came back he made Dicky Mole stand in the corner for being up on the desk where he'd no business to be.

'You've all been very quiet.' Wadey eyed us as if he knew what had been going on. '. . . so I suppose I can assume I've got some good stories to come about your holidays.'

Nobody answered.

'Well, can I?'

'Oh yes, sir.'

'That's good, Gibbs. Let's start off with you.'

'Me, sir?'

'Yes, you sir.' Wadey adjusted his glasses.

'Why me, sir?'

Wadey put on a smile. 'Because I say so, sir.'

'Well it's not much of a story, sir.' Geoff squirmed and Colin Gander sat over further against the window.

'Never mind, Gibbs. I'm sure we'll enjoy it.'

'But it's about a cat, sir.' Geoff's eyes flashed around to see if any of us were laughing.

'Don't be bashful, Gibbs. Get on with it.'

'But—'

'*Now.*' Wadey banged the desk.

Geoff cleared his throat and went 'h'her,' as if he was lifting something heavy and Colin's puffed up cheeks exploded and he wiped the spit off his chin.

Geoff took a deep breath. 'Hif you have a cat—'

'Cor!' Colin forced his head up towards the ceiling.

'If you had a cat, when it was a kitten . . .' Geoff looked helplessly at Wadey.

'Go on.'

'If you had a ca-at. When it was a *kitten*. If you didn't feed it . . . it would run away.'

'Fascinating.' Wadey sat forward with his elbows on his desk. 'Go on.'

'Well . . . it would run away . . . and it wouldn't come back.'

I felt as if I was being drowned from the inside and my ribs hurt. Colin laughed first and then we all burst.

Wadey sat shaking his head. 'Is that it?'

'Yes, sir.'

'Ab-so-lutely rivetting.' Wadey sat back and clasped his hands behind his head. 'Is that all you've got to show for nearly two hours' work, Gibbs?'

'Well, I got stuck, sir.'

'Got stuck, Gibbs! You sank without trace.' Wadey was trying to look serious but a smile was breaking through. 'And I can't see what's so funny, the rest of you.'

'Nah! See.' Geoff swung round.

'Go on, sir. Let 'im read it again.'

'No, I don't think so, Geer. P'raps we'll hear more about Gibbs's cat later on. In a little more detail maybe, Gibbs . . .? Always supposing it ever returns.'

That was one of Wadey's jokes so we could finish off laughing properly and he made Geoff wait behind when we went to lunch so I was able to get away ahead of him.

I poked about at my dinner while I looked around for the new girl until it got cold and I waited for her after school and then didn't want any tea and I let my breakfast get cold next morning so that Mum said it wasn't fit for the pigbin and

28

that my tummy'd rumble and disturb the lesson. Wadey set us some sums on the blackboard and then he called out the answers and we self-marked them while Paul Craven set out a pile of paper and an ink pad for us to print out a map of South America with a rubber roller.

'For heaven's sake, Mole!' Wadey screwed up Dicky's sheet, where he'd rolled it across the narrow side, and wiped the splodges of print off the desk top. 'Here, show him the right way round, Margaret— and Wilson's dreaming again. Do it again, Wilson.'

I printed another one and sat staring at it. It had come out properly on the edges but the middle was all faint and smeared and there were little chips of wood in the paper where the ink wouldn't dry. I tried to blot them up with the furry edges of my sum book.

'Right then. Pay attention.' Wadey tapped his desk with his ruler. 'You'll see thick lines and dotted lines and shaded bits and bits with little crosses on 'em. Thick lines're rivers. Do them blue. Dotted lines're railways. Do them black. Shaded bits're hills, brown, and crosses're forests, green. All right?'

We shuffled about borrowing crayons and then settled. The shadings and the crosses all looked the same and the dotted lines mixed in with the crosses and came out again further up or lower down and some of the thick lines had breaks in them that looked like long dots. I etched in a lot of green and followed a few rivers and railways and then sharpened my pencil into a cup-cake case in my drawer. The little chips of pencil were brown like rabbit bran and I crumpled them to dust between my finger and thumb and blew the dust away. I joined some of the dots together, where the shaded bit was patchy, so that they made a face sideways on with a slender nose sloping down and thin lips and a little chin and then I coloured in some brown above it. *She* had brown hair. I shaded in a little more brown with red and sharpened her chin. P'raps she wasn't fat after all and she couldn't help it if she had to wear ankle socks. Maybe her mum would let her come to tea. Or maybe she'd forget to ask. Maybe she didn't even—

'Simon.' It was a hissed whisper and Wendy Brewer was

twisting round in her desk and keeping one eye on Wadey at the same time. 'Si—'

'What?'

'How are you getting on?'

'All right.' I wrapped my arm around my map.

'Want any help?'

'No thanks.'

I went on colouring in the hair. She had said she'd see me again. She'd even said it twice. I made her eyelashes longer. And if she hadn't meant to she wouldn't have . . . but maybe she'd been embarrassed and had just wanted to—

'Yes?' Wadey looked up at Wendy who had her hand up. 'Go on then.'

Wendy got up and she brushed against my arm as she went out but I didn't look up.

Playtime was at quarter past ten but the minute hand looked as if it was stuck on five to. I watched it until my left leg went to sleep and then it jabbed forward a minute.

'Right. Let's see how you're getting on.' Wadey pushed his stool back and I scratched away with my brown pencil.

'H'm. Not bad.' Wadey'd been round the girls and was moving on to the boys. 'But Gander seems to think there's no forests in South America.'

'I ain't got a green, sir.'

'Well get one, idiot.' He moved on to Geoff Gibbs and muttered 'Pleasing absence of cats.'

Geoff slewed his paper round with a sick grin and then stuck two fingers up at Wadey's back as he went to Jimmy and Jerry.

'And what have we here?' Wadey was holding Jimmy's book close up and then further away. 'Phillips has discovered a river running smack through Santiago. Amazing, Phillips. Now rub it out. That's a main rail line, you twerp.' He picked up Jerry's book. 'And would you believe it, Henry's made the same discovery!'

The ones he'd seen laughed but the rest of us crayoned as fast as we could. I couldn't make out if the girl's hair should be forest or mountains. P'raps they were crosses and not shaded bits. They *were* crosses. I scraped away with the green.

'Let's see, Wilson. Oh, Wilson's of the opinion that half

Argentina's thickly wooded mountains. That'll please the farmers when they discover their cattle have deserted the plains. Rub it out, Wilson, and do try to concentrate.'

My armpits were moist as he moved off and started on the camp kids.

'Very good, Geer. I suppose I can asume all of you here at the back have got it right?'

'*I* have, sir. I been there.'

'Have you, Craven?'

'Yes, sir.'

'What, all of it? It's a big place, you know.'

'Me dad was there for—'

'Is there anywhere your dad hasn't been, Craven?'

'Oh yes, sir. Ain't been to China and—'

'Thank you, Craven. Don't tell me. Make a list of them.' Wadey went back to his desk and started to put some laces in a new pair of football boots he had in a carrier bag.

The clock had moved on to five past ten and Dicky Mole asked if he could start again. Wadey said 'yes' in a tired voice and Wendy Brewer appeared at the cloakroom door again. I didn't take any notice till she was right next to me and dropped a folded piece of paper on my desk. I reached for the paper as the door sprang back but a draught caught it and sent it spinning up and down like a leaf and it landed between Geoff and Colin. I didn't take much notice as Geoff picked it up but Wendy's face went red and then white and she reached her hand out but Geoff stuck his tongue out and I carried on colouring. They started giggling soon after that and going 'oo-oh' until Wadey told them to shut up and then he sent us out to play.

I was the first out. It was raining but I dashed off without putting a jacket on and skidded round the corner of the air-raid shelter. She wasn't there. I stared at the ground. All the footprints were full of water so she hadn't come. P'raps she wouldn't come. Milly's class hadn't been let out yet but I couldn't tell about the Guv's from here. P'raps they had started their playtime but he'd let them stay in and she wouldn't bother because of a little bit of rain.

I stuffed my hands in my pockets and leant back against

the wall and tried to stop the rain dripping down my neck. The wet was seeping through the knees of my trousers and I was cold. She was probably watching them playing draughts and looking out at the rain and thinking it wasn't worth getting—

'Hello.'

I swung round.

'You'll get wet out there.' The rain glistened on the grey hood of her mac as she stuck her head out of the entrance to the shelter. 'Come on in.'

I crept in next to her and we stood facing each other in the wedge of light. It smelt dry and dusty inside and was so dark it looked as if the inner passage was draped in a black sheet. The boys never went in there because they all said it was full of dog muck.

'I didn't think you'd come.'

'I didn't think you would.' She was shorter than me and we were standing close together so she had to look up at me. 'You're all wet. Why didn't you put a jacket on?'

'Oh, it's nothing.' I eased my neck forward away from my wet collar. 'I'm used to it.'

'I *hate* getting wet.' She folded her hood back and wiped the backs of her hands across her forehead. 'Urgh,' she said and she dried her hands on her dress.

'Shall I do it?' I pulled out my hanky. 'It's clean.'

She held her head back and I stroked her eyebrows and cheeks and down the line of her nose and dabbed underneath, in case she thought I was wiping it, and into the curve of her chin and then back up to the corner of her mouth like Nan did when she'd been eating blancmange. And with her eyes closed she looked like a baby asleep and I was standing guard over her like Saint George looking after the children and the lion cub in *Where the Rainbow Ends*.

'That tickles.'

My finger was tracing the outline of her ear.

'Oh, does it?' I started back because she was looking at me. 'Thought you'd cut yourself. Looked like a . . . cut, or something.'

She passed her finger over the lobe. 'Don't think so.'

'Up here more.' I moved her hand up and guided her

small finger along the top of her ear. The soft brush of her hair on the back of my hand sent shivers through me. 'P'raps it wasn't.' I folded her hair back over her ear carefully as if I was burying treasure. 'I cut myself there once . . .'

She was leaning against the wall with one foot hooked round the other ankle.

'Walked into a door.'

'Did you?' She had very dark eyes and her skin was a sort of pinky brown colour that looked warm to the touch.

'Yeah. Jus' swung round once to go after someone and bashed it.'

'Oh.' She was bending back more and rubbing her instep against the back of her other leg.

'Didn't 'arf 'urt.'

Her eyes were focused sideways towards the sky like a princess in a tower.

'D'you wanna come in more out of the rain?'

'It's nearly stopped.' Her head lolled over towards the entrance.

'Be warmer inside a bit.' I tried to shiver.

She edged a fraction closer to the doorway. 'Oh, I don't know.'

She was moving one way and I was moving the other and we weren't really facing each other any more. 'My name's Simon.' I edged back towards her by changing my weight to my other foot.

'I know.'

'Oh. Do you? What's yours then?'

'Janet. Janet Rolls.'

'Strewth!'

'What?'

'Nothin'.' I could imagine Gibbser calling her roly-poly or jelly roll or even toilet roll and her crying. 'Don't you mean, Rawl?'

'No-o. Rolls. Like jam roll.'

'Oh.'

'Don't you like it?' She had both feet on the ground now and she was standing up straighter.

'Well, I dunno. It's better than Glue or Mole, I s'pose.'

She sniffed and buttoned her coat up.

'But I like you . . . Janet.'

'Do you?' She looked up at me from under her eyebrows as she fastened her belt.

'Cor yeah, and if any of 'em call you names I'll bash 'em up.'

'Will you?' She leant back again.

'Yes I will.'

'Come on then.'

'What?'

'Well, kiss me. If you want to.'

The whistle had gone when I got back but I hadn't heard it. I walked in behind Wadey and he was so busy boxing Kenny Lane's ears for fighting that I was able to sit down without him seeing me. Geoff Gibbs kept pointing at Wendy and kissing his lips up at me and the others were grinning but they all stopped and looked to the front when Wadey said we were going to start *The Taming of the Shrew* and he was looking for likely candidates. I kept my head down and got a small part but he said Wendy could be Katharina because she had plenty of spirit.

We droned on through the first two scenes and Gerald Mortlake helped me with the difficult words that I had to say. Then Wadey said we could read act two to ourselves while he went up to see Milly.

As the outside door banged closed Geoff Gibbs bounced out of his desk. At the same time Wendy Brewer flew at him like a kestrel swooping on a mouse.

'Don't you dare, Geoffrey Gibbs. Give me that.'

'Get off, Windy.'

Wendy was scratching at his face with one hand and grabbing at his clenched fist with the other. 'Give it to me. It's none of your business.'

'Get 'er off, Col.' Geoff was defending himself with one hand but Colin stayed back well out of the way.

'If you do, Geoff I'll . . .'

'You'll what?' Geoff was holding her off now by clutching at her frock up under her chin. 'Nip-per,' he chanted. 'Wanna see what I got?'

'If you do—' Wendy stopped flailing suddenly and slumped down sobbing.

'You horrible creature, Gibbs,' Margaret Mole said and Maurice Geer yawned and asked what was going on.

Geoff's face went red and he seemed ready to stop but Colin pushed him towards me. 'You got a love letter, Nipper.'

Wendy lifted her head and her face was all smeared with rats'-tails of hair. Then she banged her head down again.

I unfolded the paper. 'Round and round went the hands of the clock. Let's see if . . .' I read it again. I felt like a negro slave being priced up for sale.

Wendy was back in her seat wiping her eyes and Margaret Mole, Pat Smith and Jenny Wright had their arms around her.

'She wants you to . . . cor!' Geoff collapsed laughing and the girls all turned on him like geese.

Maurice and the others were sniggering and Micky Leary grabbed the scrap of paper out of my hand.

'You give that back, Leary.'

'Come and get it.'

'He wants it. He wants it.' Geoff Gibbs was banging his fists up and down on his desk.

I made a dive at Micky's back as he was sitting down but I caught my toe against the metal strut across the back of my desk and dragged it round.

'What's all this?' The door crashed back and I felt Wadey's thick hand on my collar. 'I can't turn my back for a moment, can I, before you start skylarking about?' He dragged me to my feet. 'What'd'ya mean by it?'

'Wasn't my fault, sir. It was 'im.' I pointed at Geoff. 'And 'er.' Wendy put her hand to her chest and mouthed '*me?*'

'It wasn't them I caught scrabbling about on the floor.'

'Well, she wrote me a dirty letter.'

'I did not.' Wendy's mouth opened so wide I wondered if it would ever close again.

'And Gibbs got hold of it an' I hadn't even read it.'

'No, sir.' Geoff sat solid. 'I didn't, sir.'

'And then they started passing it around.'

35

'All right, Wilson.'

'An' it makes me sick, all that sort of thing.' My mind was racing forward to how Mum had said I was never to go into corners with girls because I'd get a disease that'd make me go blind. 'And it's disgusting and sickening.'

'All *right*, Wilson. Now sit down.'

'It's not fair and it makes me—'

His hand rested on my shoulder and he put weight on it and I sank down into my seat. 'I said, it's all right.' He left his hand on my shoulder as if I was a spring he expected to bounce back at him. 'I don't know what's been going on here and I s'pose I'll only get a pack of lies if I ask.' The weight came off my shoulder and he moved on up the classroom. 'I suggest you all settle down and forget about this. You too, Simon.'

I sat and watched the clock until my mouth went sticky and the wet streaks on my face turned to salt trails. I suddenly felt cold where I'd been hot before. Micky Leary was a friend of mine and I wondered if they'd still let me go down the RAF camp to play. I turned round but they were all working and wouldn't look up, except Gibbser who kept making faces at me and Gander grinning behind him. I went back to *The Taming of the Shrew* and gritted my teeth as Katharina and Petruchio were fighting and if Wendy was Katharina and Gibbser'd been Petruchio she'd've scratched his face to ribbons with her long nails and while he was blinded with blood she'd've hooked her little fingers under his eyeballs and ripped them out and 'augh . . .' The sound hung in the air and they were all staring at me.

'You look very hot, Simon. You all right?' Wadey sounded as if he was helping somebody old off with their coat. 'Simon?'

'Yes.' I was staring back at Gibbser and willing him to laugh.

'Good . . .' Wadey interlocked his fingers and bent his hands back together in front of him. 'But p'raps you'd like to pop out for a bit of fresh air before dinner. Good heavens!' Wadey said it before he'd looked up at the clock. 'You'd better be off else it'll *be* dinner time.'

*

36

The cold from the roller gradually worked through my trousers and made my bottom feel wet. I stood it for as long as I could and then went behind the hedge to Brindle's field and pee'd on the heart of a dock. A spider crawled out and up a stem of grass and I sloshed him off, then dashed back to our side of the hedge as one of Brindle's coal lorries turned into their yard.

'What you been up to, Simon?'

'What?'

'Bird's-nesting?' The Guv was sitting on the roller lighting one Turf off another.

'Oh . . . yeah.'

'Don't take eggs, do you?'

'There weren't any.'

He took a couple of long puffs and then blew the ash off with the smoke.

'No lunch?'

'Not hungry, sir.'

'Aren't you? I had an appetite like a horse when I was your age.'

'Haven't you now then?'

'No.' He looked down at the cigarette smouldering in his fingers. 'Not so much now.'

I knew what he meant. Denis Matthews'd told me once about a Marine boxer who'd smoked to stop himself eating so that he could lose weight but his wind had gone and he'd got knocked out by an airman in Bancock and fractured his skull on the side of the ring.

'Where's Bancock, sir?'

'Bangkok? That's in Siam, Simon. What brought that on?'

'Oh nothing. Just something I thought of.' The big boys used to spit on their fingers and rub them on the wall to get the yellow off but his fingers had it right up to the joint.

'Is smoking bad for you, sir?'

He took a long drag and trod the butt-end out. 'It's a stupid, expensive habit, Simon and I don't know why I do it.'

'You should pack it up then, sir.' Nan was always saying that to Grandad but he usually made a joke of it.

'You're right, Simon. I will.' He took his packet out and counted how many were left and then he closed it and put it in his inside pocket. 'I will. And now, will you go and get some dinner?'

'Well, I'm not really—' A grey mac flitted between the girls' toilets and the Guv's classroom. The Guv turned to see what I was looking at.

'Oh I see.'

'What, sir?'

'Why you're off your food.'

'I'm not, sir.'

'Go on. Off you go before she disappears.'

'We only feed the rabbits, sir . . .'

'Well, you'd better go and feed them then, Simon. And I must get back and finish off my marking.'

I waited on the roller willing her to come but she didn't so I sauntered over to the fence by the shelter, then ran in case she thought I wasn't coming. She wasn't by the rabbits' cage or behind the shelter so I looked inside but she wasn't there either and when I came out again the sun made me blind.

'Hello.'

I rubbed at my eyes but they wouldn't clear.

'You crying?'

'No.' I rubbed hard to make them red. 'Got dust in my eyes.'

'Couldn't we bathe them?' She was running her finger over the hard bit of my eye socket.

'Could do. In the washbasin down in Miss Anderson's class.' I grabbed her hand and we slipped from behind the shelter and along behind Milly's and the Guv's classrooms and past the bike sheds over the hard playground to my classroom.

'What we going in here for?'

'It's quicker.'

I pulled her through the door between the two rooms and into the cloakroom, like Jeremy hurrying Elizabeth away from the red elves in *One Magic Night*. I ran some cold water and splashed it into my face.

'Here, let me do it.'

She folded her hanky into a long soft finger, dipped the end in the water and ran it over my eyes.

'Better?'

38

'Cor yeah.'

She dabbed with the wet end and wiped up the drips with the flared out dry lacy corners and I could feel her warm breath where my face was damp. I opened my eyes. She was so close that I could only see her face.

'Do they ache?'

'Not so much now.'

'But you've got your hair wet.'

'Only a bit, haven't I?'

She smoothed my hair back where it came over my forehead. 'Look nice if it was back.'

'What'd'ya mean?'

'Combed back.' She smoothed it some more, her fingers coming up through my hair. '. . . or sideways.'

'It'd always flop forward.'

'Wouldn't if it was trained. Shall I try?'

'Yeah. If you like.'

I picked the bits of fluff off my comb and I gave it to her.

'Shall we sit down?'

I stared round the cloakroom. 'What, here?'

'No, silly, not in here.'

'Oh no, course not.' I made out I was joking. 'We can go in my class. They won't be back from dinner yet.'

I pulled the door towards me and saw her reflection looking at me in the glass where they'd put grey manilla over the other side and made it like a mirror.

'This is my desk. Shall we sit down?'

She stood in the gangway and I didn't know what to do with my hands so I put them in my pockets.

'Over here.' She was whispering as if we were in church and she settled down at one of the double desks and slewed round with her back against the wall. 'C'mon.' She patted the seat.

I sat down.

'Not like that. Turn round.' Her hands were on my ribs and it tickled. 'Like that, and lay back.'

I was half lying with my shoulders across her leg and the back of my head against her chest and she ran the comb through my hair. I closed my eyes.

'That nice?'

39

'M'm.'

'Has it always been this fine and blond?'

Her voice came from a million miles away and I could feel my eyes blanking over and I didn't need to move my lips. 'I had tight black curls, Mum says, when I was a baby.'

'Did you?' Sweep . . . sweep . . . I let my head fall heavier.

'Yeah. And before I could talk I used to read the newspaper by saying da-da da-da dum.'

Sweep and brush. Sweep and brush. Sideways now . . . once with the comb and once with the palm of her hand to keep it in place.

'And once I sat up in me pram when they met a vicar out on the Greatwood Road by the Redvins and said "how do you do?" and he was so surprised he gave me a shilling, Mum says.'

'How old were you then?' She held my hair in a wave for a moment and then let go.

'I dunno. 'bout two I s'pose.'

She stopped combing and let her fingers run down my cheeks and I could feel her heart against my ear.

'I can remember right back to—'

'Simon Wilson!'

I shot up and banged my head against Janet's chin.

'Whatever are you doing? And look what you've done to Janet.'

'It's all right, Miss Anderson.' Janet's eyes were watering. 'It didn't really hurt.'

'Get up at once. Whatever do you mean by skulking around in here with girls?'

'I was only—'

'I'm not talking to you, Janet. You should keep away from him. Why, he was in trouble again only this morning.'

Janet was still sitting down. I wanted to see if her chin was all right but I couldn't see her properly because her head was bent forward.

'Go on, Simon. Get off out and play some boys' games and let the girls alone.'

'Yes, Miss.' I wanted Janet to look at me as I left but she didn't.

*

Our bungalow was the last in the Close. There was a space about the width of a football pitch on each side of the road between the last bungalow and the hedge of Vine's Farm and the Close ended in a bubble where the bread van and the postman could turn. The space on the other side was all grown over with nettles, except for the pathway to the cess pit, but our side was flat and grassy where Dad and I played football. Nobody else played there and when I played with the boys we always went in the back field or up to the playing field. I sat on the chopping block with my elbows on my knees and my chin in my hands and looked along our fence. If we took our side fence down and put it along the front we could turn the space into garden. We could have a football and cricket pitch and some apple trees like Grandad's and dig out a pond and fill it with water and have some ducks waddling about and make the ditch by the fence deeper so that it was like a stream and plant roses in the hedge so that they grew up through it and have seats out there so that we could invite people for tea in the garden and maybe Mum and Dad'd get to know Mr and Mrs Rolls and—

'Haven't you changed your trousers then, Nip?'

'No, not yet.'

'What'd'ya mean "not yet"? You usually change straight after school, don't you?'

'Yes, Dad.'

'Didn't you want to go out to play?'

'Not really.'

'What's up then?'

'Dunno.' I thought he was going to sit down on the sawing horse with me but he just stood there and turned over some cut pieces with his toe. 'Nothin' to do.'

'Blimey boy, when I was your age I was off out with old Den Payton bird's-nestin' and playing football as soon as I got home. You have to make your own amusement.'

'Yeah. But I haven't got anyone to play with.'

'Stone the crows, Simon. What about Jimmy and Jerry?'

'They never want to do anything.'

'Well, suggest something then.'

'I can't.'

'Why not?'

'I can't think of anything.'

41

He turned over some more wood at the bottom of the pile and the flecks of sawdust clung to the spiders' webs. A wood louse crawled over my shoe and I picked him up to let him run on the palm of my hand but he rolled into a tight black ball.

'Da-ad.'

'Yes?'

'Did I have tight black curls when I was a baby?'

'I dunno, Nip.' He sat down slowly on the sawing horse. 'You were like a snowball time I got 'ome. Who told you that?'

'Mum did.'

'Well, you must'a done then.'

'And how did I read the newspaper before I could talk?'

'Search me. With difficulty, I expect.' He was laughing when he said it but his face clouded over. 'There's a lot I missed with you when you were little. See I didn't see you 'til—'

'I know Dad. 'til I was three and a half.'

'Yes. There you are then. Bit of a shock it was, coming home and finding you half grown.'

'Didn't you know I was here then?'

'We-ll.' He bit at the skin at the corner of his thumbnail and then started to pick it. 'I knew you'd been born but that was when you were about eighteen months old.'

'Couldn't you have escaped?'

'What? From the Japs?' He sucked at the picked bit and folded his hands. 'You couldn't. There was nowhere to run. Just miles of bamboo. And we didn't know where we were half the time. Anyway, Simon, we were too weak to walk far let alone run.'

'But you could run like a greyhound. Cabby said so.'

'Properly fed I could but we only had rice and a little bit of fish sometimes.'

In three and a half years they could have dug a tunnel under the wire and sailed down a river until they met friendly natives and Dad could have had a picture of me and Mum that he could have shown his friends at night when they were walking under cover of darkness.

'Da-ad?'

'Yes.'

'Couldn't I have a brother?'

'Strewth. I don't know about that, Simon.' He stood up. 'It's hard enough bringing one up, let alone . . . anyway, we want the best we can for you.'

'Oh . . . Dad. Can you play with me?'

'When?'

'Well . . . now.'

'Oh, I dunno, Simon. Be much better if you went off and found some pals to play with.' He looked at his watch. 'I don't know, I was going to do some wood-sawing. P'raps I'll go up to Nan and Grandad's first and then have a game with you and do some sawing later.' He brushed sawdust off his shoes. 'You coming up to 64? They'd like to see you.'

The sun was low over the trees up by the dell over the back field. Already the shadow from the hedge was creeping across the patch where we played. Soon it would be night and then morning and school again and the boys'd keep on about Wendy Brewer and Janet wouldn't want to—

'*Simon.*'

'What?'

'You coming up 'ome?'

'I don't really want to, Dad. Da-ad?'

'What now?'

'When'er we gonna build that duck pond?'

'What duck pond?'

'Out there.' I pointed towards the hedge away from where we played football. 'Like you said you would.'

'Oh, I don't s'pose I will now, Nip. Hardly seems worth it. They'll be building out there during the summer probably.'

'Oh Dad, they won't, will they?'

'Yes, course they will. Pair of bungalows each side of the road. You coming?'

A wailing feeling welled up inside of me and I made my face go stiff. 'Well, can we have a jackie then?'

'Yes, Simon. If it'll keep you amused.'

'When, Dad?'

'Later, Simon. In the summer.'

I watched as he tapped the window and called to Mum that he was going up the road and then I made believe a piece of sawn wood was a duck but I felt daft talking to a piece of wood so I slung it at the dustbin and missed.

3

I pressed my toe up under some loose bark on the leg of the sawing horse and let it spring back. It was as if Janet Rolls had never known me. She wouldn't look at me if I got close to her and she talked to somebody else if she saw me coming. I tried to give her her coat in the cloakroom one morning when it was raining but she went back into her classroom and fiddled about in her desk until the boys asked me what I was waiting for. I pulled at the bark again and it snapped off and I slung it into a puddle.

The patch of grass at the side of our house was ripped up like a bomb site. Sharp stones stuck out of the mud in the sides of the trenches and each trench was etched with a mound of earth that had been dug out wet-brown and dried off to a sandy red. They'd put a concrete mixer where our batting crease used to be and the only grass that was left was littered with dried-out mud.

The hooter down at the camp had gone at half past five and the men had dunked their trowels in buckets of water to clean them and padlocked the shed and turned the wheelbarrows over. Then they'd filled the mixer drum with water and churned it round and switched it off and left it spinning.

A sparrow flew down on to the mixer handle and sat cocking his head as if he'd left his nest there to get some food and found it gone when he got back. I brushed my hair back with my comb and then with my hand but it didn't feel like anything and just flopped forward again. A clod of earth rolled down one of the heaps. It dislodged some little pieces and fell plop, plop, plop like rain patters into a pool in the trench.

I climbed up on to the sawing horse and stepped over our fence on to a pile of bricks and jumped down the other side. I sat down by the trench and slid my legs forward and dropped into it. Standing up straight, my head was just level with the ground. The trenches were in a square with other trenches going across and one had pipes laid in the bottom that showed shiny on the inside when I trod on it and a bit broke off. It was heavy but I managed to lift it up and fit the piece back underneath where it didn't show. I'd bumped my back getting into the trench and trying to turn round to see if I'd got mud on my coat I got it even dirtier. The trench hadn't looked deep when I'd jumped in but now I had to put my arms right up to get my hands over the top and when I pulled to get out the sides crumbled and showered me with earth that went sticky in my hair. I wandered up and down looking for something I could grab to pull myself up. A car drew up and I ducked down. The engine stopped and two doors clicked open and then slammed closed.

'This is it.'

'Aye, sir.'

'A pair on either side. Get these on this side up to joist level and then start on the others.'

'Yes, sir.'

'You've got six men and a boy. Think you'll manage?'

'Oh yes, sir.'

'Right. You can start on Monday on a fortnight's trial. But I'll be watching you, mind. Anything untoward and you'll be back on the gang.'

'Yes, sir. Thankee, sir.'

They were nearly up to me.

'Want a lift to the bus stop?'

'Well, I've got 'alf'n hour for the Chichester bus, sir. Think I'll just hang on and have a look round, sir.'

'Please yourself. Eight o'clock sharp, mind. And I want any latecomers reported.'

A pair of feet crunched away through the rubble and the car drove off.

A match scraped just above me and a whiff of blue smoke against the wet of the earth and the drier tang of cement and bricks reminded me of when I was small and the other bungalows were being built. I peeped up over the trench. Black trousers tied with string and big black boots. I ducked down and then peered over again.

46

'Hello. What've we got 'ere?'

I dropped on to my knees and then stood up slowly. He was standing over me picking a shred of tobacco from his broken black teeth.

'Who are you?'

'Simon, Mr Black.'

He jerked back and his lips came together. 'How'd'you know my . . . Gawd bless me, young Simon!' He leant forward again and reached down. 'Here, giv'us yer 'and. You've grow'd up a bit, 'aven't you?' He hauled me out and I stood rubbing mud off my jacket.

'Look at you. Why, you're twice the man you were.' He slid his cap back further on his head. 'Whatever's happened to the little shaver I used to know?'

'Dunno, Mr Black.'

' 'aven't been gettin' in no mischief, 'ave you?'

'Oh no.' I tried to look away from the bits of trench that had fallen in. 'My ball came over here somewhere.'

'Arh.' He trod his cigarette end into the mud.

'Didn't expect me back again, did you?'

I looked over at the builder's board. It was the same one as when they were building our bungalow with the word STIRLING in big letters in a red circle.

'Why not?'

'Well . . .' He said it as if it was obvious but he didn't know the answer. 'Remember old Tom, the bricky?'

'Yes.'

'Well, 'e got made up to foreman an' then 'e started getting a bit above 'imself with the guvnor an' got the sack.'

'Did 'e?'

'Arh, 'e did.' George Black looked around the site at the sand and bricks and workmen's shed and mixer and along the trenches as if he was counting them. 'Buildin's a mighty precarious business if you ain't careful. Still, now I've got made up as foreman an' if I can keep this little lot goin' I'll be all right.'

'Are you in charge now?'

'Yes, I am.' He drew his feet together and stood up straighter. 'Yes, my young shaver, I am.' He sat down on the side of a half-turned wheelbarrow and stretched his legs out.

47

'Will you help me?'

'Cor yeah.' I sat down next to him and he drew away so that he could turn and face me.

'See, I'm engaged now. Know what that is?'

'Yeah. Gittin' married.'

'Aye. Getting married. And it'll be very 'andy if I can stay put up as foreman.'

'What, more money?'

'Aye. No flies on you.' His hand rubbed rough across my head and I put my hair straight. 'So I'll be needing a bit of help.'

'What'cha want me to do?'

'Oh, just keep an eye on things.' He looked around the site again. 'Don't let any kids go treadin' the sand about or fillin' the trenches in or generally muckin' about. Will you do that for me?'

'Ye-es.' I imagined myself sitting on guard on a pile of bricks with Dad's old Diana air rifle holding Gibbser and Gander at bay. 'I'll try.'

'Good lad. Now I must be off and see about that bus.'

'Simon. Tea time.' Mum was at the back door brushing crumbs off the bread board.

'Coming, Mum.'

'Well, come on then. Don't hang about.'

George'd tipped his cap at Mum but she didn't seem to see him.

'Wouldn't you like a cup of tea, George?'

George looked at the back door and rubbed his hand across his stubbly chin. 'No, better not. I'll see you on Monday. Bye, Simon.'

'Bye, George.'

He went off up the Close whistling and I waited until he was out of sight and then I climbed up the bricks and over our side fence. 'George is back, Mum.'

'Yes, I see he is.' Mum was rinsing hot water around in the tea pot. 'Just switch that kettle on again a minute, Simon.'

The kettle boiled straight away and I switched it off and turned the spout away from the wall. Long steam bubbles broke and made trails down the green gloss paint. Mum put

48

two scoops of tea in the pot and reached over me and poured hot water. 'Where's the tea cosy?'

I picked it up from under the tea trolley and gave it to her. The tea trolley was made of metal and painted green. It had wheels but we never pushed it. We carried it if we ever wanted it in the living room, in case it marked the lino. Most of the time it stayed by the cooker and Mum had put little plastic cups under its wheels to stop it getting pushed up against the earthenware jar where she kept her cooking salt.

'Why'd we get this, Mum?'

'What?'

'This trolley.'

'We got it when we were first married.'

'Why?'

She poured milk into the cups.

'Why, Mum?'

'I don't know, Simon.' She was standing with her back to me holding the tea pot and staring out of the kitchen window. 'S'pose we thought it would be nice to take the tea into the living room.'

'Yeah but—'

'Just sit in front of the fire and—'

'But—'

'Sit there nice and quiet . . .' She seemed to be gazing out of the window and pouring the tea at the same time.

'But we don't, Mum.'

'Course we do. When Nan and Grandad come.' Mum flicked her head as if she was shaking off water. 'Now look what I've done. Poured tea into the sugar bowl. What a blessed mess.' She started scooping chunks of wet sugar out and dropping them into the cups. 'Don't blame me if it's too sweet and what's all this about George?'

'You saw 'im, Mum.'

'So they're back, are they?'

'Yes, Mum.'

'Well, I'd rather you kept away from the builders. Go getting into mischief out there until all hours of the night and you'll never get on at school.'

'I won't, Mum. But blimey, it's only next door.'

49

'Nevertheless . . . anyway, here's your daddy home and he's got a surprise for you that'll p'raps occupy your mind.'

I hadn't heard the gate click but now the ticking of his back wheel was coming past the side window. I opened the back door.

'What'cha got for me, Dad?'

'Eh?'

'What'cha got? Mum said—'

'I said nothing of the sort, Simon.' Mum pushed past me and kissed Dad while he was still holding on to the handle-bars. 'I merely said you'd be giving him a . . . you know.'

'Oh, did you? Yes, all right, I s'pose so.' Dad stood his bike up in the shed. 'But give us a chance, Simon. Let's have'us tea first.'

'But what is it, Dad?'

'All in good time, Nip. All in good time.'

I kept on about it all through tea until I ran out of questions and I knew I wasn't going to like it whatever it was.

'For heaven's sake, do stop, Simon.' Dad drained the last of his tea. 'Get your coat on. We're off.'

'Where we goin', Dad?'

'Wait and see.'

'But, Da-ad.'

'Cor . . . the impatient little—'

'Hanover Park, Simon.' Mum did my coat up and pulled my hands out of my pockets. 'Now don't ask any more questions and be a good boy.'

The walk up to Hanover Park was always the same. It was uphill and the fields were flat right out to the Common Woods one way and as far as I could see towards Chichester the other. But it all changed at Hanover Crossroads. There were always cats skulking around in Brindle's Coal Yard and men loading the lorries with sacks of coal and heaving them up as if they were full of feathers and old Mr Landers was usually out with his dog, poking at the hedge with his stick. He held his dog's lead with his good hand and managed to balance his stick in between the hooked piece, where his hand should have been, and his elbow. Some people said he'd lost his hand in the First World War but I couldn't see how it had ended up as a crook because a bone wouldn't bend in a shell blast so p'raps he'd been born with it.

Over the crossroads and up Hanover Lane it was like walking into medieval times. On one side was the flint wall that ran all round the Hanover Estate. It was made out of the same stuff as they'd used when William the Conqueror built our church and Hanover Castle but I knew it wasn't as old as them because I'd heard it was built by some of Napoleon's men who'd got captured. Little bushes grew against the wall where wrens and hedge-sparrows nested and the boys reckoned there were grass snakes and adders in the long grass at the bottom.

We walked up the hedge side of the lane out of the shadow of the wall and I let the seedy tips of the hogweed run through my fingers as we passed. The smell of wild honeysuckle was thick like syrup and every now and then I stopped to look at new rabbit holes in the hedge.

'Keep up, Simon.'

'Where we goin', Dad?'

'I told you. Up the park.'

'But we *are* up the park.'

'No we're not. Not yet.'

I ran after him and climbed over the five-barred gate at the end of the lane and tiptoed over the cattle grid while he undid the small gate and walked through.

The lane and the wall curved on up the side of the park to Rook Wood. A rough field of long grass stretched away to the meadows etched with chestnut trees and up beyond the furthermost trees the ruins of Hanover Castle merged with the woods like a rock wall in an earth bank. The chestnut trees were spaced out about every hundred yards and they all looked as tall as our church. When the estate was new they'd have curved away to the castle and if William the Conqueror'd planted them they'd be about nine hundred years old. They were all dying. They'd been dying, Grandad said, when he'd first come down from Ripon and married Nan and they'd go on dying for ever.

51

'This is where we used to play football before the war, Simon.' Dad was leaning back against the gate.

'What? Out there?' It was a long slope and the patches of docks were shoulder high.

'Yes. Good pitch it was then but we didn't have any changing facilities.'

'Did you have a good team in those days, Dad?'

'Cor, I should say so. Your Uncle Steven was extra good on the right wing there.' Dad's eyes ran up and down the field. 'Young Roger could never make much of it though. You come up here much?'

'H'm. Sometimes. But only with the boys.'

'Ah.' He was staring at the field as if he could still see it marked out, with him and Uncle Steven playing in their red and yellow shirts and Cabby and Grandad and Uncle Roger and all the others watching.

'Dad?'

'Yes.'

'What we come up 'ere for?'

'Eh? Oh, just to see if we can find a young jackie. You'd like one, wouldn't you?'

'Cor! Yes please.' I nestled against his arm stretched out along the gate. 'But how we gonna get up to 'em?'

'We don't. You don't take 'em from the nest, Simon.' He leant forward off the gate and we walked along together. I could almost match his steps. 'See, they always have four in a brood and there's always one that doesn't get much food and he's smaller than the rest.'

'Why, Dad?'

'Well, cos the others grab it all and the littl'n gets littler.'

'That's not fair.'

'P'raps not. But it's true . . . anyway, they all try to fly at the same time and the squeaker – that's what they call the littl'n that's not strong enough to fly – he falls and you can sometimes catch 'em runnin' about if the foxes don't get 'em first.'

'Oh.' I stared along the line of trees. 'Where are they then?'

'Well, you only see 'em occasionally, Simon. You have to look for them.'

'All right. I'll look.' I dashed on ahead of him looking round each tree where the cows'd trodden the dry mud to powder and in the long grass and up in any hollows that I could get to. I went backwards and forwards until I got up to the sheep dip in front of the farm cottages at the side of the ruins. 'He's left it too late.' I sat back on the front wheel of a tractor and leant against the radiator. 'I knew 'e bloody would.'

Dad was walking slowly through the long grass right out from the trees swishing the palms of his hands over the seedy tops as if he was wading in water. He didn't seem to be bothering to look at all.

'All this flamin' way for nothin'.' I went and leant with my hands against the wire-meshing round the private bit of the ruins. There were lots of jackdaws sitting on the broken walls and flying in and out of the holes and a little one was standing on the mown bit in the middle but he turned out to be a blackbird when I threw a stone at him.

'What you up to, Nip?'

'Nothin'.'

'Well, you shouldn't chuck stones about there. They'll muck the mowers up.'

I turned away from him. 'Don't care if they do.' I'd wanted a jackdaw for years, so that it could sit on my shoulder and nibble my ear and pick up woodlice like Dad's'd done when he was a boy.

'Well, I'd rather you didn't, Simon.' Dad stood looking at the stone as if he was thinking of climbing the wire to get it. 'Come on, let's go down the other side.' He pointed to the thinner part of chestnut trees that ran back down the fence between the park and the cornfield.

'What for? It's a waste of time.'

'You've got to keep trying, Nip. You never get anywhere if you just give up.'

'Well, all right. But we both gotta look this time. Not just me.'

There were more jackdaws on this side but they were all fully grown and flew away as I got near them. I got to the end of the line and sat down against a tree trunk and wiped the sweat and tears off my face. 'Absolute soddin' waste of time.' I clenched my fists and tried to make myself want to kick something but I knew I'd just be sad in bed tonight on my own thinking about how it would have been if I'd had a jackdaw to play with when the boys had all cleared off somewhere and how they'd all want to come and see it and feed it and then we could play cricket or football together in the back field if we could find a flat bit.

'What's up, Nip?' Dad was standing over me.

'I'm fed up.'

'Why?'

'Cos I wanted a flamin' jackie.'

'Well, you've got one.'

'What?'

'Here.' His hand was inside his jacket and he came closer to me and opened it up.

'O-h, Dad.' His fist was clenched lightly and the bird's head was poking through the ruffed up feathers round its neck. His beak was soft and yellow at the corners like dried egg yolk but his eyes were like wet black buttons of coal. I went to stroke him but he 'jarked' at me and tried to peck me.

'You smashin' little bugger.' I said it without thinking and it didn't seem to matter. 'Try to peck me, would you? You're not scared are you, Jack?' I let my finger run over his head and then down his beak and he arched his neck so that the hair on the back of his neck stuck up even more and his eyes stared at me as if he wouldn't ever give up. 'Lemme 'old 'im, Dad.' I could feel his heart pumping in the palm of my hand and his body felt like a picked herring bone and yet I could feel the strength in his wings and legs when I held him loose.

'Not too tight, Simon. Hold him gently.'

'Yeah. All right.' I nuzzled him up to my cheek and let him bite at my ear and smelt his dark, dry, rotten-wood smell. 'Where d'you find 'im, Dad?'

'Out in the grass. I know a bit more what I'm doing on this lark than you do, Simon. They don't just crawl out the nest and drop. You don't find 'em right under the trees. They usually get out on a branch and then fly a bit before they come down.'

'Why didn't you tell me?'

54

'Well, you were off like a shot, weren't you? You wouldn't wait to be told.'

'Oh . . .' He didn't know what I'd been thinking about him. He looked so happy I wanted to hug him to make up for it. But he should have let *me* find Jack . . . I stroked Jack's head and it was like borrowing someone else's new bike . . . and the more he looked pleased the more I wanted to cry. 'Can he be mine, Dad?'

'Yeah, course he can. That's the idea, Nip, isn't it?'

'I'll try to take care of him, Dad.'

'Good. Just get his wing clipped and when it's grown again he'll be as tame as a kitten and he'll be fun for you during the holidays.'

The sun was still hot when I got home from playing in the churchyard. Mum had gone up to Nan's but she'd left me a drink of orange and two biscuits on the kitchen table and I took them out to the sawing horse and sat there with my legs stretched out and my back up against the struts where Dad fitted the wood to saw it. I had an orange box that I put my drink on so that I had the buildings on one side and our bungalow on the other. I took a long drink and crunched a biscuit and then washed the bits out of my teeth with another drink.

'Watch out, lads, guvnor's back.' George wore a jacket now and a waistcoat and he'd swapped his cap for a blackish pork-pie hat with a pheasant's feather.

'Evenin', bird-man. You're on 'oliday again, aren't you?'

'Hello, Terry.' I waved back at Terry as he went by with a barrow-load of bricks. 'Yeah. Six weeks.'

'Life of Riley, ain't it? You gonna eat all those yerself?' Freddy's head popped up from the other side of the wall he was building.

'No, course 'e ain't.' George settled himself next to me on the bricks. ' 'e's gonna give me some.'

'You can 'ave 'alf a one, George. Gotta save 'alf for Jack.' I looked round. 'Jar-hck!'

There was a muffled squawk from over by Dad's chicken

55

house and Jack flapped on to the washing line, balanced himself then flew in a curve and landed on my shoulder.

'Fly's bent, boy.'

I nuzzled my ear up against Jack's beak. ' 'e'll straighten out when his wing's fully grown.' I crumbled my last half-biscuit in the palm of my hand. 'Come on, Jack. This is for you.'

He trod carefully down my arm and stood on my wrist with his claws biting into my skin as he steadied himself, bent and stabbed at the crumbs and stood up again.

'Ah, 'e's all right.' I pressed his beak gently to make the back of his neck ruff up and his devil's eyes shone at me and then he caught the end of my finger and I could feel him squeezing and letting go. 'He's lovely. Aren't you, boy? Have to watch out for your rings and things though.'

'Oh yeah. Why's that?' George swept biscuit crumbs off his smart working jacket.

'They go for shiny things.'

'Do they? Thought that was jays.'

'Yeah. Jays do and so do magpies but jackies do as well.'

'Be better'n a guard dog then, won't 'e?'

'Oh yeah.' Jack was pecking up the last few crumbs. 'Except that we put 'im in at night.'

'But you're keeping an eye on things 'ere, aren't you?'

'Yeah, course I am. Why?'

'Oh . . .' George stood up and flexed his back and put his hat straight. 'Just that the guvnor's been getting a lot of damage and pinchin' on the other site and 'e's pretty fed up with it.'

'What other site?'

'Oh, it's not here. One in Chichester. But 'e's watchin' us mighty close.'

'What, me as well?'

George smiled. 'Well, me mainly. But you're my mate, aren't you? You and Jack.'

'Oh yes.' I gave my wrist a quick twist and Jack hopped into the air, flapped and settled on my shoulder. 'We'll see everything's all right, won't we, Jack? I'm off up the Close now. I'll be seein' you, George.'

'Aye. Bye, Simon.'

I'd started off making out I was Long John Silver but it made my leg ache having it strung up behind me and I didn't like Gibbser calling Jack 'Pretty Polly' so I'd packed it up.

Aunty Win was in her front garden getting Laurence's playpen in. I stopped to talk to her while she balanced Laurence on her hip and Laurence kept on about stroking the 'dickie-bird' until we let him, and then I went and watched Mr Stroud gardening but he told me to push off because he didn't want that damned bird pinching his peas.

I waited against the Close sign for the boys and let Jack wander up and down my arm. Every time he got to my palm he wiped his beak in the joint at the top of my fingers and it tickled. He perked his head up as Derek Brown's front door closed and hopped up on to my shoulder.

' 'lo, Nipper. 'lo, Jack.'

' 'lo, Derek.'

'What'cha doin'?'

'Nothin' much.'

'Where ya bin?'

'Watchin' the builders. What you bin doin'?'

'Nothin' much.' Derek leant up against the sign and I made space for him.

'Seen Gibbser'n the others?'

'Nope.'

I stood up straighter and leant a new bit of my back against the Close sign. Jack climbed up on to my head and then down on to my other shoulder.

'Wan' 'im for a while?'

'Will 'e bite?'

'Ain' got no teeth.'

'Well, peck then?'

'Don't s'pose so.'

'Go on then.' He went rigid and I slipped my hand under Jack's feet but he wouldn't hop on to Derek's shoulder. ' 'e don't like me.'

'Come on, Derry. 'e likes everybody.'

'Does 'e like me, Nipper?' Geoff Gibbs clapped me on the back and Jack flew up on to Harper's roof.

'Pack it up, Gibbs, you'll frighten him.'

57

'Jus' bin up me Uncle's. 'e's got a new 12-bore. Shall I get it an' we'll 'ave some target practice?'

'You shoot 'im an' I'll bloody shoot you.'

'I'm only jokin', Mush.'

' 'ere, call 'im down, Nipper an' le's 'ave a look at 'im.'

'Don't you hurt him, will you?'

'Nah. Course I won't. Ring 'is bloody neck!'

I stood away from Geoff and held my arm out. 'Jack. C'mon, boy.'

Jack squarked and flew down sideways flapping his cut wing at twice the rate of his good one and settled on my arm.

'When's 'e gonna fly proper?'

'When his wing's grown.'

'Fly away then.'

'He won't.'

'Wanna bet . . . and 'ow d'ya know 'e's a boy?'

'He just is.'

' 'ave you if 'e laid'n egg, wouldn't it?'

'Well he won't.'

' 'ere, le's ave'n.' Geoff shoved his arm under Jack's legs and Jack hopped and jabbed at the same time.

'Ouch! Bloody 'ell!' Geoff shook his hand and then held it out. 'Look at that.' He bent his finger knuckle and a spot of blood oozed out. 'Beak's getting bloody sharp.'

'You frightened him. Here, do it like this.' I took Geoff's wrist and smoothed his hand against my shoulder.

Jack looked at it and put one foot on it, like a lady stepping between puddles, and then the other. Geoff held him away from him and slowly let his arm drop so that he climbed up on to his shoulder. 'See, Mush. I got the knack.'

'Well, don't move too fast and watch out for your ear.'

'Ouch!' Geoff leapt in the air. 'Bloody 'ell!' He rubbed the lobe of his ear and Jack flapped back on to my hand.

'I told you. You 'ave to go gently until 'e gets used to you.'

'You can bloody keep 'im. An' you wanna try feedin' 'im.' Geoff felt his ear and touched at his finger. 'That bleedin', Derry?'

'Don't think so.' Derek's voice was drowned by the camp whistle.

'Where ya goin', Nipper?'

58

'Tea.'

' 'ang on.'

'What?'

' 'e's got broken legs.'

I stopped. 'He hasn't.'

' 'e 'as. Look. They bend the wrong way.'

I held Jack up to my face. His knee caps were at the back. 'See.'

'Well, he can still walk all right.'

'Need to. 'e'll never fly prop'ly.'

'Night, Simon.' We stood back as George and the others went by. 'Keep an eye on the site, mind . . .'

I turned my back on Geoff, and made out I was looking at Jack's knees.

Geoff stood spitting down the drain to miss the bars until George was out of earshot and then he drew his arm back as if he was going to hit me and scratched his ear.

'What's all that about looking after the site?'

'Nothin' much.'

Geoff grinned. 'That's what we can do tonight. Nice game'a hide'n-seek round Nipper's building site.'

'No, we're not. I'm goin' 'ome for tea.'

'C'mon, Browner.' Geoff slung his arm over Derek's shoulder. 'We'll get the others. See you there, Nipper.'

Mum had laid the fire out with crumpled newspapers, kindling, a couple of big bits and some coal and she'd rearranged the brass ornaments on the mantelpiece and put some of them in the fender. She'd changed her frock and combed her hair and powdered her nose, and she smelt like fresh washing in off the line as she brushed past me to get to the airing cupboard. I sat back in the brown armchair and played at pressing my fingertips on the polished wooden arms and watching my fingerprints dry out.

'When's tea, Mum?'

'Any minute now, my precious.' She ballooned the table-cloth out and spread the creases flat and then slewed it round so that it went on like a diamond.

A pair of ankles ran past the side window on the scaffold-

59

ing next door and then another pair in short trousers that knocked a cement bucket which fell with a soft thud.

'That somebody at the door, Simon?'

'No, Mum.'

'What was it then?'

'Just the boys. They're playing on the buildings.'

'You going out there after tea?'

'Might do. Where's Dad?'

'Oh he'll be here soon.' Mum was primming her hair up in the reflection from the china cabinet. 'He was going to make a phone call from Tangmere Corner on the way back.'

'A phone call!' I sat forward. I couldn't remember us ever making a phone call and I'd never even been in the phone box except with Jimmy Phillips when we were looking for dog ends. 'Who to?'

'Aunty at Petersfield. But we'll tell you all about it when he gets back.'

S'pose that means Old Gran, I thought, and I sat back and tried to ignore Colin Gander who was down on his knees on the scaffolding looking through our window and poking his tongue out at me.

The front gate clicked and Colin lay flat and rolled over and back against the wall.

'He's here, Simon.'

'I know, Mum.'

I sat up to the table and took a slice of bread and butter and started to spread it with strawberry jam. Mum'd put scent on and I couldn't stop noticing it. There'd never been that smell in here before. It belonged in their bedroom by her dressing table when they were getting ready for church. They were whispering in the kitchen and I went over and fiddled with the ornaments on the mantelpiece so that I could hear what they were saying but Mum only said 'Oh, that'll be lovely, darling. Thank you,' and then they came in.

'Hungry, Nip?'

'Yes, Dad.'

'And then he's off out to play, aren't you, my pet?'

'Yeah.' I looked around but I couldn't see anything special except that Mum and Dad were standing closer together than usual. We hadn't won the pools or got promoted at football and it wasn't anyone's birthday. 'Yeah. On the buildings.'

'Oh yes.' Dad was smiling like Pop did when he was doing a christening.

'With the boys . . . on the scaffolding.'

Dad just grunted and Mum cuddled in closer to him and said how I'd promised to be careful and not to get into mischief.

'Can we get going then, Mum. I'm starving.'

'Yes, course you can.'

Dad pulled Mum's chair out for her and she sat down as if she was on a bus that was pulling away and Dad tried to pour the tea out but Mum said he was doing it all wrong because he had to put the milk in first so he sat down and she stood up and I couldn't see what was so funny about that and spread another slice of strawberry jam.

'Do you know what it is soon, Simon?'

' 'olerdees still.'

'*Holidays*. Dear, oh dear, what a slovenly way of speaking you're getting into. Sooner you get into Chichester to school the better.' They looked at each other and then at the ceiling. 'Yes, I know it's the holidays. But what else is it?'

'I dunno.'

'Think.'

I wiped jam off my plate with a crust and stuffed it into my mouth and rinsed it round with tea. 'I can't, Mum. What is it?'

'It's our anniversary.' They both reached across the table and touched hands. 'Eleven years.'

'Oh.' I could feel a burp coming up but I held it back. 'Any more tea?'

'Is that all you can say?'

'Well . . . *please*?'

'Oh, Simon.'

'Leave it, Ina. He doesn't understand.' Dad let go of Mum's hand and turned to me. 'It's like this, Simon.'

I sat and listened to how important anniversaries were to women and how grateful I ought to be and what a wonderful thing it was to be married and have a happy home and '. . . do you see, Simon?'

61

'Yes, Dad.' I didn't blink so he'd know how hard I'd been listening. 'Where's my cuppa tea, Mum?'

'And so, Simon' – he stopped until I looked at him again – 'we thought we'd have a little holiday.'

'Oh yeah.'

'And you could have a week with Nan and Grandad up with Aunty at Petersfield. How'd you like that?'

Petersfield, with Nan and Grandad! Aunty lived in a pub and there was the lake but I wouldn't know what the boys were doing and—

'You wouldn't miss us too much, would you, lovey? Just for a week? And you'd have Nan and Grandad.'

'Yes, Mum.'

'What's up then?'

'Well, who'd look after Jack?'

'Oh, don't worry about that. We'll think of something.'

'Yes but—'

'But what?'

'Oh never mind.' I stood up. 'If I don't get out soon the boys'll 've gone off without me.'

'What about your cup of tea?'

'Don't want it now, Mum.'

I closed the kitchen door behind me and leant against the shed wall. The boys'd be playing on the buildings and going up the dell and over the Common and I could've helped George and looked after Jack and it'd probably rain all the time at Petersfield and . . . 'Oh, sod it,' I said to myself, 'I'm not going,' and I climbed over the sawing horse and down the bricks and crept in between the crossed bits of wood they'd nailed across the doorway of the new bungalow.

'Took yer time, didn't you?' Geoff Gibbs was sitting on the brick outline of the front window with Colin Gander and Jimmy Phillips and Jerry Henry and Kenny Lane.

'Yeah, they kept me talkin'.'

'C'mon, let's get started. Browner'll be down in a minute.'

'Where's 'ome then?'

'That fireplace.' Geoff pointed to a hole in the centre wall.

'That's no good.' Colin went over to the window. 'They'll only 'ang about in 'ere and we'll never get 'ome. Make it the concrete mixer, then they'll 'ave to come off it to get in 'ere to find us.'

'Yeah, all right. 'oo's up?'

'Let's dib for it.'

'Dib for it?' Geoff cuffed Jerry with the back of his hand and threw his cap out of the window. 'Bloody sissy thing. We'll spin for it.' He tossed his Irish penny up and caught it and covered it on his wrist and we all had to call until there were only two of us left. 'Right, it's you and 'enry then, Nipper. Push off'n 'ide yer eyes an' give us an 'undred.'

'What's the boundary?'

'The buildin's?'

'Yeah,' Colin said. 'And no crossing the road.'

'Right. C'mon then, Jerry.'

We sat down with our backs against the rubber wheels of the mixer and Jerry rubbed the sandy mud off his cap.

'You enjoying the 'olidays, Jerry?'

'Yeah, s'pose so.'

'Reckon we'll 'ave fun?'

'Dunno.'

'Spec we'll go up the windmill and Trundle 'ill and all some time, don't you?'

'We always say we will but we never do.'

'Go sledgin' if it was winter.'

'Never get any snow.'

'Or down the beach.'

'Too far.'

'Yeah, s'pose it is. We'd better start lookin', 'adn't we?'

'Yeah, s'pose so.'

Jerry yelled 'coming' and we sauntered back over to the buildings. Kenny Lane's head was sticking out from behind an empty drum by the builder's shed but we left him till last so that he'd be on the post next time.

We played three games but then ran out of places to hide and Jerry Henry hurt his ankle when he fell over a bucket going round a corner and Kenny Lane said he was going home when Geoff pushed him over on a wet cement floor for catching him having a pee in the hedge down by the pig pen.

The last rays of the sun were straining through the hedge

and it threw a long, damp shadow over the rough ground and piles of bricks and ballast.

'What we gonna do then?' Jimmy Phillips was tossing pebbles into a drum of water.

'I'm goin' 'ome.' Kenny Lane kept rubbing at his bottom where he'd sat in the cement.

'So'm I.' Jerry had one foot off the ground and was leaning against the mixer.

'An' Browner never came out after all. I'll get 'im when I see 'im. You comin', Col?'

'Where?'

'Go down your place'n . . .' Geoff cupped his hand against Colin's ear and I kicked a piece of dried concrete at the oil drum.

'Yeah, all right. Bye, Nipper.' Colin did his windcheater up and stuffed his hand into his side pockets and he and Geoff walked off up the Close.

Jerry Henry hobbled after them and Kenny Lane caught him up. Jimmy Phillips's mum called him and he yelled back that he was coming before she could shout that it was his bath time.

'See you tomorrow, Jim.'

'Yeah, spec so.' His shadow leapt ahead of him and he disappeared through his gate.

I sat down with my back against the bricks and stared at the last lines of light in the sky along the hedge by the dell.

The building site looked like a ghost town and the darkness seemed to be seeping out of it like melted tar. I crept inside one of the houses and waited until my eyes got used to the dark. The floor was covered with cement droppings that crunched under my feet. They'd have to clean the floors before anyone could move in and lay down lino or carpets. If me and Janet Rolls got married I'd do all that kind of work and she'd do the cooking and look after my baby. But Janet was always playing with the other girls now and I never even caught her looking at me. P'raps George'd move in when he got married. Maybe he'd have some children I could take for walks in their prams and play with when they got bigger and they'd call me Uncle. And if George was still a foreman when I left school he might let me work for him because he'd be so grateful that I'd helped him look after the site. I leant my head against a scaffold pole and let my hand run up and down its rusty surface. I'd probably be a bricklayer and lay a hundred bricks an hour and keep yelling for more pug. My hands were cold so I rubbed them together. Laying bricks would be cold in the winter. Maybe I'd be a fireman and come sliding down a pole through a hole in the floor. I picked at the scales of rust. The pole was rough. I tried to monkey-climb it but it was too narrow. I clasped my hands around it and worked my feet up. Maybe I could go right up and step over the wall and on to the scaffolding on the other side. I rested my back against the wall and pushed up. It gave way.

I clung on to the pole and looked round. The wall fell faster, arching over like a pile of dominoes, until it hit the scaffold poles the other side and then it broke up and the mortar spilled out like sand.

I dropped down the pole and slunk out without looking behind me. 'I didn't do that. It fell over by itself . . .' There was nobody about so I slipped in behind the workmen's hut and knelt down and put my hands together.

'Dear Lord Jesus,' I whispered so that only He'd hear me. 'This is the worst thing I've ever done. And if I'd known it was going to happen I'd've stayed in and listened to the wireless. Please help me so that they don't find out. And don't make George get the sack or I'll have to own up.' I couldn't think of anything else to say so I went through it again until my knees started to hurt and then I went out the back way and through the hedge and over the back field and came back down to the Close from Town Lane. I passed Bladder Payton on his way to the Men's Club and said 'hello,' so that he'd know where I'd been but he just said ' 'lo,' and I knew he didn't know who it was in the dark.

I tapped on the front window as well as the side one as I went round the house and scuffed my feet on the mat as I went in to make sure there wasn't any brick dust left on my shoes.

'Wherever've you been, Simon?'

'Up the lane, Mum.'

'What at this time of night? It's nearly ten o'clock.'

'Yes, Mum. I climbed a tree to wait and see if any rabbits came out.'

'Well, I called and called over that building site. Couldn't think where you'd got to.'

'Oh no, Mum. I wasn't there. The boys all went home early.'

'Well, I don't want you playing out there any more.'

'I know, Mum. I keep tellin' 'em but they won't listen.'

She went on into the living room and I ran the cold tap for a drink of water and washed my hands quietly to get the rust stains off.

'Mu-um?'

'Yes?'

'When'd we go to Petersfield?'

'I dunno. Soon I expect. Why?'

'Well, I think I'd like to go.'

'Would you, my love. What's brought that change of heart on?' She came and loved me up against her. 'Doesn't matter why. I'm ever so glad. The change'll do you good.'

*W*e'd come in to Chichester early to get a front place in the queue for the Petersfield bus in case there was a crowd so that Nan could have a seat between the wheels. Grandad had gone off to the shops and Nan'd left me sitting on my case by the bus stop so that she could go and buy Aunty Rene a pretty headscarf in Morant's. They'd given me Old Gran's spare case for my clothes because they said anything bigger would be too heavy for me to carry. I'd complained because it would only take my pyjamas and dressing-gown and slippers and short trousers but they'd said short trousers would be better so that I didn't get too hot and sticky running around by the lake and it wouldn't matter so much if I fell in. I turned the case up on its end so that it was easier to sit on and watched the rooks up on the cathedral spire. Wonder how they got up there to build the spire? Couldn't have had scaffolding in those days. The word 'scaffolding' made a shiver go down my back but nobody was watching me.

An old man with a face like dried gravy and a grey beard was asleep on the bus-shelter seat. A lady with a little girl sat down next to him but he started to snore and she moved further away. His shoes had no laces and were tied around with string and his old army overcoat was trailing on the ground. He snorted again and his mouth hung open. People veered out around him as they walked past. I kept looking across the road to Morant's big double-glass door but there was no sign of Nan.

Whoosh! A long wet streak spread out in the dust. He must've been eating tomatoes. I tried not to look but my head wouldn't turn round and I shivered back against the bus stop.

'C'mon, Simon.' I felt Grandad's hand on my shoulder and I clung to him. 'We'll get our tickets in the bus station and wait for it over there.'

'What about Nan, Grandad?'

'She not back yet?'

'No, Grandad.'

'Well, we'll wait for her over by Morant's then. She won't be long.'

I kept looking back as we went across the road and I could still see the old man, when we got across, in the reflection in the shop window. Two policemen came up to him from the direction of the Market Cross. One gave him a little push and he stood up as he fell off the seat, then he turned and staggered from one side of the pavement to the other past the cathedral. He was shouting things at the policemen and waving his arms so that his old coat flapped in the wind and he looked like a dead hydrangea flower floating down a flooded ditch.

'What's the matter with him, Grandad?'

'Drunk, Simon.' Grandad had his blue suit on and his trilby and he stood so straight that his reflection looked like one of those figures in the window showing off clothes for sale. 'Blind drunk, poor chap.'

'Do you feel sorry for him then, Grandad?'

His arm folded around my neck. 'S'sh, Simon! Here comes Nan. Not a word to her mind.'

'All right, Grandad. But she'll see the—'

'No she won't. They'll probably clear it up before we get there. Manage your case?'

'Yes thanks.' I checked the handle to make sure it hadn't got splashed and followed him as he went to open the glass doors for Nan.

'Blessed performance in there!' Nan was puffed up in her Jaeger coat and scarf like a thrush in winter. 'And we'll have the devil's own job getting a seat.'

'No we won't, Madam. There's nobody waiting for it, so I thought we'd get our tickets in the bus station and sit and wait there till it comes.'

'You sure? Yes, well, I s'pose I would come over all giddy if I had to stand for long.' Nan was fastening her handbag.

68

'So long as we don't have to have a seat over the wheel or in the back. I got a pretty little scarf for Rene, though I doubt she'll ever wear it.'

'What'cha get it for then?'

Nan slipped her handbag along her arm and her other arm through Grandad's. 'Don't be silly, Art. It's a present. It's the thought that counts, you know. C'mon, Simon lovey. You walk on my other side and don't bang me with your case.'

The bus station was up some stone steps next to the post office. It smelt of cigarette ends. Grandad went up to the hatch for the tickets and Nan and I sat down on the long seat by the wall and let the hot air from the grilles blow up our legs.

'You want to spend a penny, Simon?'

'No, Nan. Why?'

'Well, it'll be an hour or so before we get there. You hungry?'

'No.' I looked over to the bus shelter. They'd spread sand over the pavement. 'No thanks.'

Grandad was counting his change. 'Dear oh dear. Dear old business this is getting. Nearly ten bob. Was only about half a crown before the war.'

'Well, don't forget we've got—' Nan looked at me and I tried not to be listening. 'Anyway, it's only once in a blue moon.'

'Aye.' Grandad slipped the tickets into his wallet. 'Aye, so it is. Hey, what about this, Simon?' He was groping about in the shopping basket. 'Hope I haven't spilt any.'

'What is it?'

'You take a swig'a that.' He peeled off a brown paper bag and handed me a coconut.

'Cor thanks, Grandad.'

'Huh! He didn't want anything when I offered him a fruit bon-bon. And what'er you doing crumpling up that nice bag?'

'What do yer think of that?'

'Smashin', Grandad.' It was furry against my lips and sweet and cold on my throat.

'And you're surely not going to go cracking it in the bus, are you?'

69

'It's done.' Grandad winked at me and made one side of his moustache twitch. 'The assistant in the shop cracked the shell without splitting the fruit and drilled the eyes out. Lord knows how he did it.'

'Well, it'll look awful him munching coconut all the way to Petersfield and he'll get bound up to the eyeballs and then 'e won't want 'is dinners.'

'Course he'll want his dinners. Why Rene'll've done a lovely big joint'a roast beef to serve cold afterwards in the bar and thick gravy and roast potatoes and sprouts and cauliflower and—'

'All right, Art. You make it sound as if you don't get fed at 'ome. I work my fingers to the bone and—'

'What do I get for it?' Grandad and I said it together and then we both said 'Nothing'.

Nan started to get watery-eyed but Grandad said we were only teasing and then she sat back looking miffed until the bus came and he took her arm over the road and I had to carry my case and the shopping bag.

Nan took up two thirds of the seat but Grandad said he was 'quite comfor-table thank you' on the edge. They sat me in the seat in front of them by the window so that I could look out over the edge of Harting Hill when we came to it. The bus pulled out past the Market Cross and up Summers-dale and past where we'd played Lavant at football and then off to the left towards the names of places I'd only ever heard Old Gran talking about and I'd never been to before.

'How did Gran get out here in the old days, Nan?'

'What, my duck?'

'Out here. It's miles from Hanover.'

'Pony and trap, I s'pose, most of the time and sometimes on her bike, I expect.'

'What for, Nan?'

'Oh, delivering letters and parcels and things.'

'Old Grandad Grainger was up to all sorts of stunts selling things you know, Simon.'

'Was he, Grandad?'

'Bit too fond of the parsnip wine though.'

'Cor yes.' Grandad smacked his lips. 'Lovely droppa homemade he made. And he sold it.'

'Not so much as he drank though.'

'Well, I'm looking forward to a nice droppa cheese and pickled gherkin and a pint of beer.'

'One. One pint of beer. I don't want you up all night.'

A lady in the seat next to us folded her coat under her.

'Do you good to have a drop of Guinness.'

'It would not. Make me as giddy as an owl.'

The road rushed past and then the bank fell away and it was like looking down from a plane. Trees grew out of the hill and the tops of them flew past below the level of the road. The bus dived forward and it felt as if the back was catching up with the front. I closed my eyes but it made me feel sick so I opened them again.

There was nowhere like this around our way. We could have made parachutes and jumped into the tops of trees and gone fishing in the river like Tom Sawyer and gone sledging and making camps in the caves in the hillside.

'Like it, Simon?'

'Cor yes, Grandad.'

'Well, you wait until we get to Petersfield.'

'Why?'

'Well you can go swimming in the lake and fishing maybe and playing darts in the pub and—'

'They won't allow him in the bar.'

'Why not?'

'Because he's not old enough.'

'Stripe me, he's only a shaver! He's not old enough for them to bother about.'

'Course he is.'

'Well, he's got every right.'

'How'd you make that out?'

'Took his first steps in that bar, didn't he? So Mum's always saying.'

'Ah, little love.' Nan leant over and hugged me and I shrank back down again as the lady next to us looked up. 'But you were a dear little fella when you lived up along'a us.' Nan rubbed my head and I sat staring straight ahead as she did it.

*

The Downs fell away on each side and the bus levelled out round a corner and there, glinting through the trees, was the lake. The water breathed forward and back on the tiny sandy beaches and slopped up under the tree roots where the banks were high. A dozen or so rowing boats were moored on one side and there was a jetty where some people were climbing out of a boat. On the far side, about fifty yards from the shore, was an island about the size of Grandad's back garden. Three swans sailed across the lake like Spanish galleons, dipping their beaks from side to side as they went. A group of ducks were in their way but they spread and then came together as the swans went through them. Beyond the lake, banks of gorse bushes rose up like folds of icing on a wedding cake and some boys were playing cricket against a waste-paper basket by a wooden hut that sold ice cream. I turned my head until my face was pressing into the back of the seat and then the bus turned a corner and we were in the town.

The joined-together houses stood back from the road and they each had a strip of garden full of flowers and it reminded me of the cottages in Hanover. Most of the front doors were open and I could see inside the hallways, some with coats and walking sticks and some with little tables with plants on them. The bus stopped with a bump at the crossroads and I read PORTSMOUTH and WINCHES-TER one way and MIDHURST and PETWORTH the other.

'We far from home, Grandad?'

'Nigh on twenty miles.'

'Cor!'

'Aye, I shouldn't want to walk it.' Grandad leant forward over the seat and I leant back. 'This is the market. Do you remember it, Simon?'

'Course 'e doesn't, Art. He was no age at all when he was up here last.'

The bus bobbled over the grey bricks and then ground forward round the first side of the square. The square was flat cobbles and iron pig and cow pens had been put up on half of it and the other half was covered with stalls on wheels and small shops with only a coloured canvas over them or no

72

roof at all. Cabbages and cauliflowers and leeks and oranges and apples and swedes seemed to be spilling about in all directions and a man in a white overall and blue and white striped apron and a straw hat was ringing a bell in front of a butcher's stall.

'Won't the flies get on that meat, Grandad? All out in the open?'

'What? With that row going on?'

'Don't be silly, Art.'

'We'll have some of those th'ausages to bring back though, Simon.'

'We won't, you know.'

'All lovely and spicy with thick skins that burst as they fry up crispy on the inside.'

'And sprats, Grandad?'

'Stinking my kitchen out!'

'Aye, with salt and vinegar.'

'Will you stop it?'

The bus came to a stop by a line of other buses with odd names on them like Chilhurst and West Meon near a building with a stone clock on it that looked down over the square.

'That's the Town Hall, Simon. And the Market Clock. It's got a lovely chime.'

'Wake you up every hour on the hour.' Nan was buttoning her coat up and shifting her handbag into a new position. 'Wonder if Rene's got any cottonwool.'

'Want me to get some?'

'No I don't. Let's get our stuff over to the Oak first. Never see you again if you go running off round that market before we've even got here.'

The cobblestones were bumpy under my feet and I wondered how you could run on them. I followed Nan and Grandad over to the edge of the square and dabbled my hand in a stone horse-trough with a thing like a sun dial in the middle.

'Goes back to the Middle Ages that does, Simon.'

'So'll we if we don't get a move on.'

73

We turned into a narrow lane with pavements on each side and the sun bounced off the walls and made my eyes screw up.

'Here we are then.'

I stared up at the smoky glass windows with BEERS and WINES and SPIRITS written across them in wispy letters like the wind.

'We going in the bar way or up the side?'

'Oh, try the bar else I'll snag my stockings on those crates and things.'

Grandad put his case down and gripped the brass door handle and twisted it. The door opened.

A high, polished bar ran along one side with four handles in the middle with a tea towel draped over them. There were seats against all the walls with black tables in front of them, except for a space with a long rubber mat that ran up to the dart board. The light above the board was bent forward and had a dented green shade. At the back of the bar, amongst the bottles hanging upside-down and the glass cabinets of cigarettes and bars of chocolates, there were two doors.

'Shall we go on in?'

'Blimey, I should think so, now we're here.'

Grandad lifted the flap of the bar and as I walked through I smelt the flat heavy-metal smell of the empty bottles and the tin pans under the pumps that caught the drips of beer. He opened a door with a PLAYERS PLEASE poster on it and we walked into the clear light at the bottom of the stairs. The stairs and banisters wound up and round and I ran my hand over the shiny surface and the round knob like a mahogany football at the end.

'Had we better knock?'

Grandad tapped on the door and they let me in first.

Uncle Nat was asleep in the armchair. He could go to sleep at any time, they said, and I'd never seen anybody more asleep than Uncle Nat looked in the armchair. He lay with his bald head tilted back on two cushions in the niche where the arm met the back of the chair, like a duck egg in a nest of feathers with his lips going thin as he breathed in and wrinkling like creased-up rubber as he breathed out.

'Do you think he's asleep?'

'Looks a bit like it.' Grandad stood his case down gently.

The willow-pattern clock on the sideboard flicked on to quarter to one and the quarter hour chimed out like metal flower petals in an up-draught. The old grandfather clock in the corner ticked a solid trudging tick and the two of them reminded me of when the bells of Stepney sang 'When will that be?' in a light high sprinkling voice and the Great Bell of Bow said 'I really don't know' in a dark, atticy sort of way like the solicitor in *The Old Curiosity Shop* when Mum read to me.

The back door opened and an arm, with the apron sleeve rolled up to the elbow, pushed in a wicker washing basket of blue sheets.

'No, leave them there, darlin', and finish the others.'

The arm disappeared and the door blew open and then swung closed.

'Busy I expect.'

'Aye, I expect so.'

I looked at myself in the glassed back of the sideboard mirror and picked up a brazil nut and then put it down again.

'C'mon, Grandad.' I pulled at his arm as Uncle Nat grunted and carried on sleeping. 'Let's go and find them.'

Aunty Rene and Beth were sitting at the old wooden table in the centre of the yard shelling peas with two lines of washing flapping about their ears.

'Hello, Aunty.'

'Simon!' Aunty stood up and held her arms wide. 'Come'n give yer old aunty a booful love.' I felt myself smothered inside her apron and woolly cardigan and her arms gripped my head around my ears and went right down and round my back. 'What a lovely boy and getting so tall now. Now that'll be you taking after your Uncle Nat because your dad and grandad— Hello Arthur, Fran . . . they're both short but you'll see if I'm not right.' She held me away from her and gave a little laugh as if she'd won a raffle and then hugged me back again before I was ready for it and it was like having a door slammed in my face. 'How are you?'

'Not too bad, Rene, but I *do* get these awful—'

'Simon?' She caught me again but I was ready for her.

75

'Fine, Aunty, thank you.'

Nan came up and let Aunty kiss her on one side and Grandad took his cap off and kissed her on the other. Beth sat at the table humming and muttering 'dear oh dear' and dropping peas in the shell bowl and shells in the saucepan.

'I expect you're parched, aren't you? Nice cup of tea?'

'Well, I am rather, Rene.'

'Good. Well, just pop the kettle on, Fran dear.' I closed my eyes and winced. '. . . while young Beth and I finish these peas and then we'll all have one.'

Nan's jaw had dropped but she recovered enough to stand back with her legs together. 'I'm not really very sure of the Rayburn, Rene. P'raps . . .?'

'Aye, I'll do it.' Grandad put his trilby hat on the table and went into the kitchen. There was a clatter and a sharp squirt and another clatter as he put the lid on and came out dusting water off his waistcoat. 'Blimey bill! You've got some pressure there, Rene. Came out in chunks.'

Aunty Rene wiped him over with the corner of the sheet on the line and sat down again. 'Come on, Beth, watch what you're doin', darlin'.' She fished the pods out of the saucepan and dropped them one at a time in front of Beth into the basket. 'Still, I dare say the shucks'er better'n the peas.'

Grandad avoided Beth's groping hand and took a pod and ran his nose along its length. 'N'no.' He shook his head. 'Bought'ens. Not bad though.'

'Man in the market said they were today's.' Aunty tapped Beth's fingers and she took them out of her mouth.

'Yesterday's, p'raps.' Grandad squeezed the pod. 'No later.'

'Oh dear, and I do always like to serve my lodgers up fresh vegetables.'

'Well, they are fresh.' Grandad winked and put a couple in his mouth. 'Freshish.'

Nan coughed and cleared her throat and Grandad sat down. 'And how are *you*, Rene?'

'Busy.' Aunty carried on shelling peas as if she was spitting bullets with her thumb. 'I've got four casuals and two near-regulars and Mr Stodgel tonight. And they'll all want an evening meal—'

'Oh!' Nan stood up straighter. 'You know how I hate having people watching me eat.'

'Don't worry. They'll have theirs in the smoking-room after us. Except for Mr Stodgel, of course.'

'Only strangers make me come over all queer.' Nan steadied herself. 'I do wish I could get over these awful nerves.'

'Well, my knees have been playing me up no end lately and there's a hundred and one things to do and Mum's—'

'And I haven't had a proper night's sleep since I don't know when . . . last night I took two sleeping capsules and just lay there—'

'And there's a stream of washing because I do insist the sheets are changed every day, you know, Arthur . . .' Grandad nodded that he knew. 'And then Mum keeps—'

'And this awful sinus trouble.' Nan suddenly sounded as if she was talking through a tube. 'I shouldn't be surprised if Dr Collins doesn't insist I have some treatment.'

Grandad blew his nose and put his hanky back in his top pocket.

'Not that one, Art. How many times do I have to say it? Use a work one.'

'I'm not at work. I'm on holiday.'

'And Mum will keep slipping off up the shops as soon as my back's turned.' Aunty plonked the last of the peas into the pot and smoothed her hand over them as if she was setting the seal on a letter. 'And now I suppose I'll have to go and make the tea.'

'Do you want me to give you a hand, Rene?' Nan reached out to the table to steady herself as if the ground was spinning but I thought I saw her looking through her fingers when Aunty said No, she'd do it herself.

Grandad slid along the bench so that there was a blanket between him and the kitchen window and pulled out his packet of Woodbines and lit one. Beth stacked pea pods on top of one another in a square that came to a point at the top like an electricity pylon. I moved round next to her.

'Careful, my love.' Beth put her arms round the castle as if it was going to blow away.

'What are you doing, Beth?'

'Making a tower, my darling.' Beth pushed her glasses further up her nose. 'A green tower.'

'What for, a green princess?' Grandad blew smoke at the sky.

'Oh no, Uncle. You don't get green princesses.'

'No, course you don't.'

Beth pulled at her white ankle socks under the table. 'Green frogs . . . get lots of green frogs. And elves—'

'In green tunics and brown boots, made out of—' Grandad was staring at us. ' . . . leaves.'

'Maybe we'd better get off in and get this tea, Simon.' He took his cigarette end over to the border by the wall and trod it into the earth. 'After we've buried the evidence.'

I followed him and looked round for Beth but she was talking to herself among the pea pods.

Aunty'd been up to wash and change while the tea mashed and now she was back with a blue cardigan on and her hair fluffed up at the back. She had the biggest tea pot I'd ever seen and her tea cosy had been knitted and stuffed and looked like a rooster. She poured the tea quickly with one hand while she put out tea plates for the biscuits with the other.

Uncle Nat snorted and rolled over and gradually sat up like an Eskimo climbing up through a hole in the ice. 'You got here then?'

'Aye.'

'Smells my tea.' Aunty Rene wagged the tea pot spout at him. 'Sleep through a bombing raid he would but a droppa tea'd wake him up sure as day.'

'Thank you.' Uncle Nat took his cup and two biscuits and balanced it on the arm of his chair.

'And how are you, Nat?' Nan broke a biscuit and nibbled it.

'Here, drink your tea while it's hot, Simon.'

'Thank you, Aunty.'

Uncle Nat came out of a yawn that left a gap between his false teeth and top gum. 'Tired. Haven't been too good lately.' He stifled another yawn.

Uncle Nat and Grandad didn't look like brothers.

'How's the business, then?'

78

'Shouldn't grumble, Arthur. But I will.' Uncle Nat shook his head as he blew his tea. 'Can't get the brewers to do anything with this place and it's not a popular beer.'

'Be a darned sight more popular if you'd let them drink in peace and leave off about politics.'

'Well, it's gone too far.' Uncle Nat eased himself up on his elbows. 'Half the nation's nationalised and the other half's penalised. Want to get back to good old Liberal principles.'

'Well, I can't really see much to choose between them.' Nan passed her cup over and Aunty filled it up.

'Oh there is, Fran.' Aunty Rene put a half spoonful of sugar in Nan's tea. 'You ought to take an interest. But not so that it turns business away.'

'Well, I'm sure I wouldn't do that.'

'No, *I'm* sure you wouldn't.'

'What do you mean by that, Art?'

'Well, just that—'

'I wouldn't know what to do with myself if I went in that bar, with all those strange people and all that smoke.'

'Well, it's our livelihood, Fran. We can't afford to be fussy. And it's very difficult with Mum always—'

'Fussy!' Nan's cup was just short of her lips. '*Fussy?*'

'Well . . . self-conscious then. But it's very difficult with Mum always around.'

'Well, I do wish I felt better.' Nan drooped again like a flower in a jar that'd run out of water. 'You know how I like to take my turn.'

'Where is Gran, Aunty?'

'Yes, where is she?'

Aunty thought for a minute. 'I don't know. You see what I mean? She got on a bus the other day to go down to the lake and went to sleep and woke up in West Meon. The police were ever so nice about it and she hadn't got the fare to go all that way. And the *washing!*'

Grandad was choking on a half-dunked biscuit and when he'd stopped coughing he said that if the old girl did that down our way she'd end up in the sea.

'It's no laughing matter, Art. I couldn't go traipsing out all over the countryside after her.'

'And neither can I, Fran. What with Beth and all.'

'Yes, but where is she, Aunty?' I could imagine her black skirts ballooning up in the lake and her not even being missed.

'I don't know, lovey. Go and see if Beth does. And here, take her tea out with you.'

Beth's pea castle was a foot high now and she waved her hand at me and said 'careful darlin',' as I put her tea down.

'Where's Old Gran, Beth?'

'S'sh.'

'Why?'

'Nobody knows.'

'I know. That's why I'm asking.'

She came closer to me. 'We mustn't say.'

'Why not?'

'Because she said so.'

'Well, where is she then?'

'In her bedroom. She says if nobody wants to see her she'll stay on her own.'

'Well, if nobody knows she's there they can't go and see her, can they?'

'Hush, darling.'

'Why?'

'They'll hear you.'

'Oh.' I hunched my head up closer to Beth. She was about sixteen, they said, but she was very big and gentle and she had a hairy top lip. 'Can't I go and see her?'

'Oh yes, darling. You can. But don't tell *them*.' She looked all round as if she thought the Russians were after her and then got up and took me down the passage at the side of the pub. 'You go on in here.' She opened the side door. 'I'll show you but they mustn't see us.'

Old Gran was sitting by the window in a high-backed chair with green padded arms. Her face was sideways on and she looked so much like Nan's picture of Queen Victoria that I nearly walked out again backwards.

'Hello, Gran.'

She turned slowly as if she had a stiff neck but her thin lips

80

parted and her cheeks swelled up in a smile like two old Cox's apples and she held her arms out. 'Simon.' She said it as if I'd turned up from the dead. 'Oh, Simon.'

I gave her a love from the side and let my lips rest on her scaly cheek and the wisps of grey hair behind her ear, that'd fallen out of her bun, stroked my cheek like frayed silk. Her clothes gave off a kind of echo and it made me think of Christmas when I was little and shopping in Woolworth's when they still had the wooden counters and wires with metal barrels on for sending back change. I loved in closer to her and her arm reached up me but I was too much to the side so I slid round in front and put my head in her lap and it felt like a cuckoo in a hedge-sparrow's nest. Her fingers teased and tested in the hair on the back of my neck and I could feel her wedding ring slopping up and down from the knuckle to the joint and I knew she was staring out of the window and not looking at anything.

'You're all here then?'

'Yes, Gran.'

'Nan all right?'

'M'm. Not too bad.'

'And young Arthur?'

I lifted my head and peeped at her. I imagined Grandad going courting Nan and asking her to marry him by the gate in the low wall with honeysuckle and roses growing along it and Old Gran coming out of the old post office and telling him to clear off and Grandad Grainger mending his bike before he died. But I couldn't imagine Grandad being any younger than he'd been in the picture in the front room of him espaliering apple trees in Mrs Evans's garden just after the First World War. And he looked pretty much the same then as he did now.

'Eh?'

'Yes. I think so.'

'Good. Good man he is.'

'Is he, Gran?'

'Yes.' She was staring further away now – I could feel it by the way her lap moved. 'She's luckier than she knows.'

'Gra-an?'

'Yes.'

'Did you chase him off with a broom once?'

'What?'

'When they were courting?'

'Can't remember. May've done. What if I did?'

I smiled into her lap. She said it like Jack pecking at me to make out he was angry but not meaning to hurt. 'Did you, Gran?'

'Oh, Simon!' She stopped fiddling with my hair and clasped her fingers together like Nan shutting the sweet tin to stop herself eating any more. 'You do torment a body.'

'But did you?'

'Yes, I jolly well did. Him and Nat always pestering about after Fran and Rene and my Fred up to goodness knows what instead of helping out with the post office and the whole place crawling with Canadians and—'

'But that was after, Gran.'

'What was after?'

'The Canadians. They didn't come over till the war started and that was in 1914 and my dad was born in 1912 so Nan and Grandad'd've been married before they got here.'

'Well, what's that got to do with it?'

'Well, they must've been married before the Canadians got 'ere, so why did you chase 'im with a broom?'

'I've told you. They kept pestering my gals.'

'Oh.' Old Gran's lap relaxed and I lay deeper into it. My ear was pressed flat and it began to make echoing rings of tingles like the radio waves on the front of my book about the wireless that they'd let me look at when I was small but I'd never been able to understand.

'You going to sleep?'

'Nearly, Gran.' I resettled my head.

'Well, don't go to sleep there. You'll make me stiff.' She turned my face over and I slewed round so that I was sitting with my head back looking up at her.

'How's those little cousins of yours?'

'What, Michael and Jonathan? They're all right. Only see'm at Christmas and when it's Nan's birthday.'

'They won't let me see'm.'

'They do, Gran. You saw them at Nan's birthday.'

'Well, they never bring them here to see me.' Old Gran sat

forward and stuck her chin out like she'd done when she'd told Nan she wasn't going to be seen dead with me on the bus in my Mickey Mouse gas mask.

'You saw a lot of me, Gran. When I was a baby.'

'Ah yes, Simon. It suited them then. It was wartime. We had some good times then, didn't we?'

'Yes, Gran. Did we?' She'd always been pulling me to keep up with her and moaning that things weren't like they'd been in the old days and yet she'd told everybody what a good boy I was and kept on doing it until I was much too old for that kind of thing.

'Catching the old 66 over to the Admiral's to see your mum.' She leant forward and straightened the lace curtain and peered down at the street. 'Haven't been on a bus for ages.'

'What about coming up here from Nan's, Gran?'

'Young Edward brings me in the car.'

'Well, what about West Meon?'

'What about West Meon?'

'You went there the other day, Aunty said.'

'I never did.'

'You did, Gran.'

'I didn't. It was the 154 to Ashling. But they'd mucked about with the route and the old post office'd gone and they'd knocked down Valley Cottages and—'

'But it *wasn't* Ashling. It was West M—'

'It wasn't.' Gran's lips had gone like the edges of two pennies. 'Don't you think I know Ashling when I see it. And I know West Meon. Poky little bit of a place. My father used to deliver meal out there and he said it never would be anything much to speak of.'

I lay my head back and let the blood curdle at the back of my neck. If Dad was thirty-nine and born in 1912 and Nan was sixty-four and she was thirty when she had him, she'd've been born in about 1880 and Old Gran was over eighty so her dad must've been born about 1700 and something.

'And they keep hiding my pension book.'

'Do they, Gran?'

'Do they what, Simon?'

'Keep hiding your pension book.'

83

'Who's got my pension book?'

'I don't know, Gran.'

'Anybody take my pension book and I'll . . .' Old Gran sat forward again with her jaw set and her black blouse spread out over my face. I looked up into it and it got closer and then her lap started to move.

'What you doing, Gran?'

'Getting up.'

'What for, Gran?'

She leant further forward to get up and strained and made a noise like a lorry changing gear on a steep hill.

'Come on, Simon, move. You mustn't keep me up here all day. I expect Rene'll be making some tea and I'm parched. Pass me my handbag.'

She put her hands back as far as she could reach and rocked herself forward and pushed and stood up. She slipped her arm inside the straps of her handbag and drew her black crocheted shawl across her chest so it hid Uncle Steven's airman's badge that she always wore. Her back was getting so bent that it looked as if she had a hump and her head stuck forward on her thin neck as if she was turning into a tortoise.

'Have I forgotten anything?'

'I dunno, Gran.'

'Well, have a look down the sides of the chair.'

'No, nothing here, Gran.' I ran my fingers along between the sides and the seat. 'Oh, hang on. What's this? A thimble.'

'Where?' She took it and popped it on her finger and held it up to the light so that the polished silver sparkled. 'My best thimble. And they said I'd lost it.'

I held the door open for her and Beth stood back to let us out.

'Shouldn't you be doing something, Beth?'

'Yes, Granny.'

'What?'

'I don't know.'

'Well, come on then. You go first and Simon can walk at the side of me. I don't want anybody treading on my heels and sending me luddock down stairs.'

84

We went slowly so that Old Gran could keep up with us but she sprinted down the last few stairs and held Beth back at the door to the living room and stood sideways on to it with her ear against the crack.

'. . . well, if you can't and I can't we'll 'ave to think about a home.'

'No, Fran, I won't have that. I just want a break.'

'Well, there's no alternative.'

'The business is wearing me out and Beth—'

'P'raps Beth should be at a special school.'

Old Gran put her finger to her mouth at Beth.

'Nothin' wrong with my Betsy . . . gis 'nother cuppa tea, gal.'

'You wait a minute, Nat.'

'Yes, p'raps we could just take a turn around the garden.'

'You sit still, Art.'

Beth's mouth puckered and she nodded as if she was saying, 'There. That's told *you*.'

'Well, maybe Ina would. After all, we've brought Simon up here so that they can have a nice break.'

'That's not the way of it.'

'*Will* you be quiet, Art.'

I crept in closer to Gran. 'They going to put me in a home, Gran? Are they Gran?'

'S'sh a minute, Simon. Course they won't.' She turned the handle of the door quickly and marched in and Beth and I stood back and waited for each other.

'Oh hello, Mummy.'

'Come and have some tea, darlin'.'

Nan and Aunty stood up together and Old Gran bent her face to Nan as she went past to the kitchen.

'I expect the tea's been made ages.' She filled the kettle and plonked it on the Rayburn.

'I do wish you wouldn't do that, Mum.'

'Why not?'

'Because you might drop it.'

'I wouldn't drop it, Daddy.' Beth suddenly flung herself on top of Uncle Nat and the wind came out of him like a squashed football. 'And I can shell the peas and feed Tibbles and clean my shoes . . .' But nobody seemed to be listening.

85

Aunty Rene fussed over Old Gran and Nan took her hat off and had another biscuit. Uncle Nat went back to sleep and Beth went out to search for a button she had lost off her shoe. Grandad's arm reached for me and eased me back so that I was half sitting on his knee.

'What you been up to then, Simon?'

'Just talking to Old Gran.'

'What about?'

'Nothing much . . . Grandad?'

'Yes.'

I leant closer to him. 'I will be going back home, won't I?'

'Course you will, my boy.' He said it so loudly he made me jump. 'I'm off out for a smoke, Fran.'

'You what?' Nan's dunked biscuit hung above her cup and the wet bit peeled off and fell in and sent up two splashes.

'I'm off out. C'mon, Simon.'

There was no wind in the back yard. The yard was enclosed by a wall as high as the top windows with an open-fronted shed with a sloping corrugated-iron roof on one side where they put boxes and crates and bicycles. Grandad stood in under the shed and struck a match and then he walked back stiffly in his polished shoes and dropped the match through the sink grating under the kitchen window. We walked off up the side path between a high wall at the back of next door and the side of the long shed.

'Just a lot of silly talk, Simon.'

'Yes, Grandad.'

'Best forgotten.'

'Yes, Grandad.'

The path came out into a wide garden green against the rust-red wall. Some peach and pear trees had been growing against the wall but the wires that'd held them in place were hanging from the branches with the nails still wound round in them and pointing at the holes in the wall where they'd pulled out.

Narrow tracks had been trodden in the long grass that reached to the lower branches of the fruit trees and a few hollyhocks stretched up like shepherds' staffs with the tops bent over and their flowers curled up like rolls of crispy bacon.

'Dear, oh lord!' Grandad went to puff at his cigarette but it had burnt out. 'In a bit of a state, isn't it, Simon?' He walked in and around the paths to try to find something growing properly that he could look at but he finished back where he'd started and brushing grass seeds off his blue suit. 'The whole thing's a bit of a mess. Can't even find anywhere to sit.'

'What about over there, Grandad?'

'What on those bricks?'

'Yes.'

'Well, all right. But I don't want to get these trousers messed up.'

'You won't, Grandad.' I ran on ahead of him and made a seat for him on the bricks and dusted a plank of wood with my hanky.

He sighed as he lowered himself and sat down. 'This is more like it, Simon.' He stretched out and leant against the wall and a blackbird in one of the apple trees started to sing and the dry grass that was wet at the bottom gave off a mixture of dusty and earthy smells.

'You heard what they were saying in there?'

'Yes, Grandad.'

'And Gran?'

'Yes, Grandad.'

'It's unforgivable.' He banged his fist down on the board we were sitting on. 'We'll all be in the same boat one of these days.'

'Well, why'd they say it then?'

'I don't know, Simon.' The outline of his head and shoulders was black on the wall and the sun was shining in his eyes. 'Old Gran's getting a bit funny and she takes a lot of looking after and your Nan's not very well. Well . . . doesn't think she's very well. And Aunty's got Beth and the business and Nat . . . Well, it's a lot of work.'

'But Beth helps, Grandad, and she's grown up.'

'In a way she is, Simon. But in a way she isn't. She was a clever little girl, could read before she went to school and could do anything with figures. They had the same hopes of

87

her as we've got of . . . oh well – doesn't matter. And she knows the bus and train timetables backwards even now.'

I imagined her waving goodbye to Old Gran on the wrong bus but it didn't seem funny when I thought of how difficult it was for me to read and the way the words and numbers on the timetable in the bus shelter ran into each other when I tried to work out when the next bus was.

'Aye, pretty little thing she was too.'

'And what about me, Grandad?'

'You're all right, Simon. You're pretty bright and you don't give your mum the run-around and go getting into mischief, do you?'

'Don't I, Grandad?'

'Course you don't. Don't take any notice of them, Simon.' He flicked cigarette ash off his trousers. 'They'll argue until one of them gives in and then we'll get a bit of peace and quiet. But don't you worry, Simon.' He stood up. 'C'mon, let's get washed and see what's for dinner and I'll buy you a bottle of pop in the bar afterwards.'

After dinner they'd made me wash and comb my hair and put my new short trousers on that had creases in them. The parlour curtains were drawn and the room was dark so I nosed my way into the bar. It was like looking at a moving picture. Uncle Nat was leaning on the counter talking to two men in shirt-sleeves and black waistcoats and Aunty was hooking pickled onions out of a big jar and putting them on two plates with sandwiches. Beth was pulling at the handles on the bar and squirting beer into big glasses as if she was milking a wooden cow. Three or four men were playing darts and some others were playing dominoes in the corner. Two girls, who looked like the ones who stood around outside Chichester bus station, were drinking out of flat glasses with cherries on sticks and talking to a man with his hair greased back wearing a cowboy shirt.

'Ah, 'ere 'e is.' Aunty dropped the fork in the pickle jar. ' 'ere's my little beauty.' She got me under my armpits and sat me up on the bar as if I was a doll. 'You say "hello" to Mr Stodgel.'

'Hello, Mr Stodgel.' I was facing the wrong way and I tried to slew round but they all looked like cattle in a market pen. A fat hand stuck out and I shook it and followed it back to a fat red face and a rounded stomach.

' 'e's a booful boy.' Aunty had primmed her hair up and put a clean pinny on. 'And he took his first steps in this very bar.'

'He lived with us though most of the time, Mr Stodgel. Till just before he started school.' Nan had her best frock and bolero on and her black court shoes. 'Ever so happy with us he was.'

'Up and down, up and down he used to go and for ever into everything, you wouldn't credit it.' Aunty grabbed me round the waist and nearly made me overbalance and the two girls started giggling.

'I expect you remember living up 'ome don't you, Simon?'

'Yes, Nan.'

Nan was shorter than Aunty but the same shape and, standing together, they looked like the little round wooden doll Mum had that came in half and had a smaller one inside and another one inside that until you got down to the one about the size of a pea.

'Used to sit in his pram and gabble away twenty to the dozen.'

The girls talking to the man in the cowboy shirt looked up and I gritted my teeth.

'And how do you like Petersfield? Peter's-filled-'is-trousers!'

'Rh'eally, Mr Stodgel. You and your jokes. Another pint, Mr Stodgel?' Aunty took his glass and Beth pulled beer into it.

They'd left me sitting on the bar and I turned and slid down and leant my chest against it and watched Mr Stodgel's Adam's apple working as he drank. He wiped the froth off his lips with the back of his hand. 'Got an evening paper, Nat?'

Uncle Nat was talking to a man whose head nearly touched the lights and looked like a Guernsey bull but he reached under the bar. 'Here you are but there's nothing in it tonight.'

'Aren't Pompey playing?'

'No, that's tomorrow.'

'You going down?' The big man drained his glass and touched Mr Stodgel's arm. Mr Stodgel drank his off and Uncle Nat passed both glasses to Beth.

'Probably.' Mr Stodgel pinched his thumb and finger into a small silver box and sniffed up each nostril and sneezed. 'I'll be down that way on business anyway. But they're not the team they were.'

'What do you mean?' Uncle Nat placed both hands palms down on the bar.

'Won't you be wanting an evening meal then, Mr Stodgel?'

'Well, p'raps on the hot plate, Mrs Wilson.'

'Certainly, Mr Stodgel.' Aunty made a note on her pad.

'What d'ya mean, not the team they were?'

'We-ll.' Mr Stodgel sucked in through his teeth and the darts players stopped to listen. 'They're getting a bit over the hill.'

'Over the hill!' Uncle Nat's jaw stuck out and I felt the floorboards give as he planted his feet apart. 'Douggie Reid, like a rock. Jimmy Dickinson, backbone of England. Jimmy Scoular . . . Scotland. Peter Harris, best winger in the land except for Matthews. Over the hill!' Uncle Nat looked round the bar as if he dared any man to disagree with him.

'Good players all . . . in their time.' Mr Stodgel turned to the moans that came from the domino table and then at the nods from the darts board. 'It's the same with politics, Nat. You're too conservative.'

'Conservative,' Uncle Nat roared and Aunty rubbed roughly under his hands at the bar with a wet cloth. 'Confound it man, this is a liberal house I'll have you know. Now if there'd been a Liberal government in 1938 instead of that upper-class warmonger we'd've 'ad no war—'

'See you down there, p'raps.' The man like a bull finished his drink and put his cap on.

'All right, Ted. By the tunnel.'

'. . . and if we'd got one after we'd've had none of this nationalisation nonsense.'

'Not so loud, dear.'

Uncle Nat elbowed Aunty off. 'Crippling taxes and Reds popping up all over the place and they'd've—'

'I think we'd better be off, Deirdre.' The two girls stood up. 'Night, Mrs Wilson.'

'Good-night, dear. Mind how you go.'

The man in the cowboy shirt drank his beer up so quickly that it ran down his chin and he slammed the bar door after him.

'. . . and they'd've put a stop to all this pay-claim business that's making paupers of us all.'

'It's all right for you, Nat. My wages gotta go up to keep pace with your prices.' A man with his back to us turned round as he spoke, plonked a domino at the end of the row, said he was out and going home. 'They say price of beer's going up again. Good-night.' The others followed him.

'It's the same for me.' Uncle Nat spread his hands out to the empty bar and then stared at Mr Stodgel but Mr Stodgel's eyes had gone glassy and he picked up his coat and said he was going out the back.

A cigarette burned on the edge of the ashtray. The long ash dropped off and fell into a pool of beer and fizzed out.

'That soon chased them out again.' Aunty had gone tight-lipped. 'Better wash up, Beth.'

'Quicker'n God Save the King.'

'Art!'

'Sorry.'

'Lost a good half hour's trade.' Aunty wiped up so hard that the tea towel squeaked against the glass.

'Good heavens yes. Is that the time? Off you go up to bed, Simon.'

'And p'raps you'd put a drop of milk on, Art?'

'He's in the second-back bedroom next to Mum, Arthur.' Aunty's hair was beginning to wisp and she was losing a hair-grip.

'Nigh-night, Nan.' I started to edge round Uncle Nat to get to Nan but he turned and nearly trod on me.

'Whoops! Shall I lock up, Rene?'

'Course not.' Aunty was rubbing at the glasses and banging them down on the shelf under the bar.

'Ah well . . .' Uncle Nat folded his tea towel over his arm.

'May as well have a look at the paper then. Where is . . . oh damn and blast! That man Stodgel's gone off with it.'

'Oh, do stop carping on about your paper and clean the ashtrays.'

'Dear oh dear!' Beth's voice broke in as Uncle was going to answer and they all looked at her as she stood making circles in the soap suds with the scouring brush.

'Night then, Simon. P'raps you had better be off.' Aunty led me to the door and left me at the stairs.

I passed the palm of my hand over the polished wooden ball at the end of the banister and went up. The stairs curved at the top and went up another three steps to the landing. Ahead of me was a passage with bedroom doors off it and I could hear snoring. It was probably Mr Stodgel. I shivered and went up to the next floor. There was a light showing from under the door of Old Gran's room. I opened the door of the room next to it and the light from the corridor put a path in front of me. My case was on the bed and somebody'd got my pyjamas out. I flicked the light on. It was a high room and it felt like standing in the back of Cabby's removal lorry. There was a double bed and a small one with peach-coloured bedspreads and peach curtains hung in long folds to the floor. There were green rugs like door mats on the lino by the beds and I could see the handle of a china pot sticking out from under the double bed. I sat down on the only chair and undid my shoes and slipped them off. A cord hung down above the head of my bed with a rubber ball on the end with a button. I pressed the button and the light went out. I pressed it again and the light came on and then I bounced it against the wall and caught it and hung it back carefully so that it didn't swing.

There was a square dressing table between the beds with a Newcastle Brown ashtray on it. The drawers were empty and lined with pages from the *News Chronicle*. I put my two pairs of short trousers in one, my clean socks and pants and vest in another and my clean shirt and best navy-blue jumper in the third. The wardrobe squeaked as I opened it and was big enough to walk inside. The coat hangers

92

wouldn't come off the metal bar down the centre and I managed to get my jacket over one and it hung all sloppy like a dead person. I closed the door and the draught it made swept across my knees and my feet left damp prints on the lino. My reflection in the mirror was walking towards me but it stopped when I stopped. I put my head on one side and it did the same. I smiled and a sort of plastic mask came over the face in the mirror. I closed my eyes and sat down on the bed and pulled my jumper off. I undid the first three buttons of my shirt and had it over my head when I heard a ticking sound. It was coming from the far wall as if a giant blind worm was pushing through the plaster. Then the cupboard door started to open. I watched it petrified. It stopped and the ticking stopped. I sat still until I stopped sweating and then I pulled the rest of my clothes off, put my pyjamas and dressing-gown on and ran next door.

The light from under Old Gran's door came from an oil lamp she'd put on the table in the middle of her room. I knocked but she didn't hear me so I walked in. The lamp light was yellowy green against the curtains and carpet. My feet sank into the soft pile of the carpet and it filled in between my toes. The curtains were open to the street and the street lamps let a liquid glow of yellow in through the nets. Gran had parted the nets and was sitting back in her chair staring at the slit.

'That you, Simon?'

'Yes, Gran.'

'Close the door then.' I pushed it to and it clicked. 'Blessed draught round my knees and I'm nearly out of Algepan.'

I sat down on the wide window sill and looked out into the street. A cat was sitting in the middle of the road cleaning herself and, beyond, the square opened out flat and empty. A light flicked off in a house on the far side and then another one.

'Time you were abed, Simon.'

'Yes, Gran.' Her long white nightie reached to the floor and her dressing-gown was all pads of braided silk like the cape Pop wore when we marched round the Church for the Litany. Her hair was like long strands of tattered spiders' webs and it looked as if a puff of wind would blow it out of her crinkly yellow scalp. The lamp light flared for a moment and then it fell back again.

'Takes you back, doesn't it, Simon. Lamp light?'

'Yes, Gran.'

She carried on sewing and I followed the shadow of her moving elbow on the carpet.

'Remember when we used to sit and read at Nan's all nice and snug and Gerry playing merry hell outside?'

'Yes, Gran, and I can remember us going to the Admiral's and playing in the garden and going over to the church.'

'Ah yes.' Old Gran pulled the last stitch tight and bit the wool off with her teeth. 'Never knew your Grandad Grainger, did you?'

'No, Gran.'

'Nineteen thirty two he died. Seems longer.'

'I'm only ten, Gran. Well, nearly.'

'H'm?' Old Gran bared another hole in Grandad's sock between her fingers. 'Luv'us what a great big hole. Done Fran a deal more good to have concentrated on her needle'n thread than keep gallivanting off out all the ti— Lucky she's got me here to bring these socks to for mending.'

'Gra-n?'

'Yes.'

'Where did Nan go gallivanting off to?'

'Oh, out dancing and out with the Sunday School on trips all over the place and dressing up.'

'Wasn't she supposed to then?'

'And there was the post office to run and cows to milk and—'

'I didn't know you had a farm, Gran.'

'We didn't. We had a cow for a while. One of your great grandad's grand notions that was. He settled on a cow for a debt as couldn't be paid and I had to milk it.'

'Did you get much, Gran?'

'Thirty shilling.'

'What?'

'Thirty shillings.' She tried to cover a grin by making out she was yawning. 'I wasn't going to put up with milking that darned thing at five every morning and then getting the letters sorted so I sold it.'

'Did you, Gran?'

'I did.' She paused with her wool half pulled through. 'To a travelling butcher as went round the farms.'

'Cor, I bet Grandad Grainger was pleased.'

She pulled the wool through and sat forward. 'And why should he have been?'

'Well . . . thirty bob was a lot of money in those days.'

'Ah.' Old Gran grinned again and went back to her darning. 'And it still is. I put it in the post office. It's still there.'

'Blimey! Is it?'

'It is.' She said it quietly and I knew she was talking more to herself by the way her eyes were angled down. 'That's for a rainy day.'

'Is it, Gran? Good-night, Gran.'

'Good-night, Simon. God bless you.'

I lay down in bed but I had to sit up again to put the light out. The glow from the street lamps filtered through the peach curtains and I turned over on my tummy and lay with my head on the edge of the pillow and fixed my eyes on the point where the light was brightest through a thin patch. I slipped my hand under the pillow and it rubbed rough against the sheets where I'd climbed up the rusty scaffold pole. I felt my back against the wall and then the wall was gone. I closed my eyes as I heard the soft crumpling crash of bricks and then I could see George standing over them and shaking his head and Mr Stirling next to him and pointing to him to get off the site. And then George was standing in an empty kitchen talking to a lady like I'd seen in the bar and she was crying over the sink and my bed was in the corner of the kitchen with my books and my cricket bat. There was a tap dripping. The splosh, splosh, splosh got louder and it was darker and a wind started to moan and I was in a black open-fronted shelter and the rain was running onto the pavement from a broken gutter. Something moving behind me made me turn round and the old man with sicky red bits in his beard was coming towards me. His arms were stretched out to get me and I felt myself falling. I opened my mouth and tried to scream but the scream wouldn't come. I thrashed my arms to let it out but it just swelled up inside me. My wrist hit something hard and I sat up.

I lay blinking in the sunlight. My eyes felt like burnt bacon rind and my eyeballs were gritty. The market clock tinkled a downward rhythm of chimes and then donged seven. I got up and drew the curtains and sat down on the window sill. A boy was delivering newspapers and he waited for a milkman with a horse and cart to pass before he crossed the road. The market square was a mass of pigeons pecking at scraps between the cobblestones. Then the vans started to arrive with the stalls for the Saturday morning market and the pigeons took off in one rush and settled all over the Town Hall like grey leaves.

Doors opened and closed down the passage and the bathroom door lock clicked and the toilet flushed and the lock clicked and clicked again and the flush flushed again and I counted six of them followed each time by a heavy tread downstairs. They'd be half an hour having breakfast and that left me enough time to go exploring. I put my clothes on, took two and six pence of my spending money and crept downstairs. The sound of knives and forks and newspapers being turned and folded came from the smoking room and the smell of bacon and eggs wafted through from the kitchen. I peeped into the parlour but it was empty so I slipped the bolts on the side door and went out.

It was warm outside and the air felt furry on my bare legs. They'd said I had to wear the black shorts Old Gran had made for me so that it'd please her. They were a bit long and too tight round the middle because Mum'd measured me and sent the size up by post and I had to hold my two and six in my hand because they hadn't got any pockets.

The men in the square had got their stalls fixed up and were arranging the things they had for sale. My fist with the half-crown felt big and I tried to hide it but I kept looking behind me in case anyone was coming to bang me on the head and run off with it. There was a gents at the far end of the square so I went in and put my money down my sock and then went on a cigarette end until the paper burst and I rinsed the bits down the channel and through the brass grating.

Most of the stalls sold sweets and jewellery and bath salts

and stuff but one sold toys. There were tin cars and lorries and clockwork penguins and then the man brought out a cleaned-out catering size tomato tin full of pea-shooters.

'Want one, sonny? Give you hours of fun.'

' 'aven't got'ny peas.'

'You don't shoot garden peas through 'em.' He came round from the side of his stall groping in his pocket and pulled out a small round brown pea and blew the pocket fluff off it. 'These'll make the little gals sit up and take notice.' He rinsed the pea around in his mouth and pressed his red rubbery lips against the flat end and shot it at a jar of cough sweets on the stall opposite.

'Daft trick to learn 'im, Cedric.'

'Mornin', Charles.' He wiped the mouthpiece on his trousers. 'Pigeon peas. They come out like bullets.'

'Cor. Where d'you get 'em, mister?'

'Here, my young sir.' He disappeared under the stall and came up with a paper bag. ' 'alfa pounda pigeon peas'n a shooter'll be eleven pence to you.'

'Cor, thanks. But can I have that one?'

'Here, take yer pick.' He pushed the tin over to me.

I held the bag carefully so that they didn't spill and stuffed the pea-shooter into my trousers.

'Hey, don't you reckon to pay?'

'Oh, sorry. I'll just—'

'You'll just nothing. Come 'ere.' He was round the side of the stall and had me by the scruff of the neck before I could move. 'Young bugger!'

'I wasn't going to run off, mister. It's just that—'

'Just what?'

'Me money.' His hand was hurting my neck. 'It's in my sock.'

'Blimey O'Riley! Come on then.' He stood over me as I put my bag of peas down and fumbled in my sock. 'And you can come 'ere'n get yer change.'

I took my change and hurried away behind the next stall.

'Miserable old sod. I'll bet this thing doesn't work anyway.' I put a pea in my mouth, rinsed it around and took aim at him from behind a lorry when he'd turned round. There was a rattling whoosh and a clatter where I'd hit his bunch of plastic windmills. I sunk behind the lorry as he spun round.

'You see where that came from, Charles?'

'Where what came from?'

'Oh nothing. Go back to sleep.'

I hugged myself behind the lorry. 'It works. It works a treat,' and I wandered off keeping the lorry between me and the man until he was out of sight.

'Nice bottla perfume, sonny, for your mum?' A lady with big teeth and a headscarf was holding a yellow bottle at me.

'Not today, thank you.' Mum'd said that once to a man who came selling lavatory brushes at the door but as soon as I said it I felt awkward. 'E'hm. How much are they, please?'

'One and six.'

'I'll have one then, please.'

She bent down to get one from under the counter and I searched in my sock again.

'Where are you then?'

'Here, Miss.' A sixpence was trapped under my ankle bone. 'Haven't got any pockets.'

She took my money and gave me a bottle in a brown paper bag and went on arranging the things on the stall in a pattern. There were bath salts for sixpence and little cubes of soap and the piece of cardboard she stood up against the bottles of yellow perfume had 1/- on it changed to 1/6d. My shiny new half-crown was gone and instead I had one dirty penny left. I put it in my sock and it slopped about cold against my foot as I walked back to the Royal Oak.

A warm fug of cooking came out of the kitchen window but I held back on the door step. Beth was crying and waving her arms about and Old Gran and Nan and Grandad were standing round her and Aunty was turning and stirring the porridge at the same time.

'Course you can, Beth. Don't be so silly.'

'No, Mummy.' Beth's face was creased up like a pug dog.

'She must've seen me do this a hundred times and never made a fuss about it before.' Aunty had her dressing-gown on and her hair was hanging as if she'd dipped it in the porridge.

'I won't. I won't, I won't.'

98

'Oh yes you will, my girl.'

'No I won't, Granny.'

'Never mind, darlin'.' Aunty cuddled Beth with the arm she wasn't stirring with.

'Give way. Give way all the blessed time, Rene. You'll never get anywhere with her at this rate.'

'Please, just go and do something, Mum. Go and see what's keeping Nat.'

Old Gran stood her ground for a minute but then she stalked off as if she'd been starched.

Beth sat down at the yellow-topped kitchen table where Aunty kept her jars of pickles and sobbed and Nan dried some knives and forks. 'I know how she feels, Rene. Once I get myself worked up into a state there's no stopping me.'

'What's happened, Grandad?'

'S'sh, Simon. Come here.' He went into the parlour and I followed.

The table was laid for breakfast with willow-pattern plates and knives and spoons with blue crests on the handles and the silver salt and pepper pots and the sun through the net curtains sparkled on the silver legs of the biscuit barrel on the sideboard.

'What's up, Grandad?'

'Oh just Beth. She got in a paddy when she saw Aunty putting salt in the porridge.'

'Do you put salt in porridge?'

'Aye. Just a pinch.'

'What's wrong with that then?'

'Beth doesn't like salt.'

'Oh.'

He sat down in Uncle Nat's chair and pulled the creases on his trousers up at the knees. 'It'll soon blow over.'

The paper bag with my peas in was going soggy where my hand was sweating and I held underneath it.

'What you got there, Simon?'

'Pigeon peas.'

'Blimey. I should think they get enough to eat without you feeding them.'

'No, they're for this, Grandad.' I pulled my pea-shooter out.

99

'Oh, I see. You be careful with that, my lad. Don't you go shooting them at Gran.'

'No, Grandad. Why not, Grandad?'

'Because they hurt, that's why. And don't for heaven's sake shoot at Nan.'

'No, all right.'

'In fact, I think you'd better give them to me for safe keeping. Don't you?'

'S'pose so, Grandad.'

'And what's this?'

'Scent. For Mum.'

He unscrewed the top. 'Blimey bill! That's powerful stuff. Where'd you get it?'

'In the market.'

'And how much'd they rush you for that?'

'One and six.'

'One and six!' He sniffed it again. 'Phew! We'd better take it back after breakfast.'

'Why, Grandad?'

'It's too strong, Simon. And it'll probably stain.' He resettled his knee where I was heavy on him. 'Never mind. We'll get a nice little bottle of rose water or something instead.'

'But *I* chose that for her, Grandad.'

'Never mind, Simon . . . hey-up now here comes breakfast.'

Nan came first with the tea pot then Aunty with a tray of steaming porridge and then Beth with a bowl of cereal in one hand and her spoon in the other.

Uncle Nat's boots sounded up the cellar stairs and he held the door open for Old Gran to come in. She stared at Beth's cereal bowl until Aunty stopped doling out the porridge and then she tutted and said 'spoilt' and sat down.

'Hot or cold milk, Mum?'

'Neither. You know I don't have anything on it.'

'Well, you had hot milk yesterday.'

'Well, why'd you ask me then?'

'Because I wanted to know what . . .' Aunty spread her hands at Old Gran and a blob of porridge fell off the spoon and Uncle Nat watched it on to his saucer.

'Cantankerous old . . .' Aunty dumped great splodges into the bowls and passed them round. 'And do wait a minute with that Shredded Wheat, Beth darling. You haven't got your milk yet. What do you want? Hot or cold?'

'Warm.'

'I'll be darned.' Old Gran looked like a hawk.

Aunty poured from both jugs on to Beth's cereal and then she gave the cold milk to Nan.

'S'pose we all want tea now?' Nan was standing over the cups.

'Yes please.' Grandad. and Uncle Nat said it together.

'Don't s'pose my porridge'll go cold.'

'Oh sit down, Fran.'

'Well, I do hate it when it goes cold. But I like to do my share.'

Nobody spoke so Nan poured the tea out and then she said her brain was letting her down again because she'd forgotten to use the strainer.

'Thanks.' Uncle Nat took his cup. 'Dear oh lord, what's happened to this?' He balanced his spoon on the surface of the tea. 'Lucky I'm not nervous.'

'You haven't got any nerves.' Aunty stopped Beth taking more sugar.

'Ah now,' Nan sighed, 'I just wish I hadn't.'

'Took a deal of nerve to look Mr Stodgel in the eye this morning, I can tell you.' Aunty stirred her tea by wiggling the spoon in it as if she was whisking cream.

Uncle sucked at his tea to cool it. 'He was all right, wasn't he?'

'No he wasn't. Very tight-lipped he was.'

'Well, serves him right.' Uncle put more sugar in his tea and stirred it. 'Shouldn't take things to heart so.'

'You can't help it, Nat. Not when you're sensitive.'

'Sensitive? Stodgel?' Uncle's fists lay next to his bowl like two fir cones. 'He's got the hide of a rhino. He's more thick-skinned than you, Fran.'

A fly crawled up the underside of my bowl and then went around the rim. Nan's face looked as if it had been set in marble and I wondered if she'd ever blink again. Aunty took Beth's bowl from in front of her and Uncle finished his tea quietly. I straightened the cloth around my bowl and then Old Gran blew her nose.

'Ah well, better be seeing about it.' Uncle Nat stood up.

'You fancy a stroll, Nat? I've got to take young Simon down the market.'

'Well, I'm expecting a delivery at ten.'

Grandad glanced at Nan. 'Come on. Ten minutes. Then we'll sort the cellar out together.'

'Right-o.' Uncle tiptoed round the table and past Nan and led us out through the bar.

'And you can get me some of those nice hard pears, Nat,' Gran called after us. 'And I expect Fran'd like some soft ones.'

'Yes, all right. Back soon.' Uncle slid the two brass bolts on the side door and lifted the latch and we were outside.

'Blimey, that's better.'

'Aye.' Uncle Nat felt in his pocket. 'Want a Player?'

'Please.' Grandad took one and they bent over the match. 'They sell pears in the market?'

'Old Elsie Walcott's got a stall.'

'You getting the hard ones?'

'M'm, might as well. You can stay with the soft option.'

Uncle Nat stood head and shoulders above Grandad and he marched ahead through the people in the market with his bald head flashing in the sunlight. The ladies said 'Good morning, Mr Wilson,' and the men said ' 'ow do, Nat' and he seemed to know everybody.

'Where d'you get that stuff, Simon?'

'Down there, Grandad.' I pointed in the direction of the horse trough.

'What's that, Art?'

'This.' Grandad passed him my bottle.

Uncle unscrewed the top and smelt it and screwed his nose up like Grandad did when he drank whisky on its own for a cold. 'That'll be old Rosie. Oldish lady with a headscarf?'

'Yes, Uncle.'

'Rosie Smith. Right, off we go. Haven't seen her here-abouts for a while.'

Mrs Smith had taken her cardigan off and was working in her shirt-sleeves. She was passing things to customers with one hand and taking money and giving change with the other.

'Mornin', Rosie.'

Rosie looked over from passing a customer a bunch of lavender in a raffia basket and straightening a rack of men's ties. 'Mr Wilson.'

'You recognise this?'

'I do— That'll be one and three and sixpence and they're sixpence but there's a crack in it. Call it two bob.' She counted the pennies and threepenny bits as she slid them into her bowl. 'Thank you very much, sir . . . what about it?'

'We want to change it.' Uncle held the bottle out but she didn't take it.

'Yes, sir. They are hand-made. Made 'em meself this mornin'— What into?'

'Well, something a little less lethal.'

'That's good stuff, Mr Wilson— If you don't want that, sonny, don't muck it about.'

'I wasn't.' A little boy dropped a stick of barley sugar and wiped his hand down his trousers.

'*Very* good, Mr Wilson.'

'Mixed with cider p'raps it is but if m'lado 'ere's mother puts it behind 'er ear it'll probably drop off.'

'Mr Wilson!'

'Come on, Rosie. Give us some'a that rose water there and a stick'a barley sugar for the boy for our trouble.'

Rosie gave me a stare that would have cracked concrete.

'And pop round to the Oak after for a Guinness and some cheese and pickles.'

Rosie's face changed and she smiled even as she was slapping the boy's wrists off the barley sugar. 'You're a gent, Mr Wilson. I've always said so and you've got our votes for the Council. Be round about two.'

'Right then. See you later, Rosie.'

'You enjoy that candy, young man, and if your mum uses this afore she goes a'bed there'll be a chavvie-child on the way for you.'

'Cor thanks, Missis.' I took the barley sugar and Uncle

put a small red bottle in his pocket.

I unwrapped the sticky paper and took a bite and ran after Grandad and Uncle Nat who were heading for the fruit stall.

'What's all this about the Council, Nat?'

'Don't you mention it to Rene.' Uncle Nat was covering his mouth. 'Blessed if I know how she got to know about it. In fact, I haven't made my own mind up properly yet. She must be psychic.'

'What's psychic, Uncle?'

'Sort of seeing into the future.'

'Is it? And what's a chavvie-child. Is it a brother?'

'That's the gypsy's warning right enough.' Uncle Nat smiled and showed his false teeth. 'Better keep that to yourself else it'll put the wind up your dad.'

'But it does mean I'll have a brother?'

'So she says, and she ought to know.' Uncle Nat patted his pocket and winked at Grandad. 'P'raps we'd better give it to the old lady. That'd soften her cough.'

'Don't you dare.' I rummaged in his pocket. 'That's for my mum.'

Uncle Nat laughed and tousled my hair and gave me the bottle and I held it all the way home with both hands.

Mum was spelling out words on the top edge of the *News of the World*, as Nan thought of them, to see if they fitted into eleven across. Dad was checking his football coupon and Grandad was asleep in the brown armchair.

'Mu-m?'

'Yes.'

'Do you like that perfume I bought you?'

'What about "lame" Ina?'

'Don't think so, Mum.'

'Do you, Mum?'

'Yes, it's lovely, Simon.'

'Have you tried it yet?'

'Well no, not exactly.'

'Why not?'

'I will do, Simon. Why d'you keep on about it?'

'Dunno. Just want you to.'

They went on to twelve down and I looked at the pictures in *Coral Island*.

'And was he good at Aunty's, Mum?'

'Not too bad, Ina.' Nan put her cup down and dabbed the corner of her mouth with her hanky. 'But Nat was a pretty awful example.'

'Oh dear.'

'Yes, he was rowing with everybody and upset us all one morning when he accused me of being . . . well, I won't repeat it.'

Grandad's tummy rumbled and he moved to a new position.

'And Mum couldn't stand it. She took herself off down to the lake and we found her feeding the ducks and needleworking without even a clean hanky.'

'She still walks all the way down to the lake and back again?'

'Yes she does, Ina. And like a good'n too.' Grandad opened one eye and nodded his head as he spoke.

'Tidy step that is.' Dad had finished checking his football coupon and was filing his fingernails.

'Yes it is but that's not the point.'

Grandad went back to sleep and Dad put his hands behind his head and stared at the ceiling and Mum stirred her tea.

'I bought that scent in the market, Mum.'

'Did you, dear? That's nice.' Mum put her spoon in her tea to check that she'd stirred it. 'And how is Gran, Mum. All in all?'

'Not too bad, I'd say.' Nan said each word as if she was measuring it out against a ruler. 'Pretty fair really but I couldn't think of having her with me until I'm feeling a bit better.'

'Well, how long did Aunty want her to come down for?'

'Oh not long. Just until the weather gets a bit colder and she can't go slipping off so easily, or until I'm feeling more like it.'

'Well, what d'you think, dear?'

'I dunno.' Dad was drumming his fingers on the arm of the sofa. 'Be all right I s'pose. But it's got to be your decision, Ina.'

'You'd better use it soon, Mum.'

'For goodness' sake, Simon, I will. But what's the hurry?'

'Well, it might go off.'

'Think I'll take a turn around the garden.'

'That means you're going smoking again, Art.'

'Coming, Simon?' Grandad bent forward to do his shoe laces up.

'Yes, Grandad.' I followed him through the kitchen and out to the sawing horse.

We'd only been away a week but already the windows had been put in the bungalow next door and the roofs were on and the black felt was in place and they'd started tiling. The front door faced towards our house and now it was nearly finished it felt as if it was right on top of us.

Grandad cupped his hand inside his jacket and lit a cigarette. He tossed the match towards Jack who was poking about after ants in the flower border. Jack stood staring at the match until it stopped smoking and then he put one claw on it and broke it with his beak.

'That was clever, Jack. You see that Grandad?'

'Aye. He's getting stronger.'

I put my hand down to him and he hopped on and shot a white stream on to the green leaves of the forsythia bush.

'Cor. Glad I missed that lot.'

'Yes, I'll bet you are. Think he missed you while you were away, Simon?'

'Oh yes, Grandad, but Uncle Den looked after him and him and Dad used to go jackying together when they were boys.'

'Aye, I know they did.'

I stroked Jack's beak. 'Grandad . . .?'

'Yes, Simon.'

'How long'll Old Gran stay if she comes?'

'Not long I don't s'pose. Why?'

'Just wondered where she'd live if we had more people in our family?'

'Ah, that's a tall order you know, Simon. Another little mouth to feed.' He leant forward towards me. 'And that reminds me. Your mate, George, from the buildings left you these with old Ted Norbitt for helping him. Said he was sorry he missed you.'

I took the box of Black Magic and ran my fingers over the cellophane wrapper. 'Has he got the sack, Grandad?'

'Sacked? No lad. Whatever made you think that? He's moved on to a bigger site. His overseer's pleased with him. But come on. Let's get back in and see where they've decided the old lady's next port of call's going to be.'

~~ 5 ~~

I hadn't worn shoes all through the summer holidays and the new ones they'd bought me were giving me a blister before I'd left the house for school. I knelt down by the Close sign and loosened the laces and watched the ants pushing the sand up between the paving slabs. They'd taken up one of the paving slabs to relay it and the sand underneath was honeycombed and the ants were bubbling up like boiling soup and dragging eggs as big as themselves out from where it'd fallen in. The babies must be born full-grown. If I had a brother and he was born full-grown he'd be bigger than me and he'd have to sleep on the sofa and I'd have to sleep with Mum and Dad if Old Gran came to stay and—

'Hey!' Something shot me forward.

'What'cher, Mush.'

'Watch it, Gibbs.' I wiped sand and ants off my hands. 'You'd better not've made me dirty at the back. You wanna watch where you're puttin' yer boots.'

'Garn, Nipper. Was only a little shove.' Geoff Gibbs was chewing gum. 'Where you bin the last week?'

'Up me Aunty's.'

'What doin'?'

'Nothin' much.'

'Waste of a summer 'oliday, that is. An' where's yer jacky?' Geoff stared past me at our roof. 'Lost'n?'

'No I haven't.'

'He has, Mush.' Geoff nudged in closer to Colin Gander. 'See 'is eyes. You can always tell when 'e's lying. Went off on 'oliday and found'n gone when 'e got back.'

'No I didn't. We just don't encourage him to come to school with me.'

'Urgh-hur! Just listen to Mr Lardy-dar Wilson.'

Colin always seemed to be standing back from Geoff as if

108

he didn't really like him but they were never apart. 'C'mon. Let's see where the others are.'

I followed them down to Crouch Cross Corner. Jerry Henry, Jimmy Phillips and Kenny Lane were sitting on the kerb but they stood up when Geoff called out 'ten-chun!'

'Heard the latest?' Jerry Henry stepped forward and his stomach stuck out between his braces where he was bending back to make himself look taller.

'No, Jerry. What's the latest?' Geoff slung his arm around Jerry and cuddled him up and winked at Colin.

'Git orf an' I'll tell ya.'

'Tell me quiet then. We don't want you-know-who to 'ear.'

I made out I was scratching a pattern in the dust with my toe round towards Jimmy Phillips. 'What's happened, Jim?'

'It's Wadey.' Jimmy said in a whisper. 'They reckon he's left to go back to the army. Browner's dad heard it down the camp.'

'Did I give you permission to speak to Nipper Wilson, Phillips?'

Jimmy stood to attention. 'No, sir.'

'See, Mush,' Gibbser grinned. 'There's been some changes since you bin away. We got an army now and me and Col's in charge. Ain't that right, Col?'

'S'pose so.' Colin picked up a stone and sent it crashing through the bushes at the bottom of Mrs Evans's garden. 'We'd better get on up to school.'

I started after him. 'Yeah s'pose we'd better.' I put my arm over his shoulder but he pulled away.

'Go on then. I ain't stopping you,' and he held back so that I had to walk ahead of them.

It was clear and sunny when we lined up in the playground. Somebody said the teachers were having a meeting and we didn't mind waiting. Nobby Clark had been down to the Saturday night social at Tangmere with Big Bim and he'd been telling some of the big boys about it and Michael Hoskins was so frightened when Margaret Maylor, who lived in a trailer up in Common Woods, put a slug down the back of his shirt that he wet himself. But then the sun went in and it was cold and we ran out of things to talk about and started shuffling our feet and wondering where Milly'd got to.

'P'raps he's gone to the army with Wadey as well.' Jerry Henry'd been telling his story to the camp kids but then we saw him coming down past the alms houses with a new man.

'Stupid bloody nit, 'enry.' Geoff Gibbs kneed Jerry in the thigh. '' 'e wouldn't've come if you'd kept yer trap shut.'

Mr Miller said something to the new man and he nodded and dropped back and Milly came on and stood on his step where he said prayers and things sometimes before we went into class.

'Right, School.'

We all spaced ourselves out.

'Atten-chun!'

We all pulled our legs together, hands by our sides.

'At-tease!'

We all went back the way we were before. The man had a big black overcoat on and black wool gloves and a wide-brimmed black hat that made him look as if he was going to a funeral.

'Good.' Milly glanced back over his shoulder and the new bloke made out he'd been watching. 'Now this is a new term—'

'Don't we bloody know it!' Drip Williams scuffed his feet and Doreen Turner said 'S'sh'.

'And we are honoured.' Milly looked along our lines and we all wondered what he was on about. 'Mr Wade has been chosen for something very special. He's leading – yes *leading* – a team of Territorials. On a series of exercises.'

'' 'eaven 'elp 'em!' Maurice Geer was just behind me.

'He'll be away for most of this term.'

Geoff Gibbs's head poked forward down the line and he breathed 'left!' at Jerry Henry and shook his fist.

'But in the meantime we are fortunate to have the services of Mr O'Hallerhan.' Milly beckoned to the new bloke. 'Mr O'Hallerhan, welcome.' Milly stuck his hand out and Mr O'Hallerhan shook it.

'Thank you, Headmaster.' He kept on shaking Milly's hand as if they were glued together and then stepped back.

110

'You are lucky to have Mr O'Hallerhan, School.'

'Why's 'e callin' us "School"?'

'Jus' showin' off, Drip.'

'Some of you, those who don't quite get through the 11+, will be seeing a lot of Mr O'Hallerhan at the Lincs. Mr O'Hallerhan has been maths and drama master at—'

He broke off as Mr O'Hallerhan bent forward and whispered something to him.

'— and he's got a special interest in sport.'

There was more whispering.

'Oh, really? Portsmouth! Yes, and a particular interest in one of our most famous clubs.'

Geoff and Colin set up a strangled cheer and Mr O'Hallerhan beamed.

'Quiet now . . . at the Lincs for nearly ten years and he's due back there when he's quite better.' Milly flopped his great red hand on the man's shoulders. 'We hope you are soon fully sound again in wind and limb.'

'Good wind'd blow him away.'

'Shud up, Drip.'

'So we'll have Mr O'Hallerhan taking over Mr Irvine's class and Mr Irvine can go down with Mr Wade's for a bit and the rest stay as you were.' Milly got down off his step and told us to go to our classrooms quietly except for the little ones who had to wait for Miss Anderson.

The classroom smelt dusty. I'd left my ruler crooked on my desk the last day before the holidays to remind me that I wouldn't see it again for six weeks and six weeks had seemed so far away that I might not ever have to come back to school.

'Bloody 'ell.' Maurice Geer hauled Jerry out from the back seat and then stood aside to let Drip Williams in. 'We suffer Wadey for ages and when we finally get a chance to get Guv Irvine, and learn something, we land up with this twit with a face like a rasher of bacon.'

'Good name for him, that, Rasher.'

Drip Williams was trying to touch his nose with his tongue.

'Drip, you listening?'

'What about it?'

'Well . . . the Guv's a good bloke and we were supposed to be having him this term.'

'Gives out a lot of homework though.'

'How do you know?'

'Gave me brother a lot end of last term.'

'So what?'

'Watch out. 'ere 'e comes. Rasher O'Hallerhan.'

Mr O'Hallerhan stopped inside the cloakroom door and hung his hat and coat up and straightened his tie. Then he put his head down and his shoulders forward and bored in through the door to the classroom as if he was coming straight through without opening it. He had a circle of black hair round the bottom of his skull which looked like crêpe paper round a chamber-pot and a black suit and black shoes. But his shirt made me shiver. I was sitting towards the back but I could still see it. It was a dirty white colour with a big floppy collar and bubbly bits like water blisters. It looked cold and wet and I could imagine it feeling like tripe against his skin. He stood behind Wadey's desk and put his black bag on top of it.

'H'm, huh-h'm, huh-h'm' he hummed out loud and we all looked at each other. 'I like a nice-cuppa-tea-in-the-morning . . .' He pulled out a flask. '. . . and a nice-cuppa-tea-for-my-tea.' Next a packet of dry biscuits. 'On the shores of the Snitcher Knitcher the dirty dog stole her away.' He kept on singing and humming until he'd got his books and ruler and some things that looked like registers out and some pencils done up in an elastic band. He put them all down neatly as he took them out. Then he rearranged them so that his flask was at one end and the biscuits next to it and the other things going down in order to his rubber which he stood up on its thin end.

'What was Oscar Wilde's name, boy?'

'What, sir?' Everyone sitting near Colin Gander sank back.

'Too slow! "Too-too'ril'o loo'ril o'day" Full back's nipped in and taken the ball away and that's another scoring chance gone away up the Swanney River. "Way down upon the Swanney River . . ." '

112

' 'e's off 'is 'ead!'

'You boy! Oscar Wilde?' He was pointing at Michael Hoskins and then at somebody else moving from one to another before anybody could say anything. Even Wadey asked things slowly and made it look as if he wanted us to know.

'What shall it be now. Singing or sums?'

Geoff Gibbs thought he meant it because he yelled back 'singin' ' but Mr O'Hallerhan just made him sing 'Sing a Song of Sixpence' on his own and said now we'd do sums.

'You there. Little Miss Muffett, is it?'

Jenny Wright stood up.

'Just hand these out, if you'd be so kind.'

I'd never met a teacher who carried his own books around. Mr Wade had frightened us when he first came but we'd soon got used to him and Old Anderson used to yell a lot but nobody took any notice of her. I sat looking at Mr O'Hallerhan through my fingers and I had to hold my wrist to make my hand stay still. There he was. All in black except for his blue socks and the ginger moustache on his white face and—

'Simon!' Jimmy's hand nudged me in my side. 'Stop lookin' at 'im.'

'So you're Simon Wilson, are you? Family's great white hope . . .'

I blinked my eyes so that the furry mist cleared and looked at him and then I looked away. For a moment he'd been staring straight at me but I'd seen inside him and it made my flesh creep.

Rasher always sent our class on a cross-country run before we joined up with the Guv's class for football on a Wednesday afternoon. I said I didn't think it was fair but he said they were younger than us and not to be such a baby and Gibbser'd laughed and then they'd all teased me when little Harry Tanner'd kept getting the ball off me and I got a hundred lines for clipping him round the ear for kicking me. I was nearly at the end of them now and my fingers were inky and I felt hot and sticky looking out at the boys playing football and leap-frog. The ink had seeped into the gap between my skin and my thumbnail where I couldn't get at it so I put my hand in my pocket.

'You can go and get my tea now, Wilson, as you've taken up my break time.' Rasher was reading what he'd written on the board. 'Do you hear?'

Harry Tanner was showing Toby Little how to kick with your instep outside.

'Wilson!'

I stood up slowly and let the seat spring back so that it banged. 'Answer me, boy.' He was still facing the board but he wasn't reading it any more.

'*Wilson!*'

'I'm goin'.'

'You sullen little creature. Come here.' His voice gurgled as if he was drowning and he started coughing. 'They say your uncle was a fine sportsman.'

'He was. So's me dad.'

'*Is* he!' He folded himself over and coughed inside his chest with his hand trapping his mouth. Grandad was like this when he had bronchitis. Maybe he was even somebody's grandad. I wondered if he wanted a drink of water but he straightened up and stared at me from under his eyebrows, and I suddenly felt as if I was going to laugh but I was cold from being so near him, as if his saliva was poison and he was going to spit at me.

He passed his tongue over the pus on his lips. 'Get my tea.'

I walked out sideways on to him and pulled the door to behind me so that it clicked.

They always had their tea in Milly's kitchen. I rubbed most of the dried mud off my knees and put my shirt collar straight and knocked. I'd had tea here with Grandad when he was working for old Mr Mawson before I'd started school and the kitchen had always smelt as if somebody'd been baking and been crammed with cupboards and chairs and racks of pickles and jams and strings of onions, but the door opened and it was bare except for a couple of benches and a low table.

Miss Anderson stood in the doorway and the Guv and Milly looked round and then carried on talking.

114

'Well?'

'He wants his tea, Miss.'

'Who?' Miss Anderson stuck her head forward so I stepped back.

'Mr . . .' It was as if I was trying to be sick when it won't come.

'*Who?*' She moved over so that I was in full view of Milly.

'. . . O'Hallerhan.'

'*Mr* O'Hallerhan.'

'Yes, Miss.'

'Then, why didn't you say so?'

'Come on in, Simon, and get it.' The Guv shook his head at Milly as if he was apologising for something. 'Pour it out and take it to him and don't keep Miss Anderson standing at the doorway.'

Miss Anderson stepped well back, as if I had a disease, and pointed to the tea pot. There was a cup and saucer by it with some milk in so I poured the tea without using the strainer and dropped two sugar lumps in but I didn't stir it.

The path from Milly's house, in the middle of the alms houses, was made of cinders with half-bricks and flints poking through. I had to be careful where I was stepping so that I didn't trip but when I watched the ground I spilt the tea. The saucer was flooding and I stopped by the opening in the wall to pour it back into the cup. The yellow rambler roses were still open on the alms-houses wall and the wires, with what Grandad'd called lead nails driven into the cement, were still in place, but rusty now, and fallen away and the roses stood on their own. I stared at their glossy green leaves. They shone polished in the sunlight until they went hazy as if they were a thousand miles away. The roses were silky cold and wet and they smelt of Mrs McGraff's special soap at the Admiral's.

'Mummy and Daddy all right, Simon?'

'Eh?' Rasher's tea slopped again. 'Oh, hello, Miss Turner. Yes, thank you.'

'And Grandad. Is he still keeping pretty fair?'

There was the smell of lavender and dark dusty rooms with lots of polished furniture that reflected her white-spotted blue dress and wispy grey hair and skin the colour of withered leaves and . . .

'Yes, pretty fair.' She'd had to hobble round the table to the sweet tin even when I was little and we used to come up to the alms houses and give her logs when we'd been wooding up the Common. 'Thank you.'

'Don't see you about with him much nowadays.'

'No.' A fly had settled in the tea in the saucer and was struggling to get out.

'You all right, Simon?' She put her warm, papery fingers under my chin and I could sense my head against her tummy when that was where my head came up to but I pulled away.

'Yeah, course I'm all right. I gotta get back.' I stared at the school roof as I went away towards our classroom.

I stopped outside our lobby door and emptied the saucer into the cup. There was a skin on the top and it was cold when I stuck my finger through it.

'. . . and you'll all have a part to play and your mums and dads and aunts and uncles and next-door neighbours and second cousins'll think you're the finest set of . . .'

The girls in the front were listening and making their eyes go wide but the boys were mostly sitting with their chins in their hands as if they were waiting to see the dentist.

'. . . and we'll even wake old Wilson up long enough to get some sense out of him.' Rasher turned suddenly and made out he'd just seen me. 'Oh, here he is.' Derek Brown laughed and Paul Craven mouthed 'scratcher' at him. 'But he's not such a bad lad for getting my "nice-cuppa-tea-in-the-morning" even if he can't get round little Harry Tanner.'

I put his tea on his desk and sat down.

'And-a-nice-cuppa-tea-with-my-tea.' Rasher broke one of his thin biscuits and tried to catch a piece in his mouth.

'What's set him off again, Paul?'

Paul shrugged and splayed the nib of his pen out on the desk. 'Milly's said he can do a school concert and he's doling out jobs.'

'There's scenery to be painted and costumes to be sewn up and hammering and sewing.'

'We ain't gotta go sewin', 'ave we, sir?'

'No, you haven't, Gibbs. But we'll set you and Gander off building scenery.' Rasher covered one eye and held his other

116

hand out in front of him and shouted 'I see no ships!' and Maurice Geer put one finger just above his ear and twisted it and said 'daft as a brush' under his breath.

'And Wilson and Henry can paint some windows . . . wind*ers*, windows, Wilson? Where'd that come from?'

'Squeers, sir. 'e ran some school outa Dickens.'

Rasher closed one eye as if he was trying to see in the dark and went 'h'm' to himself but then he relaxed. 'Quite right, m'boy. So you can paint 'em,' and he started to tick off names on a list. His face was flecked with red streaks as if it was bloodshot. He stood back, still looking at his list, and lifted his cup and drank it. 'Cold as charity, boy,' he said without looking up. 'And thick as soup— Augh!' He shuddered and his face went rigid. 'You idiot! It's sugared.'

'Yeah, but I didn't stir it, sir.' I thought he was still mucking about and I nudged Paul.

'Come out to me, boy.'

I sat stock still and then stood up as his hand went for his strip of bamboo on the ledge on the blackboard.

'That's poison to me, you wretch. Hand out.'

Swish! Crack! The cane rose and fell a second time and the ends of my fingers felt as if they'd been trapped in a door. The third stroke caught the fleshy part of my thumb and it went limp. I closed my eyes and saw the butcher's cleaver cutting up chops and I thought I was going to be sick.

'Sit down, boy. You ever do that again and I'll flay you to within an inch of your life.' He put the cane back but it fell off the blackboard ledge and he left it and rummaged in his black bag for a silver tin. 'Be reading *The Tempest* until I get back.'

The pain in my thumb was like broken glass and I felt closed in where they were all turning round to me. Paul laid my hand out in front of him.

'Does it hurt, Nipper?'

I held my head still with my jaw set.

' 'e's gonna cry.'

'Shut up, Gibbs.'

'I'm gonna kill 'im.'

They were all looking at me now and they could see I was crying but nobody laughed.

'I'm gonna kill him. I swear it. If it takes all of my life to do it.' I wanted to scream it so he'd hear and know but my voice broke.

They gradually turned round and started whispering to each other and Johnny Harris said 'S'pose we gotta do soddin' Shakespeare.'

It felt as if they were all sitting away from me, as if I'd done the murder already, except for Paul. He wet his handkerchief in the rainwater butt outside and laid it on my hand.

I'd been holding my hand in the fish pond until it was numb and the skin on my fingers had gone white, like tripe.

'That any easier, Simon?'

'Yes thank you, Grandad.'

The sun was behind him and it put his face in shadow. He took his knife out of his pocket and trimmed a rough thumbnail back.

'Sounds like he's diabetic, poor man. Still . . . you weren't to know.'

'No, Grandad.' The bone of my thumb felt as if it was splintered when I waggled it under the water. 'What's diabetic, Grandad?'

'Oh, it's . . .' He rubbed the blade of his knife on his trousers and put it away. 'It's when you can't take sugar properly. You have to lay off it else it makes you ill.'

'Oh.'

'Better put it back in the water.'

I let my hand drop back again. My fingers were smothered in paint where Rasher'd made me help with the scenery and I'd had to hold the brush with both hands.

'What you been doing with yourself these last few weeks?'

'Oh, nothing much.' The laces on his boots were pulled tight and the welts were puckered up as if his feet were slipping about inside them. 'Just mucking about with the boys and playing with Jack and that.'

'Oh ah! Growing up I s'pose.'

A leaf dropped off the plum tree and fell on to the grass.

'S'pose so, Grandad.' The old wheelbarrow he used to take me in was leaning up against the side of the potting

118

shed. One handle was broken and the shaft was rotting and I wondered how I'd ever fitted into it and he'd changed the potting shed around inside and put up some new racks. I looked for the beer crates we used to sit on to have our tea but they weren't there.

'Ah well! Better be getting a move-on, I s'pose.' He stood up and his hand was under my elbow. 'Leg gone to sleep?'

'Yeah.' I stumbled as I stood up and my right leg crumpled. 'Gone like rubber, Grandad.'

'Be too much tearing around, I expect.'

'Yeah, we had cross-country today and played football and I got kicked. Look.' I pulled my trouser leg up and my sock down. The blood had dried.

'Blimey bill!' He knelt down like a string of cotton reels settling. 'That's a beauty. Hold still a minute,' and he touched in some Vaseline from a jar from his pocket. 'C'mon now. Let's see if Nan's got any tea brewing.'

The bushes in the front garden were ballooning out in different coloured greens from nearly black to almost yellow and the wooden posts and cross-pieces round the strawberry bed, that Grandad hung the net on, were crooked and some were broken and the passion flower over the front room window had pulled away from the wall and was hanging by its wires and the rock plants from the borders were sweeping out on to the front path. I walked behind him but I had to keep stopping so that I didn't tread on his heels. Round by the back door the vine was hanging heavy with grapes and he had to reach up through the leaves to get the soap from the little cupboard he'd made for it on the wall. The old enamel basin had splinters in it as if it'd been peppered with air gun pellets. I washed my hands after him and we took our shoes off together. Some of the boys were playing football in the school field. I could hear Gibbser picking sides but I couldn't see them through the hedge. They hadn't told me they were playing football after school and I'd've run off to join them if Grandad hadn't been holding the door open for me.

The sounds of outside fell away. It was dark in the passage and I waited for him to hang his coat up and then we went into the kitchen. The furniture was all crowded in so that there was just enough room to get round the table between the dresser and the sofa and the range. The cuckoo clock made a slow, dusty tick as if it had forgotten what time it was and the fire burned steadily in the grate as if it had never gone out. The table was laid with a tray and two cups and saucers and two plates and knives and there was bread and butter under a muslin cloth and cheese and pickles. The door to the stairs was open.

'Nan'll be upstairs, I expect, Simon. I'd better go and see.'

I sat back on the sofa and ran my fingers over the red weals on my fingers. Uncle Steven's photograph was almost hidden in the dark of the corner where the light from the window missed it but I could feel him looking out into the room from exactly the same position where Nan put him back every morning before breakfast after she'd dusted him. I got up and went and looked closer at him. He looked younger than Uncle Roger now – more like Big Bim. I picked up the metal penguin he'd brought home from somewhere during the war and started to fiddle about with the little pencil with no lead that was fixed to it by a silver chain. It was still held together with a twist of fuse wire where I'd snapped a link one Christmas. The pendulum on the clock moved into a squeak on every other swing and the old sofa bumped back against the wall when I sat down again and I had to prop the arm Nan said was 'wonky' up with a kitchen chair. Nothing had changed and yet it was all different. There was a new carpet and the new sideboard was several years old now. I only noticed the difference when I was here on my own as if I was nosing around a shop after it had closed and things came out at me from the quiet and stood up for me to see them and then went back into hiding places beyond my memory. P'raps today'd be like that and it would be as if it had never happened. And yet the further I went forward the further I was away from things as they used to be.

The bedroom door upstairs opened and then closed. They were standing at the top of the stairs.

'S'pose I'll have to cut some more bread and butter.'

'I'll do it, Fran.'

'And get another cup and saucer out and we haven't got any fancy cakes.'

I got up and went to the door to the passage. If I went now I might still meet up with the boys.

'That doesn't matter.'

'Well, it jolly well matters to me.' The third step from the bottom creaked. 'Hello, Simon. What brings you up here unannounced?'

'Dunno, Nan.'

'I haven't got any cake, my duck, and Grandad forgot to get any paste.'

'Don't matter, Nan.'

'But you'd like a cuppa tea, I s'pose?'

'Yes please, Nan.' She had her fairisle cardigan on and I wondered if she'd been to Aunty Sarah's.

'Aren't you going to kiss—'

'Sit you down then, Simon.' Grandad pulled a chair out for me. 'I could do with a cuppa tea now, couldn't you?'

'P'raps you'd get him a cup out then, Art.'

'S'all right, Nan. I'll get it.'

'Well, be careful not to bang the door and watch you don't knock the glasses.'

The sideboard cupboards were lined with old newspapers and the best knives and forks were wrapped in tissue paper. There were only sets of cups left and I looked for the beaker with a sun with a face on that I used to use but it wasn't there so I took Grandad's old enamel mug. The door rubbed up against something as I closed it.

'What's this, Grandad?'

'Eh?'

'This book. It was under the sideboard.' I held it over to him.

'Well, I'm blowed. So that's where it went.'

'Well, I never!' Nan plonked the tea pot down. 'Trust that to turn up now. Shan't get a word out of him all evening now.'

'What is it, Grandad?' It had a paper cover with a picture of a man with a knife in his back slumped over the bonnet of a racing car.

'Oh, that's one of my Sexton Blakes. Good they are, but a bit gory.'

'What's gory, Grandad?'

121

'We-ll, a bit bloodthirsty. Detective stories. You want to read one?'

'Course he doesn't, Art. Shooting and poisoning! They'd give 'oo nasty nightmares, wouldn't they, my duck?'

The pages were rough like my comic book paper but it had long words and there wasn't much talking in it so I gave it to him.

'P'raps when you're a bit older, Simon. I'll save them for you.'

Nan grumbled that she wasn't having boxes of Sexton Blakes littered about attracting silverfish and I drank my tea. Grandad offered me some bread and cheese but Nan said it was nearly my tea time and Mum'd be worrying about me. I sat and ran my thumbnail over the thin bit in the knee of my trousers until it came in a hole and then I pushed my chair back.

'I'm off now then, bye.'

A fly was walking over the handle of my spoon and I could see his reflection under him.

'Aye, I'll see you off the premises.' Grandad pushed another piece of bread in and then turned back for another scrap of cheese.

'You'll give yourself indig—'

'Yeah, bye, Nan.' I waited for Grandad in the passage and then went on ahead of him to the back door.

'I don't think Nan likes me any more, Grandad.'

'Whatever—' Grandad manoeuvred his mouthful into one cheek. 'Whatever makes you say that?'

'Well, she didn't seem to want me up 'ere for tea.'

He chewed faster and swallowed and shut the back door behind him. 'You mustn't think that, Simon. She's a bit nervy just now. See, with your Old Gran on her way back down here again it's put her on edge.' He wiped his moustache on the back of his hand. 'Course she likes you. Thinks the world of you. Especially after your uncle went missing. We both do.'

'Was he *very* good at school, Grandad?'

'Oh, yes. Yes he was.'

A blackbird was picking about in the leaves but he stopped and cocked his head and his yellow eyes glistened.

'Well I'm not, Grandad.'

'Aren't you, Simon? Well, you just make sure you do your best.'

We stood together and the sparrows hopped and chirruped in the laurel bushes and then Nan called him that his tea was getting stone cold.

I set all the swings swinging in the playing field and then went and poked some mortar out of the alms houses wall before I went down to the bus shelter. I'd cycled up the lane and across to the Redvin Woods and back over the Wobble fields but I hadn't seen any sign of the boys. It was the same every Friday but I couldn't ask them where they went because they'd know I'd been looking for them. I sat on the wall by the allotments and kicked bits of flint out of the cement with my heels. Dan Evershed was picking apples and he gave me one but he said I mustn't help myself. I sat up on the wall eating it and the 66 bus went by and the whoosh of it nearly made me fall backwards. I sat swaying backwards and forwards with my eyes closed as if I was bobbing about in the sea and just letting it—

'Your 'and still 'urt?'

I stopped and opened my eyes carefully. Geoff Gibbs was dragging his toe in the dust by the kerb.

'Yeah. Where you bin?'

Geoff hitched his trousers up over his belt. 'Up Gander's but he had to wash up so I went scrumpin' down the church. Wassa time?'

' 'bout ten past. Sixty-six went down just now. Why?'

'Oh, jus' that I don't wanna miss the start of it.'

'Start of what?'

'Oh nothin' that'd interest you. Just "Billy Bean". We watch it down Pargetter's.'

'Cor! Can I come? What is it anyway?'

Geoff sucked his bottom lip. 'I dunno. She said twelve's the limit and there was twelve there last week.'

'Oh, go on. What's it about?'

'Ain't you 'eard of "Billy Bean and his Funny Machine"?'

'No.'

'Gawd!' Geoff kicked a stone across the road and popped a couple of tar bubbles. 'Don't you know anything?'

'Go on then. What is it?'

'It's a thing on television. She let's us go and watch it for a penny.'

'Does she? What in 'er 'ouse?'

'Yeah.'

'Cor! Go on, let me come.'

Geoff squinted at me against the sun. 'Got a penny?'

'Don't think so.'

'Well, you can't then.'

'Can't you lend me one?'

'Dunno.' Geoff pulled his handkerchief out and a couple of fag cards from Turf packets and some red-tipped matches. 'It'll cost you penny'a'penny tomorrow.'

'Yeah, all right.'

'Right. You can pay me at pictures.'

I jumped down off the wall and walked along beside him. 'I don't know if I can come. I'll have to ask me mum. But if I can't I'll pay you after church.'

'I ain't goin' church.'

'Well, I'll see you up the field after.'

Geoff put his hand and his penny back in his pocket and slung his arm over my shoulder. I ducked.

'Nervous, ain't'cha?'

I smiled. If I said 'no' he'd probably thump me.

'Come on. But I'll give it to her, see.'

'Yeah. Thanks.'

We walked down past Dan Evershed's boot repair shop and up the rough road that led to the slaughter house, and Geoff let me in the side gate to Mrs Pargetter's back garden. I'd always thought the shop was just a shop but it was quite big at the back with rooms built on top of rooms under a flat roof below the level of the shop roof as if the living part was hidden behind the shop. The garden was like a picture on a chocolate box; a little patch of grass like a square of sticky paper from school with a silvery tree at one side with strings of things for the birds and borders all round with small flowers at the front and bigger ones at the back and red and blue and orange stacked up against the red-brick walls as if

124

they were painted on to strips of cardboard. I trod carefully on the white gravel of the path in case I spoilt it. Geoff stopped by the French windows and tapped. The door opened just enough for him to squeeze through and I followed him into darkness.

There was a light like a reflection from a mirror on one wall with people moving about on it. 'It's like the pictures,' Geoff whispered and I stumbled up against some legs and a voice came up from the floor, 'sit down.' I tried to walk in the path of light from the screen but some more gritty sounds of 'out the way' came out of the darkness and Jimmy Phillips edged me back and moved his feet for me to sit on the floor.

'Shift over, Mush.' Geoff seemed to sink out of sight on the other side of the room and then his face was lit up as the door opened.

'Haven't you forgotten a little something, Geoffrey?' Mrs Pargetter was in the doorway.

Geoff heaved himself up off the sofa by forcing his hands down on Kenny Lane and Derek Brown's laps. 'This is mine and Nipper's.' There was a clink as their hands crossed like the clasp of friendship on the football coupons and he sank back again half on top of the others and there were mutterings about squashed goolies and 'git orf!' until they settled still in front of the flickering light. There was a buzzing sound and a wave of silver rolled up and down the screen under a blanket of flickers like a steaming kettle with the lid off. And under this you could just see a man with a stick pointing out what the weather was going to be like tomorrow and then his legs started to slip down underneath the edge of the screen and the whole thing started to spin and when it stopped it was the end of the news. The screen went blank and then some jumpy music came on and a picture of a thing like a mechanical bedstead floating in the sky with a little man on it who looked as if he was made out of potatoes. 'This is Billy Bean and this is his Funny Machine,' came from the television.

'An' this is Geoffrey Gibbs an' Nipper owes me tu'pence.'
'S'sh.'
'Pack it up, Gibbser!'
Billy Bean landed on a planet with no vegetables and the

people asked him to help them and he went off to another planet and pulled some levers and the Funny Machine started digging and raking and sawing and planting and watering and then a big sun came out and made them all grow. Jimmy Phillips shifted my leg over so that he could stretch out further.

'Looks like it's snowin', Jim.'

'S'sh.'

The cabbages and lettuces were just hearting up and the beans were swelling and the potatoes were growing like trees when some wicked people came along and started ripping them up and smashing them with clubs with nails in the end but Billy Bean jumped into the Funny Machine as the music got louder and pulled some more levers and the Funny Machine suddenly grew legs and a lot of flaps opened and mechano arms shot out with boxing gloves on and bashed them all on the chins. I laughed and cheered with the others but I couldn't see how a machine knew where to hit and how to make them bump into each other like that. My right leg went to sleep and I rolled over on to my other side. 'You playing after, Jim?'

They were flying back now with crates of cabbages and cauliflowers and lettuces and stuff and all the people cheered and then they were sitting down to a great big meal and the music got louder again and some wiggly writing rolled through as if it was on a mangle. Mrs Pargetter pulled the curtains open and we sat blinking in the light.

'Right. Off you go, children. And remember, no more than twelve next week.'

We trooped out in a long line, ducking under Mrs Pargetter's arm, through the door. The boys were nudging each other to show how the baddies had got socked in the eye and fallen back and bashed into each other and saying that Billy Bean must have been travelling at a thousand miles an hour to get all that way in five minutes and Kenny Lane said there was an old car left over from the war up in Redvin Woods and why didn't we make a Funny Machine.

Jimmy and Jerry were waiting for me by the railings of the electricity thing. 'You should've come last week, Nipper.' Jerry was unwinding some strands of bindweed off the bars.

'He chopped down a whole forest in a day.'

'What for, Jerry?'

'I dunno. Wood I s'pose. What's it matter?'

'Well, it takes a long time for 'em to grow.'

'For buildin' log cabins,' Jimmy said. 'Bet'cha it was for log cabins.'

'Do you *like* television?'

'Cor yeah!' They both said it together. 'Don't you?'

'Oh yeah. Yeah. It's smashin', I s'pose.'

We walked on up the road together and they talked about the programme today and then the one last week and then bits of other ones and it made me wonder whether I'd been watching it properly. I went on ahead to see if they'd catch me up and then I said 'I'll see you after tea' but they were still talking so I started kicking a stone along the pavement until I turned into the Close.

Mum wasn't watching for me from behind the living room curtains as I came in the gate and she hadn't taken the tea tray in from the kitchen or changed the tablecloth for tea. And it was nearly six o'clock. The bathroom door was open so she wasn't there and she wasn't in the garden. P'raps she was at Aunty Win's— but she never went to Aunty Win's at tea time. I ran back into the garden and then up to the chicken house. 'Hello, Jack. Where's Mum? Mum!' I called back in the kitchen and then louder 'Mummy, where are you?'

'In here, Simon.'

'Where, Mum?'

'In my bedroom.'

I dashed in through the living room and banged the bedroom door.

'Over here.' She was sitting by the dressing table with her head resting on the window sill.

I knelt and put my head in her lap. 'I couldn't find you. I didn't know where you were.'

'Didn't you, my darling?' She sounded like she used to when she sang 'What are the Wild Winds Saying?'

'What you doing in here? Got a headache?'

She ran her fingers over my face as if she was looking for a light switch in the dark. 'No . . . I'm just thinking.'

'What's the matter then?'

She made a sst't sound and shook her head and smiled. 'Oh . . . nothing you'd understand, Simon.'

'But what's up, Mum? What've I done?'

She patted her knee as I sat up and I let half my weight down on her.

'What is it?'

'Well, Simon . . .' She gazed out over the back field. 'You know Nan's not very well?'

'Yes.'

'Well Aunty at Petersfield needs a break from Old Gran.'

'Does she, Mum?'

'Yes. So she's coming down to stay with us for a while.'

'Why, Mum?'

'Why what, Simon?'

'Why does Aunty need a break from her?'

'Because she's not very well. And I don't think Nan'll be able to cope with her for some time.'

'But what's wrong with her, Mum?'

'She forgets things and she can't get to sleep at night and when she does she can't wake up to go to the . . .'

Old Gran always forgot things. She always had. She was always losing her darning and her pension book and once, when she was in Chichester, she forgot where she was supposed to be going home to until an inspector at the bus station looked at her return ticket and I wouldn't have thought staying awake was such a bad thing if she got off eventually and—

'. . . and there's lots of extra washing and drying and ironing and we've only got the two bedrooms.'

'Well, that's all right, isn't it?'

'Haven't you been listening to a word I've been saying, Simon? She'll have to have your room.'

I turned her bottle of rose water round on her dressing table. 'You used any of this yet, Mum?'

'Blowed if I know what we're going to do.' She picked up her hairbrush with the picture of flowers on the back and straightened the lacy thing under it and put it back. 'Or how long it will go on.'

If Gran came to stay they might let me stay up later until they went to bed and then I could listen to Paul Temple and boxing and then p'raps Mum'd have my brother. 'Poor old Gran, I don't mind if she stays in my room, Mum.'

She pressed my hands together between hers, but they were cold. 'That's nice of you, Simon. But there's more to it than that and we want you to be nice and fresh for school because it's ever so important that you get to the High School.' She sighed and moved the net curtain along so that it hung in even folds. 'But I expect you'll be wanting to get off out to play now, won't you?'

I looked at her out of the corner of my eye. 'Well, I did think I might have my tea.'

'Oh, my poor darling!' Mum bounced off the chair and shot me off her knee. 'Whatever's the time? You must be famished and what in heaven's name's happened to your father. Dear oh dear and I haven't got a thing ready.'

The kettle filled up and the cups and saucers crashed on the tray and the saw knife bit into the bread.

I lifted up Mum's little green and white ballerina. I'd always thought she was looking at me in my bedroom at Nan's and sometimes I made out I was looking the other way and tried to turn quickly and catch her out. She'd looked like a lady then but she was only about my age now and her eyes were really just dots of blue paint and she looked china'y. I put her down carefully so that she faced the mirror and looked over the top of her as if I was a giant in a forest. I'd got more freckles this year. I tried to smile but my face went like cardboard so I breathed on the glass and drew a stick man on it.

Mum'd laid the table and was watching out of the window in the living room and pressing the earth down round her cactus.

'Where in the world's he got to, Simon? It's after six o'clock.' She dusted the earth off her fingers and started twisting her handkerchief. 'He's never been this late before.'

'Dunno, Mum.' I stared at the glass face of the clock and imagined the roundabout by the White Swan and him cycling around it with cars whooshing by but they came too close to him so I imagined him on the straight Westerton Road. Grandad said that was a bit of Watling Street that the

129

Romans had made and I saw the Roman soldiers marching along two abreast to leave space at the side of the road for the chariots. They'd probably be going to attack the Saxons on Trundle Hill. Wonder who'd be chief of the Saxons? Not Rasher because he was Irish and not Wadey, he wasn't noble enough, and the Guv was too soft and Grandad was too old. Could have been Grandad when he was in his army uniform, but I didn't think he'd've liked fighting. Bladder Payton would have been warlike but—

'Here he is at last. Thank goodness.' Mum dashed to the back door and I followed her.

Dad put his bike in the shed and slipped his cycle clips over the handlebar and straightened his trousers.

'Oh my darling,' Mum flung her arms round him as he turned. 'Wherever *have* you been?'

'Cor, steady on, my Ine. I've got—'

'We've been worried sick, haven't we, Simon? Thinking something awful'd happened.'

There was a little round stone in the mortar by the back door and I picked it out.

'Stop that, Simon. You're too fond of picking about at things.'

'Well, I've got some good—'

'And Mum's been on at me about how she can't have Gran again. I really don't know how we're going to manage.'

'Hold on, 'arf a minute.' Dad kissed her and I followed them into the living room.

'I've been . . .' He lit a cigarette and blew the lighted spill of paper out and flicked the burned end on the bars of the range. 'I've been up to county hall to see the valuer.'

'What, at this time of night?'

'No not work, Ina. For an interview. He's offered me a job at half as much again as I get at Rapson's and going up for the next five years.'

Mum stood still as if she'd seen an accident and then she put her arms round him again and started to sob and Dad said I ought to go and see if there were any carrots worth pulling.

The sun was angled down on the back of the chicken house

and the corrugated iron was warm through my shirt. I called for Jack and he flew down on to my shoulder from a holly tree down by the pigs and we sat picking green flakes of paint off the chicken-house wall. 'Half as much again, Jack! Blimey, what does that mean?' I multiplied it by two but that came out to ten pounds and it couldn't be that much. Dad got five pounds ten shillings a week. I'd found that out from a bit of paper in the drawer that showed what it was spent on and there was another figure called 'Army Pay' but he'd kept crossing that out and it was nearly gone. Five pounds ten shillings! I put five stones down on a flat piece of flagstone and stared at them. That's what he got now and half again – I put two more stones down and a little one – that made five, six, seven and a bit over. Nearly eight pounds. I sat back and closed my eyes. Nobody else I knew got that much. Things were always 'tight' when he was trying to grow his own tobacco and mincing up old bits of toasted bread for the chickens and it was never worth paying a bus fare into Chichester even if things were a penny or two cheaper than down the shops and— Gibbser! 'Watch out, Jack.' I jumped up and ran down the path and hurdled the clothes prop and into my bedroom.

'What's up with you, Simon?'

'Nothing, Mum. I promised Gibbser something.'

I had an old kitchen knife in my bottom drawer for getting at my money box and I slid a penny ha'penny out without making it rattle and grabbed a Buck Jones comic.

'I promised 'im this, Mum. Are we rich now, Dad?'

'Phew, I dunno about rich, Nip. And I hate leaving Rapson's but the tithe work's not worth what they pay me to collect it and—'

'But we'll be rich*er*?'

'Well a bit better off p'raps.'

'Good-o. Shan't be long.'

'But, Simon. Don't you go telling anybody, mind,' followed me from the living-room window.

'And what about your tea?'

'Not hungry, Mum.'

*

131

There was a quick way to Geoffrey Gibbs's house past the cess pit and through old Mr Errity's garden where Grandad used to take me to get my hair cut. I forced a way through the stinging nettles and squeezed between the stakes in the fence where one stave was broken. The grass was long under the apple trees and Mr Errity's mower, that he'd always kept clean and shiny, was lying under a tarpaulin with a bramble bush growing over it. Last year's runner beans were still clinging brown and withered to their trellis of hazel poles and some cabbages were flowering yellow. The roof of his shed was lifting at one corner and the felt was ripped where a twig from the apple tree rubbed under it in the wind. Old Mr Errity was down by the house with his back to me arranging a pink and orange and blue crocheted blanket over a wheelchair. He looked so bent and old that I doubted he'd see me if he looked at me. His black car, that I'd been able to see my face in and Grandad said ran like a sewing-machine, was up on blocks of wood in the barn built on to the side of the house. He'd used to reverse it out when I went for a haircut and give it a wipe with a cloth from his back pocket as he came back. Grandad always had his hair cut first so that I didn't have to stand about with hair down my neck. Once he'd nicked my ear with the scissors because I wouldn't hold still and they'd stuck it up with stamp edging. A wind whipped through the grass and he tucked the blanket in round his wife's shoulders as if he was making a bed. I crept back towards the hedge. He'd always showed Grandad his garden when we came down and he had the best cabbage and sprout plants in the village and Mrs Errity was always smart and smelling of rose water and now it seemed as if their front gate had been closed and locked and rusted up and the garden was growing up around them. I squeezed back through the fence and stung the back of my hand.

If Geoff was in he'd be having his tea and if he'd had his tea he'd be out so I went up Crouch Cross Road towards the playing field. There was a slope where the pavement by the new houses ran down to the road. Wally Hamick and the new kid from the farm cottages and Derek Brown were lying face down at the top of the slope.

'What'cha doin'?'

'Playing racing cars. Wanna game?'

Derek Brown was going b'rmm b'rmm on his hands and knees. 'No thanks. I gotta find Gibbser. You seen 'im?'

'Nope. You go first this time, Browner.'

I walked on up past Phil Alker's house and picked some shoots off his box hedge. His little girl was lying in the back garden in her knickers reading a book. I made out I wasn't watching and stripped the skin off the shoot and ran my thumbnail down the stem and split it. There was a whoosh from the kitchen door and some washing-up water shot out and I carried on up to the end of the road. I stopped outside Teddy Perrin's house and trod on some ants. The more I trod on them the more they came out and they started to crawl up over my shoes. They might be little soldier ants. I'd read about some soldier ants once in a book at school who'd eaten a man to death when he was asleep in a rowing boat in Brazil. He'd thought he was safe moored out in the middle of the river but they'd crept across the rope and got him. Wonder if they'd waited until they were all there. If the first one'd started nibbling, when he was on his own, the man could have squashed him or cut the rope but p'raps they knew they had to stand around and attack in force . . . attack in force! . . . I'd heard that somewhere—

'What you doing, Nipper?'

'Eh? Oh, hello, Teddy. Nothin' much.'

'Well, you'd better move on and do it cos me Mum reckon's you're starin' in our window.'

'Course I ain't starin' in your rotten—' I was going to say something horrible about his mum but he was watching me as if he hoped I didn't. Teddy was taller than Dad now and he'd started playing rugby as well as football and cricket at the High School. 'I'm lookin' for Gibbser. You seen him?'

'No. Still, I ain't been looking for him. What you want to go around with him for?'

'I don't go around with him. Not really. But I owe him some money.'

'Oh, yeah. What you been up to?' Teddy reached up to a branch of a tree in the hedge and did a couple of chins.

'Oh, nothing like that. Just for . . . just for some sweets.'

'You wanna lay off sweets.' He pulled up for two more

chins and then dropped to the ground. 'They'll ruin your teeth.'

'M'm . . . coming up the field?'

'What for?'

'Find Gibbser.'

'And if he's not there?'

'I dunno. Go down the bus shelter.'

'No thanks.' Teddy stepped over his hedge and changed the milk order on his front door step. 'Is that all you do? Wander about from the swings to the bus shelter?'

'No, course not. Sometimes we go up the common or to the dell.'

'What a flamin' waste of time. You can do better than that, Nipper. Look, when you've found Gibbser, come back and we'll have a game of cricket. But for heaven's sake don't bring him with you.' He bowled an overarm with a piece of earth and went through his back gate.

'Yeah, all right, Teddy. I'll see.'

We weren't supposed to play in the school field in the evenings but we did if we thought Milly was out and Geoff Gibbs's gran'd told old Mrs Ballard once, when they were sitting on the wall outside their cottages, that we had every right to play there because they'd all taken a penny a week to school to buy the field when she was a girl. The grass grew tall and spindly up through the fence where the cows couldn't chew it from my side and where the school mowers missed it on the other. I pulled a piece to chew but it was dusty. Tiny blue butterflies, like icing crisps off a cake, flittered about in the long grass and I knelt and crept up on a Red Admiral but he swerved away up and down and zigzagged towards the football field. The grass was long all over the pitch except for in the goal mouths. Dad'd tried to get them to turn the pitch round but they wouldn't because they didn't want to have to keep getting over the school fence to get the ball. There was nobody on the swings or playing round the village hall. We always crept past the village hall in case anybody saw us and thought we were going to mess about in the outside toilets that they didn't use now. There was an elder tree by the toilets that was easy to climb. One branch overhung the roof and I climbed up level with it. The roofing felt was flaking and when I pulled a bit to make it level it tore off like a skin. It was shiny underneath and I kept on pulling it to make it straight but it went all jaggedy so I pulled some more off. The rafters underneath were worm-eaten and thick with spiders' webs. They ought to mend the roof or it'd leak. I put the bits of felt back and climbed down. The hinges were rusty and I had to squeeze in against the door post. Long dusty cobwebs hung down like curtains and the bucket looked as if it had been dipped in tar. The ceiling was sagging in one corner. I poked at it with a stick to push it back but a crack opened up across the middle. I dropped my stick and ran.

The crash was like when they brought down Westgate Brewery chimney. I dived into the grown-over back door to the hall and peeped out from behind the buddleia they'd planted to hide the new drain. There was a sort of settling silence and then puffs of chalky dust seeped out of the door and through the roof.

'P'raps it's on fire,' I said to myself and looked around to see if anyone was listening.

The nettles by the wall were powdered with chalk and a thin haze settled against the sun. A black beetle scuttled past my toe and then a couple of sparrows landed on the telephone wire that stretched from the corner of the alms-houses to the middle bit where Milly lived. I slunk out between the alms houses wall and the hall and crossed the road before I got to the school.

The gravelly stones up the lane past the entrance to Mrs Evans's garden crunched under my feet and I veered off by the side of her wall through the waist-high grass to the Old Boys' Club Uncle Steven'd run before the war. I couldn't see in through the windows because my reflection kept getting in the way so I got down lower and held a bit of tin with 'Gold Flake' on it over my head. The billiard table was covered with a green canvas sheet and it was dark inside like a tomb. Dad said Joe Davis could get the red and the white wedged in the corner of the pocket and bounce the other white off them all night. Then they'd made it illegal. He must've stuck them there with his hands. I rubbed the window clear and wiped my hands on my trousers. There was a round army stove at the far end in the middle of the wall. It looked like the one Johnny Duke used in his camps but this one had a long chimney. We could make a good camp in here. I tried to push the door open but it was locked and when I tried to open it with a piece of stick it broke off in the key hole.

Mr Ewings was taking the cows in past the ruins of the old part of the church for milking. I leant on the iron fence and watched. A cow rubbed against it and I felt it bend. Her feet stabbed at the ground like a fat lady in high heels and her veins stood out through the hair where her belly was full of milk and her head turned so stiffly and was so heavy that I thought she'd flatten the fence. Wonder if Mr Ewings knows how strong they are and what would happen if they all turned on him. He was slapping one on the rear to stop her going through a hole in the wire to the ruins and she jumped her back legs and ran on after the others as if she was going to tell them what he'd done.

The jackdaws swooped and dived into the holes in the crumbling flintwork and I measured with my eye to see how many of me it was up and sucked my teeth and wondered whether Jack would ever grow up enough to want to go away.

Grandad said it was too dangerous to climb the ruin and that's why they'd put the fence round it. He said it'd been falling down ever since Henry the Eighth'd smashed it up to get at the monks' silver. I rubbed the dents in my arm where they'd been resting on the fence and ran in and out of the apple trees by the path to the church and slipped up under the laurel bushes where there was a tumbledown shed against the wall that looked over the kitchen garden. Grandad'd planted a peach tree against the wall and made the branches grow along and fixed them with wire tied to nails we'd driven into the mortar. The peaches were ripe. If I tied my cap to a piece of string I might be able to let it down and knock the peaches into it. That'd mean coming straight here from school when I'd got my cap on. I leant over and reached down. The wall was bowing out and it made me dizzy as if the ground was pulling me. I hauled myself back and brushed the bits of moss and grit off my pullover.

'Never take anything that's out of reach.' I said it to myself and tried to screw one eye up like Grandad did but it didn't sound like him and I kept saying it to myself as I went through the wicket gate to the churchyard.

There was guttering all round the church roof that I hadn't noticed before and the down-pipe was square and made of lead. I scratched at it with a sharp flint and made a face and wrote G.G. under it but then I scratched the letters out. Maybe the boys had seen me coming and were hiding.

The grass was growing long on Grandad Grainger's grave and I knelt beside it and smoothed it all one way. If I pulled it low down and did a bit every day it'd look as if it had been clipped. And the flowers had wilted in his vase and the water stank. I slung the flowers over the orchard fence and tipped the water out. The daisies were still flowering amongst the long grass and I could arrange them with some sprigs of yew. P'raps do a bit of grass pulling first. 'I dunno, though. Better put the flowers in and see what time I've got left.' I took the vase and walked along the concrete path by the church wall. The grass sloped down so that I was walking in a sort of moat that went around the side of the church to the tap by the main door. The tap had sacking wrapped around the joint where it leaked and it was corroded as if it had been in the sea but the handle was polished where people had twisted it and it shone red gold. Maybe it *was* gold. Maybe the monks had melted it down when they heard Henry the Eighth coming and they'd made it into taps and pipes and things and I was the only one who knew. I scratched a piece of flint lower down the handle and then on the pipe. It skidded off the cold steel and chipped and made no mark. I turned the tap on and a few drops came out but then it stopped. I twisted it full on but nothing happened so I gave it a kick to see if it was stuck and then I couldn't turn it back again. P'raps it was broken. I tried to knock it loose with a piece of broken gravestone but I'd forgotten which way it turned so I left it.

All the puddles had dried up and the vases on the graves amongst the trees were empty. Darting from one to another I felt like one of the body-snatchers from when Queen Victoria was queen and the pictures in our history books showed people standing back in horror as men with whiskers and check coats and caps with ear-pieces grabbed the coffins in the light of lanterns . . . or p'raps that was Sexton Blake or Sherlock Holmes . . .

I tried the tap again but it still wouldn't budge so I went into the church porch to see what they kept in the broom cupboard by the hat and coat stand. I tugged at the door but it was stuck. I slid the blade of my knife behind the lock and wrenched again. S'srarck! A crack opened up like lightning on a larch tree down the whole length of the panel. I slid my knife out and walked away from the cupboard until I was sure nobody was watching and then I ran back and fitted the split piece back so that the crack didn't show.

The church smelt of cold stone and incense and sunlight slanted down in pillars through the stained-glass windows on to the paved floor by the font. The font was shaped like a big buttercup of granite covered with carvings of babies and vines and deer. It was covered with an oak lid that came apart in the middle so that it could be lifted off for christenings. A basket of dried flowers stood in the middle of the top step and I was careful not to brush against it as I reached up on tiptoe. I lifted one side and stuck my arm in but it was dry. I lowered the lid gently but it slipped and crushed my little finger. Yellow spots dived in from the corners of my eyes and I forced my breath against my chest and made my arms go stiff so that my veins stood out and the blood churned down to my fingertips. As I turned my trouser bottoms caught in the basket and I lost my balance. The basket spun down and sideways and a clanging whooshing sound rang out on the flagstones and echoed around in the church roof. The basket went one way and a white enamel jug behind it shot the other. Water sprayed all over the floor. I dived at the jug and sent dried flowers spinning like confetti. The water spread out in the shape of a Saracen's sword and the splashes settled.

I leant my head back against the font and lay my finger in the puddle. The throbbing bubbled over a flat ache and I closed my eyes and pretended it hadn't happened. P'raps a cat had got in and knocked it over, or maybe a dog had chased the cat and the dog had done it, or I'd seen them run in and chased after them to get them out and accidentally knocked it over. But I couldn't think what the dog had looked like and if they asked me and watched my face as I was talking and trying to think how it might have happened they'd know I'd done it.

The sun warmed my face and I sat round so that it was full on me. I screwed my eyes up and squinted through the lids. The light was a spinning, dusty purple where it was strained through the capes of the Roman soldiers and, above them, Jesus was bleeding on the cross with a thief on either side and Pop reckoned he'd died as a propitiation for our sins. His head was lolling over and I could see He was dead because in the next picture a man in a white cloak was reaching through the crowd with a long pole with a claw on it to grab a jewel or something from Jesus's crown of thorns. And in three days' time he was going to be rising again according to the scriptures and be sitting on the right hand of God the Father in heaven and . . . then he'd see everything that happened on earth for ever and ever.

I sucked my finger dry and stood up. I bowed to the altar and tucked my trousers up under my belt.

It had to be cleared up with something but the broom cupboard was locked and grass was no good. I searched all around the church and up behind the organ but there wasn't a newspaper or bit of rag or anything. I wandered back down the aisle and sat down in the end of a pew. I knelt forward with my elbows on the wooden ledge so that my finger wouldn't hang and hurt and lowered my knees on to the hassock. It was soft and had a fringe round the edge. I leant back on my heels and shut my eyes. 'Gentle Jesus, meek and mild, look upon this little child, pity my simplicity and . . . let me find something . . . something soft!' I let my hand down on to the hassock.

The splashed spots of water soaked up easily and then I started blotting the puddle from the outside. The hassock got heavier and sank in the middle as I lifted it by the cloth-lip handles and a thin stream of water ran out of it. Grandad Grainger's vase was lying next to the jug. I stood them up side by side in the middle of the pool and let the water run out of the hassock into first one and then the other. As the trickle got thinner I bent the cushion up until it was as far as it could go and then I blotted some more. I moved gradually round the edges blotting and squeezing as I went, and it got smaller and the flagstones became a sea and the puddle was dry land and I was a sort of spirit of the sea and I was commanding the waves to gobble up the land and Grandad Grainger's vase was half full and the jug had a couple of inches in the bottom. I soaked up the last of the water, wrung the hassock out and put it under the pew and put the jug back on the step. The sun had dropped to the bottom of the window but they'd probably leave the church door open so the rest'd dry . . . but I'd better be safe than sorry. I slipped my shoes off and danced up and down on the wet patch in my socks and then rolled over it a few times. 'Neat but not gaudy . . . the monkey said as he tied the elephant's tails in knots.'

I stood the wicker basket up and straightened its handle. The hydrangea flowers and the Chinese lanterns went at the back with the dried leaves and a few ears of corn amongst them. Then the little crisped brown cornflowers and stuff in front. It looked a bit like Geoff Gibbs's head after he'd had a haircut but it'd have to do. I bowed to the altar and said 'sorry' to God and ran out with Grandad Grainger's vase.

The yew trees flung out pools of black shadows on the long grass of the old part of the churchyard and the cool evening air chivvied my wrists against my wet shirt sleeves. I filled the vase with yew sprigs and daisies and I went and started to tell Grandad Grainger I'd do them for him again next week but I could imagine him lying there listening to me and all the other dead people hearing as well and one or two opening their eyes and some others starting to sit up as if it was the last day and— I shot out past the church doors without seeing if the patch on the floor was dry or giving the tap another kick and kept on going until I got to the end of the church path where it met Church Lane. The lane was empty so I slipped out through the gate and scuffed along through the deep grit at the side of the road.

Mr Norbitt was watering his runner beans by the light from his kitchen door, from a watering can he dipped in the rain-water butt. His wireless was on and the eight o'clock pips were going. Mr Ewings was shooing his chickens from their run into the hen house and the last drainings of the sun were sliding down behind the roof of Ray Whittle's house like soapsuds down a milk bottle. I leant back against the telegraph pole and let the midging and flaffer of the insects in Mrs Evans's hedge blend into a hazy grey hum.

'This is your Conservative candidate, Joynston Hicks!'

I jerked up against the pole and banged my head. A white van with blue ribbons and lights on the bonnet was coming down past the Men's Club as if it was leading something big or dangerous.

'Vote for your Conservative candidate, Joynston Hicks, at the parliamentary general election!' It sounded like a wireless. 'This is your Conservative candidate, ladies and gentlemen,' it wailed at the empty street. 'Now is the time to get some order into government before the Labour Party bankrupts us all.'

Cedric Kyle was driving and a bloke next to him was talking into a thing like a paraffin jug.

I stepped into the road but as the van turned up Crouch Cross Lane I saw the boys were running along behind it.

' "Vote, vote, vote for Leslie Cot-ton. Throw old 'icksy in the ditch." What'cha, Nipper. Fun ain't it!' Colin Gander broke off from the others. 'Come on. Where ya bin?'

'Lookin' for Gibbser.' I fell in behind them as they loped after the van. 'Where is 'e and what'cha doin'?'

'Chasin' this bleedin' thing. We bin all up round Greatwood and Hanover. The bugger keeps speedin' up but we catches 'im most'a the time.'

'What'cha yellin' for then?'

Colin hung back as if he didn't want the others to hear. 'What'cha mean. He's Conservative,' and he stuck two fingers up at the van.

'So what?'

'Well, you're not, are you?'

'I dunno. What should I be?'

'Labour a'course. Your ole man works, don't 'e?'

'Yeah, course 'e does.'

'Yeah, well . . .' Colin rubbed his chin. 'Office work . . . I s'pose that's work of a sort. You don't want the snobs to get in again, do you?'

141

'I dunno. What's bangtrup?'

'Bankrup? I dunno. But it's lies whatever it is. C'mon.'

We all ran after the van yelling about slinging Mr Hicks in the ditch until Mr Kyle stopped the van and said he'd get the police after us if we didn't stop acting like hooligans so we went for a sit-down in the bus shelter.

'Seen Gibbser, Col?'

'No. We lost 'im up the Redvins. He went for a crap in Christie's spinney.' Colin had started coughing now he'd stopped running and Jerry Henry and Jimmy Phillips were sitting down and rubbing each other's feet.

'Run ruddy inches off my legs tonight. Reckon we'll get in trouble.'

'Dunno, Jerry.' Derek Brown was drawing an aeroplane on the concrete floor with chalk. 'There was a lotta blue posters up round Hanover.'

'Trouble? What can they do? They want Conservatives to win and we wants Labour. We got a right to say our piece.' Colin coughed and spat out of the bus shelter into the dust. ' 'ere, you got Gibbser's money?'

'Yeah. Why?'

'Well 'e said give it to me else it'll be tuppence tomorrow.'

' 'ere 'yar then.' I handed over the penny ha'penny and made Jimmy Phillips witness it.

The boys squabbled and argued and Colin trod on Derek Brown's fingers by mistake but Derek ran off saying he was going to tell his mum anyway and I went home wondering if the boys'd say I'd been with them all night.

The Nine O'Clock News had finished but I couldn't sleep. Dad was still up at Nan's and I could hear Mum sighing at the clock in the living room and wondering 'where the deuce he'd got to'. I'd tried opening the curtains and counting the stars but I kept forgetting where I'd got up to and finding I was thinking about school and Rasher and the way the sums he was teaching us just bounced off my brain like snowflakes off a window pane.

Click. That was the front gate. Dad's footsteps came down the path and they were hurrying. The living-room door opened as the back door closed.

'Simon asleep yet?'

'Of course he is, I expect. Whatever's the—'

'There's been a hell'ov'a row up at the Hall . . .'

'Oh no!' I shrank back in bed.

'Dad had to hear it all and Pop was there and all the others and P.C. Howlett—'

I put my hands together. 'Oh no, please. Please don't let me be in trouble.'

'. . . told him after they'd been to lock up the church.'

'Shall I get him?'

The light flicked on in the passage and I buried myself.

'C'mon, Simon. Daddy wants you.' Mum prodded me through the bedclothes. 'Whatever were you thinking of to-night and what've you been messing about with these curtains for? You'll have them down if you go pulling on them.'

Mum stood aside as I walked through and tried to blink in the light of the living room. Dad was standing in front of the fireplace and he pointed at his feet and I stood there.

'I want a full explanation.' The vein above his right eye was bulging and I stared at it. 'C'mon. Out with it.'

'It wasn't me, Dad.'

'What do you mean "it wasn't you"?'

'Well, I was with the boys all evening.'

'Strewth alive!' He bent forward and banged his fist against his leg and I winced. 'That's the whole point.'

'I'm sorry, Dad . . . what've we done?'

'Are you daft or something?' He came down closer to me. 'You were all in it. The whole pack of you.'

'If you can't keep out of mischief, Simon, you'll have to stay in evenings.' Mum was next to him now. 'Oh dear oh dear. What *is* to become of you?'

'But I haven't done any—'

'Up-at-the-Hall . . .' Dad was poking his head up and down in my face. 'Pop and Mr Peters and Grandad and Lord knows who else. They were there for a church council meeting, Ina. And they got P.C. Howlett up.'

'But I wasn't up at the hall when there was any meeting on.'

'Stop interrupting and listen. It was disgraceful behaviour . . . making a spectacle of yourself chasing after that van and—'

'O-oh.'

'Don't you "oh" me my boy.'

'But . . . well, was that all, Dad?'

'All?' Dad's voice went so high it disappeared. 'I don't think you've quite got it into your head yet.' His hand was on my shoulder and his fingers were clenching. 'You *don't* race around like a young savage hurling abuse at adults—'

'Or anybody else for that matter.'

'No, Mum.'

I kept staring at Dad without blinking until the tears came and then he rolled a cigarette.

'His mates stood up for him apparently. Lord knows why. But old Cedric Kyle said he was there.'

I scratched my toe into the carpet and wondered if it was still wrong if you were blamed for something you hadn't done if you couldn't tell the truth about what you had done.

'And you shouldn't stand there looking so innocent, Simon. Poor little Derek Brown! Fancy dragging him into something like this.'

I sniffled as I said 'sorry, Mum' but I was wondering who they'd blame for the roof in the old toilet and the broken tap.

'Well, you're to stay away from the other boys from now on.' Dad relit his cigarette. 'And I want a written apology to Mr Kyle and Pop and you'd better go up and say you're sorry to Grandad.'

'Yes, Dad.'

'And then you'd better think about what you want to hang on to out of your bedroom.'

'What, Mum?'

'Old Gran's coming down tomorrow. Your Uncle Edward's going up to fetch her. It was all fixed up this evening. So you'd better start behaving from now on, Simon.'

They'd put Old Gran in my bedroom and it smelt of Evening in Paris. The bed had a new blue eiderdown and Nan'd got her friend, Mrs Kaley from Eastergate, to make some new curtains to match. My brown armchair by the fire always had a cotton bag of darning wool and tins of pins and bits of material in it and I had to start keeping my elbows in at mealtimes. Mum and Dad'd started off sleeping me on a mattress on the floor at the bottom of their bed when Gran first came but it was like a coffin between their bed and the dressing table so they let me go in with them. There was plenty of space in their bed when I first got in but I always woke up squashed so I started staying out longer with Jack and going to bed later.

Jack had grown up all of a sudden. He wouldn't go into his cage at night and kept backing up my arm when I tried to put him in until I had to give up. Then he was nice and tucked his head around the back of his neck and stood on one leg and made out he was going to sleep. I loved him more then because he was stubborn and I fixed up a perch for him under the overhang of the chicken-house roof.

When he saw me coming out of the back door after tea he jumped and flapped and glided down on to my shoulder in a curve as if he was freewheeling and we went mushrooming in the back field most evenings. We rarely found any mushrooms so I'd given up taking a basket and we just wandered over to the dell and back. There was always something happening. Some days some new rubbish had been tipped into the dell that we could sort through or we'd find a fossil or nearly catch a rabbit. They'd ploughed the field up yesterday and now they'd covered it in farm muck. I held my breath as I climbed through the fence into the dell field and waited while Jack scuttled on to my back and stepped over the wire. The smell from the manure was wet and stinging and I stepped on something that squelched. I started to run but it was slippery and then my foot caught in some strands of baling twine and I fell. My hand landed in something wet and sticky and my face was almost in the straw. An eye was staring up at me. I could see it was a dead piglet and maggots were crawling around its mouth. I eased myself up and ran and I just got to the lane and was bending to climb through the fence when I remembered Jack.

'Jack. Where are you?'

The field was empty. I listened but there wasn't a sound except for a tractor churning away over towards the Redvins.

'C'mon, Jack. Don't muck about. I gotta get home.'

I stared up into the trees behind me but he wasn't there.

145

'Ja-ack!' My voice rang hollow through the trees. 'P'raps he's over by the dell.'

I started to pick my way through the straw and muck but the stench made my throat curdle so I ran back to the dell. It was cool and dark and empty there now.

'Ja-ack!' My voice was wailing and I closed my eyes and counted to fifty and willed for him to be there when I opened them. I ran back to where I'd fallen over and looked around. There were some black birds pecking at stuff around the wheels of a trailer but they were all rooks and they flew away as I got closer to them.

'Please come back, Jack. Oh, please come back.' My voice echoed around the dell as if it was laughing at me. I walked back slowly along the rim of the dell on the path that was left where the plough had got in close to the barbed wire. My jacket caught on it as I was gazing up into the trees. I unhooked it but it had ripped already and I ran back to the lane. Every movement in the bushes sent me scampering in to look and I called and called but there was no answer and as I got nearer to home it felt as if I'd never had him. My legs felt stiff as I climbed through the fence and my wellingtons dragged through the long grass in the back field and I didn't hurry into our back garden even when I saw Farmer Vine's manager coming up out of the farm lane with his gun.

'Where in heaven's name have you been, Simon?' Mum was tipping the tea leaves round Dad's cabbages. 'You're late.'

'I've lost Jack, Mum.' I tried to grab round her.

'You can't have. Where?'

'Up the dell.'

'Oh, Simon. How many times have I told you not to—'

'But *Jack*, Mum.'

'I don't care about—'

'Wha-at?'

'Well, of course I care. But I don't suppose you've lost him for a minute. I've told you a thousand times not to go up that blasted dell.'

'But I've lost Jack, Mum.'

'Oh and, Simon. Just look at your jacket.' She'd pulled me round and put her fingers in the hole. 'Don't know how I'll be able to mend—'

'Oh sod the rotten jacket.'

'Simon!'

'Ouch!' I felt the weight of Dad's hand at the same time as I caught sight of a black shape in the holly tree down by the pigs.

Jark!

'Jack!'

Bang!

It all happened together. Like a frozen moving picture, Farmer Vine's manager had taken aim as my ears were ringing and Jack had jarked at me and the puff of smoke had come from the shotgun and then the bang and I'd shot up the garden and dived over the fence and was panting and punching and clawing at his face.

Firm hands clamped my arms to my sides and the nut-brown stain smell of the shotgun butt pressing into my shoulder mixed in with the wax and turpentine of his khaki jacket filled my nostrils and they picked me off him like taking a stag beetle off a bare arm so that the claws don't rip out.

'. . . didn't seem right 'im just sitting there. I'm ever so . . .'

'Can't be helped.'

I imagined Superman climbing out of a wrecked car that'd gone over a cliff on Saturday-morning pictures. 'He might still be al—'

'No, Simon. He's not.'

'It was the boy's, was it?'

'Yes. He was ever so attached to it.'

I bit my teeth together so that my cheekbones stuck up through the skin.

'What can I say? I'm so so—'

'You can give me that gun.'

'What?'

'Simon!'

'If you're so sorry, gimme that gun and I'll—'

'Simon. How—' Clout! '. . . dare you.' Dad frogmarched me to our bit of the fence and heaved me over bodily and plonked me down in front of Mum.

Mum's face was grey like burnt-out log dust and she held me in place until Dad got through the wire.

147

'In . . . at once.' He marched me in through the living room where Old Gran was sitting looking over the top of a cup of Ovaltine and into my bedroom and out again and into theirs. They forced me down on the bed and lined up in front of me.

'Is that the way to talk to Mr Lennox-Hills?'

'He shot Jack, Dad.'

'It was an accident.'

'But he shot Jack.'

'I know that. But aren't you listening?'

'Aren't *you* bloody listening.'

Clout!

'I don't care. You can hit me as much as you—'

'S'sh, Simon.'

'Yes, mate. You'd better be quiet.'

Dad had taken a step backwards and I could have got to the window but it was closed and as I looked at the grey evening outside and the outline of the trees up by the dell my legs went suddenly heavy.

'Your face, Simon!' Mum knelt in front of me. 'I think you'd've . . . well, I don't like to think what I think . . . if you'd got hold of that gun.'

'Jack's dead, Mum.'

'Yes, I know he is. But Mr . . . well, he's ever so sorry.' Her face was smeared with hair where she'd been crying. 'What more can we say . . . or do?'

'Losing his temper won't help.'

'Just have to face up to it, my lad.' Mum put her arms round me but I pushed her away. 'Try saying your prayers.'

'What for?' I clenched my fists and forced my eyes to stop crying. 'There isn't a God.'

'Simon!' Mum and Dad drew together.

'He's s'posed to love little children and now He's killed Jack. But I'll get even with Him.'

'Simon. Don't say such things. George! Say something to him.'

'Yes, come on, Nip.' Dad put his hand on my shoulder 'It was an accident, really. Mr Lennox-Hills is ever so sorry.'

'What good's it being sorry.' I twisted away from him. 'I hate him for killing Jack and I hate Go—'

148

'Stop it.' Dad's hand caught me across the cheek and left my ear stinging. 'There's no need for all this.'

'And you can jolly well get that temper of yours under control, my lad.'

My nose was running and I felt as if I'd wet myself and I could see Jack sitting there and the bang and him dropping.

'Did you hear me, Simon?'

'Yes, Mum.' I sniffed to clear my nose. 'But I won't.'

'You won't what?'

'I won't control it. I'll kill . . .' I gritted my teeth and held my breath until my face quivered.

'You'll kill who? Us?' Dad stood up straight and folded his arms.

'Of course not, George. He's just upset.' Mum took round me again and I let her lead me to the bathroom.

'I wish I was dead, Mum.' I held my arms up for her to pull my shirt off over my head.

'Course you don't, old funnikins.'

'I do. I wish I was dead and—' Mum's bottle of rose water was on the window sill and the water in the toilet was stained pink.

'And what?'

'You been putting that in the lav?'

Mum stared down and bit her lip slowly. 'Well I—'

'You have. You've been chucking it in the bog.'

'Well, just a drop. It smelt so nice that I—'

'But that was for you. I bought that for you so you'd have a bloody—'

'Right, my lad!' The bathroom door crashed open. 'That's about enough for one evening.'

I cowered back against the toilet as Dad came for me but he didn't hit me. They both said they hoped I'd ask for forgiveness and be a good boy from now on and that I could make a start tomorrow at church with Grandad.

I was asleep when they came to bed and I stayed over on one side and just let my hand dip into the warmth of Mum's back.

*

149

My back ached where I'd been sleeping on Dad's elbow. I leant back against the chicken house and stretched my legs out and then bent my knees so that I didn't scuff the backs of my shoes. My pullover smelt of Persil and the wool was rough and stiff on my wrists. I dabbed my finger on some little red mites running about on the bricks. Dad said they weren't red mites and that red mite was a disease chickens got and that they were insects but they looked as if they ought to be called red mites so that's what I called them. Jack would have watched them for a minute and pecked at one but they were soft and didn't crunch and he'd have preferred woodlice.

'What you doing, Simon?' Old Gran's head poked round the side of the chicken house.

'Nothing, Gran. What you up so early for?'

'I'm going to church with you. I don't want you in any more trouble.'

'But they said I'm going with Grandad . . .'

She came round behind the chicken house and settled herself slowly on Dad's box of chicken pellets and moved her hand for me to stand over in front of her.

'You were out with the boys the other night, weren't you?'

'Oh that.' I stared at the path and edged my toe towards a crack between two stones. Maybe I'd be able to see if they'd fixed the tap at church this morning and if the crack in the broom cupboard door showed.

'Stop messing about and answer me.'

'Yes, Gran.'

'Yes, Gran, what?'

'I was with them a little while but not all the time. And they were chasing that van already and if I don't do what they do they don't like me and I finish up on my own and . . . now Jack's gone.'

Gran spread her arms to me and I slipped inside and sobbed so that my chin banged into her shoulder.

'Ah there now, Simon. Don't take on so.' She felt like a bundle of sticks. 'It'll all come right. You'll see.'

'I don't know what's happening, Gran. I keep on getting into trouble and it's happened before I know it and I can't stop it if I don't know it's happening, can I?'

150

Old Gran stood back and pressed under my chin with the side of her finger. 'Naughty's naughty, Simon. You know that, don't you?'

'Yeah, I s'pose so. But I can't see why it is half the time and it all seems a lot of fuss about nothing . . . and I get so bored. And now Jack's gone.'

'Well, I really don't know what we can do about that. Certainly the devil finds work for idle hands so you'd better concentrate at school else that'll be another thing you'll be for the high jump for. Come on now. Dry your eyes and let's be off to church.'

I counted every crack in the pavement as we walked up the Close and when Old Gran made me take her arm I wanted to disappear.

'Mornin', Mrs Grainger.' Geoff Gibbs and Colin Gander were clearing leaves out of Colin Gander's down-pipe.

'Morning.' Old Gran slipped her arm further through mine.

'Goin' church, Nip— Simon?'

I ground out 'Yes' without looking at them.

'Pardon?'

'Yes, I am.'

Old Gran's heels clicked on the pavement and I could hear them hooting behind me. 'Nice polite boys, Simon.'

'They're not, Gran. They're the ones that got me into trouble the other night.'

'Oh, are they?'

'Yes. And how is it I get all the blame and not them?'

'Because you're our responsibility and we love you.'

'Do you, Gran?' I took her arm and made sure she didn't kick up against the uneven slabs but she dropped my hand when we got to Grandad's gate.

'Morning, Simon.' The sun had risen over the ridge of Grandad's roof and I was facing into it. 'How are you?'

'All right, Grandad.'

'Sorry about your jacky.'

'M'm.'

'Made your feelings known to Hills though, didn't you?'

'Yes, Grandad.'

'I've known him for years, Simon. Straight as a dye. And

then there was that business the other night too, wasn't there?'

'Yes, Grandad.'

'Won't do, Simon.' He opened the gate and took Old Gran's arm and led her up the road ahead of me. 'Won't do at all.'

Toby Little hadn't turned up to carry the incense and Shifty Bright had a sore throat so Grandad carried the cross and I had to be incense-boy and wear a surplice with a frilly collar. The boys came in late and sat up at the front and I knew they were laughing at me and then I spotted a jackdaw up on the railings behind the organ and it looked so much like Jack that I started to cry and my censer went out and Grandad had to get it going again with his cigarette lighter and blowing on it before Pop could shake incense smoke over the altar.

I kept trying to look at Grandad to see if he'd smile at me but he was always looking the other way, even when I said 'amen' out loud when Pop gave a blessing on the bans-of-marriage-for-the-first-time-of-asking for Nathanial Herbert Gibbs, who turned out to be Gibbser's uncle, and a lady from Lavant but he tapped my knee to listen when Pop went down to the pulpit at the front and rested his arms on the eagle with the spread-out wings.

'It behoves us all . . .'

I closed my eyes and tried to remember that bit so that I could see how it tied in later on.'

'. . . respect and obedience to those to whom it is due.'

My head had fallen back so that when I opened my eyes I found I was looking at the shields and mottoes of the saints and William the Conqueror's men on the church ceiling.

'. . . unto Caesar what is Caesar's.'

Uncle Nat reckoned we'd all be taxed out of sight if the Conservatives got back and that we'd all get shipped off to Siberia if they didn't.

'. . . and that this unfortunate incident will have taught them a lesson and that from now on they'll be a credit to the school and the village and behave especially well when they visit the Festival of Britain. Amen.'

152

'We going to the Festival of Britain, Grandad?'

'Yes you are, Simon. Although you almost put the mockers on it the other night. Miller was all for cancelling it but Pop said it wasn't fair to penalise the innocent with the guilty.'

'Cor, did he?'

'Yes he did. But we're not having any more skytes like that, are we?'

'No, Grandad.'

'That's it. You start off now with a clean slate.'

6

*W*e were all crammed into Miss Anderson's class sitting on the desks with our feet on the chairs waiting for the coach. The Guv had a plan from *The Times Festival Supplement*, that Pop'd given Milly, spread out on a pair of paint tables and Doreen Turner and the other girls were huddled over it like pirates over a treasure map. Kenny Lane and Derek Brown were playing at stamping on each other's toes and Jack Smith was complaining to Nobby Clark that he didn't know why he had to wear a tie just to go to 'Lunnon'. Paul Craven'd had his hair cut short and he'd put lots of Brylcreem on so that it stood up like black needles. He was leaning against the door post to the Guv's class with his hands together and his arm back flicking the light on and off with his elbow. Michael Hoskins walked past him with a box under his arm and Paul tripped him up.

'What'cha got there, Hoskey? Cheesey ones?' Paul pointed at the box with a picture of a lady's shoe on it. 'Phew, what a pong!'

'All right, Paul. That's enough and leave that light alone.' The Guv looked up with his finger on the plan. 'It's what's in them that counts.'

'So what you got?'

'Dripping.'

'Dripping!'

'That's enough, you two.' The Guv looked back to his plan. 'See, that's where the river goes.'

'*And* Marmite.' Michael Hoskins stuck his jaw out at Paul. 'What you got?'

'Corned beef and tomato an' two apples an'—'

'I said, *that's enough*.' The Guv slapped his hand down on the newspaper on the desk. 'Do you hear me, Craven . . . Hoskins?'

'Yessir.'

'Yes, sir.'

'Then sit down the pair of you.'

The wind gusted up under the eaves and Paul came over and stood next to me.

'Right, come to order then.' Milly'd been polishing his glasses and sorting through some papers on Miss Anderson's desk. 'I want you all to go to the toilet before the bus gets here. We've got a schedule to keep to and I don't want . . .'

'What's a schedule, Paul?'

'Dunno. List or something. 'ere. You wanna sit with me on the bus?'

'Pay attention, Wilson and Craven.' Milly's finger was pointing at us. 'We'll have one stop midway and I don't want any misbehaviour. You can sit where you like. Mr Irvine will take the top deck and I'll look after the lower. Mr O'Hallerhan will be staying here to look after things with Miss Anderson and don't start eating your food until we get there because it'll be a long day and the prices there'll be . . .'

I folded my fingers over the purse with my pound in it Mum'd given me. I'd have taken it out to look at it but she'd said not to flash it around in case of pick-pockets. She'd sewn a tape into the purse with the other end fixed to the inside of my pocket and then made a button-over bit I could fix so that my pocket was sealed up. A whole pound! I'd never had a whole pound to myself in my life before except a pinched one and that wasn't just for me, and I didn't know why she'd given it to me because it would be wicked to spend it all. And if the boys saw me with—

'Wilson, you're not listening. I said you're to stay together. But if anybody does get separated you must find a policeman or some other grown up and go to the Lost Children's Room.' Milly put his hands flat on Miss Anderson's desk. 'Have I missed anything, Mr Irvine?'

'Strangers . . .?'

'Ah yes. Thank you. Now you must be very careful of—'

Crash! The door flew open and Barbara Harris and Susan Farley and some of the other kids from Tangmere came in with Janet Rolls and her brother behind them.

155

'Nice of you to join us!' Milly glowered at them but he went red as an arm in air force grey held the door back and Skip Matthews's head poked in.

'Sorry they're late. My fault. I offered 'em a lift in the camp wagon but I got delayed at the NAAFI droppin' off some football kit for the tub. Have a good day.'

Milly was saying it was quite all right but Skip'd gone. 'You'd better fill them in with what I've been saying when we get on the bus, Doreen. Right then!'

'H'hm.' The Guv put his hand to his mouth.

'What is it now, Mr— Oh, yes, very important.' Milly leant further forward. 'Don't go off with anyone. On no account . . . and don't accept anything from anybody and . . . well, keep away from strangers. Do you understand?'

'Yes, sir.' We all said it together like learning our three times table in the Infants but I wondered what he meant. The Festival was going to cover umpteen acres, Mum said, which was bigger than the whole of our village but it was only the tiniest fraction of London and London was the biggest city in the world and I didn't know anybody there so they'd all be strangers and I couldn't see how I was going to get found again if I got lost if I could only ask people I knew because if I knew them I wouldn't be lost and anyway . . .

'Now, lastly, we'll have a little prayer.' Milly closed his eyes and made his face go soppy. 'Oh heavenly Father . . .'

We all put our hands together and closed our eyes. A car or something went by and I wondered if it was the coach but I couldn't see because Jack Smith and Nobby Clark were standing in front of the window and the blinds were pulled half down.

'. . . and especially that our good friend, Mr Wade, finds us.'

' 'e's not back, Paul, is 'e?'

'No. Just for the day. 'e's already up there.'

'A-men.'

'Arm-en.'

'Right then. Pair up and you can go out two by two. Into the ark as it were.'

A couple of the big girls tried to laugh and Maurice Geer whispered 'bloody twit.'

156

I looked for Janet Rolls but she was standing with Susan Farley and holding hands with a new boy from the camp. Susan was taller and slimmer than Janet. She was even prettier than when we'd been too shy to kiss each other in the ammunition store down at Tangmere years ago and I felt shy again when she saw me staring at her and I made out I was looking at the clock and then I moved closer to Paul. A double decker had pulled up outside but there was nobody in it.

'Lead off then, Paul.' The Guv put us at the front because Paul kept treading on Jenny Wright's heels.

'We goin' on *that*, sir?'

'Yes you are. And don't be cheeky.'

Paul and I walked out together.

'You'd've thought they could've got something better than a Southdown wouldn't you, Simon? Hope the driver knows the way.'

'Pack it in, Paul. You'll get the Guv in a mood again.'

Paul went towards the back of the bus but the Guv hauled him back and made us sit in the middle where he could see us. Geoff Gibbs banged up against me as he went by and said 'Sorry, Nipper. Was that your leg?' and Gander did it as well.

'Why don't you sort those two out, Simon?' Paul craned his head back over the seat. 'I bloody would.'

'P'raps I will one day.'

'Right then.' Milly's head poked up above the rail leading to the stairs. 'Anybody who's not here had better say so.' He was holding Miss Anderson's clipboard. 'Beaven?'

'Yes, sir.'

'Craven?'

' 'ere, sir.'

Sometimes the answer came from downstairs and Geoff Gibbs got told off for saying 'think so' and the Guv said he was only ever half here anyway.

The bus pulled away up to Hanover Corner and I lay back and watched Hanover go by and then Warehead and out past the lane to the Windmill and further out to places I'd only heard about.

The bus seemed to roll from side to side and up and down

157

and I closed my eyes and felt the sun on my eyelids and I didn't wake up until we got to a place in Guildford called the Pantiles and stopped for a drink and to go to the toilet.

After Guildford the towns came closer together until they all ran into one. My mouth was dry and my legs ached and I wished I was at home. The bus stopped and started and stopped again and the Guv muttered 'traffic jam' and then the noise of the engine changed and we were going over the Thames. Somebody said they could see the Houses of Parliament and they all scrambled over me to see.

The bus stopped and the engine died and the Guv stood up and stretched. 'We're here!'

We were in a car park that was the size of the aerodrome playing field. A few cars were scattered about at one end and a long pointed thing was sticking up in the sky and there were lots of buildings and tents and huts with a wooden fence all round them and a black dog was cocking his leg by the entrance. There were spatters of rain in the puddles and it didn't look as if it was open.

'This is the greatest city in the world, ya know, Paul.'

'Yeah, I know.'

'Right now!' Milly was halfway up the stairs again. 'This is the Festival of Britain. It's been set out to show how great Britain really is. The first one was a hundred years ago when Queen Victoria was on the throne and it was held in the Crystal Palace that we'll be reading about next term which was built all out of steel and glass and got tragically burnt down . . .'

I stared at the tents and wooden buildings. Bet they'd go up if somebody put a match to them if they ever dried out. '. . . pick out one seventh of the globe coloured in red and that was the British Empire on which the sun never sat, er, set and . . .'

Paul leant forward and loosened his laces. 'Bloody new shoes. They're killin' me.'

'. . . and now we're getting sorted out after the most terrible ordeal this country's ever faced, when we stood alone against . . .'

'My dad was a navigator on Lancasters in the war, Si. What was yours?'

'A prisoner.'

'Oh.'

'. . . the greatest country on earth.' Milly stopped so we looked up. He was red in the face and looked as if he'd got something in his eye.

'Lead on from the back then.' The Guv held on to the silver knob on the corner of the seat and pulled himself up. 'You lot at the front come last then we'll all be together.'

They made us line up in pairs to march across the car park to the main gate where Milly was trying to find our tickets. He had lots of pound notes in his wallet and he pressed them back in as he took out a brown envelope.

'All right. C'mon then and we'll count you through.'

The man in the box by the turnstile slewed round on his stool and opened a side-gate to let us through and he patted each of us on the head as he counted us like they did on the farm when the cows were going in for milking.

'Let's go to the Skylon.'

'I wanna see—'

'Where's the fun-fair, sir?'

'Round here, please.' The Guv had pulled his coat collar up and his hair was blowing about. 'And I don't want you keeping on about that darned fun-fair, Gibbs. You'll only go there if you behave yourselves and . . .'

Milly kept looking at his watch and then he went back and spoke to the man on the turnstile.

'I think he must be at the other gate, Mr Irvine.' Milly pointed towards a tower with a lip at the top and a round glass house above it. 'You hang on here.'

'Where's he going, Guv?'

The Guv muffled his head and lit a cigarette inside his coat and craned his head back and puffed until it was well away. 'Find Mr Wade.'

' 'ope they both get lost.'

'I beg your pardon, Craven?'

'Sorry, sir.'

Some of the boys started to spread out but I leant against the fence out of the wind. There was a groan from the boys at the front and some of the girls said 'oh no' and they all came in round the Guv again. The Guv smiled and said 's'sh' and stood up straighter and took his hands out of his pockets.

'There now.' Milly was rubbing his hands together. 'Here we are all together again.'

'Cor! 'oo's that smashin' bird with 'im?'

I stretched up on tiptoe. 'Dunno, Paul.'

'Glad you could make it, Mr Wade.' Milly stared at us until we muttered something back. 'And Iris as well. Your convent has released you to us for the day, have they?'

'That's Wadey's niece, Nipper. She's a nun or something.'

'Oh yeah.' She was tall and slim with long brown hair and I just couldn't believe she was a relative of Wadey.

'We'll divide into three parties, go our separate ways until lunchtime and meet at the entrance to the Dome of Discovery at half past twelve. Smith, you pick twelve and go with Mr Wade.'

'Very good, Headmaster.' Wadey had a yellow pullover on and clumpy boots like mountaineers wore.

'And Doreen, pick a dozen and come with me and Mr Irvine can have the rest.'

Jack Smith counted off some of the bigger boys and the girls gathered around Doreen Turner. I thought they'd missed me out and I could go with the Guv but Jack was one short. 'Come on then, Nipper.'

'Oh, but I was going with Paul and—'

'For Pete's sake, Wilson.' Wadey had his hands stuck in his jacket pockets. 'We'll find somebody else to hold your hand.'

Geoff Gibbs had been bending down pretending to do his shoelace up but now it'd been sorted out who we were going with he stood up and laughed and said something about ' 'oldin' 'andies' and the Guv took him by the ear and told him if he didn't behave he'd put him in the Shot Tower and drop something heavy on him but then he laughed and gave him a friendly shove and I watched as they disappeared into the crowds and then I turned and followed after Wadey and the others.

It was like walking through a giant toy town. In and out of the Power and Production Pavilion we went with its rows of

160

gleaming, greased machinery standing there as if it was somebody's best set that was too good to use and then out into the Country Pavilion with more tractors and things and I wondered how they'd managed to get them in through the doors without ruining the flowerbeds ... then into the section called Homes and Gardens that was done up like a lot of rooms in a house with a make-believe garden like a picture in an advertisement. I just looked at them and thought 'Yes, that's cups and saucers and tables and chairs and lawn mowers and carpets and things but why are they here?' Then Wadey herded us into a pitch-black tunnel to a place called the Periodic Table of the Elements with dotted lines and arrows on the walls and lights that flashed on and off. He reckoned it told you how the weather got made but one of the boys said he'd found John Cobb's racing car so we didn't really hear what he was saying. There were hundreds of people round the car and Wadey and Jack Smith and Nobby Clark stood up on tiptoe and said 'Yeah. Cor. Look at that' and then they moved on because it would take ages to get near it. I wanted to mark the tyre with my thumbnail so that I could see where I'd touched it and look at the leather seat where he'd sat going as fast as a plane, but I had to run to catch up with them.

They all stopped under the Skylon. It was thin at the bottom and came out thicker in the middle and then went thin again at the top so that I had to keep stepping back to see more of it and the higher up I looked the more it felt as if something was pushing against my forehead to get my head back further and I stepped back more and— Whoops! My head was spinning. When I tried to stand up I fell over again.

'That was clever, Wilson.' Wadey set me up on my feet and a lot of dots came zooming in on me from the corners of my eyes. 'There's notices plastered about all over the place about guy ropes. Here, Clark. Look after Wilson, will you? He's trying to bring the Skylon down.'

They'd made some concrete ponds in front of a row of shops and water was gushing out of them down a channel with rocks set up like a waterfall. A man chucked a cigarette end in and it got right over the rapids before the paper frayed and the shreds of tobacco sprayed out like a stain. The Guv's group was already waiting outside the Dome of Discovery and Wadey said he was early and we'd better wait for Milly before we ate our sandwiches.

Milly had most of the girls with him and they were late because they'd all wanted to stay at the exhibition on penicillin.

'A bunch of budding nurses we've got here, Mr Wade.' Milly was carrying Doreen Turner's carrier bag.

'Oh, that's good, Headmaster. Don't know that my lot've learnt much except Wilson, who's rediscovered gravity.'

We sat and ate our lunch in a paved square with concrete seats. Milly put a white hanky over his lap and unwrapped his sandwiches from yards of greaseproof paper. Wadey had a pie like a slice off a football in a paper bag with a picture of Britannia's head on a spike and he said it cost him one and six. Geoff and Colin had eaten all their lunch on the bus and they bought chocolate-spread sandwiches off Dicky Mole for a penny each, until his sister said he had to have one himself, and then they nipped off to get ice cream and crisps. I wasn't hungry. I wished I could've given them mine but Mum'd made me cheese sandwiches and they'd probably have said they were like old socks. I kept chewing one but it got more and more tacky so I ate the apple Grandad'd given me instead.

The sun'd gone in and it was cold and my stomach felt as if it had a lot of water swilling about in it.

'Where's the toilet, Nobby?'

'Nipper wants the bog, Guv.'

'Quiet, Clark. They're over there somewhere, Wilson.' Wadey waved in the direction of the Skylon.

'Shall I come with you, Simon?'

'Oh sit down, Mr Irvine.' Milly licked the end of his fingers. 'He'll find it. Off you go, Wilson.'

I had to walk past them all and I was glad when I got in amongst the crowds. The people crowded over me so that they had to bend from the waist to miss me and the tents and buildings and flags all looked the same and I couldn't see where I was going or where I'd been. I kept my hand on my purse in my inside pocket and tried to look as if I had a bad arm. My stomach was gurgling again and I held my bottom in and started to run. I had to dodge to get through and as I swerved to miss a man with a dog on a lead I tripped against a step and banged into a waste-paper bin. It hung sideways and an arm in blue with a black glove put it straight.

'Who are you, m'lad?'

'Simon, sir.'

'Who you with?'

'School, sir.'

'Oh and where are they?'

'Back there, sir.'

'Don't you know better than to go chasing around and knocking things over?'

'Yes, sir.'

'Up you get then.' His hand was lifting under my elbow. 'What you hanging on to in your pocket?'

'Me mum gave it to me. I'm looking for the toilet.'

'Oh, I see.' He bent down and dusted some grit off my knee. 'Here. Come with me and then I'll see you back.'

He gave me a penny and showed me how to put it in the slot and pull the knob back and he waited for me and made me wash my hands. All the people looked at us and whispered as we walked back with his hand resting on my shoulder.

'And they let you go off on your own, did they?'

'Yes, sir.'

'*Did* they know you'd gone or did you just slip off?'

'They knew, sir.'

'And where did you say they were?'

'Over there somewhere.' I pointed past the Skylon.

'And who's in charge of you?'

'Mr Miller, sir. He's our headmaster.'

I couldn't remember any of the places we passed. P'raps I was taking him the wrong way. Some people dressed up in old-fashioned clothes were doing a play in a little square that I hadn't seen before.

'Is this it, son?'

'No, I don't think so . . . yes it is.' Gibbser was chasing Kenny Lane and Milly was looking at his watch.

'Come on then.'

163

Doreen Turner spotted me first and she whispered to Milly as we came out of the crowds.

'Mr Miller?'

'I'm Mr Miller.' Milly stepped out from behind Wadey.

'Right. I want a quiet word with you,' and he went away and stood by a flowerbed set in concrete.

'You in trouble, Nipper?' Jimmy Phillips got in close to me but he kept out of sight of the policeman. 'Milly was going on about you holding us up.'

'What d'you do then?'

'Nothin' much.'

'You must'a done to get caught by the coppers.'

'I haven't, Gibbs.'

'What's up, Nipper. Get caught in the ladies?'

'Shuddup, Gander.'

'Watch out. 'e's coming.'

The policeman said something to Milly and Milly's face went all blotchy.

'Bye, son. Don't get separated again.' The policeman was moving away now.

'No, I won't. And thank you.'

'What was all that about, Head—'

'Nothing, Wade. Nothing at all. But . . .' Milly turned Mr Wade away from us and said something that made him look back at me.

'All right, Wilson. You're with me from now on. Tied to my boot laces, see!' He prodded me in the back. 'Lead on and we'll finish off the Power and Production Pavilion.'

Gleaming chunks of machinery and bits of coal as big as buses and flashing, swinging things that somebody said were atomic made me look in every direction at once and I wondered if the place'd blow up if anyone struck a match and every time I stopped to look at something or made sure my purse wasn't missing I found the others had gone off a different way. Wadey kept yelling at me not to daydream and my legs ached and I wanted a drink. We trailed from one building to another and we'd just come out of the People of Britain Pavilion when I met Jimmy Phillips coming the other way.

164

' 'ere, Mush. Seen the thing like bein' on the pictures? You can see yerself on it.'

'Can you? Where?'

'Jus' down there. Gibbser and Gander're there. I'm tryin' to find Jerry.'

'Won't you get lost?'

'Nar, it's all right. The Guv's showed us where the big clock is. He's stayin' there all the time an' we gotta get back to 'im by five.' He shot off into the People of Britain Pavilion and I followed on after Wadey. There was a wide doorway on the right with people coming in and out. Geoff Gibbs dashed out and then sprinted back again with his head down as if he was in a potato race. Mr Wade had stopped to look at some pictures of Saxons or something so I slipped in. It was dark but there was a big screen at the end.

'What'cha, Nipper!'

'Oh hello.'

'It's me. Colin. I saw you come in. Up there on that.'

I stared up at the screen. People were walking in out of the light as if they were coming towards me.

'See. There's Gibbser. 'ere 'e comes again.'

Gibbser was running on the picture and then he ran out of it and I felt something hit me in the back.

'Gibbser! But you were up there . . .'

'Yeah, I know. Good in'it? Takes yer movin' picture as you come in. Go on, Col. Show 'im.'

Colin disappeared out into the daylight and Geoff squinted at the screen. ' 'ere yer. Watch as 'e—'

'Wil-son!'

Wadey was on the screen and I could see his mouth moving.

'Wilson, are you in there?'

'Oh, bloody 'ell, what's 'e want?'

' 'e's keeping tabs on me. They reckon I got lost.'

'Well, tell *'im* to get lost. Miserable old sod.'

'Wilson.' The crowds parted. 'Didn't you hear me calling you?' His hand thumped down on my collar. 'I said, didn't you hear—'

'Yes, sir.'

'Well, why didn't you come then? I'm fed up with chasing

165

around after you. You can go and sit under the clock with Mr Irvine.'

The stone seat under the clock was hard. I counted eight cigarette ends by the Guv's feet and his heel lifted and he trod out a ninth.

'Enjoying it, Simon?'

'Not much.'

'What's up then?'

'Everyone keeps getting on at me and I'm fed up with it.'

'Oh dear.' He yawned and looked at his watch. 'Four o'clock. Fancy a walk?'

'I can't, sir. I gotta stay 'ere.'

'Oh. I thought you had to stay with me.'

'I have, sir.'

'Well, come on then. *I'm* going so you'll have to come with me. Where'd you want to go?'

'Dunno, sir. Anywhere.'

We walked slowly and it was like Petersfield market but posher. I picked up a bottle of scent and the lady let me sniff it. It was stronger than the one I'd taken home for Mum that the gypsy'd said would make her have a baby and it was lime green. I sniffed it again. It didn't have to be a brother, a sister would do.

'How much is this, please?'

'That one's half a crown, son.' The lady reached for a paper bag.

'No, I don't think so, thank you.' The Guv guided me on to the next stall where a lady was singing 'A Nightingale Sang in Berkeley Square' and she was selling some cloth that had a picture of the song printed on it.

'Make a nice present for ya Mum, son.'

'Pardon?'

'I said it'd—'

'He's with me.' The Guv put a hand on my shoulder.

'Ah, fine boy, he is. You must be proud of him and him wanting to be buying his mother something.'

'I'm his teacher.'

166

'Oh are ya now, sir.' The lady had a sharp nose and her hair was black against her pale skin. 'Now wouldn't you say his mother'd like one of these lovely scarves?'

'Come on, Simon.'

It was Mum's favourite green and it had a picture of a tree with a bird in it and buildings all around it that'd faded into the background like a dream and it was fluffy and silky at the same time and it would settle against her face when she had powder on.

'She'd like that, Guv.'

'You think so?' He bent down and rumpled a bit between his fingers. 'You got any money left?'

'Yes. I haven't spent any yet.'

'Well, it *looks* all right. How much is it?'

'Ah well now, sir. That one's six shillings.'

'C'mon, Simon.' The Guv turned away.

'Oh but, sir.'

'Six shillings, Simon!'

'Oh, I can't stand to see the disappointment, sir. Here, I'll make a small reduction.' She bent closer. 'Maybe I could knock a sixpence off.'

'H'm.' The Guv made it sound as if it was still a lot of money.

'Five bob dead, sir.'

'I'll take it.' I scrabbled about at my inside pocket while she put my scarf in a paper bag and I took it in one hand and my change in the other.

'Put your ten-bob note back inside your purse, Simon, and keep the five shillings in your trouser pocket.'

'Yes, all right. And thank you,' I called to the lady but she'd turned away.

'You did well there, Simon. They're twice that price in the shops.'

'Are they?' I peeped inside the bag and felt it. 'Cor, that's good, isn't it?'

'Yes. You're not such a bad— Hey, now then. What about something for you?'

'Cor, yeah! But what, sir?'

'Well, what about a crown?'

167

'A what?'

'A Festival Crown. They're five bob but they're bound to gain in value.'

'How much are they worth now?'

'Five bob. I told you.'

'What's the point of that then?'

'You great twerp! It's a souvenir.' He rested his arm over my shoulder so that my head lay against his side as he walked. 'The idea is that you keep it and show it to your children and—'

'I don't reckon I'll have any children, sir.'

'Oh, don't you?' He laughed out loud and ruffled my hair. 'I bet you will. I wouldn't worry on that score.'

I held the box flat in my lap and peeped inside at the crown. It was so heavy and shiny that it must be valuable . . . the Guv'd left me sitting on a low wall around a space that had a massive iron engine inside it that he said was a sculpture. He'd got me an ice cream and gone off to get more cigarettes. I licked at my cornet.

We always had a cornet when we went to Bognor. Mine usually melted before I'd finished and my fingers got all sticky and covered in sand and I had to go down to the sea to get myself clean and bring back some water in my sand bucket for Mum and Dad. I hadn't seen my sand bucket for ages and I was too big for that sort of thing now. It'd been nice at the beach with Mum and Dad and going up to Butlin's on my own with a shilling for a go on the bumper cars and the rifle range and walking on the hot pavement in my bare feet but we wouldn't be going there so much now that we had Old Gran to look after and— a shadow fell across me.

'What'cha got there?'

'What?'

'There. In yer 'and.' He looked about Big Bim's age but he had a man's hat on that was pushed back so far that it balanced on a curved wave of black Brylcreemed hair. He was standing forward with his hands in his trouser pockets so that his long mac was trapped behind him.

'Ice cream.'

'Not that. Uvver 'and.' He stuck his hand out. 'In the box.'

I drew the square green box back closer to me and hunched myself over it. 'It's a crown.'

'Yeah, ya don't say. Gis'a look.' His face was lined like the Guv's though he was only Jack Smith's age and he had clear blue eyes. He probably lived in London and came here every day and got children to go with him into those small dark streets we'd passed where you could see ways in but no ways out . . . and two men in the Sunday paper called cosh-boys'd killed an old lady in a sweet shop and taken two pounds ten and— 'C'mon. What's up wiv ya. I only wanna look at it.' He was so close now I could see the black bristles growing under the skin on his cheeks and his hair smelt of lavender but like frying as well.

His raincoat was hanging open. That must be where he kept his cosh. They were made out of rubber with sand inside, Bim said, and one bash on the head could kill you.

'Yer ice cream's drippin'. It's drippin' all over the option.'

'Oh is it?'

'Got 'anky? Go on then wipe it up while I 'av'a look . . .' He took the box and lifted the lid and I watched him watching the silver reflecting the light. There it lay in the palm of his hand. Saint George was rearing up on his steed and the dragon was writhing under him on its back with its bloated belly swelling out for Saint George to get him through the heart. He slid it back into the box. It was so silver, set against the black velvety stuff inside, that it looked oily. The edge was sticking up. It was so thick they'd been able to put some Roman writing round the edge.

He turned the box over and it dropped into his hand again.

'Cor. Cold in'it?'

'Yes.'

'Smashin' though, in'it?'

He turned it over and a wet print, where his thumb had been, dried off so fast it looked as if it was melting into the silver.

'Can I have it back, please?'

169

' 'ang on.' He turned it over and held it up to the sun. 'Five bob, wan' it?'

'Yes.'

'Ain't worth five bob. There's 'undreds of 'em around. Watch'a wan' it for?'

'Because it's special. It's a Festival Crown and . . .' What else'd the Guv said? 'And I'll be able to show it to my—'

'S'only metal. Not even silver and you can't spend it.' He held it towards me. 'I'll give ya four bob for it.'

'No thanks.'

'Four'n six then?'

'No.'

'All right. Don't shout.' He bent closer. 'Don't bleedin' shout. What you wan' it for anyway?'

'Well . . . cos it's mine. And I'm gonna save it for my little boy.'

'You what?' He stood back so that his shadow fell over me. 'Chrise alive! 'ere yar then!' He dropped it back in my hand. 'an' watch out you don't get it nicked.' He peeled his cigarette off his lips and ambled off.

'Who was that, Simon?'

I jumped as if I'd been caught doing something wrong. 'I dunno. Nobody, sir.'

'He didn't try to get you to go off with him, did he?'

'No, sir. He just wanted to look at this.' I slipped the crown back into the box and put it in my pocket.'

'What made him stop and talk to you then?'

'Dunno, sir. 'e just came over.'

The Guv felt at a place where he'd cut himself shaving. 'I don't know, Simon. Trouble just seems to follow you around, doesn't it?'

'Yes, sir. But I was waiting for you to come back, sir. Why were you so long?'

'Well, I . . .' He'd flicked his head back as if he thought I was being cheeky. 'Well, Simon, there was a queue and they had to get change. But never mind about that now. It's time we were getting back.' He reached his hand out for me and I grabbed it. 'We've got that perishin' fun-fair to suffer next.'

*

Most of our lot were standing in front of the Big Dipper and they were all looking up. Ray Whittle and Susan Farley were standing close together and they were holding hands down the sides of their legs so that nobody could see. Susan had long socks on and buckle shoes like her Mum wore and a coat with a belt that came in at the waist; her face looked fluffy soft with powder and I wondered if she smelt creamy from it and if she sat at a dressing table with a mirror to put it on in just her knickers and—

'Stupid ole fool!' Jack Smith was craning his head back and he moved sideways as the Big Dipper car flashed by. 'Sittin' there as if 'e's bored just to make out 'e don't need to hold on. I'll bet 'e's pissing 'imself!'

'All right, Smith, that's enough.' The Guv nodded towards Iris who was talking to Doreen Turner. They all swung round and Ray Whittle dropped Susan Farley's hand.

'Sorry, Guv.' Jack said it without laughing but then Nobby giggled and they all started.

'Come on, Guv.' Jack nodded towards the car with Wadey's bald head disappearing behind the blue-boarded scaffolding. 'Did you see 'im?'

'H'm.' The Guv made a laughing sound through his nose. 'I expect he learnt to keep his balance in the army.'

'What for?'

'What for? Well, I don't know what for.' He wiped his nose on the hanky from his top pocket and turned a jagged cinder over under his toe so that the sharp bit was flat. 'That's just the sort of thing they do in the army.'

'Yeah!' Geoff Gibbs jumped up and tipped Jerry's cap off. 'My uncle was in the commandos and—'

'Commandos!' Maurice Geer and Paul Craven pressed down one on each side of him until his knees buckled and he was kneeling. 'RAF'd beat the daylights out of the clod-'oppin' army any day.'

'Didn't say they wouldn't, did I? And get 'orf! The bloody stones're cutting into my legs.'

'Yes, c'mon you two. Let him up. Can't let poor Geoffrey go getting himself into trouble with bad language, can we?' The Guv put his hand under Geoff's elbow to help him up and the other two went back to watching Wadey.

171

'Where've you been all day, Simon?' The voice was close up behind me.

I let Jimmy and Jerry press forward and Janet Rolls came in close to me.

'I had to stay with the Guv.'

'I've been looking everywhere for you.' She had one of those fluffy jumpers on that looked roughed up and soft at the same time and her coat was unbuttoned. Her eyes were black in the ragged flashing lights of the fairground and she had powder on and she'd let her pigtails down. 'Come on. Let's slip off. They won't see.' She took my hand and squeezed my fingers together in the palm of her hand and moved backwards between the people who'd gathered behind us to see what we were looking at.

'You could have sat with me on the bus, you know.'

'I didn't think you liked me and you were with—'

'Who?' She stopped and a man and woman with a dog and a little girl walked around us and over us at the same time. 'Who was I with?'

I wanted to scratch at my nose but she'd see and think I was picking it and if I said I'd seen her with that new camp kid she'd know I'd been watching her.

'Well. Who was I with?'

'I dunno.' I stared back towards the Big Dipper but there were crowds of people about now and some groups of big boys like men, with slouch hats and coats with straight shoulders, were dotted about by the side-shows and the roundabouts talking to girls. 'I met one of—'

'Who was I with?'

'Susan . . . Susan and the others.'

'Oh.' She said 'oh' again more softly and squeezed my hand. 'What did you say? About who you met?'

'One of them.' I turned my back on the group of men nearest us who were talking to two girls in long frocks that stuck out and high-heeled shoes that made them stab as they walked like sheep on hard ground. 'One'a them. He was after my Festival Crown.'

'Was he? Who were you with?'

'No one. Well, the Guv. But he'd gone off somewhere.'

'Weren't you scared?'

172

'Nah, not really. He was like a spiv or a cosh boy. S'pose he was really.'

Janet looked past me and pulled a face. 'My dad says I've got to keep out of their way.'

'Why?'

'Well, you know. Being rude and knocking people about.' She was still holding my hand and I wondered if I should be holding hers instead. 'Hey look, Simon. No. Carefully. Don't let them see.'

'What? What's happening?'

'Look at that girl.' Janet was tugging at me. 'Can you see? She's got a chain round her ankle.'

I turned round and stared. 'I can't see. What's it like?'

'A thin gold chain. Yes, she has. See? And it's on her *left* ankle.'

'What's the matter with that then?'

'Simon, don't you know what it means?'

'No.'

'Well, they stand out on the road. My cousin who works in Woolworth's told me. Out on the pavement up against the railings.'

'What'd they do that for?'

'Because they . . .' She pulled my head down and whispered in my ear so quickly that I only caught some of the words. '. . . for money . . . and sometimes they don't wear any at all.'

'Cor.' I stared at the girls. They didn't seem real any more. They were both smoking and one of them was letting one of the men put his arm around her and I wondered if they'd— 'They don't do it in front of . . .? Well, I mean—'

'No, course they don't. They go in bushes or under bridges or something. Simon?'

'Yes?'

'Shall we go for a little walk?'

'Where?'

'Over there.' She pointed past a fat man with a straw hat and a yellow shirt and braces who'd taken his coat off and was swinging a big wooden hammer to try to make a thing like a giant thermometer shoot up and hit a brass bell.

173

'Come on.' She squeezed my hand and her voice went softer but it sounded as if she was in a hurry. 'Please, Simon.'

Whoosh. A red line surged up the machine and the bell clanged.

'This way.'

'Where we going?'

'Just over here. Why?'

'Nothin'.' I stood up straighter and tried to look as if *I* was holding *her* hand. 'Only Milly'll do me if I go missing again. Hey, Janet, where we going?' She'd walked right past the coconut shy and was pulling me round the back after her.

'Close your eyes.'

My head was spinning.

'Tight . . . oh come on. Bend down.' The warmth of her was against my face. She bent back and her lips folded over my mouth. It felt like a hot sponge and I didn't know what to do with my hands. She was moving her head slowly from side to side. 'Come on.' The words squeezed out from between us and the air left a cool patch against the sticky feeling. 'Come *on*.'

'What?'

'Open your . . .' Her tongue was against my lips and forced my teeth apart. 'Ah . . . that nice?'

A hot liquid shiver went down my back and made a heavy melting in my tummy.

''scuse me!'

We froze together and a man in a frayed brown jacket dumped a wooden box with lots of coconut shells down and took a new box off a pile.

'Bit young fer that lark ain't'cha?' He humped the box to get a better grip and went back round the front.

'Do you think he saw?'

'S'pose so.' She didn't turn round. 'Doesn't matter anyway.'

'Doesn't it?'

'No, course not. They all do it.'

'Do they?'

'Course they do. Else how'd you think babies get born?'

'Yeah, I know but . . .'

'Simon, would you like to—'

'No, Janet. We mustn't.'

174

'*Simon.*' Her face went red to the roots of her hair. 'I was only going to ask if you'd like to sit with me on the way back.'

'O-oh . . . yes please.'

'Come on. Hurry up.' Milly was standing on the bus platform ticking us off on his list. 'I suppose now we'll have the pair of you forever getting lost.'

The boys all wolf-whistled as we got on and Paul Craven did an extra loud one by putting two fingers in his mouth and the noise made Dorothy Newton put her hands over her ears. Going down the middle of the bus was like doing the collection at church and walking back facing the congregation. I hoped all the double seats would have been taken but Gerald Mortlake slid over next to Michael Hoskins and Janet sat in his place. I stood looking for another seat.

'Go on, Nipper. Snuggle in next to 'er.'

'Shud-up, Gander.'

'You don't *have* to.' Janet's lips pouted and she stared out of the window.

'But I want to.'

'He wants to. He wants to.' Geoff Gibbs rolled around in his seat and he and Colin nudged each other. 'Go on, Nipper. Get 'em down. Yer on next.'

'That's enough, Gibbs.' The Guv shot up and swiped Geoff around the head with his newspaper. 'We've had quite enough of your uncle's influence for one day. Now sit down and shut up.'

The chattering downstairs faded away and the distant music from the fun-fair sounded through the rattle of the engine.

'Had just about as much as I can stand today.' The Guv was standing up in the gangway as if he was going to swat the first head that came into sight and the way he said 'yes thank you' when Milly asked him if everything was all right made us duck down even further.

'Is he annoyed with us, Simon?'

'S'sh, no. Gibbser.'

Janet's hand crept down to my side.

'Don't. They might see.'

175

'No they won't. We can put them under my coat here.'

It was warm and snug and secret. Janet was looking out of the window as if I wasn't with her but her fingers were linking inside mine and nobody knew what we were doing. The bus rocked out into the traffic and I wanted the ride home to take all night but I caught Geoff Gibbs watching me and Janet from round the side of his seat and he mouthed 'I'll get you!'

The lights from shops and pubs and cinemas passed us by until the traffic thinned out and the bus throbbed on gently through the dark and wreaths of blue smoke hung above the Guv. A snuffling sound came from the back and Margaret Mole said 'no' a couple of times quietly and then it sounded as if they'd all gone to sleep. Janet said she was tired and she rested her head on my shoulder and I slid my arm around her so that she'd be more comfortable and she slipped my hand under her armpit and squeezed her arm down on it and edged my fingers round to her front so that she wouldn't slip and then she put her face up to me and her eyes were closed and I could feel her breath sweet through her lips and I made out I was stretching over her to look out of the window so that I could see if anyone was watching us in the reflection from the glass.

I stayed like that until my neck began to hurt and then I lay back and let my eyes close and my head hang loose so that it rolled with the movement of the bus. The swaying lulled me to sleep and when the bus turned a corner or stopped it woke me up and it was nice to keep drifting off again with Janet's head on my shoulder and wake up and find it still there. My head rolled a long slow roll to the right, as if the bus was tipping over in deep water, and then it stopped and Milly's voice sounded up the stairs.

'Fifteen minutes if you want a drink or to go to the . . . Doreen, my dear, p'raps you and Mr Wade'd take the lower deck to the toilet while Mr Irvine's seeing his lot fixed up with drinks. Then they can go after.'

'But I can't wait. I'm burstin'.'

'All right, Craven. You slip out first and join up with us later.'

'Thanks, Guv.'

176

'Yeah. Thanks, Guv,' several others chipped in.

'Hey, not all of you. Are you that desperate, Dorothy?'

'Must be . . . after what she was up to with—'

'Thank you, Gibbs. Now button your lip. Well . . .?'

'No, s'pose not, sir.'

'Leggo!' Paul had got to the end of the gangway but Nobby Clark had him by the ankle and was looking around making out he didn't know where the noise was coming from. 'Lemme go else I'll bloody go all over—'

'Craven, how *dare* you. And you let go at once, Nobby.' The blood was rising up the Guv's neck but Nobby smiled and put his head on one side until the Guv grinned. 'You bloomin' 'orrible lot.'

'Tie a knot in it!' Geoff Gibbs called out of the window as Paul walked stiff-legged across the car park but he turned and pointed to his bottom and the Guv told Nobby he could count himself lucky.

'I don't want to go, Simon.'

'What?'

'Not that, silly. And stop blushing. No, I just want to stay here with you.'

I cuddled her a bit closer. 'Yes, but they'll know and if they put the lights out they might say . . . and you'd like a drink, wouldn't you and a packet of chocolate fingers? I've still got some money left, you know.'

'Hurray, Old Lord Snooty's paying. C'mon kids.'

'Shut up, Gibbs. You're not gettin' any.'

'All right. Quietly now.' The Guv was standing up inside his seat and he beckoned us past him. 'Lead off from the back now.'

It seemed like a lifetime since we'd been here this morning. The Pantiles sign was picked out by a square light fixed in a metal box in the lawn like a searchlight and there were dozens of cars drawn up outside and a lot of the tables had people sitting at them all dressed up. A lady who'd been mopping up this morning was wearing a white frilly apron and a black dress that was so tight it looked as if she had a cushion stuffed up the back. She was taking the dinners round and she had the plates balanced all the way up her arm.

'Get a coupl'a bottles'a pop an' we'll 'ave a burpin' contest, Col.' Gibbser peeled off from us and sat down at a table putting his hand on the chair next to him and a man and a lady moved to another table.

'Well, give us the money, then.' Colin had pushed into the queue in front of Jerry. 'Nip over an' get 'is money, 'enery. I'll save you a place.'

'Would you like to sit down, Janet?'

'Yes, thank you, Simon.'

I moved the chair back for her. 'Could you look after this for me?'

'What is it?'

'A scarf for my mum.'

She opened the bag. 'It's lovely, Simon.'

I was doing something for her like Dad would've done for Mum. I stood up straighter and got in the queue and I didn't put my hands in my pockets. The camp kids were always talking about going steady and I wondered if this was what it felt like.

'Move along there at the front.' Wadey's voice came up the queue over the heads of the others. 'Second contingent's comin' up.'

I moved forward. Colin had two bottles of Tizer in one hand and two glasses in the other and he was staring at two packets of crisps on the counter.

'Pour the drinks in the glasses and carry 'em on that saucer and carry the crisps in yer other but not too fast!' He was sloshing it in so that it rushed all frothy up the glass. 'Here look. Do it slowly, like this.' I tilted the glass and poured slowly with the neck of the bottle resting on the edge of the glass.

'Cor, we got an expert 'ere, Doris.' The lady on the till put Colin's change on the counter.

'I watched how they do it at my aunty's. She's got a pub in Petersfield.'

'Oh has she?'

'Bloomin' posh you are, Nipper. And they won't fit on this saucer.'

'Take one in each hand then and carry the crisps in your mouth.'

178

'Oh yeah, thanks.' Colin gripped his crisps in his teeth and left.

'A cup of tea and a lemonade in a glass and a packet of crisps and one-a-them please.' I pointed at some chocolate biscuits.

'Right you are, sir.' The lady dinged the register. 'One and three please.'

'I think I've got that.' I counted the money out into her hand.

'Oh and that boy's left his change.' She pointed at Colin's three pennies.

'I'll give it to him.' I picked the coins up as I put sugar in my tea.

'Want a tray?'

'Yes please.' I stacked my drinks and stuff on the tray and moved slowly out of the line.

'What a nice young man,' she said to another lady who was washing-up and I made out I hadn't heard.

Janet was sitting with Geoff and Colin. They were giggling and she was trying not to look at them. I sat down next to her without getting too close and put her lemonade and biscuit where she could reach them.

'Nipper's got a girl-friend.' Geoff poked Colin in the ribs. 'You'll be payin' out for the back row in the flicks soon, Nipper. Gettin' wound in—'

'Pack it up, Gibbs.' Colin wiped his chin. 'You'll make me spill this.'

'Pack it up yer'self. And where's my bloody change?'

'Oh sod it. I left it on the counter.'

'But I picked it up. Here—'

'You thieving so-and-so, Wilson. Gis it 'ere.'

'I was going to.'

'Yeah. We know you.'

'I was, Geoff. Ask the lady.'

'Well, why didn't you give-it-us?' Geoff's hand shot across the table and gripped my wrist.

'I was going to . . .' People were looking round at us and Janet had broken her biscuit and was pushing the crumbs into a little pile.

Geoff was twisting my arm.

179

'Get off, Gibbs.' I wrenched my arm away and he let go suddenly. Crash! My tea spread over the table and drip, drip, dripped into Janet's lap and on to her coat and Mum's scarf.

'For heaven's sake, what's going on now?'

'Nipper wouldn't give me my change, sir.'

'And look at the tea, Simon. That'll stain her coat you know and it's ruined that scarf. Who knocked it over?'

'He did, sir. And he wouldn't give me my—'

'Well, go and get a cloth, Si— no, you'd better go, Colin.'

'Oh, but I could get it.'

'Sit down, Simon. You've done enough . . . and did you have his money?'

'Yes, but—'

'Well, why the deuce didn't you give it to him?'

'Well, he was—'

'Simon, I'm talking about *you*.' The Guv was gripping the back of Janet's chair. 'For heaven's sake, boy.'

My face went stiff and I stopped breathing. Janet was staring at the spots on her coat.

'Oh, I give up. Come on, Janet. Let's see if we can get your coat cleaned up.'

They went over to the counter together and he showed one of the waitresses her coat and then they disappeared into a room at the back.

Geoff and Colin sucked at their drinks and blew bubbles through their straws and then they ate my crisps. Mum's scarf was soggy in its bag in a puddle of tea. I stood my cup up.

'Out of the way then, sonny.' A lady with a mop and bucket pushed past me. 'Lot of cleaning up after you lot. You're not coming back this way, are you?'

'No.'

'And I should think this can go in the bin.'

'No, miss.' I reached for Mum's scarf.

'I'll rinse it out for you then. But I expect it's stained.'

I watched as she mopped up and then she draped the scarf in its wet bag over the handle of her bucket and went into the kitchen.

'Look, Mush. 'e's booin'.' Geoff was grinning at me with his mouth full of crisps. 'Look, Jerry, Jim. Mr Big-I-am's—'

'Shud-up, Gibbs.' He was all hazy now and my voice was breaking.

'O-ooh!' Geoff whooped as if he was edging something heavy over a cliff. 'Look at 'im.'

I bent my fingers back until my knuckles cracked and then I dived at him. 'I'll fuckin' kill you, Gibbs.' My fist crushed his lip against his teeth and they dug into my knuckles.

'Simon *Wilson!*' Milly's chair went over and he had me by the scruff of the neck before I could defend myself.

Out through the people he carried me with my head level with the table-tops. He had me round the chest with his other arm around my legs to stop me kicking.

'Vicious little devil,' a man eating ice cream with a cherry on top, said to the woman with him. 'I'd give him what-for if he was my son.'

Milly'd gone. They'd made me stand up while he told them what I'd done and not to interrupt and then they'd both gone to the front door to see him off and left me on my own in front of the fire. I stood fiddling with the flap of loose skin on my knuckle and watching Old Gran knitting in the brown armchair.

'Not much of a day then, Simon?'

'No, Gran. But it wasn't all my fault.'

'Rarely is. But—' She clicked off a couple more stitches and then lay her needles down. '... I don't hold with swearing and foul language.'

'Sorry, Gran.'

'There's really no excuse for that. We can't think what's come over you lately.'

'What, even Grandad, Gran?'

'All of us. Why'd you do it.'

I stuck my thumbs in my trouser pockets and let my shoulders slump. 'Dunno, Gran.'

'Si-mon!' I could see her thinking of me when I was little. 'Whatever's come over you?'

'I don't know, Gran. Everyone keeps getting on at me. And now I've lost Janet.'

Old Gran looked up as if somebody was at the door. 'Who's Janet?'

'Girl at school.'

'You fond of her?'

'I love her.'

'Oh, I see. Does she love you?'

'Thought she did, Gran.'

'Well, if she does and she's worth anything she'll stick by you.'

'Will she, Gran?'

'Course she will.'

'And what about other people, Gran. Like Grandad, say?'

'H'm.' Old Gran touched out a cocoa drip at the corner of her mouth with her hanky. 'Ever so fond of you he was. Still is of course. But come on now. You'd better get off to bed.'

7

*I*t got dark early when the clocks went forward and by the time I'd got home from school and had my tea it was cold out and it'd usually started to rain. Old Gran was always cold and Mum lit the fire early each morning and kept it in until after I'd gone to bed and Dad got our winter fender out of the loft with the woodboxes at each end and I used one to sit on with my back up against the chimney breast to look at books and throw bits and pieces on the fire. I sat as close as I could to the fire with my pyjama trousers rolled up so that they ballooned out at the top, like a Spanish soldier in Mexico, and the heat made my thigh go mauve and mottled like blackcurrant stains on plastic.

Sometimes I got inside the airing cupboard and sat behind the hot tank on the hot water pipe until Mum said I'd send it crashing down and scald myself and probably suffocate as well, so I started listening to the wireless more. They never told me the truth when I asked which programmes were on because it meant me staying up too late, so I worked out how to read the programme page and once I'd got a few words right I could guess the rest and then I started to recognise them and to be able to make out most of what they were writing on the blackboard at school and even whole books when I knew what the story was about already. Most evenings I rushed home to look at the programme page before Mum and Gran got back from Nan's and then hid in the airing cupboard reading until tea time and then I listened to 'Ray's a Laugh' and 'Much Binding in the Marsh' and 'Take it from Here' and 'Educating Archie'. I got all sweaty in the airing cupboard one night and I was still wet in the morning and they took my temperature and said I had flu and they closed the door and left me in bed and I had wild dreams all through a black night with red flashes in it until it was morning.

I lay back in bed with my eyes closed and realised I was awake. The sun shone on my face and I lay deep into the pillows and let my mind go wandering. Geoff Gibbs and school and everything went spinning round and down and I was floating over mountains with somebody who looked like Janet Rolls but wasn't and then, out of the darkness, I heard Mr Wade having a cup of tea with Dad and saying he was thinking of moving to teach at Walberton School but that we could go over to visit if he did, and if they wanted me to have a chance of passing the 11+ they'd better send me to the Central Boys' School in Chichester for my last year. I couldn't think what Mr Wade was doing in our house, but it didn't worry me because I didn't feel as if I was here anyway, especially when I opened my eyes and found Iris sitting on the side of my bed holding my hand under the cover.

'Hello. I thought you were at school?' My voice felt rusty.

'It's half term.'

'Oh.'

She had freckles and looked like a wood imp and when I stretched my other arm out she lay down and snuggled into me and she smelt like honeysuckle but when I woke up again it was dark and she'd gone and there was only a dent in the pillow next to me that'd disappeared by morning. And later Aunty Win next door brought me a blue leather book called *The Children's Encyclopaedia* and I sat up in bed and didn't feel so sleepy. There was everything in this book from wirelesses to Red Indians and poems and the pages were cool and smooth against my fingers. But when I read my eyes got tired and I dreamt about Iris and Janet Rolls and the boys and Susan Farley so that they got all mixed up and I could change from dream to dream like jumping from one paving slab to another.

Mum put 'Housewives' Choice' on each morning at nine and on Saturdays it was 'Children's Choice' but I didn't like that because they didn't have Kay Starr or Guy Mitchell or Johnny Ray records. When I finished having flu they said I had whooping cough and then mumps and measles and then something else that made me yellow but I felt the same whatever it was as if my body had no weight and going to sleep and staying awake were both the same. I read all my

184

books and Mum's about the Barons and the Civil War and even started one of her love stories and then they started getting them from the library for me and Grandad sent me some Sexton Blakes. It was getting on for Christmas and they said Mr Miller thought it wouldn't be a good idea for me to change horses mid-stream but that I'd have to stop dreaming and work like stink or else I'd never pass the 11+ and then the bedclothes started rubbing my heels and bottom and my neck ached from sitting up against the bedhead.

'Where's Gran, Mum?' I'd woken up one morning with a headache and I felt as if my body was coated in lead and the room smelt as if it was full of stale socks.

'Up at Nan's, my love. She's been there for ages. Since you first took bad.'

'Aren't I still bad then?'

Mum felt my forehead and stuck a thermometer in my mouth.

'No. You're on the mend now. You've lost that awful flushed look.'

'Well, I feel terrible.'

'That's because you're getting better.'

'Not much point me going back to school before Christmas though, is there?'

'Course there is,' Mum rinsed her finger round in my glass of orange and fished a bit of fluff out. 'There's nearly a month to go before school breaks up and you've got a lot of catching up to do. Drink this up now. Doctor says you're to have plenty of liquid.'

'When's the doctor say I can go back to school then?'

'As soon as you're up and about.' She switched the light off and drew the curtains back. 'And you can get up for a while and sit by the fire in your dressing-gown.'

I lay and looked at the rain. It'd still been sunny when I'd got ill and I'd missed half term but I didn't feel as if I wanted to go out to play and they said I'd lost nearly a stone.

I had to wear braces again because I'd gone so thin my trousers kept slipping down and Pop prayed for me in church on Sunday and Milly told the boys they mustn't be rough with me until I'd got fit again.

'We thought you was dead, Mush.' Geoff Gibbs and the

185

boys were all round me arguing about who was going to sit next to me.

'I didn't feel that bad. Kept having these dreams and things. It was good really.'

'Skiving!'

'No I wasn't, Browner. Is Wadey back?'

'No, not yet.' Geoff hauled Derek Brown out of the way and sat down.

'Isn't he? That's odd. I heard something about him going to Walberton but I thought I'd dreamt it.'

'He's helping out there a few days a week. Poor sods. But he's not leaving.'

'So that means we keep Rasher?'

'No it doesn't. He's going back to the big school after Christmas.'

'Ah well, at least we'll get rid of—'

'Morning, Wilson. Get rid of what?'

The boys parted and Rasher was standing behind them. He looked thinner than ever and his neck stuck out of his shirt like a stick of celery. 'What do you want to get rid of?'

'Headache, sir. It's left me with a headache. I nearly died, sir.'

'Die boy? You won't die. Old Nick's not ready for you yet. Come on now, you motley crew.' He drew his hand back as if he was going to swish them all. 'Let's put the finishing touches to this jamboree.' The boys scattered and he went back to his desk.

'What's he on about, Geoff?'

Geoff sniffed and hoiked in his throat. 'Bloody pantomime. We thought they'd forgotten about it but now it's on again. 'ere, did you get a cold when you was ill?'

'I dunno, why?'

'Well, I'm getting one. I'm going back with Col. I don't want your bleedin' germs.'

He went over next to Colin and I slid into both seats and lent my elbows on the desk with my chin in my palms. I'd been away for so long I didn't feel as if I belonged here any more. I closed my eyes and I could hear the other boys whispering to each other but I didn't even bother to listen.

*

Rasher was madder than ever. He kept hopping and skipping and putting his hand to his eye and saying he could see no ships and he'd got friendly with Gibbs and Gander because they supported Portsmouth and they sometimes sang 'Play up Pompey' together but Paul Craven told me to watch out for him mid-mornings and afternoons until he'd had his insulin injection. I watched him doing it once through the cloakroom window and with the sun reflecting off the glass he looked as if he was on fire. It made my flesh creep to see his scaly skin bend under the needle and then spring back as it went in and whenever I saw him I remembered how his eyes screwed up and he held his breath and strained as he pushed the plunger down and then closed his eyes and let his head sag as he pulled it out.

They did lessons in the mornings but Rasher said I'd missed so much I could just sit and read and in the afternoons they went up to the hall to fix the scenery for the pantomime and to practise and he made me be a villager in a play about the Pied Piper. I didn't have to say anything and I just stood at the back listening until I knew everyone's lines and then I started taking a book with me to read. They had one or two good books about Frederick the Great but the rest were too easy so the Guv lent me one about the Kings of Serbia and the Kaiser and I read it at school and in the airing cupboard at home and in bed until the battery in the torch Old Gran had left down the side of my bed went flat. I finished it in the kitchen up at the village hall the afternoon of the pantomime as they were getting everything ready.

'You'll strain your eyes reading in this light, Simon.' The Guv was folding up raffle tickets and putting them in a drum.

'I've finished it.'

'Enjoy it?'

'Yeah. But where's Prussia now?'

The Guv rubbed his chin. 'Oh, that got mixed in with Germany after the First World War.'

'So it isn't there any more?'

'Yes it is. You can call things a different name but they're still there.' He stopped folding tickets and I took a handful and started crumpling them up. 'In fact the Second World War was inevitable after the way the first one finished.'

187

'What's inevitable?'

'Certain, Simon. Had to happen.'

'Oh.'

'See, Germany was shattered in the First World War and . . .' He carried on talking about things called war debts and inflamation where people carted their wages home in wheelbarrows and they weren't worth the price of a loaf of bread by the time they got to the shops and Rasher said the children were going home and was Mr Irvine going to stay here all night and he just smiled and told me about everybody being unemployed and the Krupp factory made guns even when they weren't allowed to and stuck the barrels up so that they looked like factory chimneys and it got so dark that I could hear him but I couldn't see him except for a shadowy outline against the window.

'Didn't it blow about, sir?'

'What, Simon?'

'All that money in them wheelbarrows. If the wind blew.'

'I'd never thought of that. I expect it did.' He stood up and groped his way to the light. 'Didn't much matter though. It was almost worthless. But come on, you'd better be getting home for tea else it'll be time for you to come back again.'

'Aren't you going home, sir?'

He was leading me down through the rows of chairs to the hall door. 'No, I'll just get back to the school and have a cup of tea with Mr O'Hallerhan.'

I pulled away from him. 'Do you like him, sir?'

'Simon. What a question!'

'Sorry, sir.'

It was all over so fast it felt like a dream. Grandad was out for a smoke in the light of the hurricane lamp in the shed but he followed us in when he saw how fast Mum was walking. Old Gran was darning in Grandad's place by the wireless and Nan was in her usual chair but she jumped up when Mum slumped down on the sofa.

'Whatever's the matter, Ina? Simon, is she all right?'

'Yes, Nan.'

188

I went and kissed Old Gran and rubbed my hand on her ear the way Grandad used to rub mine and straightened Uncle Steven's photograph.

'It's all right. Just let me catch my breath.' Mum's head was hanging back and she was panting.

They'd been sitting with just the oil lamp on but Grandad clicked the electric light on without asking Nan if she wanted it on and drew the curtains. 'Steady on then, Ina. What's happened?'

'Oh, Dad . . . first of all . . .'

She told them about how we'd been late getting up to the hall because I'd been dallying about on the way home from school and then the stage curtain'd fallen down and bashed Milly on the head and then Rasher'd come in and roared 'silence' and how she'd felt like a criminal when he'd carted me off because I should've been down in Miss Anderson's class with him waiting to do our play and why hadn't I told her that I wasn't allowed to go up to the hall with her and not make such a fool of her.

'And *would* he hold my hand, Dad, in the dark coming home? He would not. Running off out in front of a car . . . Why won't you hold my hand, Simon?'

'Yes, my duck, you should do as Mummy says, you know.'

'S'pose he thinks he's too blessed big and independent for that now, Mum.'

I sat back on the sofa where Dad sat and thought of Mum's frightened face when Rasher was telling her off. Then I put my hands behind my head and leant my head back. The electric light made sparkling patterns on Uncle Steven's photograph. His hair was thick and wavy and his eyes were set wide apart and I couldn't believe they'd ever thought I'd be like him and that he was dead and I was alive and they'd never see him again.

'. . . and then apparently Mr O'Hallerhan had some sort of fit in the classroom when he'd lugged Simon back and had to be carted off to hospital and that just about put the tin lid on it. I do hope you didn't bring that on, Simon. And they gave it up as a bad job and sent us all home.'

I'd let my hands slip forward over my ears and closed my eyes against the picture of Rasher wheezing and heaving. I could see Uncle Steven's plane coming down in flames with petrol spilling out of the bullet holes and spattering over his face and catching fire until it burned and crinkled and his arm reached up to get the cockpit open and it was burning.

'I hate him!'

'What, *Simon?*' They all looked up and the fire crinkled and the clock ticked.

'I hate him. O'Hallerhan.' I pressed my hands against my head until I squashed my ear lobes. 'Oh, Grandad, I'm sorry.' I ran over to him and laid my head in his lap. 'But he's awful. He's like a murderer.'

'S'sh now, Simon.' He ran his hand gently back and forth over my head and it felt like the sway of the horse and cart when I was little and we used to go wooding up Common Lane. 'Blowed if I know what to make of things lately. Have to get you interested in something that'll occupy your mind I s'pose.'

We always went to the common for holly and ivy. Grandad worked out how much he needed for wreaths and crosses and then he added a bit for decorating their house and ours and then some extra for the old ladies at the alms houses. They said I could go and get it this year because Grandad was busy over at Mrs Evans's and I was old enough to go on my own and anyway it'd give me something to do and might keep me out of mischief. He'd given me his old pair of secateurs and two sacks and he said if I filled them both it would be more than enough and not to go climbing about after mistletoe in case I fell and broke my neck and we didn't want it anyway.

I finished my cocoa and rinsed the cup out for Nan and went out into the shed. I folded the sacks up in a long roll and tied them with the string Grandad'd given me and slid the secateurs into my trousers and under my belt like escaped convicts did with their guns because they hadn't got a holster and if he'd been coming with me on the old horse and cart he could've been Bertie Brewster on the chuck wagon and I could've ridden shotgun.

Pauline Tennant and Colin's sister Margaret were sitting

on the school gate as I went by and I made out I hadn't heard when Pauline said to Margaret that she expected I was going rabbiting.

The cows'd broken the ice on the puddles through Price's farmyard but it was dry up the lane where the frost was still hard in the churned-up mud and the sun couldn't get at it between the hedges. The sky was like our colour wash at school and the blackbirds and thrushes stood singing on the bare bramble bushes that were spangled with dripping icicles that glinted pink and violet with the sun shining through them. I made a sling of my rolled sacks and slung it over my shoulder so that I could swing my arms and the cold on my fingers and cheeks burned and my feet sprang easily off the crisp ground and I walked fast and sang 'I love to go a-wandering' in time with my steps and I kept sweeping my hair back out of my eyes and then I yelled out 'I don't give a sod' and I listened to the sound echoing amongst the trees of the common and wondered what had made me do it.

It was bitterly cold on the common. The sun filtered through in one or two places but the bit that Mrs Reader had marked 'Keepers Spinney – Private' was mainly laurels and holly trees that didn't lose their leaves. I ran through it and kept on going until I got to where the wood widened out into bramble patches and hazel thickets and I followed the path in the sun up towards the Eathram end where Gander and Gibbs played bike races. Most of the holly trees had blacky green leaves so I knew they were male ones and wouldn't have any berries but I found one that was loaded and there was a dead oak near it with ivy hanging down almost to the ground. I cut and snipped and pulled and stacked the holly into the sacks so that the bends in the branches went the same way and they fitted together like spoons and I rolled the ivy into balls and put it on top of the holly, and then I tied the tops of the sacks and cut a hazel stick and slotted it through the holes in the top of the sacks Grandad'd made so that I could carry them over my shoulder the way he said Arab women in the bible carried water. Dad'd let me borrow his old watch that didn't go properly and had numbers in two little boxes on the face instead of hands. It was still ticking but it was only ten-fifteen. I hid my sacks in amongst

191

some ferns and sat down on a log beside a holly bush and started picking at the bark. I could build a camp if I wanted to or go up to Tally Hills place by the gravel works and pinch some eggs and cook them if I had any matches or—

Smack! Something fell and I saw it hit the dead leaves. It struggled and stopped and then a figure appeared from out of the trees carrying a bow.

'What you doin' 'ere?'

'Been gettin' some holly.'

'A'rh!' They said Johnny Duke was half animal and almost lived in the woods and he was watching me as he pulled the arrow out of the squirrel's neck. 'Where'd you get it?' He wiped the arrow in some leaves and slotted it into a quiver in his belt.

'That one over there. Why?'

Johnny shrugged. 'There's some better down by the barn.'

'I've got enough now thanks. Can I see the squirrel?'

'Why?'

'I've never seen one close up.'

'S'dead.'

'Yes, I know.'

'Go on then.' He stood back like a cat over a mouse.

I knelt in the leaves and ran my fingers along its flowing tail and felt its claws and pressed its eyes closed. 'It's smaller than I thought.'

'Tree rat . . . with a tail.'

'But it's beautiful. Why d'you kill it?'

'Money.' Johnny slid a long knife out from a sidepocket in his quiver and slashed and when I opened my eyes the tail was sticking out of his pocket. 'See . . . it's just a rat now.' He laughed and slung the little body into the bushes.

'You get paid . . . for doing that?'

'A'rh. Ninepence a tail and I get five bob for a fox.'

'You don't! Who pays you?'

'Never you mind.'

We rarely saw Johnny Duke. He was supposed to come to school but he'd only been a couple of times since I'd been there and the camp kids called him the Wild Man.

'Don't s'pose you get all that much money?'

'Dunn I?'

'Do you then?'

'Got nearly sixty now.'

'Sixty! Cor, can I see 'em?'

'No you can't. They're hid away.' He twirled the knife round his finger where the blade met the handle and slipped it back into its sheath. 'And you'd best not say nothin' about it. I don't want you kids up 'ere lookin' for me.'

Johnny started to walk away and I followed him. I expected him to tell me to scarper but he let me catch him up and he explained how he'd tried to tip his arrows with lead and stick cut-off nails down the end for points but now he'd started to bake the sharpened ends over a fire and then leave them in an inch of water to weight the end and the best way to make a bow was to bend it between three fence stakes while you strung it with fishing line. He shot two more squirrels and a pheasant on the way back but the pheasant was out in the field and he said he'd leave it till it was dark in case anyone saw him. We were getting on down towards the Tangmere Road by this time so I said I'd better be getting back.

'Aye, but 'old on a minute.' He reached up and chopped out a fir branch, slit the twigs off it and then he held it up against me and lopped a bit off the thinner end. 'Slot that in along your fence like I told you and string it and cut some hazel shoots and bake'm and see how it goes.'

'Cor thanks, Johnny'

'And don't you bring the other kids up 'ere, see.'

'No I won't. Bye.'

Pauline Tennant and Margaret Gander were still hanging about outside the school as I went by with my sacks and sticks and there was a lorry parked outside.

'See, I told you he wasn't rabbiting. He couldn't catch a rabbit no more than fly.'

'Couldn't I? You just wait till I get this going. Johnny Duke gave it to me.' I made as if I was shooting an arrow at them.

'Bows and arrows . . . how childish.' Pauline Tennant cocked her nose in the air as Margaret nudged her.

193

'S'sh. Here he comes. Isn't he gorgeous?'

A man of about eighteen with a brown face and crinkly black hair and a moustache was wheeling a barrow down past Miss Anderson's class.

'You go and play cowboys and indi-bums, Simon Wilson. We've got a real man here.'

I said 'up yours, Gander' and left but I wished I hadn't because Pauline Tennant had a lovely face and I thought I might like to go out with her when I was old enough to go to the pictures in Chichester on my own.

I left the sacks of holly in Grandad's shed and pinched one of his Turf out of his gardening jacket and went up behind the woodpile but I didn't really want it so I went back and slipped it back in his pocket.

The shed still smelt of dust and paraffin and old apples and sooty cobwebs hung from the scythe and a couple of fag-hooks on the wall.

I edged the old last he used for keeping the door open back with my toe.

'What you doing, my duck?'

'Just putting the secateurs back, Nan.'

'Thought you'd gone.'

'Yeah, I forgot them. I've got the holly.'

'Have you? Cor, that's a nice lot. Hope the berries don't drop off and go getting trodden into the carpet.'

'Fran!' The back door opened. 'You seen my 'andbag, Fran?'

'Dear oh dear.' Nan pushed the last back along the floor. 'She's had me on the go all morning. You off home now, Simon, only I'd better close this door to stop the leaves blowing in.'

'Yeah, well, I only came to put the secateurs in.'

'Fra-an.'

'I'm coming, Mum.'

I walked out over the bricks at the back and went and stirred the water in the rain-water barrels until the little worm things in the bottom swirled around and then I climbed up Grandad's ladder that was standing by the woodpile against the Arnolds' plum tree. The sun had thawed out the frost and their chickens were scrabbling

194

about in the mud and pecking at the stalks of the few long weeds that were left. I pulled a dead branch off the plum tree and slung it at the chickens. They flapped and scattered and when they settled down again I went out through the hedge and across the corner of Brindle's field to the footpath that ran through their yard.

Mrs Brindle was tipping potato peelings into her dustbin. She had a white dressing-gown on and her hair in curlers and she was grey in the face as if she'd never been out of the house before. She stared at me with her dustbin lid in one hand and her bowl in the other and I stared back at her because this was a public footpath and she couldn't stop me and then she went back indoors.

I took the bow shaft and arrows round the side and bent the bow in between the slats on the fence between our garden and the new bungalow next door. The new people, called Keen, had moved in several months ago and they'd got a baby that was so small you could have put her in a milk jug when she was first born, and a fluffy dog called Florence. There was a bend in the wrong place and I pulled it along until it looked about right.

'What you doing, Simon?' Mrs Keen spoke to me as if she'd been here for ever and it was me who'd just moved in.

'Making a bow, Mrs Keen.'

'What, for shooting arrows?' She was sweeping her front step but it didn't need doing.

'Yes.'

'Well, you be careful you don't put it through the window.'

'Oh, I won't. I don't want to mess up the points.'

'Oh . . . good!' She gave me a funny look and went in.

I left my bow in the fence to get properly bent and sharpened my arrow points and took them indoors.

'What you up to, Simon?' It was Wednesday and Mum was cooking the fish and mashed potato and cauliflower.

'Nothing, Mum.'

'Well, don't get into mischief doing it then.'

'No.' I knelt in front of the fire and turned an arrow above the flame.

The tip darkened and singed and started to scorch and the

flame leapt up to it and I lifted it and teased the flame up higher. Sap began to drip off the end and it fell spitting into the fire. I trimmed the blackened end back to a point with my knife and toasted it again and then did the others.

'Whatever *are* you doing, Simon?'

'Making arrows, Mum.'

'Well, you're making a mighty smell. And just look at the mess on that polished front. Oh, you are a naughty boy.' She dashed off into the kitchen for a wet cloth.

'It's only sap, Mum.'

' "Only sap, Mum." That'll burn on and be the very devil to get off.' She got down on her hands and knees and rubbed until the cloth steamed.

'Mu-um?'

'Ye-es.'

'Got any string?'

'What for?'

'My bow.'

'Oh, I don't know, Simon. There's some about some-where. Have a look.'

There was none in the cupboards and the sideboard drawers, or on the bottom of the tea trolley, so I went out into the shed. There were some small bits amongst Dad's tools but I didn't want a bow with knots in so I climbed up into the atticy bit above the door where he kept the good wood he used for jobs and my old high-chair. I scrabbled about with my hands until my eyes got used to the light and then I started to move things around. The old Diana air gun was hidden in a sack by the wall and there was a rusty green tin next to it. I took it towards the light and opened it. Air gun pellets!

'Simon, where are you? It's dinner time.'

'Coming, Mum.' I slipped down quickly and just got the ladder back as Dad came round the corner.

'What you up to, Nip?'

'Looking for string, Dad. I wanna make a bow.'

'Oh yeah.' He winked and opened his bike saddle-bag. 'This any good? I got this specially for mending the football nets.'

'Thanks, Dad.' It was damp as if it had been dipped in linseed oil and it twanged as he cut a piece off.

'You be careful what you're doing with that, Simon. It looks mighty powerful to me.'

A sparrow was standing on my bow picking at his claws when I came out. He stayed and watched me from the gutter as I slipped my arrows into my belt and then he flew away. I pinged at the string and slid the bow off the fence. It was nearly as tall as me and still a bit too bent at one end but I shot an arrow up the garden and it went right over the hedge and into the back field and I had to pull it out flat to the ground where it had sliced into the thawing frost under a thick patch of grass. I cut a notch in the top of the arrows for the string to fit and took aim at a rook lazing around in the air currents miles up, and let fly. The arrow shot up and up and up. It hung flat for a second and then turned and speared down and stuck in. I ran to it and twisted as I pulled it like Uncle Roger did when he was playing darts. I looked around and then wiped the arrow tip in the grass and pretended I'd shot a squirrel. It only took me six shots to get from our fence to the dell field and four to get from the dell field hedge to the dell.

In the dell I shot at big leaves for a while and then at bottles I stuck up on a tree trunk until I'd smashed them all and then at an old oil drum that'd been lying down and gone lacy with rust. I pretended it was a German tank and I'd made a new weapon that could pierce its armoured plating. I stood back further and further to see how far I could get away and still hit it and one went through a hole I'd already made and stuck in a tree behind.

'Where'd you get that, Nipper?'

I squinted up. Gibbs and Gander were outlined amongst the trees against the blue sky on the rim of the dell.

'Ol' man been spoilin' you again?'

'No, he hasn't. I made it. Johhny Duke showed me how.'

'Go'n!' They slid down the side and ran over to me. 'He wouldn't 'ave anything to do with you. Le's 'ave a look.'

They sighted it up and twanged it and said it was bent crooked and took an arrow each.

'What shall I 'it?' Geoff pointed it at the ground. 'Your foot.' He shot and I jumped back.

'Careful. That'd go straight through.'

'Go'n! Wouldn't cut butter.'

'Bloody would. Look at that one.' I pointed to the tree.

'Cor look, Mush.' Geoff pointed and Colin nodded. 'It's all poxy where it's gone rotten but it stuck in. Let's see if we can put one next to it.'

'No don't, Geoff. You'll bust the points.'

'I won't. You watch.' He drew the bow back until I thought it would break and let fly.

The arrow glanced off the side of the tree and then off a branch further on and shot out into the field.

'Cor, see that go, Mush? You got a good one 'ere, Nipper. Go an' get it.'

'Gi's the bow then. And that arrow.'

Geoff hung on to the bow and Colin put the arrow behind his back.

'You just go and get that one. We'll give you twenty and then we'll try to get you.'

'Don't you dare.'

'Go on. Go and get it.'

'No, you get it.'

'I think 'e's coming funny, Col.'

'Yeah. Thinks 'e's Johnny Duke!'

'Gimme that bow back.'

'Come and get it.' Geoff held it back towards Colin and they both held it.

I dived at Geoff but he let go.

'What's up, Nipper? I ain't got your rotten bow.'

'Give it, Col.' I walked over to him.

'What?' He tossed it over my head. 'He's got it.'

'Come on, Gibbs.'

Geoff edged back and tossed it wide of me and Colin picked it up. I anticipated it the next time and caught Geoff as he was reaching up where his shirt had pulled out of his trousers. My fist buried itself in his stomach up to the wrist and he hit the ground like an egg. I picked the bow up and moved away from Geoff as Colin came over to him. He rolled over and I picked up the arrow Colin'd dropped and fitted it into the bow. Geoff climbed to his knees and Colin bent him forward and slimy saliva ran out of his mouth.

198

'Bloody 'ell, Nipper. I'll murder you for that.'

Colin helped him up and they both started towards me. I raised the bow and pulled it back. They stopped.

'You wouldn't dare.'

I squinted along the arrow. 'Right between the eyes.'

'I think 'e means it.' Colin moved away from Geoff.

'You bet I bloody mean it.'

'But 'e's only got one arrow.'

'Yeah, but sod you, Col, it's pointing at me.'

I stood rigid and I felt like Billy the Kid.

'We'll see you later, Nipper.' They edged back. 'When you've calmed down a bit.'

'Keep going.'

'What's up can't you take a joke any more?'

'No.' I raised the bow and followed them. 'And I never could.'

I stood at the bottom of our garden and looked at the lights in the kitchens. They all had lacy curtains up and some had bright lights and some were dimmer. Our light had a greenish tinge where it reflected off the walls and our curtains hung in stretched folds because we had an expanding cord along the bottom as well as the top. A car came down the Close. Its headlights traced out the bungalows one by one and then it disappeared. I could feel the damp on my jacket collar against my cheek and my fingers were cold and stiff and I imagined myself curled up in the brown armchair with a book, shut away from the outside. I crept into the kitchen and the warm air hit me.

'You're late, Simon. Where you been?'

'Up the lane, Mum.'

'Didn't get into mischief, did you?'

'No, Mum. But I feel sick.'

'Oh dear. Better have a lie down.' She had her sleeves rolled up and was mixing a Christmas cake in the brown earthenware bowl. 'Really should have got some more mixed spice and cinnamon down at the shop. This taste all right to you?' She held the wooden spoon out to me and I picked a bit off with my teeth.

'Dunno, Mum. It's not cooked.'

'Course it's not, you fat-head. That's why I'm asking you.'

'Oh.'

'And you're not playing about with that thing in here, are you?'

'No, Mum.' I held my bow and arrows upright so that they didn't bang the china cabinet and went into my bedroom and stood them against the spare roll of lino behind the door and drew the curtains. My socks were wet so I took them off and then my jacket and I kept on going until I had nothing on. I stood looking at myself in the mirror. When I let my shoulders go forward my stomach stuck out and I imagined all this stuff inside it. My knees weren't dirty but my cheeks were smudged so I put my dressing-gown on and went down to the bathroom and ran a basin full of water. The steam hung on the frosted glass and when I dried myself I still felt damp under my arms and round my neck. I rubbed and rubbed until I felt sore and then I put my dressing-gown back on.

'You're not going out any more, are you, Simon?'

'No, Mum. I've had a wash.'

'You've what?' Mum's head came in through the door. 'So you have. Whatever's come over you?'

'Dunno, Mum. Just felt like it.'

'And you're getting your pyjamas on. Good boy.'

'I probably won't go out nights any more, Mum.' I opened the door from in front of her and reached across her to pull the light cord. 'And I'll probably stay in most of the holiday and read.'

'Will you, Simon? Well, that'd be a jolly good idea but I expect you'll soon get bored with that and get off out with your friends.'

'No, Mum. I don't think I will.'

'Why ever not?' Her head went back and her nostrils quivered. 'Heavens above. My pudding!' She bounded down the passage and I followed after her and went into my bedroom. The saucepan lid clanged and Mum said 'Jiggeration!' and then, 'Oh, I dunno. P'raps it's all right,' and then she filled the kettle.

I sat on the edge of my bed and traced my toe over the

pattern in the lino. The dark outside seemed to be pressing on to the window as if I was inside a diving-bell and going down and the pressure was building up. The walls felt as if they were coming in and the ceiling got lower. I stood up and went to the window and shielded my eyes against the light to see out. It was like looking through a hole into a box. I flicked the light off and the darkness fell back. I leant with my elbows on the window sill and let the throbbing feeling in my head flatten out against the cold of the window pane.

The grass was going crisp in the frost and the layers of darkness feathered back like black snowflakes. A cat crept out from under our hedge and stood on our path for a moment and then she slid over the top of our gate like a piece of black velvet and the darkness swallowed her up and spread back like a heat haze.

'The boys'll be out there somewhere.' I strained to hear the outside and tapped the window pane with my knuckle but the sound came back to me. My stomach felt better but my head ached and I was sweating.

'Sod it.' I jumped back from the window. 'I'm off out.' I dressed quickly, put on clean socks and found some gloves and a scarf and my old balaclava, pushed my bow and arrows out of the window and rushed out.

'Bye, Mum.'

'Where you going? Thought you were going to have a nice evening in.'

'I been in every night lately. Shan't be long.'

My feet crunched in the grass and my breath hung in the air and I kept in the moon shadows so that I could see out from the darkness into the light. I started off with my bow over my shoulder but it got mixed up with my arrows so I carried it like a gun. I slipped over Crouch Cross Lane and up the bank where Derek Brown lived so that I was in the shadow of the houses. The light was on in his front room so I waited. Derek Brown's dad rode by on his bike. His back tyre was flat to the rim and his backside hung down so that I couldn't see the saddle. I watched him as he climbed off his bike and pushed it up the path. He passed the light from his living room and his side gate clicked closed. His back wheel ticked and then stopped ticking and I heard his back door scrape against its draught-excluder.

'Daddy's home,' came from their house. 'Derek . . . Lu-cy!' The light went off upstairs and feet thudded downstairs and I could imagine old man Brown bending down to Derek and his sister.

I shook my hands and then blew in the palms and rubbed the warmth in while it was still in the wool of my gloves.

Jerry Henry's dad pulled up at the pavement opposite me and kicked a piece of frozen dog muck off his grass on to the road. I slipped an arrow into my bow and took aim. He rode a girl's bike with stuff like string going from the centre of the wheel to the mudguards with plastic over it which Jerry said was to keep ladies' coats out of the wheels and I wondered how other ladies managed to ride bikes without one if it was worth putting one on his dad's bike.

My Dad rode past now with his head down. His shadow with his cap on looked like Donald Duck and I followed with my bow as if I was going to ambush him.

' 'ow do, Johnny.' Dad waved to Mr Henry.

Twang!

Whoo-arh!

I looked from my gloved fingers where the arrow'd slipped to Dad's bike as the back wheel reared up. He rolled over the handlebars as if he was doing a forward roll and on to his back on the grass and I dived backwards behind Derek Brown's box hedge.

'You all right, George?' I could see Mr Henry through the stalks of the hedge. 'What happened?'

'Search me. Blasted stick or something.' Dad straightened his cap. 'Can you see anything?'

'Oh God oh God oh God.' I let go of my bow as if it was burning my fingers.

'I heard a snap or something in the front wheel.' Dad was picking himself up. 'Unless it was my light slipped down the front.'

'Wasn't that.' Mr Henry spun the front wheel. 'You've got a couple of spokes bent though and one's broken.'

'P'raps that was it.'

202

'Yes. Yes. *Yes*.' I crawled along under the hedge on my stomach with my hands together. 'Please, let me get out of this.'

'We'd better get 'em straightened out. You got a spoke-true?'

'Don't think so.'

'That's all right. I have. And I'll get the missis to make us a cuppa tea. You sure you're all right?'

'Yeah. No bones broken, I don't think. But Ina'll be . . .'

'Oh yes. Poor Mum.' I crawled faster and tried not to get my knees dirty. 'Poor Mum and poor old Dad. I could've killed him. Oh please stop me being so naughty.' I lay waiting for them to go in and then I ran down the road and the frosty air made my face go into icy strips where I'd rubbed my tears away and I had to bang my knee up against the wall until it bled so that I could tell Mum I'd fallen over and she bathed it for me and gave me a piece of hot Christmas cake she'd baked separately.

They'd given me a new cricket bat for Christmas and a real leather ball because I needed them and they'd been in a sale in the autumn. They smelt nice and I said they were 'very nice thank you' but they didn't take long to unwrap and I couldn't play with them and I got a game of Lexicon without any instructions and a box of chocolates that I ate up behind the chicken house when I'd got ready to go up to Nan's, and a book. The book was called *Amazon Adventure* and they'd let me take it with me. We'd had a goose for Christmas dinner. They all said it was too greasy but I said it was lovely until I started to feel sick and then Grandad's hand had slipped and he'd missed the Christmas pudding with the brandy and put a bit more on top and it flared when he lit it and set fire to the bit of holly at the bottom where it'd collected on the plate. Old Gran said it was a wicked waste of good brandy and that they shouldn't be buying it anyway and she'd had the silver threepenny bit. They'd washed up and Grandad was looking out over the long front garden.

'Any sign of them yet, Art?' Nan was putting the plates and knives and forks away in the dresser.

'No. Not yet. Not just yet awhile.' He'd taken his jacket off for dinner and his khaki braces made his shirt look like pyjamas.

'Get later every year.' Nan straightened on her knees and then stood up one leg at a time. 'Be leaving it until after the King before long.'

'You going to open this cream now, Mum, or later?'

'Oh, later I think, Ina.'

Mum stood in the doorway to the passage and turned the small blue tin over in her hand. 'Only we forgot it last year. And it'll be a nuisance to whip it at tea time.'

'It was nice and cool on the cold slab, Ina. And did you get some more Ginger Wine, Art?'

'George did.'

Dad nodded. 'It's down by the cider.'

'I could whip it in a basin and then put it on the cold slab but it'd go all hard on top.'

'I'd rather you left it.'

'Leave it, Ina. Strewth alive!' Dad uncrossed his legs and I marked the place in my book with my finger.

Old Gran sat forward in Grandad's chair and cut the wool off her darning. 'Put a damp cloth over it, Ina.'

'What good'll that do, Mum?' Nan was setting out the tea plates and knives and forks.

'Stop it clotting.' Old Gran spread the sock out on her outstretched fingers and then pulled it off and folded it with the other one with their tops together. 'You got any more darning you need doing, Fran?'

'Oh, don't fuss me about that now, Mum.'

'You haven't got another tin-opener have you, Mum?' Mum was back at the door with the blue tin.

'*Will* you leave it, Ina. Here give us it.' Dad jammed the opener in the tin and gripped the handle and squeezed.

'Careful, George.'

'Damn and blast.'

'Just look at that.'

'Get a damp cloth, Ina.'

'Oh you and damp cloths, Mum. You've got damp cloths on the brain.'

'Better hurry up.' Grandad stood back from the window. 'They're here.'

I slid off the sofa and walked carefully round Dad. Uncle Edward's black Reilly had pulled up at the bottom of the garden and Michael and Jonathan were wedged in the back door trying to get out together.

'Just look at those two little monkeys.' Nan had her hands together under her chin.

Michael and Jonathan both pushed and they popped out like a cork.

'They got Roger and Doreen with them?' Old Gran leaned forward and pushed with her hands on the chair arms.

'Yes, and there's young Stephen and little Rachel in the back there as well. Talk about a squash.'

We were all up at the window now except Mum and Dad. Mum was rubbing at Dad's inside leg with the dish cloth and Dad was getting in her light looking down to see if it was coming out.

Michael and Jonathan ran on up the path but Uncle Edward called to them and they went back and walked up slowly in front of him and Aunty Sarah. Aunty Doreen was carrying Rachel and Stephen was holding her other hand and walking sideways reaching back to Uncle Roger. Uncle Edward was carrying a shopping bag, but it wasn't a very big one.

'Do you think they've brought any presents, Grandad?'

'Aye, I expect so, Simon. Let's go and see.'

We trooped off out into the passage and stood waiting inside the back door. Footsteps sounded on the bricks and the door opened.

'Happy Christmas, Sarah.'

'Mummy!'

'Edward!' Nan fell off Aunty Sarah and into Uncle Edward.

'Mum . . . Dad. Happy Christmas.' Uncle Edward clutched Nan with one arm and shook hands with Grandad past Nan with the other. 'George . . . Happy Christmas.'

'And to you, Edward.'

'Where's Ina?'

'I'm in here.' Mum's head stuck out of the pantry where she was stirring a fork in a pyrex dish. 'I'd hoped to get this done before you came.'

'A'ha . . . yes.'

Uncle Edward stood aside from Nan and she loved up to Uncle Roger and let Aunty Doreen kiss her and then she made out she'd just found Rachel. 'And 'ow's my ooful-booful little girl den?' They all gathered round Rachel and poked her and held her and I watched Mum but she just stood stirring the cream in the basin.

I crept round the side of them to where Michael and Jonathan and Stephen were standing against the wall.

'Hello, you lot.'

'Hello, Simon.'

'Did you bring any presents?'

'Yes. Mummy's got them.'

'Spec' we'll have to wait to open them until after tea.'

They'd finished kissing each other now and shaking hands and Nan and Aunty Doreen and Aunty Sarah went on into the kitchen and made a fuss of Old Gran, and Grandad and Uncle Edward followed them talking about how the apples were keeping this year and Dad and Uncle Roger went last. Mum licked the cream off the fork and left it on the cold slab.

'P'raps we'll just make a cup of tea, Ina, to have while the King's on.'

Mum filled the kettle.

'Do we have to listen to the King's speech, Mum?'

'Well p'raps the boys would like to hear it.'

'Would you?'

Jonathan crept up closer to Michael and Stephen and put his thumb in his mouth.

'Well, would you?'

'Don't speak to them like that, Simon. Let them make up their own minds.' Mum fitted the lid on the kettle and went into the kitchen.

'You don't wanna hear the King's speech, do you? Let's go in the front room and play darts.'

Michael came with me as far as the front-room door and stood holding Jonathan's hand with Stephen on his other side. Michael was nearly as old as me but he still wore short trousers for best and pale blue pullovers and white socks and sandals the same as Jonathan and Stephen who was only five. They were all pink and smooth like blancmange made with milk and I liked it when they came out to Nan's but I wouldn't have wanted the boys to see them.

'You coming then?'

'I'll just ask Mummy.' Michael went into the kitchen and Jonathan and Stephen drew closer together.

'I won't bite'cha!' I poked Jonathan in his tummy and he tensed back but Stephen giggled when I did it to him and hung on to my arm.

'Must you, Michael?'

'Well, Simon wants to.'

'What's that?' Nan was watching to see Mum didn't put too much milk in the cups.

'Darts, Mum. They want to go playing darts.'

'Do 'oo, my dears?'

I looked round from playing with Stephen. Nan was looking over at us through the open door and then she turned back to the others. 'Well, I s'pose they can. But won't they want to listen to—'

'Shouldn't think so, Mum.' Uncle Roger laughed and winked at Dad and tweaked the crease in his grey flannel trousers. 'Not if they're anything like we were.'

'Let 'em play.' Grandad was tuning in the wireless. 'Simon knows what to do.'

'And young Michael's very responsible.' Uncle Edward turned Michael round with his hand on his shoulder and led him back out to us. 'So you want to play darts, Simon?'

'Yes, Uncle.'

'Off you go then. But come for me if there's any trouble, Michael.'

'Yes, Dad.'

'And don't stand too close, my loves, in case one flies back and catches you in the eye.'

'No, Nan.'

I closed the door and pulled the green curtain back from over the dartboard.

'She always says that, Michael.'

'Does she? Do they fly back?'

'Yeah, sometimes. You just have to jump out'a the way. Dad says it's a 'noccupational 'azzard'. I pulled the darts out of the board and gave them one each. 'You wanna practise?'

207

Michael had played before and made it stick in the board but Jonathan hit the soft board covering the back of the door and Stephen's got hung up in the curtain.

'We'll play round the board and it can be me and Stephen against you and Jon.'

'What's round the board, Simon?'

'You go for one, then two, then three.' I pointed to each panel on the board in turn. 'And you get out on a bull.'

'What about if we miss?'

'You keep going until you get it. Nearest the bull starts.' My dart hit the treble wire and Michael nearly got a twenty-five. 'Right. You start then.'

Michael and I threw first and we both got a one. Jonathan threw two into the door and one settled sideways in the top of the board. Stephen held the darts in his fist and threw them from his other fist. I tried to show him how to grip it gently and raise it once, level with his eye, and then back, and throw it like Mr Stodgel did.

'Up and back and throw and let go.'

Stephen pumped forward and back, threw and let go. The dart plopped at his feet. His black eyes looked up at me.

'You let go *as* you throw. Not when you've stopped. Pick it up and have another go.'

We had to wait for Michael to tuck Jon's shirt in and then we made a new rule that they could stand halfway and kneel on the piano stool. My team got well ahead but we couldn't get a twenty-five and Michael said Jon's arm was aching.

'Nearest the bull then?'

'Yes, all right.'

My shot hit the wire and bounced out and Michael made his stick in.

'You having another go, Simon?'

'No. That's it. You've won.'

'Oh . . . good.' Michael put his hands together and Jon and Stephen stood with him looking at me.

'What'cha wanna do now then?'

'Don't know.'

'Wanna nut?'

'Yes please.'

I sat them down in front of the fire and got the nut bowl

down and the flat iron that stood by the piano. Michael took the nut crackers out and put a brazil nut in them. He squeezed but nothing happened. I found a walnut that was loose and put it on the hearth. I tapped it with the flat iron and opened it up and picked the two halves out.

'Want a bit, Stephen?' I pinched a piece of bad out and gave it to him.

'Jon?'

'Yeth?'

'Want a bit?'

He opened his mouth and I popped a piece in. His cheeks were round and creamy pink and they felt as soft as they looked when my fingers brushed against them. Michael was still straining with the crackers.

'You won't get far with those, Michael.'

'Why not?'

'Brazils are too hard and if you do crack it you smash it up and probably pinch your fingers.'

'How do you do it then?'

'Here, like this.' I laid it on the hearth and gave it a bash and it cracked across sideways. I pulled the shell off from each end. 'There you are. A whole one.'

I showed Michael how to crack hazel nuts with the crackers and I kept the others supplied with brazil and walnuts and then Michael had a go with the flat iron and Stephen put the shells on the fire and made a little blaze of his own.

'What did you get for Christmas then, Michael?'

Michael scrabbled round in the hazel nuts for a brazil. 'A garage and some cars and a painting set and a zither.'

'What's a zither?'

'It's like a flat harp with steel strings.' Michael banged the nut and it shattered.

'What's the point of that?'

'Well, you play it.'

'Can you play it?'

'Yes. A bit.' Michael scooped up the crumbs of nut and shell and tossed them on the fire and they flared up. 'There were some instructions and Daddy taught me.'

'Oh yeah.'

'What about Jon?'

'Go on, Jonathan.' Michael sat round next to him. 'Tell Simon what Father Christmas brought you.'

'A scth'ooter.'

'Did he, Jon?'

'And what did it have on the back of it, Jonathan?'

'What?' Jon put his finger in his mouth and stared at his brother.

'What you tread on to make it stop.'

'Oh yeth, a brwake.'

'Cor, that's nice.'

'And some sthweeties and a chocolate angel and some goldfish and—'

'You are a lucky boy, aren't you? Proper chatterbox when 'e gets goin', isn't 'e, Mike.' Michael flinched when I called him Mike.

'And what about you, Stephen?'

Stephen was still gobbling up nuts and he had to stop chewing and swallow before he could answer. 'Some crayons and a colouring book and a horse with a cowboy on it and a gun with some caps that you bang.' He clapped his hands and made Jonathan jump.

'Cor, that's all right, isn't it? I got a cricket bat and a real cricket ball. I didn't get any toys this year. Course, I'm older than you lot. S'pect I'll get some toys for my birthday.'

'But it's not the cricket season, Simon.' Michael was nearly as old as me and as tall but he'd got asthma and his shoulders drooped forward. 'You play cricket in the summer, don't you?'

'Yeah, I know. I'll be playing for the school next summer. I don't suppose you play cricket, do you?'

'Oh yes. We play sometimes but I don't like it much.'

'And I got some nuts in my stocking.' Stephen scrabbled his hand in the bowl. 'I like nuts.'

'Blimey, I can see you do.'

'Tea time, you boys.' The door opened and Mum came in.

I slid the nut bowl behind my leg.

'My, you look nice and snug in front of the fire. What's up, Simon?'

'Nothing, Mum.'

'What are you hiding there?'

'Nothing, Mum.'

'Yes, you are.' She came into the centre of the room and I sat back from the nut bowl. 'Have you eaten *all* these nuts?'

'Not really, Mum.' I looked down at the few that were left.

'Oh, Simon, how *could* you?'

'We didn't mean to, Mum. We were just talking and . . . well . . .'

'And stuffing yourselves silly. Dear oh dear. I don't know what Nan's going to say. Especially if you don't eat your tea. Go on in and apologise.'

'Oh, Mum, do I have to?'

'Yes you do. At once.'

Mum marched me in front of her and Aunty Doreen and Aunty Sarah looked up as she stood me over beside Nan who was standing over the tea tray.

'Sit down then, my duck.'

'I can't, Nan.'

'Oh, why not?'

'I gotta 'pologise. We've eaten the nuts.'

Dad looked over at me from talking to Uncle Edward.

'What, my duck? Speak up.'

'I'm sorry, Nan.' I turned away from Dad as much as I could. 'We've eaten the nuts.'

'What *all* of them?'

Uncle Edward stopped talking and I closed my eyes. 'Yes, Nan. More or less.'

'What's he done, Ina?'

'Eaten all the nuts. Precious nearly cleared the bowl.'

I gritted my teeth and stared at the hot-water pipe that ran down the wall by the cooker.

'That was pretty piggish, wasn't it, Simon?'

'Yes, Dad.'

'And look at me when I'm speaking to you. Now sit down.'

I sat down opposite Michael and breathed 'you as well' but he stared at the tablecloth.

'Right, come on then everybody.' Nan passed a plate of bread and butter to Aunty Doreen and another one to Grandad. 'No point crying over spilt milk as long as they all eat a nice tea. Want some of Nan's trifle, my love?'

I squirmed when Jonathan didn't want any and Stephen said he didn't like it but Michael took some without cold custard and I took a piece of bread and butter to eat with mine without being asked.

'Doesn't seem a year ago since we were all sitting down together, does it?' Nan put a spoonful of trifle in her mouth and licked a strawberry seed off her lip.

'April wasn't a year ago, Fran. We were all 'ere in April.'

'Well, I know we were, Mum. But you know what I mean.'

'No, it certainly doesn't. My goodness how time flies.' Mum nibbled on a cherry stone and put it on the side of her bowl with her spoon.

'Sitting here over Christmas tea's what I meant.' Nan stood up and poured milk into the cups.

'Soon comes round.' Grandad looked down the length of the table and then nodded at Uncle Edward next to him as if he was putting a stopper on a full bottle.

'Yes.' Uncle Edward smiled as if he'd heard a joke but didn't quite understand. 'Time is the scarce commodity nowadays. If I . . .'

'Sarah.' Nan was stretching forward with a cup of tea. 'Pass that on to Roger.'

'If I had thirty-six hours in every day I'd—'

'You still not taking sugar, Doreen?'

'Just half a one, Mum, please.'

'. . . much point slimming now.' Uncle Roger said that but he said it behind his spoon and the others missed it as Uncle Edward told them how busy he was.

I watched Aunty Doreen from low down. She laughed a lot and loudly as if she was really enjoying herself. If she wasn't slimming she must be going to get fat again and when she did that she usually had a baby. There was barely room for us all round the table now that my high-chair had come down again and there'd be even less if she had another one unless they moved Old Gran's chair back when she was at Petersfield. There weren't many families that only had one child and they usually came one after the other fast and then stopped like an illness that has got better. Babies were a bit like caterpillars, all soft and spongy and Old Gran was

212

beginning to look like a chrysalis. P'raps when you died you went off somewhere for the winter and then came back again brand new, and if that happened while she was with us we could keep her and I'd have a—

'More trifle, Simon?'

'What, Nan?'

'You're dreaming again.' Mum bent over my bowl. 'And don't stare at Old Gran like that. Whatever are you thinking of?'

'Nothing much.'

'Well, eat some bread and butter then.'

'Yes, all right.' I took two slices and spread one with Bovril. 'Can you pass the cheese please, Aunty?'

Aunty Doreen winked at me.

'You've spread that already, Simon.'

'I know, Dad.'

'Well, what you want cheese for?'

'It's nice. Bovril and cheese. Dicky Mole has it at school.'

Uncle Edward wrinkled his nose.

'P'raps it is. But it's expensive. Don't know how the Moles afford it on farm wages.'

'Course, they get free milk I expect, George.' Aunty Sarah cut Jonathan's bread into soldiers and dabbed jam on them. 'P'raps they make their own.'

'Can I, Grandad?'

'Precious little cheese-making going on now, Sarah.' Nan helped herself to a fancy cake.

'Well, you never made it anyway, Fran.' Old Gran's beady eyes fixed on Nan.

Nan chewed slower.

'Any cheese-making to be done I did. Churning away until I darn near set myself.'

'Well, you wouldn't let me. Oh, Edward, the things I've missed from having such poor health.'

Old Gran's jaw stuck out and her face was set but she settled back and pinched one of Nan's specially thin cut slices of bread.

'. . . and I was never able to touch cheese again.' Nan turned from Uncle Edward and shot a glance at Old Gran that Old Gran didn't see.

Uncle Edward blinked. 'Amazing. I'd never have believed it.'

We all had more tea and then they cut the Christmas cake and Mum half cleared the table and they dished out the presents. We all gave them to each other and stacked them up in front of us before we opened them. Grandad's pile was nearly all long round ones and Dad's were squarish and Mum's were short and fat and Uncle Roger's were flat and square. We opened them when Nan had finished her cake.

Grandad squeezed his and said they might be sausages and he hauled out pair after pair of socks. His odd-shaped present was cigars that Nan said'd make him chesty but she said they were to be kept for special occasions when he said 'thank you' to Aunty Sarah and Uncle Edward. Dad and Uncle Roger opened tins of tobacco and boxes of handker-chiefs alternately and they swapped one over when everyone was looking at Mum getting excited over bars of soap and bath cubes. We boys got mainly sweets and crayons and colouring books and then I came to my last one that felt like hankies but it was a bit stiff for hankies and I wasn't really watching what I was doing as I opened it.

'What you got there, Simon?' Grandad'd been watching me.

'Dunno, Gra— It's a book. *New Old Bible Stories*.' I stared at the picture of Joseph and Mary on a donkey cuddling the baby Jesus under the stars. 'Who gave me that?'

'Well look, Simon. Strewth alive, you ought to read who it's from.'

I scrabbled amongst the wrapping paper. 'To Simon, from Aunty Doreen and Uncle Roger. Cor thanks, Aunty.'

'Good. We hope you enjoy it.' Aunty Doreen had a lovely smile. She showed all her teeth when she smiled. 'Look inside.'

I turned to the inside cover and read it and then read it again slowly.

'What's it say, Art?'

'I don't know. I can't read upside-down long distance. Not through the chutney jar anyway.'

'Read it out, Simon.'

'Writing's not that bad is it, boy?'

214

'Oh don't tease him, Roger.'

'Here. Give it here.' Grandad reached over and I let the book go. He opened it. 'To dear Simon. You should enjoy this because you look like . . .' He stopped and looked at me and I stared back at him without blinking. 'Er-hur. Because you look like an angel . . . Happy Christmas from Aunty Doreen and Uncle Roger.' He finished off quickly and closed it.

They were all staring at me. Old Gran was nodding and Aunty Doreen was smiling and Uncle Roger was smiling at Aunty Doreen. Mum was redder than I was and Dad looked as if he wanted to go to the toilet.

Somebody said 'm'm!' and some of the others started to fold up their wrapping paper.

'Here, Simon, you'd better frame that.'

'Yes, Grandad.' I took the book back.

Aunty Sarah and Aunty Doreen piled the plates up and Nan passed the kettle over to Mum to fill. Old Gran tipped all the crumbs on to one plate and went out down the passage to the back door to put them out for the birds. Nan collected the paste and Bovril and jam together ready to go out to the pantry and she put a few soapflakes in the galvanised bowl for somebody to wash up when Mum brought the kettle back. Grandad led the men into the front room and Michael and I sat on the sofa with Jonathan and Stephen between us. We'd left our presents in four piles on the table but I was holding my book and the glossy dark green cover stuck to my fingers.

'Who's this then?' I jammed my finger on the front cover.

'Jesus.' Stephen's dark eyes stared up at me and then he giggled and squizzled back into Jonathan. 'Mummy told me.'

'Oh, did she?' I turned the pages over and looked at Samuel telling Eli about his dream and Rebecca at the well and Pharaoh's palace with Joseph standing in front of him where he's just been dragged out of the pit his brothers had slung him into.

'Didn't think the King sounded too well today.' Aunty Sarah stood back wiping a plate so that Aunty Doreen could get in and pick up some spoons. 'Bit chesty.'

215

'Never been very strong, poor chap.' Aunty Doreen shook the water off the spoons into the old tin tray where Mum was putting the ones she'd washed up. 'Don't think he's ever got used to suddenly getting landed the way he did overnight.'

'It's a crying shame it ever happened.' Mum stood up to give her back a rest. 'I think it's shameful the way they hounded the Duke of Windsor out.'

'Ah . . . he put his sweetheart first.' Nan sighed and I went 'ugh' and covered it over with a cough.

'All right you lot.' Mum wiped her hair back with her forearm. 'You can go in the front room now your tea's settled but mind what you're up to.'

There was plenty of space in the front room until the ladies came in and then they took all the seats and me and Michael had to sit on the floor and Jonathan sat between Aunty Sarah's legs and Stephen stood up by the arm of his dad's chair while Aunty Doreen nursed Rachel. It was always the same. They talked about work and what an awful summer we'd had and where you could get things cheaper in the shops and Mum said they always put a penny or tuppence on everything down at the shop and Old Gran told us what you could get for a shilling when she was a girl. Uncle Roger said didn't she mean a groat, and Aunty Doreen laughed and Nan told him to shush and then he went and loved into Old Gran and said he was only kidding and she didn't know what he meant and told him to get off and not be such a great silly. Then Nan asked Mum to pass the dates round and Grandad told us how he could've had them by the bushel in Mespot if he'd stayed there and that he'd spent six months there when he'd worn nothing but shorts and it was the happiest time of his life and he'd've stayed out there after the war if he'd had his way and Nan told him the flies'd've sent her round the bend and he must've been mad to want to go carting her off to such a place and would anybody like a nut because she had some more in the kitchen cupboard if anybody really wanted one. They all said no, they'd had all they could eat, except Stephen, but Uncle Roger said 'no thanks' over him and they had another date each and then Grandad stood up and went to the cupboard at the side of the fireplace under the shelf where the glass case with a pair of stuffed sparrow-hawks stood.

'And what would we all like to drink?'

They all mumbled and thought about it as if they were too polite to say no. I said 'cider please, Grandad,' because that's all they'd let me have anyway.

'You just wait your turn, Simon.'

'Yes, Dad.'

'Edward. Spot of whisky and ginger wine?'

'Yes please, Dad. About half and half.' Uncle Edward was standing in front of the fire with his hands behind his back.

Grandad was twisting at the ginger-wine bottle but the top was stuck.

'Here give it to Edward, Art. Else we'll be here all night.'

Uncle Edward took the ginger-wine bottle and put it down and measured out the whisky and then he stripped the plastic off the top of the wine bottle.

'You great silly, Art. No wonder it wouldn't come off.'

Grandad's lips went tight.

'What about you, Sarah?'

'Got any sherry, Daddy?'

'Aye, and port and gin and brandy and cider and—'

'I'll have cider, Grandad.'

'Simon!' Dad started forward and I slumped back.

'. . . and lemonade 'ere and bitter lemon.'

'Just sherry, please.'

'And me Dad, please.' Aunty Doreen nudged Aunty Sarah. 'We'll get tiddly together.'

Grandad stood the glasses up and filled them and they dripped on the back of my hand as he passed them over. I waited until nobody was looking and licked up the drops. It was sweet, like syrup, and I tasted a bit off my pullover sleeve.

'What about you, Fran?'

Nan shook her head and sighed. 'I really don't know. It feels so awful to be out of things, especially at Christmas.' She turned to Aunty Sarah and Aunty Doreen and they nodded and looked sad and held their full glasses in front of them and I wondered why they didn't drink a bit now they'd got them. 'I used to like a drop of port wine but it doesn't like me and the very smell of sherry turns me over.'

'Little spot of whisky and ginger?'

'Edward!' Nan's hand went to her throat. 'I couldn't possibly.'

'We-ll.' Uncle Edward drew himself up and I could imagine him making a speech up at the Golf Club. 'I think there's nothing like it . . . in moderation of course. And it might' – he leaned forward – 'be the very thing for you.'

'Do you think so?'

'Might be just the thing. After a long day. With all the responsibility . . .' He stood up straight again. 'Good meal. All the chores over?'

'Well, there's still the mincepies.'

Uncle Edward held his free hand out in front of him. 'Just the very thing. I'll pour it for you.'

'Well, if you think so, Edward.'

Uncle Edward turned and poured one short and then one long and I could see the reflection in the veneer of the black lacquered shelves over the fireplace. 'There we are. Just a spot of Highland Glory and a nice measure of ginger wine.'

'Thank you, Edward.'

'And what about you, George?'

'Port wine please, Dad.'

'And me please, Dad.'

'Right then. What about you boys?'

'Cider please, Grandad.'

'And for Michael?'

'Just a drop, Dad.'

We finally got our drinks and Stephen sat sniffing the bubbles on his lemonade and Grandad stood up so straight I thought he was going to fall back in the fire, and stuck his glass out.

'A very happy Christmas one and all and a peaceful and prosperous New Year and many of them.'

They all said 'cheers' and 'hear, hear' and Aunty Doreen said 'amen'. Then we all drank.

'Cor.' Nan's face crinkled up and she coughed and shook her head and looked up at Uncle Edward as if she'd caught him pinching her fruit bon-bons. 'This is strong, Edward.'

'Ah, that'll be the ginger wine, Mum. Just take little sips and don't breathe it in.'

Nan put the glass to her lips and wet them and ran her tongue over them. 'Strong,' she said, 'but very warming.'

Uncle Edward smiled and raised his glass. 'To your health, Mum.'

Nan blushed and thanked him and took another taste and said it was quite nice really.

'I suppose I'm included in all this?' Old Gran was sitting on the piano stool between the piano and the card table where Nan stacked the playing cards and dominoes.

'Dear oh dear. You get forgotten tucked away behind there, Gran?' Aunty Sarah looked for somewhere to put her glass.

'It's all right, Sarah.' Nan nodded at Grandad. 'But you don't usually.'

'A little drop of ginger wine please, Arthur. But none of that other stuff.'

They said 'good health' to Old Gran and I strained the last of my cider through my teeth. Stephen dropped down on his knees and crawled over to me and measured his glass up against mine.

'Are you having any more, Simon?'

'Dunno, Stephen. Don't expect so.'

'I'd like some more.'

'What's that, my duck?' Nan held her glass down on her lap. 'Didn't Grandad give you very much. Poor little chap. Here give 'em a drop more, Art. Before you get settled.'

Grandad had pulled the creases of his trousers up and straightened the garters on his socks and was letting himself back into his chair.

'Sit still, Dad.' Uncle Roger stood up. 'Come on, Nipper.' He took Stephen's glass and mine and poured some lemonade in each and then he gave Michael some and gave Jonathan his glass back because he hadn't finished. 'Now that's your lot.'

'Can't think where they put it.' Aunty Doreen patted Jonathan's little tummy. 'He's got hollow legs, hasn't he, Rach?'

Jonathan looked down at his legs and felt them. His knees were chubby, with a crease across the middle like lips.

' 'oo 'asn't got 'ollow legs, 'as 'oo my booful?' Nan leant forward but she couldn't reach him. 'Cor, is it getting 'ot in here or is it me?'

'It's you.' Grandad had his eyes closed. 'If we put another log on it'll cool down while it burns up and that'll do us for the evening.'

Uncle Edward moved over and Dad bent and poked at the fire. He made a nest of red ashes and laid a log on it and Uncle Edward moved back.

'Soon warms up in here when we all get in.' The new flames were licking up round the log through his legs. 'Course the curtains make a difference.'

Nan smiled and nodded with him and he rinsed the rest of his drink round in his glass and drank it and looked at the inside of the empty glass. 'Nice drop of whisky that, Mum.'

'Good.' Nan put her hand to her mouth and said 'excuse me'. 'Course I shouldn't touch it. But you didn't put much in, did you, Edward?'

'No – no.' Uncle Edward put his finger and thumb close together. 'Just the merest spot.'

I looked at the bottle and then at him and then I felt Mum's toe in my back pushing me.

'What, Mum?'

She shook her head and shushed me and I finished my lemonade and played Michael at dominoes until it was time to go.

They stood at the back door saying good-night to each other and Nan and Grandad and then they started talking about other things as we picked our way down the front path in the dark and then they had to say good-night all over again at the gate as Uncle Edward sat with the driver's door closed waiting for them to get in.

'Looks as if there might be a frost, Edward.'

Uncle Edward wound his window down. 'Pardon, Ina?'

Mum let go of my hand and I stood with my hands under

my arms as she stepped down off the path into the road. 'I
say it looks frosty.'

'Oh . . . yes.'

'There's often a bad bit just this side of Hanover Corner,
Edward. Want to take it easy there.'

'Yes. Thank you, George.' He started to wind the window
up.

'In fact, it might be better to go Tangmere way.'

'Gawd.' The window stopped moving.

'Don't worry. I'll be careful. Good-night.'

'Yes, good-night.' Mum and Dad moved and stepped back
up on to the path together and turned and waved again.

'Blast it!' Mum stopped moving and put her hands on her
hips.

'What's up now, Ina?'

'That blessed cream. I whipped it all up and left it in the
pantry.'

'Well, it's too late now.'

'Yes. I know but—'

'Can't we go now, Dad?'

'Yes, of course we can. Whatever's up with you?'

'Well, you said we couldn't play dominoes any more and
we had to get ready to go and we've been hanging around for
bloomin' ages since then.'

'Cor, I think that's a bit strong, Simon. C'mon, Ina.'
Mum and Dad followed up behind me. 'Off you go. You
can't just leap up and say "cheerio" and dash off, Simon.
You have to say goodbye properly.'

'Well, I wish we could do it indoors. It's perishing out
'ere.'

'Cor stone the—'

'S'sh, dear. He's tired and he's been pretty good today.'

I walked a bit faster so that they didn't tread on my heels
and we stayed on the Smithy's side of Crouch Cross Lane
past Ray Whittle's barn.

I was carrying my book and I kept changing hands so that
I could put the other one in my pocket. The other presents
were in Mum's shopping bag.

'I'll have to be looking your gloves out, Simon.'

'Yes, Mum.'

'Do hope Dad keeps free of bronchitis this year.'

'M'm.' Dad was doing deep-breathing exercises.

'It'd help if he wrapped up properly. Especially when it's wet.'

'What is bronchitis, Mum?'

'Oh, it's an illness on your chest, Simon . . . like a very bad cold and you can't get your breath.'

'Is that what the King's got?'

'Don't know really, maybe.'

'What's the Royal disease then?'

'Simon!' Their footsteps stopped behind me and I looked around to see what was the matter. 'Wherever did you hear that?'

'I dunno, Mum. What's special about bronchitis?'

'Not that . . . the other.'

'I don't know, Mum. What is it?'

'Well, really!' Mum looked at Dad and he said to let it go. 'It's not something you ought to know anything about and I don't want you to mention it ever again.'

'All right.' We carried on up Crouch Cross Lane and down the Close and I tried to think where I'd seen it. 'The Royal disease . . .' it was cutting yourself and bleeding to death or something and I thought I'd seen it in a book about the Roundheads and the Cavaliers.

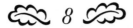

*T*he newspapers said the 2nd February 1952 was a sad day in our history and the pages of the *Daily Express* were etched in black and it said that Princess Elizabeth'd been up a tree in Africa when she'd heard the news. I looked down from the elder tree at the turning circle at the bottom of the Close and picked off some of the little green buds. The trees in Africa were mainly small because it was so dry so they could have called it up to her. But how could you call out to somebody that your dad'd died? And they wouldn't't've sent just anybody to go out and tell her. They'd probably have written it on a card and put it in a sealed-up envelope on a silver tray to be carried out by a black soldier in a red jacket and helmet and shorts and army boots carrying the tray in front of him in both hands as if he was taking it from the front door to a room inside a house. There wouldn't have been a door to knock on and they wouldn't have whistled or called to her. Maybe they'd sent a little black boy up so that he could climb in bare feet without making a noise. Prince Philip'd probably been standing on a platform on the branches making sure she didn't fall while she was looking out over the plains or having something pointed out to her by somebody from the government and the note'd've been passed up to him and he'd've waited till she'd finished talking and then whispered it to her and looked after her for a while while she cried privately. I sat round more on the branch and put one foot up and let the other one dangle. Must've been a hell of a tree for three of them to be up it, and just stand around. Maybe it wasn't out on the plains but on the edge of the forest or on the side of a mountain. The *Daily Express* said it was a place called 'Tree Tops' so p'raps there were tall trees there.

Jimmy Phillips's gate clicked. He looked up the Close and

223

then came down to the turning circle and stood under the tree.

'What'cha doing?'

'Nothing much. Coming up?'

'Might do. 'ere, you 'ear about the King?'

'Yeah. Course I have.'

'Reckon there'll be a war?'

'Shouldn't think so. Why should there be?'

'Well, my grandad reckons they'll all gang up on us now we're gonna 'ave a Queen.'

'Oh.' I grabbed the swinging branch and swung down. 'But we still got a Prime Minister, haven't we?'

'Oh yeah.'

'An' Churchill won the last war, didn't he?'

'Yeah, s'pose so.'

'Well then.' I gave Jimmy a push to cheer him up but he just fell with it and stood still a bit further away from me. 'C'mon, Jimmy, what's up?'

'I told you. My grandad reckons there's—'

'Yeah. All right.' I sat down in the hollow where the elder tree divided. 'But look . . . who's gonna fight us for a start?'

'I dunno.' Jimmy squatted down on his hands so that he was level with me. 'Germany?'

'Don't be daft. They haven't got an army now and they've been split in two. The Guv told me.'

'Russians then?'

'N'no.' There'd been a lot in the paper about Stalin lately and the wireless kept on about a cold war. 'No. Shouldn't think so. Didn't you read the paper today?'

'No, why?'

'Well, they said who's coming to the funeral. All the Kings and Queens around and Prime Ministers and all and Stalin's comin'.'

'Is 'e?'

'Yeah. Course 'e is. 'e wouldn't come to the funeral if he wanted to start a war on us, would 'e?'

'No. S'pose not.'

'There you are then.' I stood up and wiped the green off my trousers. 'Coming up the—'

'Simon . . . dinner.'

224

'I gotta go. See you after dinner.'
'Yeah. All right. If it doesn't rain.'

It rained all afternoon and I didn't even bother to go over for Jimmy Phillips. It eased off just before tea but then it started again and kept on for a week. I read *Tom Sawyer* and *Huckleberry Finn* and the *Gorilla Hunters* and *Nicholas Nickleby* and the paper every day when I got home from school and when my eyes ached I listened to the wireless. At first the paper was all sad about our tragic loss and the funeral of state and everything was black but they soon cheered up and started on about the Coronation and how we were all going to be new Elizabethans under Good Queen Bess and they had a song on the 'Billy Cotton Band Show' about it and I wondered if we'd have to start wearing those daft trousers that billowed up round your bottom like they'd done when Elizabeth the First was on the throne.

It rained for weeks and when it finally stopped the Easter holidays were over and Dad got angry when I went off to school saying I was browned off.

A misty rain was sweeping down the Close so I hunched forward and pulled my windcheater over my head. The damp cold got inside my coat and made my shoulders feel stiff and my eyelids felt heavy as if the drops of water on my lashes were drips of lead. Jerry Henry came out of his house in front of me and Derek Brown and Jimmy Phillips were behind me but I didn't catch up with Jerry and they didn't catch up with me and by the time we got to school the water was coming through the knees of my trousers. Milly made us line up in the rain and he told us that whilst it was a shattering thing for a country to lose its King, we could look forward to a new beginning under Queen Elizabeth. The water was laying amongst the bricks and cinders of our assembly playground. I scuffed some gravel and old ashes into a pile at the end of a canyon between two bricks and pressed my toe down in it. The water built up and then flooded and Milly said this was the point where we'd come together under the new Queen Bess and that we must pray she'd take us on to greater things than ever.

'What's 'e on about, Paul?'

'Don't you listen, Nipper. We got to go to bleedin' church.'

'Church!'

'Yeah, church, some sorta m'orial service or something and then we gotta work out our timetable.'

'Strewth alive!' I dug my hands deep into my trouser pockets and tried not to think about how it would feel to kneel down praying in wet trousers.

The church had a weekday feel about it. They'd left the big oak doors open and the rain and dead leaves had blown in and Mrs Norbitt was cleaning the lobby with a pail of grey water and sloshy mop in an apron with a headscarf wrapped round her head. Pop had his gardening jacket and corduroy trousers on and there was a smell of furniture polish in the pews where I'd got used to incense and a workman in overalls was fiddling about with some pipes by the vestry and he'd laid his jacket down by the wall and put a red flask and a sandwich tin next to it.

I didn't close my eyes when Pop prayed for strength 'in-nadversity' and I let my hands fall apart when he got on to 'all pulling together' because it felt awkward having my hands together when we weren't kneeling down and it didn't feel very holy to be sitting up and praying just because we might get the hassocks wet. Then Milly got up in the pulpit and said we mustn't let our grief get us down and that there'd be a celebration for the Coronation and that would be about the time the church got its new boiler. He nodded towards the man working by the vestry and the man turned round on his knees and waved a spanner back at him.

Pop prayed some more and a squeaking noise came from the pipes as the man started to unscrew them and then there was a clang and 'bloody hell' rang out and Pop said 'amen' quickly and Milly led us out.

It was still raining as we trudged back under the apple trees past the Old Boys' Club and Mrs Evans's garden. I looked in for Grandad but I didn't see him and the leaves were lying thick on the driveway past the old pigstys and apple store and there were two tracks in them where the bread van and milk and coal lorries went.

226

'Hurry along now.' Milly was walking back down our line. 'I want you all to go up to my class. I've got an announcement to make.'

'What's up now then, Paul?'

'Don't ask me.' Paul Craven clipped Michael Hoskins's ankle as we crossed the road and looked the other way so that he thought it was me. 'About whose class we're going in p'raps.'

'Not another change is there?'

'Have to be now Rasher's back at the Lincs.'

'Oh, good. Wonder who we've got now.'

'Dunno. Have to wait and see.' Paul ran on and I ran after him to get a seat near the stove.

The walls of Milly's class were covered with pictures of the Commonwealth countries and they'd put plants along the window sills that looked like green lamps set against the window panes furred with mist. I stared at them and let my eyes go glazed so that the light from the half-shielded bulbs sparkled on the misted panes and broke up into flecks that ran into each other and—

'Pst, Nipper.' Drip Williams nudged me. 'Wake up!'

I shook my head and my eyes focused. Marie Maynard and Pat Smith were standing by the stove giggling and Christine Lloyd was staring at my front.

'Sailors on deck,' Drip whispered it like we did on the stage when it had to reach the back and he stood across in front of me.

'Sod it. Must've been like that since before we went into church.' I did my fly buttons up and the other children lined up in front of us and Milly's voice came up over the shuffling of feet and the banging of the seats attached to the desks.

'. . . great asset to us but the time had to come when he'd be well enough to go back to the Lincs and no doubt some of you'll be seeing him again.'

'That means we got to pass the 11+ to avoid Rasher again, Nipper.'

'Yeah, some hope!'

'But we've got good news of Mr Wade who will be back with us tomorrow.'

'Sod it.' Paul was smiling like Peter Brough from 'Educating Archie' so that his lips didn't move.

'Mr Wade'll take the under tens. Mr Irvine is going to look after the ten to twelves because most of you'll be doing the 11+ next Easter and he'll be going on to the Lincs with you, and I'll take the rest.'

'Bloody 'ell. Eleven-plus, that's us.'

'Could be worse, Nipper. At least we've got the Guv.'

'Now just hang on a minute and I'll call out the names of those going to Mr Irvine.'

Drip and I had to wait to the end because our names both began with 'W' and there were no seats left together. I sat with Fatty Morris on the edge of a group of camp kids and Drip had to go up at the front with Michael Hoskins. The Guv stood at the front dusting chalk off his fingers until we got settled and then he came forward and perched on the edge of one of the front desks.

'Let's see now.' His eye ran down three double rows of desks. 'I've got to split you into two groups. Those who are doing the exam at Christmas and those doing it next June.'

'What's the difference, sir?'

'Age, Geer. You see the High School has been extended and they'll be taking in a lot like you who are twelve going on thirteen. Now let me see.' He looked down his list and ticked the names off with a red pen and a pencil. 'M'm.' He tapped his pencil on his clipboard.

'You're not so far adrift as you are. But I think we'd better just have you two over here and, Simon, you and Gerald move back by Godfrey and we'll have Messrs Gibbs and Gander a bit closer to the front and Pat and Jenny back a bit. There, that's better. Now we've got all those of you' – he ran his hand down the line with most of the camp kids in it and up again to Pat and Jenny – 'who'll be doing it at Christmas and the rest of you the following summer. So you first lot have got some work to do and the rest of you needn't think you can play about because a year is no time at all.' He looked back at his list. 'And the boys in the top group plus Gander will be going with the Seniors to Arundel on Wednesday mornings to do woodwork.'

'What about me, sir?'

'What about you, Gibbs?'

'Well, aren't I going?'

'No, Gibbs, you're not.'

'Well, if Gander is, why ain't I?'

'Because Gander's eleventh birthday falls before 1st September and yours is after.'

'But 'is is end of August and mine's 3rd September.'

'I know, Gibbs. That's what I said.'

'Well, that's not fair.'

'No, Geoffrey. Life often isn't but there it is and you, Marie, and Jenny and Pat will be going with the big girls for cookery.'

'Yes, sir.'

The Guv waited for Gibbs to stop mumbling 'ain't bloody fair' to Gander and then he handed us out a sheet of paper each and a new pencil and told us our timetable.

I was sitting next to a new boy called Godfrey Willis and I wrote my timetable down like he did so that I could see a whole week together and then I borrowed his ruler to draw lines between the days but I'd written 'athletics' too big and it cut through the 'c' at the end.

The Guv took us back through long division and fractions and decimals and on to percentages and I noticed Godfrey Willis listened to what he said and then did some sums of his own with a short wide ruler with a bit that slid up and down in the middle. The Guv looked at his work sometimes when he was walking up and down our line and occasionally he pointed to something and Godfrey Willis looked at it and sometimes he changed it and sometimes he looked up at the Guv and the Guv checked the rule and smiled and went on. Godfrey's stories always came back without red ink as well and he knew all about Geography and History. But he was hopeless at football and cricket.

We'd had a student, Miss Edgely, from the Bishop Otter Teacher Training College, start two days a week for training. Milly said she was going to teach P.E. and English and she was doing the high jump for Young England. Godfrey Willis was still packing his books away in his satchel and tucking his glasses into their case in a side pocket when she came in to clear the last of us out. She bounced in as if she had springs in her plimsolls and her short green pleated gym slip flared up as she walked and showed her white pants at the back.

'Come on, Simon, and you, Godfrey.' She bent and did up one of the laces in Godfrey's satchel. 'You coming, Maurice?'

'Cor, I am now.' Maurice Geer had started to stand up but he'd stopped halfway and was staring with his mouth open.

'What's up? Have you never seen a lady's legs before?'

'Yes, Miss. But not like that.'

Miss Edgely started to smile but then she blushed and went out.

Maurice ran after her. 'Come on, Si. What you waiting for?'

'Godfrey . . . we won't be long.'

Godfrey fussed and tidied at his drawer and then had to repack his satchel because his Aviation magazine was getting crumpled. 'I don't like all this running about.' He tested the weight of his satchel. 'And jumping in that sand makes my feet sore and when I rub it off, it stains my fingers.'

'Oh come on, Godfrey. Don't be an old woman.'

'I can't see that I'm like an old woman in any way.' He blew his nose and refolded his hanky. 'I just object to jumping into a sandy old pit because a girl no older than my sister says I've got to.'

'Well, Milly told her to.'

'That isn't the point.' Godfrey put his cap on and folded his coat over his arm and leant back against the weight of his satchel. 'In fact, it makes it worse. The headmaster should know better. But come on. I suppose we'll have to suffer with the rest.'

The boys were all laying down on their tummies in a line on the grass with their chins resting on their hands propped up on their elbows. Their heads turned slowly as Miss Edgely ran up to the bar, skipped and cleared it.

'Got it now?' she said as she rose up out of the sand.

'Not quite, Miss. One more time.'

'Well, for goodness' sake, watch this time, Maurice.'

'I am, Miss.'

'He is, Miss.' Paul Craven winked at Maurice. 'He's watching ever so hard.'

'Well, pay attention then.' She bounced forward. 'Up.'

'Cor!'

'. . . and over.' She did the western roll this time with her legs towards us and Maurice thumped the grass with his fist. 'Did you get it that time, Maurice?'

Paul Craven spluttered 'not 'arf!' and he and Maurice let their hands drop on the grass as if they'd fainted.

'Right. Get up. You first, Maurice. Over you go.'

We all lined up and ran and jumped in turn except Godfrey Willis who showed her where he'd cut in between his toes on a bit of grass and we kept on doing it until Milly came and said he wanted a word with Miss Edgely and then the whistle went.

We sat on the grass and rubbed the sand out of our toes and slipped our trousers on over our shorts and put our shoes and socks on. Maurice stood up and bent his bottom back and wiggled.

'Gone down yet?' Paul was tying his lace.

'Nope. Yours?'

'Think it's broke.'

They started laughing and nudging each other and followed the others over towards the air-raid shelter where the Guv was giving out the gardening tools.

'What was all that about?' Godfrey finished retying his tie.

'Don't you know? Didn't you see her?'

'Well, yes.' Godfrey rubbed his glasses on the piece of cloth from his glass case. 'But she's a teacher . . . well sort of.'

'P'raps she is. But she's . . . well, she's ever so pretty.'

'H'm. S'pose so. But I really can't see what all the fuss is about.'

'Never mind, Prof. You can't know everything. C'mon. It's gardening now.'

The Guv was giving out a fork and spade between two and sending everyone over the other side of the school garden wall to dig. Godfrey and I were the last in the line.

'P'raps you'd take a spade and the wheelbarrow and edge along there by the—'

'Geer! Come here!' Milly burst out from the side of the

shelter and marched between the Guv and me. 'Here, this minute. You little . . .'

Maurice had jumped over the wall and was trotting over but he slowed down when he saw Milly's face.

'I'll teach you to—' Milly grabbed my spade with one hand and Maurice with the other. 'You filthy-minded little—' Thwack! 'Don't you ever—' Crash. The flat of the spade caught Maurice across the back of his knees. 'I'll—' Crack . . . Another one in the same place.

'Argh!' A noise like the sea in the distance rose up from over the wall. The boys' heads were lined up like a row of hallowe'en masks.

'. . . give you something—' Whack!

'Stoppit! Get off.' Clatter, clatter, bang. Spades and forks and rakes and hoes rattled on the top of the wall and the sea of faces merged into one as others crowded in behind.

Milly held Maurice outstretched by the collar of his jacket. He lowered him and his fingers relaxed their grip and Maurice's jacket settled back around his shoulders. Milly bent and lay the spade down. He glanced at the line of faces above the wall and turned and walked away. The faces dropped back behind the wall but there was no slicing sound of spades going into damp earth or clink of flints against metal. The only sound was a starling singing in the beech tree by the sand pit.

I stood rigid as the Guv picked the spade up and gave it to me.

'You all right, Maurice?'

'Yeah think so, thanks.' Maurice walked away carefully as if he was on a tight rope.

'Did you see the way he hit him?' Godfrey was biting on one of his fingers.

'Yeah. So did that bloke over there.' A dark-skinned man in workman's clothes and wellingtons with the tops rolled over was standing level with the end of the air-raid shelter. He was punching one fist slowly into the palm of his other hand.

'Who is he, Simon?'

'Dunno. Workman or something. He was up here during the Christmas holidays doing some work for Aldred's. I'll bet he's a spiv when he's not at work.

*

The Aldred brothers had a builder's business and their yard was down on the Tangmere Road near the garage. They had two lorries and two concrete mixers and they laid paths and built bits on to houses and mended drains and things. One of their lorries was parked outside the school one morning and when I went into the back playground by Wadey's class I saw the dark young man with an older man digging a trench. Janet Rolls was watching them with Dorothy Newton and Susan Farley so I watched too. Janet had narrow shoes on with block heels that made her feet look thinner and she wasn't as fat as she had been. She had one hand in her coat pocket but the other one was hanging by her side and it didn't seem possible that she'd once let me hold it. I put my hands in my pockets and tried to look casual by standing on one leg but I overbalanced and nearly fell in the trench. Janet turned round.

'Hello, Simon.' She had a lovely face when she smiled.

' 'lo, Janet.'

'I didn't hear you come up.'

'Didn't you. 'lo Dorothy, Susan.' Dorothy and Susan looked at me and looked away. 'What're they doing, Janet?'

'Why don't you ask them, Simon Wilson, if you're so nosey? C'mon Sue.'

'You coming, Jan?' Susan and Dorothy were holding hands.

'M'm.' Janet smiled at me as she turned. 'Yes. All right. See you later, Simon.'

'Sure. Yes. Wh—' I stopped myself. 'Yes, all right.'

They went off together with Janet slightly behind and Dorothy turning round to her as they walked and she looked as if she was telling Janet off. I watched them until they turned past the bike sheds to the Guv's class and when I looked back down the trench the young man was leaning on his shovel watching me.

'What's your name then?' He had a fluffy voice and a squashed nose.

'Simon. And what you laughing at?'

'Oh, not really laughing. Just thinking you're a lucky lad to have three of them.'

233

'What do you mean?'

'She your girl-friend?'

'Who?' I felt my face going red.

'The one they called Janet.'

'No, not now. She was. Till Gibbser made me spill tea over her.'

'Who's Gibbser?'

'One'a the boys. You'll see him. His trousers are saggy at the back and he swears a lot . . . and what d'ya mean "three of 'em".'

The man laughed again. 'Well, the one called Janet was all over you and the other pretty one was as well and the one who looked like a prune was jealous of the both of them.'

'Were they?'

'Yeah. Course they were. Weren't they, Perce?'

The older man leant his shovel against the side of the trench and blew his nose and looked at what had come out. 'Don't ask me, Charlie boy. I was working and I think you'd better do a bit or you'll have to turn pro.'

'Turn pro?' I looked harder at Charlie. 'You play football?'

'No.' Charlie spat on his hands and took a couple of swipes with his pickaxe that sent sparks up off the stones. 'Boxing. I box amateur for the Boys' Club. I never played football.'

'Cor, do you? Could you teach me?'

Charlie swung in the trench again and scraped the loose earth back. 'Yes. If you like.'

'Right. I'll see you lunch time.'

You could hear a pin drop in our class. The Guv had set out our work for the whole year up to Christmas and it filled up four pages of our exercise books. He called it a programme and it took the older ones up to the time they sat the exam and he said the rest of us could do it again between Christmas and Easter as revision. I read the same things over and over again until I knew the numbers and words off by heart but I couldn't see how they hung together and when it said 'therefore equals' I couldn't see why. Godfrey Willis kept writing things down for me in different ways to make me understand and his pink face went red as he said the same thing over and over until he just sat there muttering 'If this is equal to that plus that and that then that *must* equal that. Do you see, Simon?' I watched the way his fingers held his pen and how he had nice curved nails and half-moons on his fingernails as if he didn't have to push the hard skin back with a nail file and said 'yes' to please him and made out I was concentrating but I just let my mind go so that the lines and numbers all ran into each other and I could think about taking Janet Rolls for walks in the woods and playing inside right to Stanley Matthews for England and winning the heavyweight championship of the world at Haringey and being on the wireless. The Guv came round and he spent longer and longer with me and then he had me up to the front. I followed the first bit of what he'd told me but when his face lit up and he tapped the page with his pencil expecting me to understand I had to shake my head because it was like a curtain being drawn across a window and not even a speck of light could get through. I felt really sorry for him. He looked so disappointed that I wanted to tell him it wasn't his fault and it didn't really matter and I just said 'yes, sir, thank you, sir,' when he suggested I concentrate on English and Geography and History and hope sums would come easier next time. And now I'd given up percentages and other things that got my brain in a knot I could sit warm and quiet reading about the Saxons and the Ancient Britons and the Druids and Brazil and Argentina and slavetraders and the Greeks and Romans.

Pam Smith and Jenny Wright were getting better all the time and they both had satchels and wore straight skirts and nylons and never smiled and I heard the Guv telling Milly that they were turning into fine young ladies. Drip Williams and Maurice were taking the exam at Christmas and they started working harder and it made me nervous to be sitting so close to them and enjoying History and Geography and writing stories when they were creasing their foreheads and moaning and scribbling sums that I couldn't do. But then the evenings got warmer and I could go out and I was glad we weren't getting homework like the others.

Charlie was working with his shirt off now and he looked

more like a boxer than before. He had muscles in his chest and back as well as his arms and somehow I found out he was Maltese and one morning he had a black eye.

'I spent ten bob on Saturday night.' He was leaning back against the school-garden wall one lunch time.

'Crikey, what on?'

'Pictures with a girl. Box'a chocolates for her and some fags for me an' a cuppa tea after.'

'That doesn't leave much for the rest of the week, does it?'

'No.' He brushed his fingers over his moustache. 'I'm only on one pound ten a week. Apprentice.'

'Where d'ya get that black eye?'

'Had a fight Friday night. Bloke from Bognor. Good he was but I got him on points.'

'Did it hurt?'

'No not much. Here d'you wanna come to pictures one night?'

'Dunno. When?'

'Saturday night. We're gonna see *Zulu*.'

'I can't. There's a Coronation social up at the Club.'

'Well, come Wednesday night. We go again on Wednesday in the one and nines.'

'One and nine! They'll never give me that much.'

'That's all right, you'll get in for ninepence. But you need to meet me outside cos it's an "A".'

'Yeah, all right. I'll see what me mum says. I gotta go now. There's the whistle.'

As soon as I sat down I regretted it and wanted to run and tell Charlie I couldn't go. Drip and Maurice were beavering away and Godfrey was working out sums and drawing lines with his ruler and going over on to new pages as if he was a machine. I got my old book out and looked at where I'd got to and checked it against Drip's book. He was twenty-three pages further on than me and I sat sweating over some percentages I'd done before until I made one come out right but when I tried it with money I finished up with more than I'd started with and if I went out with Charlie and to the social and kept playing in the evenings and dreaming at school I'd never catch up but if I tried I still couldn't understand so there didn't seem much point. By the time it

was quarter to four I was nearly in tears and all I wanted
was to run away up into the woods and lie down and go to
sleep and wake up without a memory but I just went and sat
in the hedge behind Nan's woodpile until I was hungry and
then I went home for tea.

They'd bought me some new trousers for the Coronation
social and a white shirt with a big collar that almost covered
my tie when I pulled the knot tight and a blue blazer with
silver buttons that Dad'd got from a man at work whose son
had grown out of it. I felt in all the pockets but I only found a
bus ticket.

'That fits very well, Simon. You pleased with it?'

'M'm, it's all right, Mum.'

'Well, you could be a bit more enthusiastic. And hold still
while I straighten your tie.'

'Could I wear it to the pictures then?'

'Pictures. What pictures?'

'In Chichester. Charlie asked me. You know. Charlie Milo
that's working up at the school.'

'When, for heaven's sake?'

'Wednesday.'

'Oh, Simon.' She sat down on one of the dining chairs and
drew me up to her. 'Why do you spring things like this on us?
You won't stand an earthly of getting to the High School if
you start chasing around with people twice your age and
filling your head with pictures nonsense. And I don't like the
idea of you going off into Chichester on your own.'

'Well, I won't be on my own, Mum. I'll be with Charlie.'

'But we don't know him, Simon. He might be anybody.'
She held me away from her with her hands on my hips.

'Well *I* know him, Mum.'

'Oh really, Simon. I don't know. Beats me why you want
to. We'll have to speak to your daddy about it. But you'd
better get off there now or you'll be late.' She saw me out to
the gate and across the road to Jimmy Phillips's house. 'And
mind you're not late, Simon.'

Mum and Dad didn't want to go to the social and said
they were 'perfectly content with their own home, thank you'

and they didn't see the need to keep going off to socials and pubs but they said they had no objection to my going so long as I stayed with Mr and Mrs Phillips and came back with them. Mr Phillips looked smart in a tweed sports-jacket and white shirt with a red tie, light grey flannels and brown suede shoes and his tanned face and short pointed nose and brush of grey hair made him look like a snowy owl. Mrs Phillips had a light pink frock on with a darker pink collar and cuffs and a wide band round her middle tied in a massive bow at the back. It came tight at the middle and flared out at her knees so that she looked like a Christmas cracker. She had some little pink sandles that her feet bulged out of and when she'd finished turning and twisting in the mirror she stuffed them in a big pink handbag and put her wellies on.

It seemed as if the whole village was going to the social. Lights were flicking off and front doors were slamming and garden gates were clicking all up the Close and down Crouch Cross Lane and by the time we got to the hall there was a real crowd.

'Is it right there's free cider tonight, Jim?'

'Think so. Gibbser said there was.'

'Think we'll get any?'

'Dunno. They'll probably give us lemonade. You ever had cider?'

'Yeah, course I have. My nan gives it to me.'

'Move along then, you boys.' Mr Phillips pushed Jimmy forward.

'What's it like?'

'Nice. Tastes appley and fizzy. I expect they'll give us some for a toast.'

'What's a toast?'

'Don't you know?' I raised my eyebrows to Mr Phillips in the light from the hall doorway but he was looking over my head. 'It's a special drink you have when you say Happy Birthday or Cheers or something. S'pect we'll have one tonight.'

'Why?'

'Why? Blimey, it's obvious, isn't it? It's because . . . so that . . . well, a bit like saying amen at the end of a prayer.'

'Oh.'

238

'I think I'll just go and change in the ladies, Fred. I'll see you inside.'

'Right.' Mr Phillips moved over into the space Mrs Phillips had left and she tramped down through the mud to the side entrance holding her pink frock up above the level of her wellingtons.

We moved forward till we were inside the warm smoky hall.

The whole of the roof had been thatched on the inside with fir branches and the walls were draped with Union Jacks and pictures of Queen Elizabeth and the Duke of Edinburgh, in naval uniform with loads of medals and ribbons, facing each other with a circle in between made out of '2nd June 1953'. In the middle of each wall was a picture of the golden coach and somebody'd painted the black horses in on sheets of cardboard. All the chairs had been set out in a double semi-circle round the walls with the gap up by the stage and they'd made a doorway of it with the two brass standards that stood in the church and their banners'd been dusted or shaken or something because we could see the colours in them where they hadn't been folded back properly. There were groups of people standing around talking and some of the little kids were playing chasing in their best clothes and sliding on the floor that'd been dusted with white stuff that looked like icing sugar.

A few of the chairs had handbags or caps on them but Colin Gander was the only one sitting down and he was right at the front by the stage and he looked daft because he had his hand on the seat next to him as if he thought somebody was going to pinch it.

'Going up with Gander, Jim?'

'Can do.'

He stepped carefully over the icing sugar. It was slippery.

'Where's Gibbser then?'

'Gone for a shit. And get off, Phillips, I'm saving this seat for 'im. 'e's bin out there for ages.'

'Has 'e? He's usually in and out like a dose of salts.'

'Ah, that's when 'e's 'ome. 'e's bin saving this one since yesterday. 'e reckons there's rats down 'is garden an' 'e always goes when 'e's out if 'e can.'

'Why didn't he go at your place then?'

'Cor.' Colin wrinkled his nose. 'You must be joking.'

'Oh.'

' 'ere, keep our places a while. I wanna 'ave a slide before too many get 'ere.' Colin waited for us to sit down and then he took his coat off and dashed a few yards and pulled up sharp. His feet flew from under him and he shot feet first like an arrow and carved through the people at the inner door and disappeared into the hallway.

'Bet 'e'll say he meant to do that.'

We shifted over one as Gibbser came out through the curtains.

'Git orf ya thievin' beggars.' Geoff grabbed us by our ties.

'Git off y'self. We was savin' 'em for ya.'

'Where's Gander then . . . oh, there 'e is.'

Colin Gander was walking forward looking back and brushing behind him. 'Cor, you see that, Mush? It was smashing. I got right out through the door.'

'Yeah, but you didn't mean to.'

'Course I bloody meant to Phillips. 'ere give us a brush down.'

'What, was you slidin'? I could do that easy.' Geoff bent to push off but his toe must have hit a knot on a floorboard because he fell forwards and scythed through the people head first on his chest.

He came back holding his ear and he had Cedric Kyle and Bert Ball on either side of him and they told us that if we did any more big skids we'd be off home before it got started.

Geoff sat down looking sick. He told Colin he'd squashed his goolies and that if we laughed about it he'd do us and then he left Colin to look after his seat while he went out to see if they were all right.

The hall was nearly full now and almost all the seats were taken. Most of the boys were here but they were with their mums and dads and people had come from as far as Westhampnett halfway to Chichester. We sat looking to see what funny mums and dads some of the kids at our school had and then the curtains rolled back and the lights went out and Bert Ball who Grandad said'd kept the Men's Club going single-handed during the war, and always came to church when the Duke of Esher did, stepped forward into the

240

spotlight in a Union Jack waistcoat with his sleeves rolled up. There was an enormous cheer from the floor and an even bigger one when he turned round and showed he had a picture of John Bull on his back. He lifted his arms to make the cheering die down.

'We're 'ere to salute 'er Majesty.'

'Hooray.' Somebody blew a whistle.

'And we're gonna do it in style.'

More cheering.

'We got a sandwich buffet.'

Cries of 'goodo'.

'And me concert party.'

Cries of 'oh no'.

'And a bar.'

Loud cheers.

'And . . . from the Earl of Mayne . . . free cider!'

Wild cheering.

'We'll have a drink and some h'entertainment and then we've got games for the children and refreshments and the Sky Bohemians from Bosham for the dancing and a few songs to round things off.'

There'd been a rumbling sound outside in the passage while Mr Ball was speaking and a bump appeared in the curtain but he clapped his hands and we all looked back at him. 'But first Father Pope wants to . . . Father.' Mr Ball waved his hand down as if he was shaking out a paintbrush and melted backwards.

Pop stepped out into the spotlight. He had his black frock thing on with the high black collar that he wore for outside occasions and his hair shone like frosty cottonwool in the light. 'Dear heavenly Father . . .' we all stood up and put our hands together. 'We pray for peace and prosperity in this land and for our new Sovereign Queen Elizabeth. May she rule over us with wisdom and justice and grant us the peace of your Holy Spirit this night and for ever more. Amen.'

' 'men. Arm-en. 'en.'

The lights came on and somebody sat down and then everyone sat down and they leaned forward as the rumbling started again behind the curtain and Mr Tennant and Mr Brown came in pulling a barrel on a trolley on wheels.

'Blimey, is that full of cider?'

'Dunno.'

The barrel was about the size of one of Grandad's rainwater butts and it was lying on a nest of woodwork trestles that stood on a wooden cart on wooden wheels. Mr Brown took a small enamel dish hanging from the back of the barrel and put it on the floor and they wheeled the barrel forward so that the front came over the dish and then he passed Mr Tennant a gimlet and a wooden hammer.

'What they doing?'

'Taking the bung out.'

'It'll go everywhere.' Geoff Gibbs was craning forward. 'They must be mad. It'll never go in that saucer.'

Mr Tennant knelt down and Mr Brown stood next to him with something in his hand. Mr Tennant screwed the gimlet, did a test pull and heaved. Mr Brown knelt beside him. Mr Tennant leant close over the cork again and for a moment they looked as if they were praying to the barrel. Mr Tennant heaved again and there was a plop and a splash and then Mr Brown jammed another cork with a tap on it into the hole. He tapped the nose of the tap with the wooden mallet and turned the handle until a clear flow came out and they both stood up.

Everyone clapped and Mr Ball came forward with a clean tea towel and they wiped their hands. He told Mr Tennant and Mr Brown he'd never seen it done better and invited them to take the first drink but old Digger Payton near us was shaking his head and saying to some of the old men that they'd lost the knack nowadays because everything came in bottles.

Mrs Pargetter and Mrs Latteral and some other ladies lined up with trays and Mr Tennant poured out pints of cider and Mr Ball stood up on the trestle behind the barrel and told everybody to sit down and the ladies'd serve them. There were some little glasses amongst the big ones from the Anglesey and I noticed they gave them to children down to about eleven. We'd either all get one or none at all.

It took ages for them to give everybody a drink and when we heard bumps and whispers from behind the curtain which had been closed again, Geoff Gibbs stuck his head under it to see what was going on but somebody brushed it back again with a broom.

242

'Bloody fool could've blinded me.' Geoff rubbed at his eye. ' 'ere, seen this, Mush?' He pulled his tie out of his pullover and we huddled round him.

'Cor, where'd you get it?'

'Bet she'd get cold when the frost set in!'

'It's me uncle's. He got it in Pompey. It's a spiv's tie.'

'Your uncle a spiv then, Gibbser?'

'Watch it, Nipper. Don't you let 'im 'ear.'

'I suppose you lot want one.' Mrs Pargetter's tray was above us and we drew back so that she could lower it. 'Rheally, Geoffrey. Shameless hussy! Put that away at once. Well, do you?'

'Cor, yes please.' Our hands darted around looking for the biggest one.

'Drink it slowly. It's quite strong so they say and you need to keep some for later.'

It didn't look very strong. It was almost clear except for a few bits floating about in it and it wasn't fizzy at all and it just tasted sweet. Bladder Payton drained his glass and put it back on Mrs Pargetter's tray and took another one and winked at her.

'Nice droppa scrump, Bert?' Wobble Terry nodded at his glass.

'Not bad at all.' Mr Alderton who played the organ in church looked quite different with a beer mug in his hand. 'These nippers'll have to watch it.'

Wobble looked down at us and they walked away.

'Bleedin' gnats piss this is.' Geoff Gibbs drank his off.

'I don't like it.' Jimmy curled his lip.

'Gis it then.' Geoff's hand shot out and he grabbed the glass.

Colin Gander's dad came over and put his glass on the stage and rolled a cigarette. He'd put lavender hair-cream on and I smelt it as he bent to pick up a match. He lit his cigarette and then took a sip and screwed his face up.

'Blimey, it's like treacle. Here d'you lot want it?'

'Yes please.' Gibbser held his empty glass out and Mr Gander filled it up and gave me and Colin some. 'Get'm to rinse this sugar-water out and get a nice pint of mild. Too sweet for me.'

'This is all right, ain't it?' Geoff's eyes were sparkling wet and he was grinning as the lights flicked off and the curtains opened and we sat round towards the stage.

'Right. Quiet everyone.' Mr Ball held his arms out until people stopped talking. He was done up in a sheet and some white painters' overalls and white wellingtons with a baker's white cap and some glasses and a face mask but we could see it was Mr Ball. 'We thought we'd do a sketch on the British Hempire this being a sort of landmark in the British Hempire but we couldn't get the British Hempire on this 'ere stage so we're gonna start off with a doctor scene so if yer at all squeamish you'd better 'ave some more scrump.'

The curtains closed again and the big light went off and a smaller one came on and, when the curtains opened, we could see somebody lying on a table behind a white sheet. The outline of two surgeons came up and cut him open and took lots of things out but I knew it couldn't be real because you couldn't swallow sausages whole without cutting where they joined together.

Then there was another sketch about a tramp and a rich farmer and then some tap dancing and Mrs Lane singing 'A Bird in a Gilded Cage' and then they all came together in their costumes and linked hands and sang 'Good Old Sussex by the Sea' and 'Land of Hope and Glory' until the curtain came swooshing across and we found ourselves blinking in the light.

'That was good, wasn't it, Si?'

'All right, I s'pose. I liked the funny bits more'n the singing.' Jimmy's shirt collar was up so I turned it down. 'Wish we could 'ave Guy Mitchell or something like that.'

'Does your dad let you listen to that, Simon?'

'Well . . . on "Family Favourites" and "Housewife's Choice" and that, 'e does.'

'Wonna listen to Luxemburg, don't 'e, Gibbser?'

'Yeah.' Geoff stuck his head forward as he spoke. 'Got any more'a that cider?'

'Get a drop when you go up for food.' Colin was looking towards the hatch as a queue formed. 'We'd better get in there else it'll all be gone.'

There were sandwiches and quarters of eggs and little sausages and sardines on boat-shaped bits of toast and tubs of potato salad and jars of celery and plates of cut ham and corned beef. They let us help ourselves to sandwiches and stuff but Mrs Latteral smacked Colin's fingers with a fish-slice when he went to take some meat and she said we could have one piece each and she would help us to it. We had to wait in the line because Geoff Gibbs stacked his plate until there wasn't any more room on it but old Cedric Kyle stopped him and made him put some back.

'Gish novver drink, Col.' Geoff sounded as if he'd had a tooth out.

'Do you think they'll let us have any more?'

Mrs Latteral heard me and called 'Get these boys another drop of cider, Win. They've only had one little glass each so far.'

Mrs Pargetter wasn't walking as fast as she had at first and was carrying her tray in both hands in front of her instead of on one hand at shoulder level. 'Can't they help themselves? They've got glasses and surely they can turn a tap on?' She stopped in front of Bladder Payton as his hand reached out across her. 'Not another one, Henry. You go on at this rate and you'll burst and we'll all drown.'

We put our plates down on the edge of the stage and Colin and I took two glasses each to the barrel and filled them. When we got back Geoff Gibbs'd found four more and he waited a while and then made Jimmy Phillips go with him. We put the full glasses under our chairs and sipped the others and watched the little kids playing Pass the Parcel and Musical Chairs with old Digger Payton playing his squeeze-box and then they put some chairs in a circle and played Squeak Piggy, Squeak until Mr Ball appeared on the stage with his bow-tie crooked and one shirtsleeve rolled up and the other flapping and called out that if they didn't start the dancing soon the Sky Bohemians'd fly off back to Bosham. The Sky Bohemians didn't wait for him to finish speaking but struck up a tango and the women hauled the men out on to the floor.

'Bloody 'ell. Dancing!' Colin chewed on a sandwich and dropped the crust down behind his chair. 'I hate dancing.'

The way he said it made me laugh and I couldn't stop even when I began choking on a piece of sausage. I was still laughing and spluttering sausage when Susan Farley came to ask me for a dance but when she saw how I was laughing, she walked straight past me and asked Colin instead. The way he said 'get lost' without moving his lips started me off again. She turned to Geoff next but he just sat there grinning and licking his lips so she sat down again. The way I couldn't stop laughing was beginning to make people look at me so I went out to the toilet.

Mr Alderton was doing up his flies as I went in. He watched me as he washed his hands.

'You're very flushed, Simon.'

'Bin laughing, Mr Alderton.'

'Had much cider?'

'Glass'n a half.'

'You want to be careful. It's pretty powerful stuff. Do you feel at all swimmy?'

'Dunno.' I did my buttons up and washed my hands because he was still watching me.

He came up behind me. 'Here bend forward.'

'Why?'

'Because I'm going to put cold water on the back of your neck.'

'You'll get my shirt wet.'

'No I won't. Here, I'll do it with the corner of the towel.' He wet the towel and wrung it and folded it across my neck.

It took my breath away and the two pairs of eyes I could see in the mirror came together.

'That better?'

'Cor yeah, it's nice. Leave it there a minute.'

'There's a good lad. Now you'd better just go outside for a few minutes. It's a lovely clear moonlight night and you'll feel better.'

'But I feel all right.'

'You take my tip, m'lad.' He led me to the side door. 'And take another one and don't have any more cider. In fact I think I'll tell them not to let the children have any more.'

'Thanks, Mr Alderton.'

I went out into the moonlight and let the cool air settle on my face. I felt as light as a feather as if I could run a mile at full tilt if I wanted to but I didn't want to. I was just going to

246

get back to my spare glass of cider before Gibbser got at it when someone behind me said 'Simon'.

I couldn't see who it was until she came out from the glare of the side door. 'Hello, Susan.'

'Are you all right?' She had her blond hair in a pony-tail and a long white dress with black spots and a little jacket made out of the same stuff that did up at the front.

I'd been shy of Susan ever since we'd been in the ammunition store together when we were still in the Infants because I'd never really known why she'd run away and I'd never liked her enough to pluck up the courage to ask her. But she looked so lovely as she came towards me that I felt myself lifted above it and standing over her.

'Yes. I just came out for some fresh air. It's smoky in there.' I took in a deep breath and held it the way Dad did when he was football training.

'Are you with your mum and dad, Simon?' Susan was standing next to me and slightly behind me.

'No. I came with Jimmy Phillips. Are you?'

'No. Daddy brought me up and I'm staying at Pauline Tennant's house tonight.'

'What, sleeping there?'

'Yes.' Her face was up to me and the yellow moon glow cast a shadow from her nose over her cheek. 'Yes I am.'

I leant back and sideways and she came forward and her shoulder fitted my armpit and my arm rested easily along the top of her back and my fingers felt her skin where her short sleeve ended and I rested my cheek on her head. Her hair was soft and smelt of Vaseline shampoo.

'Didn't know you were friendly with Tenny.'

'Her dad works with my daddy.'

'Why didn't you go to the do down the camp then?'

Her head tilted a bit and I re-rested my cheek. 'They work together in the store.'

'Oh yeah. But why didn't—'

'So I can stay here until they all go home.'

'Oh that's good but—'

'Oh listen. They're playing "Moonlight Serenade". That's lovely. Come and dance with me.'

She'd stepped round to the front of me and her legs and

tummy had to press against me because she was shorter than I was and she had to bend back to look up at me and her pony-tail hung down and tickled my fingers.

'But I can't dance.'

'Course you can. It's only waltzing and I've seen you doing that at school. Come on.'

She let her hand drop down my side and it fell into my hand and I let her lead me back through the side door into the swirling half light that came from the stage out on to the floor. Couples were drifting by with sleepy grins on their faces, like Mr Peters when he was praying to himself at the end of the service, and we picked our way into the middle. Susan held her arms ready and I took her round the waist with one arm and held her hand with the other and we slid our feet together. The music swirled over and around us and I could feel her close to me as if we were swimming joined together in a small jar of water and when it stopped we stayed together but the next one was a polka and Bladder Payton and a big lady from Hanover went crashing about like elephants through a cornfield so we sat down. Jimmy Phillips had moved over to the other side.

'What you doing over here, Jim?'

He screwed his face up and pointed. The chairs had been put straight and there was a big wet patch on the floor. I stood aside and let Susan in first and we sat down in the row behind Jimmy.

'What happened?'

'Gibbser. He drank another three glasses and was sick all over—'

'And where's Colin?'

'. . . all over Gander. He kept—'

'Yeah, all right, Jim.' I'd felt Susan wince.

'And it smells terrible over there.' Jimmy sniffed at his pullover. 'Want a sandwich?'

'No thanks, Jim.'

'Drink?'

'No, I think I could do with some fresh air.'

Susan held my hand as we walked out but if anybody'd looked I doubt if they'd have seen because most of them were doing the Blue Danube with their eyes closed and the others were sitting in huddles talking and drinking.

248

The moon was so big it looked as if it was only a couple of miles up in the sky. We walked with our heads back looking at it and my feet felt as if they were treading on spongy rubber.

'Where're you taking me?' Susan stopped and our arms were stretched as if I was pulling her. We'd got to the fir trees that ran along the edge of the playing field.

'I dunno. Sorry, I was dreaming.'

'It's lovely, isn't it?' Susan came closer and rested her head on my shoulder.

'Yeah.' I folded my arm along behind her neck and down her arm.

'There was a story once when I was little about an owl that used to gaze at the moon and want to fly to it but he wasn't strong enough. I don't remember it very well but he got a sixpence and melted it down and stretched it to the moon and walked to it like on a tightrope.'

'How did he get it there in the first place?'

'I dunno. Never thought about that. P'raps it was a dream.'

I felt her head move and her hair on my cheek. 'Oh, Simon, you are funny.'

'Am I. Why?'

'You're so dreamy when you're on your own and . . .'

'And what?'

She'd turned and was facing me and her face was glowing yellow as if she was made out of gold and she looked Egyptian. 'Do you taste of that horrible cider?'

'Don't think so. Didn't have much. Why?'

'You've never kissed me. You almost did once.'

'Yeah.' I slid my arms around her and joined my fingers at her back and she lay against me. 'We were only little then.'

'Well, we're eleven now.' Her tongue parted her lips.

The soft fir branches brushed my face and the warm scent of the pine needles closed over us.

The music had stopped when we got back but the doors were still open.

My head ached as if my skull was being stretched and I felt as if a horse had kicked me in the stomach. I kept looking

249

at Susan to see if she was any different but she didn't seem to be and clung on to my hand and smiled and I had to force my mouth and cheeks into a smile back at her. The hall had emptied while we'd been out and those that were left were sitting round the cider barrel with their glasses. A drawing pin had come out of one of the cut-outs of the black horses and it looked as if Queen Elizabeth and Prince Philip were going to nose-dive down the wall in the royal coach.

'You do love me, don't you, Simon?'

'What?'

'You do love me?'

'Oh . . . yeah.' I was watching the people around the barrel. Either they were spinning or I was or p'raps we all were. I felt Susan pulling me and followed her with my feet angled outwards as if I was roller-skating around the rim of a saucer. A girl called Margaret Maylor's dad was rocking backwards and forwards and trying to sing with his arm round her little brother, and then we went outside.

I held on to Susan's hand all the way down the road but she kept falling away and then bumping back into me and I started to laugh and couldn't stop and I gave her an extra hard pull to bump into me again but she missed and I spun round up against Grandad's fence. She took me all the way home and leant me against the gate and I watched the moon rolling from side to side and I rolled my head with it and when I looked around she'd gone and it sounded as if someone up the road was crying quietly in the dark.

Mum just stared at me when I got home and she gave me a drink of orange and hustled me off to bed. She'd looked at Dad as we went through the living room, as if the house'd caught fire but she didn't say anything.

When I woke up it was pitch black and I felt as if I was still in a dream. I was standing in a pool of moonlight that led away like a path into the trees and as I got closer to it I smelt the appley smell of Susan's hair and the musty stinging green of the pine needles and the walls of my stomach felt as if they'd collapsed on to broken glass and I dreamt we'd been seen and chased until I woke up again and wrapped an elastic band round my fingers so that the throbbing kept me awake.

All through Sunday I felt something was going to happen. I went up to look at the hall but it hadn't burnt down and I stayed away from the fir trees in case anybody saw me and remembered seeing me going in there with Susan and I rubbed Marmite into my pants where they had spots of blood on them so that Mum'd think I'd had them on back to front. I didn't know where it'd come from but I guessed she'd find out and I'd finish up in trouble again. Then I heard they'd taken Geoff Gibbs to hospital with a suspected twisted gut and Dad made a fuss about grown men who should know better than to feed whompo to children and Mum said I was a precious lamb and shouldn't have to watch out for such things. I felt worse on Monday morning and, as I waited at the side of the road until the bread van stopped before I crossed over, I thought it was because I was scared of seeing Susan again but when Jerry Henry came dashing up behind us I knew something else'd happened.

' 'ere, Mush.' He rushed straight in between Geoff and Colin. 'You 'erd the latest? Old Ernie Henty was telling my mum.'

The stabbing feeling was in my stomach again.

'Old Margaret Maylor's mum and dad got drunk as lords Saturday night and they were swaying about all over the Eathram Road when a car came round the corner and hit 'er little brother. Fractured 'is skull. 'e's in 'ospital in a coma.'

'Go away, 'enery. You're always 'avin us on.' Colin pushed Jerry off. 'You didn't see 'im in there, did you, Gibbser?'

'No I didn't.' Geoff was still looking green. 'And don't keep on about that.'

'Course he didn't.' Jerry put his tie straight and walked half backwards in front of Geoff and Colin. 'Cos they took 'im to the special 'ospital in Pompey.'

They didn't believe Jerry but I did and when we got to school and saw Milly's black armband we knew it was true.

There was a lot of talk in the village about how wicked it was to get drunk and Pop preached a special sermon about it but when I closed my eyes to pray I could only think about what it would be like to have had a little brother and for him to get killed and it made me so angry that I went up behind the toilets after school and punched the boards with my fists until I skinned my knuckles and Grandad had to stick the shreds of skin back together with Vaseline and bandage them.

Charlie Milo had to go to learn building on Mondays but I stood talking to him by the gate after school on Tuesday. Dad hadn't been at all sure about me going to the pictures with him when I said I'd skinned my knuckles on a sack of newspapers learning to box and he'd said he was a bad influence and he was going to see Milly about it tonight on his way home from work. Charlie'd got another black eye sparring on Friday and I worked him away from the road in case Dad saw him.

'It was an accident.' Half of Charlie's face smiled. The bump that almost closed his eye was the size of an egg. 'I hit this bloke in the stomach and his head caught me as he doubled up. My own fault you could say. Lucky it didn't break the skin. What you done to your hand?'

'Got in a temper and bashed the bog wall. You gonna teach me, Charlie?'

'That's the first thing you've got to learn. Losing your temper's like giving a free hit. You might as well close your eyes.'

He scraped at some loose gravel in the bottom of the trench with his shovel and then took a soft swipe at it with his pickaxe. 'I'd better take this down another few inches. You coming tomorrow?'

'Dunno, Charlie. I'll find out tonight.'

'Well, if you're coming, I'll see you outside the Gaumont at half past six.'

'Yeah, I expect I'll be there. Bye.'

I drew a stick along the school railings and watched where it left a mark against the black paint on each one as it rat-tat-tatted along and when I got to the end I looked to see how straight the line was by bending down and looking along so that I could see enough of each rail to make it look like a solid wall of black. Nurse McLaine's dog rushed out like a hairy dumpling and started yapping at me through a hole in her hedge so I threw my stick at him like a spear and

252

it stuck in the ground just in front of him. Grandad was digging at the bottom of his garden where we used to plant cabbages and sprouts. He was digging very slowly and the spade went in and lifted and turned and the earth fell off and he'd lean forward and shake the dirt off the bigger weeds and toss them backwards into the wheelbarrow and prod at the lumps until the soil was crumbly and then move down a step and dig again.

'Hello, Simon.'

He'd straightened with his foot on the spade and turned with his hand resting on the spade handle.

'Hello, Grandad. What you planting this year?'

'Brassica.'

'What's that?'

'Winter kale . . . sort of cabbage.'

'Sounds 'orrible.'

'Good for you. Puts muscles in your spit.'

'Oh does it? Bye then, Grandad!'

'You off then?'

Something in the way he said it made me want to turn back but the boys said it was sissy to hang around your mum and dad and grandad so I didn't even look back. I tried spitting with muscle in it a couple of times and I wished I had a cold to make it more clogged up but then Mrs Latterel caught me up and told me to stop it and that it was a disgusting habit.

Dad overtook me on his bike at the top of the Close and I ran to keep up with him.

'You're late home, Simon. Where've you been?'

'Up the school talking to Charlie and then Grandad.'

'Oh yes. I've been to see Mr Miller about the amount of time you're spending with him.'

'Nothing wrong with it, is there?'

'Well I dunno. But going off to the pictures at night's a different matter.'

'What's the verdict then?'

'We'll talk inside. And don't speak to me in that off-hand way.' He speeded up but I still kept pace with him and beat him in through the gate and was indoors sitting down before he'd put his bike away.

'Stuck here waiting for you both until nearly a quarter

past six and then you both turn up at once.' Mum felt the tea pot and then put the cosy back on.

'It's not ten past yet, Mum, and that clock's fast.'

'Not much it's not.'

'But it is fast.'

'Oh don't be so argumentative, Simon, and take your shoes off in the house. How many times do I have to tell you?'

I scuffed my shoes off without undoing the laces, but then I heard them coming from the kitchen so I undid the laces and put them neatly in the fender to dry.

They came in together with their heads up high as if I was something they didn't want to see. Dad pulled his chair out and then made it straight with the table and lifted the overhangs of the cloth as he sat down. If Milly'd said he didn't think I should go, they'd have said so straight out. Dad straightened his knife up next to his plate and Mum stared at me as she rinsed the tea leaves out of her cup into the slop bowl.

'It's a good film, Mum.'

'Tea, dear?' She held Dad's cup out to him.

'Thank you. Stirred?'

'Yes.'

I clenched my fist. 'Mum?'

'Bread and butter?'

'Thank you.'

'Gawd'n Bennett.' I gritted it through my teeth.

'I think it's a bit much so soon after that late night up at the hall, don't you think, dear?'

'M'm.' Dad never spread jam with the side of his knife. He scratched lines of it with the end.

'A lovely night at the social that would have kept most boys of his age quiet for months.'

'They're never satisfied nowadays.'

'Would you sit up please, Simon?'

I sat up.

'They certainly do seem to expect a lot.' Dad was still scratching with the end of his knife and there were just shreds of jam against the pale yellow of the butter.

'And what time is he expecting to be home for heaven's

sake, I'd like to know?'

I said 'bleedin' midnight' to myself and took a piece of bread and butter and jammed my knife into the jam pot.

Dad chewed fast and swallowed and choked out 'bl—rewth alive!' and pointed at my bread and swallowed again. 'Put some of that back, Simon. What the devil you think you're playing at?'

'Well, I wanna taste it, Dad.'

'Bloomin' pig. You've got half a pot there. You just want a little dab.' He pointed at his half slice. 'See.'

'Can't, Dad.'

'Why not?'

'Nothin' *to* see.'

Dad clicked his tongue against the roof of his mouth and Mum said 'huh'.

'Really. The way he speaks to us nowadays, George. It's a wonder he speaks to us at all. Let alone ask for anything.'

'Well, you wouldn't like it if I'd just gone without saying anything.'

'You're jolly right we wouldn't.' Mum stopped with her knife halfway through her bread. 'And if you don't keep a civil tongue in your head, you won't go at all, my lad.'

'Oh good. Does that mean I can go?'

Mum stared at me and then sat up straighter. 'I don't know. Ask your father.'

'Can I, Dad?'

'Beats me why you want to go at all. I haven't been once since the war and I haven't missed it. And I never went when I was your age. Certainly not on my own.'

'Well, they didn't have flicks in them days and I'm not going on my own, I'm going with Charlie.'

'What do you mean "didn't have pictures". Course we did. And don't get into that Americanised way of talking. We used to watch Charlie Chaplin and Buster Keaton and the Crazy Gang and . . . who was that other one, Ina?'

'Abbott and Costello?'

'No. They were later. Cor, stone the crows, what was his name? Jack something or other.'

'Keystone Cops, Dad.'

'No, Simon. There was them but that's not who I'm

255

thinking of. Blessed annoying when it's on the tip of your tongue.'

I sat and waited and Mum's arm lowered where she was holding Dad's empty cup out in front of him but he didn't notice when she rattled it so she filled it without asking him.

'I *will* think of it sometime, I s'pose.'

'In the meantime *who is* this Charlie man you're so all-fired fond of all of a sudden, Simon?'

'It's not all of a sudden, Mum. I've known him for ages and his name's Charlie Milo.'

'Well, what's he want with you? He's ever so much older than you, Simon. It all sounds fishy to me. And he's . . . well, he's not English.'

'No, he's Maltese, Mum.'

'There you are, George.'

'M'm, Maltese. The Messina brothers're Maltese and they're a proper pair of 'erberts from what I can see of it in the paper.'

'Well they're gangsters, Dad, and he's nothing like them. And he's not that much older than me. He's only eighteen.'

'Eighteen!' Mum put her hand to her mouth. 'Oh, whatever can he want with him?'

'P'raps he'd've liked to have had a brother as well, Mum.'

'What do you think, George?'

'H'm.' Dad'd been stirring his tea as if he'd forgotten he was doing it.

'What'd Mr Miller say?'

'That he seems a nice enough bloke. Didn't seem to think there was anything funny about it. Didn't have any real objections.'

'But didn't he think it was strange?'

'We-ell, a bit p'raps, but— Got it!' Dad dabbed his spoon down in his cup and leant forward with his hands on the table. 'Will Hay. It was Will Hay. Proper character he was, Simon. Went in for all sorts of stunts, climbing along cranes and up on the top of trains and all kinds of capers. He was never as big as Charlie Chaplin and some of the rest of them and he seemed to go off the boil all of a sudden but that's who I was thinking of.'

'Oh was it, Dad?' I'd never heard of him and he didn't

sound very funny but he seemed to have put Dad in a good mood.

'Well, what about it, George?'

'What's that, my Ine?'

'This blessed pictures business. Shall we let him go?'

'Don't see why not. So long as he behaves himself.'

'I will Dad and thanks.' I got up and slung my arms round him.

'Steady on, Nip. You'll spill my tea.'

'Well, I shall worry the entire time, Simon.' Mum was biting at the inside of her lip. 'And you're to catch the quarter to ten bus home and heaven help you if you're a minute late.'

I walked past Colin Gander's house on the way to the bus but I didn't see any of the boys until I got to the stop by the school. They were up by the hall and when I stepped out into the road to stop the bus, Gibbser yelled out something about a pro getting hold of me in Chichester and they all laughed.

Inside the bus, I got my ticket from the conductor who was sitting on the long seat downstairs and went upstairs. There was nobody else there so I laid out my flashy red tie and the piece of toilet paper I'd put some Brylcreem in on the seat next to me. I used the reflection in the window as a mirror and put my tie on and pulled it and pushed it till it looked like a Windsor knot and then I scraped the Brylcreem off the paper and smeared it on the front of my hair. I combed and combed from Westhampnett to Chichester to try to get it to go back but it kept springing up and falling forward so I combed it flat sideways and smeared it down with spit. Now my hands felt horrible so I rubbed them with an old paper bag I found up at the front until we got to St Pancras and then I got off.

I crossed over opposite Stevey Bacon's clothes shop and walked along to the Gaumont. It was twenty-five past six and Charlie wasn't there. There were pictures from the film outside on a sort of three-sided box on the wall but it didn't look very good: just lots of tables with food on and trollies and cushions. Then I saw the word 'restaurant' and realised they were pictures of a café or something upstairs and that the real pictures were down the sides. Coming next week was the *Sioux Indians Uprising* with Captain Custer firing both his guns at masses of Indians with three arrows in his back and I wished it was on this week. The pictures of *Zulu* weren't nearly as good, they were all of black men dancing except for one of a little camp of white men with columns of Zulus marching across the plain towards them and I thought I recognised it and when I read the writing underneath and saw it was Rorkes Drift I got excited and wondered why they hadn't called it *Rorkes Drift* in the first place.

'All spivved up then?'

I turned and stood up straighter. 'Hello, Charlie.'

Charlie bent at the knees to look in the glass and pulled his comb through his hair which was shiny and black and his DA folded in at the middle instead of sticking out like a cox's comb like Gibbser's did when Dorothy Newton did it for him. He resettled his padded shoulders and hitched his trousers up to show his yellow socks. 'Better be getting in, hadn't we?'

'Reckon so.' I tried to do something with my jacket but it wouldn't stay up so I hitched my shoulders.

'Got your money?'

'Yes.'

'Let's have it then.'

'What, all of it?'

'No.' He took ninepence out of my hand. 'Just your picture money. I'll have to get you in.'

Charlie kept his hand on my shoulder as we got our tickets but he let go of me as we went through the curtains. I bumped into him in the dark and then a light shone on the tickets in the palm of his hand and we followed it right down to the front until it felt as if the screen was a black and white wave that was going to break over us. I pushed past legs and grunts of ' 'lo Charlie' and sank under Charlie's hand into a seat. I tried to watch the pictures of the Coronation but I was half watching the leg that was draped half across me and up on to the seat in front because it belonged to a very big man cleaning his fingernails with a knife and he had the longest DA I'd ever seen. 'And the Coronation year Cup Final also lived up to expectation. The 1953 Wembley show piece . . .' I sat forward and watched Stanley Matthews beating Bolton but it was over in a flash and two ladies with big fur collars sat down in front of me and the man next to me dropped his leg down so that I had to sit sideways and look between them. The picture broke up into an exploding circle and a cockerel's head came out of the middle and crowed and then there were some adverts and what Charlie called the trailer. It made the Indian film look good but just as I got interested it stopped and the screen went blank and the curtains came across.

'Has it broken, Charlie?'

'No. Hasn't started yet. You get two films. This is what's on with it.'

'Is it a cowboy film?'

'No, gangsters.'

'Oh. That's all right.'

The curtain peeled back and lots of writing came up about who'd done the wardrobe and the hairstyles and photography and things and then it was just a picture of a river through a town with smoke and mist over it and a man in a raincoat in a doorway and I knew something was going to happen that Mum and Dad wouldn't want me to see. The music went low and shadowy with a warning shivery bit coming in and out like hot Oxo on a bad tooth. The film showed two feet walking along a cobbled pavement and treading in puddles and then it showed a cat all hunched up and then there was a jump and screams and running footsteps and I couldn't see what had happened but the music pounded away and I held on to the back of the seat in front of me until my knuckles hurt and the lady turned round and said if I wanted to sit next to her I could but to leave her back alone. I didn't know if she was angry or not but her lipstick was so thick and shiny that I couldn't see how she could be very nice and she might be one of the ones who'd try to get me in a corner Mum'd told me about when we went to the Festival of Britain. Two men came out through the curtains under the TOILETS sign. They stopped and one spoke to the other and walked past the screen and the other came into the same row from the other end and sat down next to the girl in front of me. The girls parted and bent towards the men and I could see between them. A man in a raincoat and slouch hat parted some bead curtains with one hand and raised his other hand inside his mac pocket. Then the camera moved on to the face of a Chinaman frying some eggs.

'Bang.'

'Got 'im,' came a voice from behind me.

The Chinaman crumpled up and fell sideways and pulled the frying-pan off the cooker.

'There goes your breakfast, Charlie.' The man next to me changed legs and I pulled in closer.

'I'm Maltese not bloody Chinese.' Charlie yawned and stretched.

'Shurrup you lot.' The girl in front of me half-turned. 'Some of us are trying to watch the film.'

'No, you're not. You're watching where Gary's 'ands're goin'.'

I tried to watch the screen but the two couples were kissing so hard and making such a noise that I couldn't keep my eyes off them.

'Big picture'll be on in a minute.'

'Do you think they'll watch then, Charlie?'

'They'll have to watch it if old Alice's boy-friend turns up.'

The two heads in front of Charlie parted. 'You mind your own business, Charlie Milo. He's not my boy-friend and he's doing a removal up to London anyway.'

'Not when I came out at quarter past six, he wasn't.'

The four heads came together in front of us and then the four of them got up and left.

'Is her boy-friend really coming, Charlie?' I could imagine the man next to me getting involved in a fight and what Mum'd say if I got stabbed.

'I dunno.' Charlie stretched out and stared at the screen. 'Doesn't matter. At least I can see now.'

The man in the raincoat was getting away in a stolen car and he was shooting back at a police car. He swerved round a corner and hit a dustbin and the car skidded and overturned and everything went quiet. Just one wheel spun through the smoke. The big man next to me refolded his *Sporting Life* and licked his pencil.

'Do any today?'

'Got a third at Doncaster. Didn't cover me bet.'

'Put a coupla bob on me for Friday night.'

'Who ya fighting?'

'Bloke called Tommy Green from Selsey.'

'Dunno about that, Charlie. He's a bit 'ard.'

'You know him?' Charlie sat forward and round me.

'Yeah, his old man's a fisherman. He's hard. Dirty too.'

'Ah well.' Charlie smiled and settled down again. 'Worry about that on the night.'

The lights came up and the curtains closed and I looked around while Charlie got us both an ice cream. There were a lot of people of Charlie's age in the first few rows and then a wide space of empty seats and then lots of older people. The lights faded in the ceiling as Charlie gave me a choice of a tub or a choc ice and I chose the tub and dropped the spoon. It was all dust and cigarette ends under the seat and the man next to me asked me 'what I was ferreting about after' when I said 'excuse me' and he got angry and shifted his legs out the other way. I couldn't find my spoon so I made a scoop out of the carton top until it went soggy and then I drank the ice cream when it melted.

Rorkes Drift didn't look at all like its description in my book of *Daring Deeds* and my eyes went glazed looking up at the Technicolor. We were so close to the screen that I could see the dots in the film that made up the picture and they fuzzed and fused together and the voices didn't really come out of the people's mouths and I kept looking back because it sounded as if it was coming from behind me and I thought I could see somebody there who looked like Grandad. The Zulus' bare feet beat up and down in the dust as they worked themselves up into a frenzy. They must have had very hard feet because it nearly crippled me when I trod on a thistle in bare feet and the spikes on some of the bushes they'd shown at the start were like nails and even if they didn't have any in their camp they'd be bound to tread on some as they ran across the hills and plains to Rorkes Drift.

The picture moved out, as if it was being carried on the drum beat, towards a sunset of rolling furrows of fire in the sky and the wooden beat went hollow and distant and then the picture dropped and we saw Rorkes Drift in the distance and it drew closer as if we were going towards it in a Land Rover.

'They're coming this time, Lieutenant. There's a new sense of urgency in the drums.'

'Bloody rubbish.' The man next to me twisted in his seat. 'They'd never hear them at that distance.'

'Sound carries out there, John.' Charlie bit at his thumb and looked at where he'd bitten. 'The air's thin.'

'Urh.' John yawned and slumped further back in his seat and I went back to the film.

They'd drawn carts and water barrels across in between the wooden huts and the hospital was in the middle. In my book of *Daring Deeds* they hadn't done that: they'd just defended the hospital doorways with mealie bags and biscuit tins and there'd been one man with a broken leg who'd had his other leg broken as they dragged him out when the Zulus attacked and the roof fell in. We went inside the hospital. There weren't any mealie bags or biscuit tins and nobody with a broken leg. There was a pretty nurse there who dodged about dabbing the faces of men who hadn't shaved with a clean cloth that never got dirty but she hadn't been in my book at all. The Zulus all charged across the plain and I wished the people who'd made the film had read my book because in the book they crept up on the station at night and were there in the morning and some got right up close by crawling up a dried-up stream. Doing it this way they got shot down before they got within throwing distance of the station and they were throwing long spears whereas in my book they used short things called assagais that they could throw or stab with at close quarters and then they started to talk to each other in English and the nurse started kissing one of the officers so I got up and went to the toilet.

I stood in front of the rows of marble sections where you had to go and couldn't go. They were always made by Shanks from Coventry and I couldn't understand how they got them so smooth. P'raps they had a special curved plane that cut marble. My hands were freezing cold and still sticky from the Brylcreem and the water in the tap was cold so they felt worse when I'd washed them than they did before. The towel was wringing wet so I finished them off with toilet paper.

'You missed a good bit.' Charlie drew his knees in. 'That lardy-dar lieutenant got a spear through the leg and now they've retreated.'

'Have they?' I sat down and watched the nurse who shouldn't have been there in the first place bandaging up the lieutenant's leg.

'How'd they get the spear out, Charlie?'

'I dunno. They didn't show. Why?'

'Well, they got a spike on them. You couldn't pull it back and you'd have to drag the handle through to get it out the other way.'

'Or cut it off.' John rolled his head my way. 'She's a bit of all right, eh Charlie?'

I looked back at the film. The nurse was crying to the lieutenant that she'd never loved anybody before and now she'd met the one she'd been waiting for they were going to get murdered.

I yawned and looked at the clock . . . twenty-five to . . . I jumped up. 'Watch out, Charlie. My bus is just going.'

'Hang on, Simon.' Charlie dragged his legs up. 'It's just coming to the best bit.'

'Can't. It goes at quarter to.' I shot up the aisle dragging my overcoat and nearly knocked over an usherette who was sitting on a stool by the exit eating an apple.

It was dark outside and the road was bathed in an orange glow from the street lamps and it felt very late. I ran along to Goodridge's and kept running until I got to the bus stop. A lady was waiting with a shopping bag and a parcel.

'Sixty-six gone yet, please?'

'Don't know, Sonny. I'm going to Lavant.'

'But it goes at quarter to ten, doesn't it?'

'I dunno. Anyway it's not quarter to nine yet.'

'Wha-at?' I stepped out into the street and looked towards the clock on the Market Cross. 'Oh sod it. I've come out of the pictures too early.'

'Oh, have you? Well, I think it's plenty late enough for a boy of your age to be out and I don't like that sort of language.'

She turned away from me as she spoke and an empty Woodbine packet blew along the gutter by the kerb and I stepped over it and back on to the pavement. My hands were still clammy and I tried to dry them by rubbing them together but it felt as if the spivs and their girl-friends outside the Rendezvous Café would be attracted by the sudden movement so I made out I was looking at the bikes in Goodridge's window and then I crept along the side of the pavement by the wall of Shippam's Meat Paste factory and crossed over opposite Pine's Hardware to catch the five past nine 57 to Tangmere Corner from the Market. There was nobody waiting for the 57 and I wanted to go to the toilet so badly that I nearly went up against the broken Gales Ales sign at the side of the Horndean Arms but a man came along with his dog and by the time it'd sniffed around the bus stop pole and sprayed it the bus came and I had to get on.

I sat with my legs crossed all the way to Tangmere Corner and just managed to hang on until all the people who'd got off the bus had gone in to the camp before I felt it coming and I went behind the bus shelter. Standing there in the dark with the wind whipping up my fly buttons I felt more lonely than I'd ever done before and the wind howling through the trees on the road from Tangmere to the outskirts of the village made me hug in close to the edge of the pavement in case I ran into something in the dark. I didn't feel safe until I got to the shop and then it started to rain so I stuffed my hands in my pockets and ran up to the bottom of Grandad's garden. The light was shining out round the edges of the kitchen curtains through the apple trees and I fancied I could smell their log fire and the oil lamp and sprats frying. But they'd got electric lights now and Grandad couldn't eat sprats any more because they repeated on him and I wished I wasn't old enough to go to the pictures on my own.

I walked home with my head down trying to miss the cracks in the pavement and cold shivers went through me when I trod on the slugs that crawled out of the hedge to lie on the paving slabs and I crossed over on to the road when I got to the Close and went in without tapping on the window. Mum and Dad were sitting on the sofa together.

'You're early, Simon. I didn't hear you come in.'

'No, Mum. I got the time wrong and came out early.'

'Did you my love?' She stood up and left Dad's arm

dangling where it had been round her shoulder. 'And just look at you. You're soaked.'

'Yes, Mum. It's raining.'

'Well, you just get into a hot bath this minute my boy. You don't want to lose any more schooling between now and your examination, do you?'

'No Mum.' I pulled my shirt off without undoing the sleeve buttons. 'Can I go to bed now, please?'

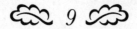

*T*he papers all said 1953 was going to be the start of a new era of opportunities but England'd only drawn with 'The Rest of the World' at Wembley and Mum said I'd been spending far too much time with Charlie and down at the camp. There was a new boy down there called Dicki Jamieson who'd played for Hampshire Juniors and wore very short shorts and a roll-top pullover to play in and smoked Abdulla cigarettes out of a silver case and had a pair of green gabardine trousers and went out with Micky Leary's big sister. He'd said I was a good crosser of the ball and I'd been practising centres every evening for him to hit in with Rumbletummy Morris's brother Harry in goal. Dick and Harry looked like film stars and I hoped that if I played with them I might look like one too. But time was running out.

In three weeks I'd have to learn enough to get to the High School and Dad said if we didn't strengthen our defence we'd have a hard job against Hungary. I tried to remember what I'd learned at school but my mind went blank and I could only see Hungary sandwiched between Bulgaria and Rumania and East Germany. None of the Rest of the World team came from Hungary so they couldn't be very good and Dad said four-all was a daft score and we'd probably let them draw with us because it was only a 'friendly'. I shifted to a more comfortable position on the meal box behind the chicken house and took a last look at the headline 'Magyars Fly In' on the back page of the *Daily Express* and then folded it up and opened my homework book. I'd half coloured in a picture of the Union Jack and crossed out some things that didn't fit in a section called 'Comprehension' and put in some commas and full stops in a piece of writing that didn't make sense, when a fly crawled over my knee. I folded the book back and swatted it. There wasn't anything I could do in it anyway.

Mum's footsteps sounded up the path and I counted the clicks of her heels on the bricks and stopped as she stooped under the clothes-prop and then counted again until she stopped.

'What you doing up here on your ownsome then, laddi-kins? Shouldn't you be getting back to school?'

'There's no hurry, Mum. They don't go in till quarter past one.'

'But don't you play football and things at lunch time?'

'Yeah, but they just muck about.'

'What about the boys from the camp then?'

'Oh, there're all right but they don't really play at school. And most of my friends down the camp're older.'

'Oh, like who?'

I faced away from her so that the sun shone on my other cheek. 'Like Dicki Jamieson and Harry Morris'n John 'arris.'

'Well, the Harris boy goes to your school, doesn't he?'

'M'm.'

'So why don't you go with him?'

'I do. Well, I can do. But he's with the other boys.'

'Can't you be with them then?'

'Yeah, s'pose so.'

'Simon?'

'Yes, Mum.'

'What's the matter?'

'I dunno. Nothing really.'

'But you don't seem very happy.'

I could feel a pulse beating down in my stomach where I was stretching back and my mouth was dry and my nose felt blocked up but there was nothing to blow on and I wondered how long it'd be if I waited for Jimmy Phillips to call for me instead of me going round for him.

'Eh, Simon?'

'I'm all right, Mum.'

'Well, I should have thought you'd be ever so excited at the prospect of watching the game today on Mr Miller's television.'

'M'm.'

'Well, aren't you?'

267

'Oh yeah.'

'Well, for goodness' sake snap out of it and be a bit more cheerful. Have you been going to the toilet regularly?'

'I dunno. Think so.'

'Because that can make you feel all lapsey, you know. Not going.'

'I have, Mum.'

'Never mind. I think you'd better have a dose of Syrup of Figs before you get off.'

'Oh no, Mum. It's horrible.'

'But it'll do you good. Come on now.'

I leaned forward off the chicken-meal box and let my arms drop down by my side.

'My, you're getting a great lollopy chap.' She put her arms round me and squashed me against her.

'Get off, Mum.'

'Whatever is the matter, Simon? What's got into you lately?'

'Nothing, Mum. I gotta be goin'.' I eased myself away from her but she hung on and let go suddenly.

'Go on then. Let's give you something to sort your tummy out and then do try to come home in a better humour.'

The girls had all got miffed because we were going to watch the football match on Milly's television so he'd put Miss Anderson in charge of them having a six-a-side netball tournament which meant the Guv had to look after her class. He'd tried to make out he didn't really mind missing it and he set us riddles until a quarter of an hour before the kick-off but I could tell he was disappointed because he kept looking out of the window to see if it was raining and the girls would have to come in. I looked out too. It was windy but there was no sign of rain.

Marie Maynard ran past sideways bouncing the ball. She had her skirt tucked inside her knickers and stood with one leg straight and one back and bent like a lazy capital A as she leant forward to have a shot. All the other girls were under the basket like birds in a nest waiting to be fed and the cries of 'Marie, Marie' changed to 'Dot' and 'Phyllis' and 'Jen-ny' as they stretched in their cardigans and bare legs and quivered their arms up each time anybody new got the ball. Janet Rolls followed the pack that followed the ball up and down the pitch and it looked as if her legs would get sore where they rubbed together at the top. Susan Farley stood upright when she ran and she watched Janet instead of the ball. She had long arms and legs and long blond hair that looked silky to the touch and her tummy was flat even though she had a hollow back and her legs were light brown against her shorts and she was nicer looking than Janet from a distance and I wished she had Janet's face.

'What's the answer then, Simon?'

'Wish I knew, Guv.' I smiled at Susan but not as if I really meant it. 'What was the question?'

The chalk dust from the blackboard settled slowly.

'I beg your pardon?'

'I'm sorry, sir.' I pointed out of the window. 'Only I was—'

'I know perfectly well what you were doing.' The Guv was halfway down the gangway towards me. 'You've been dreaming out at those girls all afternoon. I did think that you would do me the courtesy of trying to be interested until the game starts.'

I stared at him without blinking and wished he was on his own so that I could tell him I was in love with two girls half each and what could I do about it.

'Blasted cheek!'

I dropped my head. 'Sorry, sir.'

'M'm.' He stood looking at me a moment longer and then checked his watch. 'Off you go then. But walk sensibly and take your shoes off before you go into the headmaster's house. Maurice, p'raps you'd nip down and tell Miss Anderson I'll be there in a minute.'

I waited for the others to go out and when the Guv turned towards the door I caught him up.

'Could I have a word, sir, in private?'

He looked down on me with his grey eyes and I could feel him saying, 'No. Go away.'

'What, now?'

'Well, yes please, sir. If you've got time.'

'What is it then?' His face was still stern but he sat on the corner of the desk with his blazer flap draped over the edge.

I slid the brass flap over the ink-well. 'Coat might get inky, sir.'

He turned and looked behind him and smiled. 'Thank you, Simon. What's up?'

The girls were still playing netball. Janet was prancing up and down after the ball and Susan was watching her. Then she looked our way. I glanced up at the Guv. He'd seen her look at me.

'Ah!'

'Don't really know what to do, sir.'

'Well, just take your time, Simon. No hurry, eh?'

'No, sir. S'pose not.'

He stood up and patted my shoulder towards the door. 'Off you go and enjoy the match. When in doubt, Simon, *don't*, eh!'

They swamped the chairs and sofa and were spilling forward on to the floor right up to the television set. Milly was sitting in a big armchair over in the corner with a small table with an aspidistra in a brass bowl next to him and a cup of tea and a plate of biscuits. Mrs Miller was standing in the doorway in an apron wiping her hands on a tea towel.

'I don't want mud all over my carpets, Fred.'

'They've got their shoes off, dear.'

'And I don't want it stained with sweaty footprints.'

'No, dear.'

'Well, how you going to stop it?'

'They haven't been running about, dear. They shouldn't be hot.'

Geoff Gibbs tapped his finger on the toe of my shoe and whispered 'get 'em off' so I went back out into the passage and put my shoes under the long oak chest with the others and then I came back and looked for somewhere to sit. Nobby Clark was crammed into the middle of the sofa like a big book in an overloaded bookcase.

'Move up a bit, Clark and let young Wilson sit down.' Milly wiped the corner of his mouth with his handkerchief.

'I can't budge, sir.'

'Sit still now all of you.' Milly was craning forward like a tortoise. 'They're coming out.'

I stood and watched. The two teams were walking out amongst the crackles and spots and wiggly silver snakes and I recognised Stanley Matthews. Nobby squirmed to his feet behind me and pointed to the space between Paul Craven and Derek Brown.

'What?'

'S'sh.' He put his finger to his lips. 'Sit down.'

'What about you?'

Nobby bent forward and whispered. 'I don't like being squashed and I can't stand football . . . I'm gonna find my boots.'

'Qui-et!' Milly paddled his hand at the side of his chair. 'Be quiet!'

Nobby tiptoed out on the balls of his feet with his big-toe nails twinkling in the dim light from the curtained windows and crept out of the side door like somebody coming in late in a cartoon in the Sunday paper.

'What's so funny, Simon. And you, Gibbs. What's tickled you?'

'That bloke there, sir. Number ten. The fat one. He'll never play football.'

'Number ten . . .' Milly turned to the back page of his newspaper and kept his eyes glued on the screen. 'Pus-kas, pronounced Poo's-kus I s'pose. He's inside left.'

'Inside left! Jimmy Dickinson'll get across an' murder 'im. 'e won't get a smell'a the ball, will 'e, Col?'

'Just quieten down now, Geoffrey. We're going to enjoy this.'

The England players were passing the ball to each other warming up and somebody took a shot that Gilbert Merrick pushed over the bar and Stanley Matthews did a little run down the wing like a sparrow on ice and centred and then he stopped and touched the tops of his socks and stood with his hands on his hips looking just like somebody's uncle.

The captains had tossed up and Hungary were kicking off and the picture moved from England warming up to the Hungarian forward line.

'Cor, look at that!' I couldn't believe what I'd seen. The

271

man on the centre spot was flicking the ball up and down on his toe as if he was a juggler and then he flipped it to the man next to him who caught it with his foot and balanced it on his instep. 'That's brilliant.'

'They'll have to do more than play patsy with it.' Milly's arm groped for his cup of tea.

'Yeah, that's only fancy stuff, Nipper. You're all fancy stuff, in'e, Col. Fancy stuff don't get you nowhere.'

The referee blew the whistle and we settled back but before my eyes had got used to the flashes and lines the ball went up through the Hungarian team to a man called Hidegkuti and the net billowed and Hungary had scored. Then they did it again and by half time our team looked as if they didn't really want to play the second half. The second half was worse and it made my stomach muscles knot up like they did when I was trying to tackle Dad and he moved the ball every time I kicked at it and it was just like a pantomime towards the end when a Hungarian man who'd been cheering and jumping behind the goal took the goalkeeper's place and jumped so high that he hit his head on the cross-bar and nearly knocked himself out. Then the referee blew his whistle and it was all over.

Milly turned the set off. He stood over it as the light went to the centre and down a hole in the middle. The camp kids turned in towards each other but they didn't speak and Jerry was crying.

'Wasn't bleedin' fair.' Geoff Gibbs smashed his fist down on the floor and caught Jerry's fingers. Jerry's mouth went from tight-lipped sobbing to a noiseless howl and Geoff looked where he'd hit. 'Not ruddy fair.'

Milly stood up from the television and straightened his back. 'No, but we've got to accept it, Gibbs.'

'You're not supposed to pussy about like that are you, sir?'

'S'goals that count.'

'Thank you, Craven.' Milly swung round and Paul ducked down amongst the camp kids. 'It's not the way *we* play, Geoff. It's certainly not the manly, straightforward way we showed the world. And, Craven, it's not the way I want the game played here. They caught us by surprise. Hopping about like a lot of nancy boys.'

'Has it finished?' Mrs Miller was at the door again.

'Yes it has. Off you go, boys. Back to your classes.'

We elbowed each other as we got our shoes back on and Paul Craven caught Jerry in the eye and set him off again.

'For goodness' sake, Henry.' Milly was standing with his back to the door with his hand on the handle behind him. 'As if we haven't had enough to put up with this afternoon. Wipe your nose else it'll drip all over the—'

'Over the what?' Mrs Miller was tugging at the door from the other side.

'It's all right, dear. They're just going.'

Walking back to our classroom was like waking up on a wet Monday morning and realising it was the first day back at school after a holiday. The Guv had his coat and scarf on and Mr Mantle was mopping the floor in between the desks but he stopped as we told the Guv what'd happened.

'Hang on, Geoff. You say we lost six-three. They got six?'

'Yessir.'

Mr Mantle leant back on the handle of his mop and reached for the dog-end behind his ear.

'But that's not possible.'

' 'tis, sir.'

'Well, what happened, Simon?'

'They juggled it, sir. And passed it around.'

'There was this little fat—'

'. . . Puskas.'

'Pussy-pussy!'

'Shud up, Gibbs!'

'Crawler!'

'They were just too good.'

The Guv looked up. 'Were they, Paul?'

'Flippin' fancy stuff.'

'Watch out, Gibbs. Stoppit!'

'Gibbs . . . Gander.' The Guv stood up off the desk. 'He's entitled to his own opinions. But dear, oh dear . . .' He put his trilby on and cocked it to one side. 'Six-three. That'll take some living down. C'mon now, you'd better be off home.'

We all pressed out of the door and spread out on the tarmac at the back. I'd done my shoes up but one tongue was rucked up so I had to do it up again and when I stood up I

273

found I was in the middle of Paul Craven and Maurice Geer and Micky Leary and David Harris.

'What you think of them, Si?'

'Why?'

'It's all right. We won't shout about it.' Paul was looking after Geoff Gibbs and the others who were in a group around Milly. 'Good, weren't they?'

'Brilliant.'

'We could never play like that.'

'Matthews was good.'

'Yeah . . .' Maurice Geer eyed me. 'But you're not on the side of barging and kicking and all, are you?'

'No, course I'm not. I just wish we'd won.'

'Yeah, well, so do we. But we didn't.' Maurice pulled up Micky's sleeve and screwed his watch round. ' 'ere, I gotta be goin'. See you tonight, Paul.'

'What you doin' tonight, Paul?'

'Playin' football.'

'Can I come?'

'Why ask, Nipper. You usually do.' Paul slung his arm over Micky Leary's shoulder. 'But we're playin' like the continentals.'

'Yeah, all right. I'll wear my plimsolls.'

The fire crackled and Old Gran gave a muffled snort and licked her lips and went back to breathing regularly. She went to sleep most afternoons and then went to bed early and woke up at about three o'clock and reckoned that somebody'd got in and fiddled about with her clock and Nan said she couldn't stick it anymore so Old Gran'd moved back down with us because we hadn't got any stairs for her to come head-first down. Mum'd laid the table and brought the tray in and she was sitting on the arm of the easychair by the china cabinet watching for Dad. They'd left the winter fender down as Old Gran needed a fire and I'd got used to sitting on the woodbox. The seat of the woodbox was made out of sacking covered with plastic. It'd cracked where I'd been sitting on it and sawdust in the seat underneath was spilling out.

274

'What you doing tonight then, laddikins? Going to do some studying?'

'Dunno, Mum. Might go down the camp.'

'Oh, do you think you ought to, Simon? Your exam's not far away. How you getting on at school now?'

'All right, Mum.'

'Well, shouldn't you?' She straightened the folds in the curtain and sat back.

'Shouldn't I what, Mum?'

'Be swotting or something. Aren't you listening?'

'Yes, Mum.'

'Well, sound as if you are. Here comes your daddy. We'll see what he thinks about it.'

I sat back against the chimney breast and picked at the cover on the seat of the woodbox. It would rip along the front but not up. Must be the way the thread ran. The sawdust was thicker and coarser than Dad's: probably came from a factory. Old Gran's knitting was rising and falling on her stomach. Each time it rose and fell one needle slipped forward and a few stitches came off. I leant over and held the needle between my finger and thumb and slipped them back on with the other hand and resettled the pile with the needle sticking into the ball of wool.

'What you fiddling about at, Nip?'

'Just stopping Gran's knitting falling, Dad.'

'Oh.' He sat down and put the tablecloth straight. 'Saw a placard that said "Wembley Upset" on the way home. We didn't lose, did we?'

'Yes, Dad.'

'Wha-at?' He swung round in the chair and screwed the tablecloth up with his elbow. 'How many?'

'Six-three.'

'Six-three!' He suddenly looked as if he hadn't shaved and the back of his chair creaked and then he smiled. 'No, come on, Nip. You're kidding me.'

'I'm not, Dad.'

'Strewth!' He sunk forward as if he'd been punctured. 'What happened?'

'They ran circles round us. And when they got fed up they banged it in the back'a the net.'

275

'Found what in a net?' Mum came in with the teapot.

'Football. Hungary beat us six-three today.'

Mum stood with her mouth open and then she remembered she was carrying the tea and put it down. 'Dear oh dear. That was unexpected, wasn't it?'

'Unexpected! Yes, course it was unexpected.'

I sat up and spread jam on my bread and butter.

'Mind you, I've seen it coming, Ina.' Dad was stirring his tea without looking and Mum leant forward and put some sugar in. 'Transfer fees getting on for thirty thousand and some of them are getting twenty-five pounds a week. Takes away all the incentive.'

'Cor! Wonder how much the Hungarians get. They're much better than we are.'

'Simon!'

'It's all right, Ina.' Dad held his hand up and Mum relaxed. 'Six-three's pretty convincing, unless . . . we didn't have any injuries, did we, Simon? Weren't down to ten men?'

'No Dad.'

'No-o. See my point is, Ina, they're amateurs.'

'What Dad? They were brilliant.'

'So you keep saying, Simon. And you may be right but—' Dad stopped stirring his tea and took a sip. 'They don't get paid for it. They're not professionals. Most of 'em 'er in the army, so it said in yesterday's *Express* . . .' Dad turned and fiddled under the sofa cushion.

'I threw it out.'

'Oh, doesn't matter. See, they play for the love of it, Simon. Put money into it and that's all they think about.'

'Yes, Dad.' I finished my cup of tea and stood up. 'Well, I just love playing too. I'm off down the—'

'Hey, just a minute, my lad.'

'Let him go, Ina.'

'That was pretty clever, Simon.' Mum was still looking as if she was going to stop me. 'You knew I wanted you to do some studying tonight.'

'Oh, let him go, Ina.' Dad passed his cup over. 'He won't be able to concentrate tonight and one night won't make much difference.'

I bolted for the door as Mum was saying 'jigger-it-all he

never does any' and I just got out of the back door as Dad called me and ran down the garden and out through the back field before he came after me.

I ran until I got to the barbed-wired track from the farm and then I slowed down and walked in the ditch inside the hedge along the side of Vines' tennis court. I knelt in the dead leaves and looked across at the Vines' back garden through the stinging nettles growing up the tennis court fence. The lawn was mown in tram lines and the evening sun glinted off a paddling pool. A tartan blanket was laid out on the grass with some baby's toys on it and a long-legged long-haired dog was asleep by a pram with its head laid out on its forepaws. I moved my hand to relieve the pressure on my knee and it knocked up against an old tennis ball buried in the leaves. It had a slug underneath it and its slimy wetness made me shiver. I crawled out of the hedge as quickly as I could and went down the field past the policeman's house and across the road and into the camp married-quarters.

Groups of dads were standing by their back doors talking and Godfrey Willis came out of his house up on 'The Level' with his satchel.

'Where ya goin', Godfrey?'

'Hello, Simon.' His satchel weighed him down on one side and he looked like a mum who'd been shopping. 'It's my violin lesson.'

'Your what? You don't wanna play the stupid violin, do you?'

'We-ell.' He settled his bag straight and rubbed his glasses on the soft pad from his case. 'I wasn't terribly keen to begin with but I'm beginning to quite like it. And it does make a change.'

'A change from what?'

'Well . . . from the other things I do. Now I really have to go.' The way he bent down and tested the handles on his satchel before he picked it up made me think of Grandad checking the weight of sacks of manure to make sure the bottoms weren't rotten. 'Do you want to come, Simon?'

'Me-e? What'd I want with violin playin'. I'm off down to play football.'

277

'Oh all right.' Godfrey set the peak of his cap straight. 'I'll see you tomorrow.'

'Yes, bye, Godfrey.' I stood trying to grin after him but my legs felt suddenly heavy as if I'd been walking all day in wellingtons and I went and sat on the swings.

It didn't matter any more if I didn't play for England because England were no good now and Godfrey was so good at school and he could afford to go off playing the violin and still pass the 11+ and I couldn't even remember what we'd learned this morning and somehow I'd been looking forward to the match today so much that it hadn't seemed possible that there'd be anything after it.

I felt ill for a week and blamed it on the Syrup of Figs but Mum said it was because I'd got so worked up over that blessed football match. I went back to school before I was better because I couldn't stand being at home on my own but I had to keep going out and the boys laughed at me until the Guv said I should be at home in bed. I didn't want to go home so I set off the long way towards the church but when I got to the entrance to Mrs Evans's garden I slipped in and sat in the leaves under the Spanish oaks. It was dry amongst the evergreens and I stayed there until they'd come out from school and gone home and I went back there all the following day. It was so close to the schoolyard that I could hear them at playtime and sometimes I crept forward and watched them through the ivy that grew over the wall. Miss Anderson's class was just like babies. They wandered about playing with the old wooden cart full of play-bricks, building them up and knocking them down, and holding hands and sucking their thumbs.

Grandad had always gone home for dinner at twelve and come back at one. All those years had passed and he was doing the same thing at the same time and I wondered if it felt any different to him not having me walking beside him and holding his hand, or if he even remembered. He was so close, trudging along through the leaves down the drive and tying things up and making things grow and unwrapping mints – no further away than I could throw a stone. And as the days went by I spoke to him in my mind as he walked past and closed my eyes and thought he answered me and once he looked straight at me but he didn't see me.

I sat there for days imagining the lessons I should have been doing and I wrote stories in my head and plays and sometimes I acted all the parts until I had to stop because I was talking to myself and getting angry, and then I practised decimals and fractions and percentages but the numbers kept getting mixed up so I made Roman chariots out of leaves and held them together by pushing the stalks through the next leaf and sticking the other end with birds' droppings. Then one day it rained. I tried standing against the tree but the water dripped off on to my head so I lay down to cover myself in leaves but when I went to throw the flat bottom of a broken bottle away it turned out to be a curled-up slow-worm that could've been an adder so I went up to the hall and hid until they came out of school and then I went home.

Mum was waiting for me by the front window and she met me at the back door.

'You're early, Simon?'

'Am I, Mum?'

'What you been doing today?'

'All sorts, Mum.'

'What in particular?'

'Fractions, decimals, percentages'n stories.'

'My, you have been busy. How're you getting on?'

'All right.'

'Do you think you'll pass?'

'Dunno, Mum.'

'Well, at least you're making an effort and that's what counts.'

I watched myself in the mirror. My face didn't move and my eyes didn't flicker. 'I'll try even harder tomorrow, Mum.'

'Tomorrow, Simon?'

'Yes, Mum.'

'But it's Saturday tomorrow. You feeling all right, Simon?'

'Oh yes, Mum. So it is.' I could see my mouth moving but it looked as stiff as if it was frozen. 'I was forgetting. What's for tea?'

'Same as usual.' She said it slowly as she poured three cups of tea. 'Here, pass this to Gran. But wake her up first, gently mind.'

Old Gran woke up as if she hadn't been to sleep and when she'd finished arguing with Mum that she hadn't had her dinner she wanted to know what I'd been doing and I had to struggle to remember what I'd told Mum.

'You'll probably get something on General Knowledge, Simon.'

'Will I, Mum?' I buttered two slices of bread and sliced the cheese thick.

'Yes, I expect so. And shouldn't you be waiting for Dad? Didn't you have any dinner?'

'Course I did.' I gulped and made out I was choking. 'Shepherds pie and potatoes and cabbage and—'

'You don't like cabbage, Simon. Bet you didn't eat it.'

'I did, Mum. You can ask—' I took another mouthful of sandwich and waved my hand as if I was saying a name. 'Do you really think there'll be General Knowledge?'

'Shouldn't be surprised.'

'Crikey!' I filled my mouth again and swallowed some tea.

'Where you going?'

'Up Teddy Perrin's.' I slipped my coat on and stuffed a piece of shortbread into my pocket. 'He's the only one around here who goes to the High School. He'll know what we'll be getting.'

Mum jumped up and said something about me getting indigestion and didn't I want another cup of tea and what was the hurry and when would I be back.

'It's all right, Mum. I'll go on my bike.'

'But it's no distance at all up to Teddy's.'

'Then I'll be home sooner, won't I?'

My front wheel slid off the path on to the border as I reached over the handlebars to open the gate but I was away before Mum could get to the window to tell me not to ride in the garden. I rode up past the school and through Hanover and Warehead and I was at the bottom of the lane to the windmill before I'd thought where I was going.

The path to the windmill was a track of rain-washed flints. The flints hurt my feet through my plimsolls so I walked up on the bank and threw pebbles and clods of turf down into the chalk pit to make landslides until I got to the end of the lane and climbed the stile into the field. The clouds rolled back from the sun and the wind died as if somebody'd closed a door and I sat on the stile watching the peewits and a lark hovered and sang and then shot straight up as if a spring'd been sprung. I sat back against the post and closed my eyes. Exams . . . it was like when I had to go to the school dentist. I'd heard I had to go, but not until after Christmas so I forgot it. But Christmas came and went and I still had to go, but not for a few days. And then it had been the next day and I'd just closed my eyes and opened my mouth and accepted it.

I sat more upright and lifted my legs up on to the long stile step and breathed in deeply and held it. The peewits wheeled and swept as if they were riding the breakers of invisible waves and I imagined Peterkin and the others standing on the beach in *The Coral Island* looking across the calm lagoon towards the towering seas beyond the barrier reef.

'Ah well, can't be helped.' I stood up and stretched. 'Sod 'em all, says I,' and I picked up a piece of dead branch and shot Israel Hands out of the rigging of the *Hispaniola* and ran back down the path to where I'd left my bike.

The air was grey and dusty dark and the white faces around me stood out like mushrooms on a murky morning. They'd swept the floor and mopped it and it still smelt of wet floorboards and Dettol. The desks had been spread out so that there were spaces between them all and they'd been numbered from one to sixteen. There was a picture of the room stuck on the glass of the cloakroom door with sellotape with squares to show where the desks were and their numbers and our names against each one. Mine was number seven, in the middle, and I sat down to the side of Jerry Henry and in front of Gerald Mortlake and behind Colin Gander. A man in a black suit was standing at Milly's desk taking folders of papers out of a brown attaché case. He had strips of sandy hair plastered down to his bald head and freckles and thin-rimmed spectacles with thick glass that

281

seemed to spiral like old-fashioned windows. He came to each of us in turn and put three bits of lined paper and another foolscap sheet face down on each desk and whispered 'don't turn that over until I say so' to each of us like Pop saying 'take this in remembrance of me' to everyone taking communion at church.

I'd pinched a bit of Dad's chewing gum and I chewed it with my mouth open when the man'd gone past me and looked around our thinned-out classroom. Pat Smith and Jenny Wright looked like High School girls already. They had grey pleated skirts and white blouses and satchels with rulers poking out and grown-up block-heeled shoes. Godfrey Willis finished sharpening his pencil into his cleaned-out Vaseline tin and blew the shavings out of his sharpener and fitted a new nib into his pen. Wendy Brewer was picking balls of fur off her jumper and Paul Craven was carving little strips off the edge of his desk with the penknife Dicky Mole'd given him for borrowing his bike at lunch time for a fortnight and Jerry Henry was as white as a sheet and looked as if he was going to die. I didn't know whether to laugh or cry so I looked out of the window.

The sky had got blacker and it was so low it looked as if it was going to crush the elm trees along the side of Brindle's field. Two streaks of yellow slashed across the sky above Teddy Perrin's house as if a black boil'd burst and the pus'd oozed out and the wind got up and rain hissed against the windows.

'Right. Attention please.'

The minute hand clicked and jumped to five to nine.

'You've got five minutes to look at your papers. Turn them over now.'

We reached and turned them over.

'Do not write anything yet.'

I pressed my palms into the desk.

'Read the instructions carefully and complete the front sheet when I say so. *When I say so.*' His arm came out like a knight charging and I ducked and he pointed over my head. 'When I say so.' He lowered his arm and his coat sleeve slid back down. 'Commence work when I say so. Not before.' He looked at his watch and then at the clock and bent his arm in

282

front of him so that his watch face showed and my hand crept towards my pen. 'Com-plete *front sheet.*'

Our hands shot forward and the nibs dipped and some scratched. I'd dipped my pen in too far and I had to hold it halfway up the shaft and the paper felt sticky when I held it in place. They wanted my name and age and address and school. I wrote '11' in against 'Age' to see how the pen felt on this new paper and watched the man as he walked slowly down between the desks. He stopped and twisted his head to read upside-down.

'*Is* your name Jerry?'

'Yes, sir.'

'Were you christened "Jerry"?'

'Don't know, sir.'

'Cross it out and write "Gerald". Neatly.'

He walked on down the aisle and I could hear him stop and turn and as each footstep came up behind me I felt his shadow crawling up my back. The clock clicked and the minute hand quivered.

'Ready . . .'

Click!

'Be-gin.'

I grabbed at the question paper but I watched the others and didn't open it. Godfrey Willis and Jenny Wright and Pat Smith were scratching away and Paul Craven was chewing the end of his pen. Jimmy Phillips was writing as well and I felt like throwing something at him because he knew less than I did.

'. . . finish at ten o'clock precisely and have a break for a quarter of an hour and sit your next paper at ten-fifteen.'

I watched as he walked past clenching and unclenching his fingers. He got to the end of our line and turned. I looked back at my paper.

It had something at the top about what we had to do but I saw it was 'English' so I got on with the composition where we had to describe somebody. I scratched the inside of my ear and thought about Cabby McAndrew and Winston Churchill and Rasher and Wadey but they'd think I was being cheeky if I described them so I made myself think of Pop. Pop had white hair and a pink face and was always getting worried without getting angry but there wasn't much else I could say about him and it was ten past nine and I hadn't started writing yet. I turned the paper over again and wrote in my name and address and then went back to the composition. I chewed at the end of my pen and picked the splinters of wood off my tongue. If a composition was a story how could it be a description of somebody because if it was just a description it wouldn't have a story. When they'd said 'write a composition' in class and I'd written a story I'd never got told off but this said describe somebody. I sat staring at the light until it glazed and a half light shaded out from either side and said 'describe' to myself and 'comp-o-sition' until they were soft and pappy and didn't mean anything any more.

There was a fly crawling over the face of the clock and I willed him to walk along the minute hand. The minute hand jumped and left the fly in mid-air. It was twenty past nine. Twenty off sixty left forty. Forty minutes and we'd be out and I could run to the furthest fence in the playground and look out at the world outside and I fancied I was on a heath beyond the Downs where it was too far to bike ride and I'd never been before. It was high up overlooking a long valley. A river ran down through the valley and wiggled at the end and disappeared into a grey-blue mist of sky and trees. The sparrows whittered and hopped in the gorse bushes beside me and the coarse grass burst and sent up a dusty scent as I turned and trod through the tuffets. There was a hollow behind me like an enormous grassed-over pudding basin and it was a mass of yellow kingcups. I'd never seen kingcups growing before but they were just like the ones in a colouring book Grandad'd given me once with Puck sitting in one with his green hat tilted back playing his pipes. I stepped over the brim of the bowl but there was a movement off to the side and my head flicked as if I was falling.

The teacher unscrewed his flask and poured some coffee. He lifted the flask cup to his mouth and the steam misted his glasses. I dipped my pen in the ink and touched the nib on the china bowl of the well to take off the blob at the end and wrote 'The' on the paper. The . . . the what? 'The fly stood on the second hand.' It looked daft. I could imagine the bald man with freckles reading it and wondering what on earth was coming next. I giggled and the man looked up and stared at me and then he looked at the clock.

I dipped my pen again and scribbled 'and the second hand moved and made the fly jump.' Do flies jump? '. . . and made the fly jump and he landed on a bald man's head who was drinking coffee.' From then on I scribbled about the man watching us and how he blew on his coffee as he drank it and how the hairs in his nose touched the rim of the cup on the other side and how it felt like a flood of freezing molten lava coming towards me as he· walked down the aisle and back again. And I knew molten lava couldn't freeze and that flies couldn't jump and that Puck'd've been too heavy for a kingcup and it'd've bent under him but it was all down now and I couldn't even go back and see if I'd spelt the long words right because if I hadn't I couldn't put them right because I'd written the lines too close together.

'Two minutes.' His voice sounded as if it was coming through a tube that had been pushed through the roof from outside and he was kneeling over the whole classroom and talking into it like the giant in *Jack and the Beanstalk* watching his golden hen.

I wrote in a sentence that said something cheeky about people who stayed in hot classrooms all day growing to be ten foot tall and as white as a lily and then I put my pen down and flexed the stiffness out of my fingers.

'Time's up. Put your pens down.'

A sigh went up and we looked around at each other. Colin Gander stood up in front of me and I grabbed for my pen to cross out my last sentence but the man whisked my paper away and brushed my head with his elbow as he passed.

'Out you go then for a quarter of an hour and be back at ten-fifteen for your next paper.'

He stood by the door as we trooped out and those who were out first hung around by the door and I had to push to get by them.

'How did you get on with number three? And stop pushing, Simon Wilson.'

'Well, get outta the way'n gas, Smith. We can't walk over ya.' Pat Smith had a lovely round face and big black eyes like polished sloes but she thought I was a hooligan. 'Anyway, what number three?'

'Number three. The grammar. But you wouldn't know anything about that, would you?'

'P'raps we didn't have to do it.'

'Of course we did. And the comprehension. Did you do that?'

'Yeah, course I did.' My stomach fell away and I felt sweat oozing out of my armpits. 'Think I'm stupid or something?'

She looked down at me as if I was a rat in a sewer and then turned and carried on talking to Jenny Wright. I stood still until they'd forgotten me and then went over to Godfrey Willis who was fitting a new lead into his propelling pencil.

'You do a story, Godfrey?'

'I wrote a description. Here, hold this a minute.'

I let his satchel lean against my shin. 'You do two and three?'

'Yes of course I did.'

'Where were they then?'

Godfrey tapped the end of his lead and put his pencil in his inside pocket. 'On the back page.'

'Oh.'

'Didn't you see them then?'

'No. I didn't turn the page over.'

'Didn't you read the instructions at the top?'

I shuffled my toe against his satchel until it overbalanced.

'Aha! Old Lord Snooty's dropped a bollock.' Geoff Gibbs dug Colin Gander in the ribs. 'Now you'll be on the scrap-'eap with the rest'a-vus.'

'Shuddup, Gibbs. I might still pass.'

'You won't pass. You ain't got the brains. They all said your uncle was a flash in the pan. Poor little Grandad's boy.'

'What's my uncle got to do with it?' I could feel the tears coming and how they'd all go quiet up at Nan and Grandad's and talk about something else and not notice me when we were having our tea.

'Give it up, Nipper. You ain't posh. You're just like the rest'a-vus.' Geoff's face was forward of the rest around him and they looked like a pool that could open and swallow me up. 'Better come with us to the Lincs.'

286

'But I don't want to go to the Lincs.' I could see myself walking to the High School on my own and the boys in a group going the other way. 'And anyway, you ain't even taking it, Gibbs. Why ain't you takin' the exam?'

Geoff Gibbs's lip curled and I thought he was going to hit me but he slung his arm over Colin's shoulder. 'Come on, Col. Let's leave the snotty bastard,' and they went off with Kenny Lane and Derek Brown.

'Why *isn't* he taking it, Jim?'

Jimmy Phillips shrugged and looked after Geoff until he was out of earshot. 'The High School uniform's expensive. His gran said they couldn't afford it.'

'Oh.' I could see where Geoff's belt had slipped up over the top of his trousers at the back where the loop'd broken. 'Be hard lines on 'im if Gander passes, won't it?'

'M'm, don't s'pose 'e will though. Don't s'pose any of us will.' Jimmy turned and I turned in towards him and we draped arms over Jerry Henry in the middle of us. 'What *is* grammar, Simon?'

'Dunno. Never got to it.'

'No, neither did I. C'mon, let's 'ave a pee before we have to start again.'

The arithmetic paper was easy to start with but it got harder like going up a hill until it was so steep that by half past ten I couldn't go any further. I watched Godfrey Willis writing and blotting and working out with his propelling pencil on a piece of scrap paper and wondered if that was allowed and then I looked at the outline of Pat Smith against the glassy surface of the laurel bushes through the window until she looked up and away from me. P'raps when we were all grown-up and I was taller than her she'd start liking me. Maybe Janet Rolls'd get thinner and Susan Farley'd start being interesting so that I could like her without trying. Maybe if I practised football and cricket all the time I could still play for England and not have to worry about not being brainy and be in the newspapers and have my photograph taken and then they could still be proud of me.

'Time's up. Blot your work and make sure your name's on it and be back at eleven-thirty for the last paper.'

I stood up like Kenny Lane's sister's clockwork postman and wondered if my legs'd ever work properly again. I went to the toilet but I couldn't go so I just stood there with my forehead against the cold marble and let the shivers run through my neck into my back.

'You all right, Simon?'

'M'm. Yes thanks, Godfrey.'

Godfrey unbuttoned his flies and wee'd and buttoned himself up and put his cap straight.

'Do we have to pass all the papers, Godfrey?'

'Yes, I think so.'

'So if we fail 'rithmetic and pass the other two we still fail?'

'Yes. But you might get a chance to sit it again next year.'

'Sod that!' I leant back and spat into the channel. 'I'm not going through this again.'

Godfrey smiled as if the swear-word had hit him and he was trying to make out it didn't hurt.

'Come on, Old Prof. Let's get this last lot over with. Shan't be seein' much of you soon, will I?'

'Well, I don't know, Simon.' The worried look was gone from his face. 'Nothing's certain, you know. But I have been working quite hard. Although it's not really so hard because I enjoy it.' He looked up at me with a sad, lonely look on his face. 'You see I'm no good at games and I haven't really got any friends so it's lucky I like the work.'

I felt myself looking at a dried leaf in the channel beyond where the water reached and I imagined Godfrey as one of those plaster boys they dressed up in clothes shop windows with their socks pulled up and turned over and creases in their trousers and polished shoes and a tie and shirt collar that fits and crinkly brown hair that can't fly about and open blue eyes that can't see.

'And yet I'd give anything to be brainy like you, Godfrey.'

'Would you . . .? You are odd, Simon.'

'Yeah, so're you.'

'M'm.' He lifted his satchel and I draped my arm over his shoulder. 'S'pose we both are,' and we walked back to the classroom together.

I'd got nothing to lose. I didn't fidget with my pen and I waited a second or two after the man said we could start and sat watching him until he saw me and then I smiled at him and shook my head and read the instructions. I had to answer all the General Knowledge questions in sections A and B, and ten from section C. It was easy. Either I knew them or I didn't. I went through answering the easy ones and then thought about half the harder questions and got most of them right. I was surprised how many I did know and I could have answered more than they wanted me to but it was quarter past twelve and time was nearly up so I straightened my papers into a neat heap and walked up to the man at the desk.

'What is it?'

'Finished.' I put the papers down in front of him.

'But it's only—'

'I know but I've finished. And I'm going.' He looked so surprised and upset that I said 'bye' as kindly as I could and left.

Christmas was coming and I watched for the postman each morning and dashed to the front door each time he came up the path but he only brought Christmas cards or football coupons. I told myself every time that I didn't want to see a letter addressed to 'The Parents of Simon George Wilson' which would only say that I'd failed and the longer it took the better but as the holidays got closer I started running home at dinner time to see if anything had come in the second post. All Christmas Day and Boxing Day I sat with my stomach screwed up trying to read a book and Mum and Dad said they'd never known me better behaved and was I feeling all right? By the end of the holiday I was sure they'd lost our examination papers and I felt miserable that I'd spent all the time worrying but when we got back to school the Guv said they had hundreds of examination papers and they all had to go up to London to be marked and it'd be months before we got the results so we could forget about it until well on into the summer.

Those of us who'd taken the examination were moved up to Milly's class where we did revision of what we'd done last year and Shakespeare and gardening and games. When we got the cricket stuff out I found I was the fastest bowler in the school and Geoff Gibbs said he'd stop beating me up if I promised not to bowl body-liners at him at playtime and he promised to stop putting glue on the underside of Godfrey Willis's ruler as well.

Milly didn't mind much where we sat and he gave us the arithmetic book with the answers in so that we could work the sums backwards. I sat with Godfrey and he showed me where I was going wrong and he made me repeat after him how you did them and it gradually sank in. By the time it was May and I'd had my twelfth birthday I was sure they'd lost all our papers and I hoped we'd have to do it again because I knew all the sums they'd set and Mum said I should be kicking myself for not trying harder earlier. I tried kicking myself up behind the toilets one day but I couldn't get a good swing at it so I kicked the wall instead. It was then I realised my trousers were so short that the tops of my socks almost showed and Geoff Gibbs started asking me if my cat'd died and I'd got my trousers at half mast but I got him in the goolies one playtime and the Guv gave him out LBW.

We saw less and less of Milly, and Denis Matthews and Jack Smith and Nobby Clark and all the other big boys were either in part-time work to see if they could get jobs when they left school or stone-picking at the new Lincs playing field so that me and Paul Craven and Maurice Geer were virtually in charge of our class. Geoff Gibbs still bullied the weaker ones and pinched Dicky Mole's chocolate-spread sandwiches and kept letting-off in class, but Margaret pulled his hair and Maurice thumped him occasionally and Paul kicked him when we played football and I body-lined him at cricket and between us we kept him under control and the Guv announced that he'd be transferring to the Lincs with us after the summer holidays. His classroom joined on to ours and we gradually moved in with him and sat around chatting and reading stories and learning how to do spinners and seamers and as the summer drew on I spent more and more time with him on the roller in the shade under the elm tree. He seemed happier somehow and liked it when we made jokes.

We were sitting there one day talking about setting up a

six-a-side tournament against Westdean and Charlton and Lavant and Slindon when we realised the Guv wasn't really listening.

'You payin' attention, Guv?' Maurice was good at remembering what they'd used to say to us.

The Guv was looking over our heads and shielding his eyes against the sun. 'Hang on. The headmaster wants me.'

'Go on then.' I was going to say 'don't be long' but the difference between being funny and being rude was as difficult to find as holding the air-bubble steady in the builder's level so I shouted 'see you soon' to make up for it, but he didn't look round.

We could tell by the way they were standing together that something had happened. The children melted away from their games and came together around the Guv and Milly as if they were standing over an accident and the whisper went up that the exam results were out. The little ones stood back as we walked through and stopped short of Milly and the Guv.

Milly was holding a sheet of paper in one hand and a brown envelope in the other.

'I want you older ones up in the top class. I've got something to tell you.' He turned and we followed him in.

The afternoon sun streamed through the windows but its warmth fell short of us in the middle row and I shivered in my shirt-sleeves. I sat wedged in the seat, sliding my legs forward to make them thinner so that they weren't so squashed. My elbow was resting on a nerve on the desk top and my fingers were quivering like a dead claw. I twisted my arm over and the quivering stopped.

'These are the results of the 11+.' Milly put his glasses on and picked the sheet of paper up off the desk. 'Wright and Willis—'

My stomach surged at the 'Wil . . .' and fell back as he finished and a black, sick dizziness closed my eyes.

'The rest of the boys will be going to the Lincs with Mr Irvine. And the new girls' school is on the same site so you'll still see something of each other.' Milly took his glasses off and scratched the side of his nose. 'Try not to be too disappointed. There weren't many places available at the

High School and they could only take the best. And you'll have a lovely new school with . . . what is it? Nearly nine hundred children, Mr Irvine?'

'Eight hundred and forty, Headmaster.'

'Over eight hundred children . . . so you'll get the very best facilities.' Milly put the paper down. 'Congratulations, of course, to Willis and Wright, but the rest of you'll need to make the best of your remaining time here. Off you go now. We'll suspend lessons for the rest of the afternoon.'

We lined up by the door and went out singly. Milly had his back to us. He was pinning the letter up on the notice-board. I looked past him as we edged forward and looked down the list. 'Wilson, S. G. – Failed.' Six years of school and that's all I had to show for it. I repeated the word 'failed' under my breath as we strolled out into the playing field and I drifted away from the others gradually saying it more loudly until I was behind the air-raid shelter looking across at Grandad's back garden.

How could I have failed? They'd been expecting me to be dressed up and going off to the High School like Uncle Steven ever since I'd been born. I gripped my hand around the top strand of barbed-wire in the fence and squeezed. And now they'd know for ever that I'd never go. The rust on the barbs fell away as the points dug in. I squeezed tighter. There was an explosion in my palm and my hand went stiff. I forced my fingers open and drew my hand off the wire. The blood collected in my palm with rust scales floating in it.

'Where's Nipper?'

'Dunno.'

I flexed my palm and made rivers in my life lines.

'What'cha want Nipper for?'

'Game'a cricket.'

'I'll play. Bags I bat first.' Geoff Gibbs hoiked and spat. 'Nipper won't wanna play. 'e'll be sulkin'.'

'Oh will I, Gibbs.' I stooped and brushed my hand in the long grass and finished it off in my hanky and walked out round to the front of the shelter. 'Where's the ball?'

The little ones followed us and Dicky Mole gave me the ball. Drip Williams had the stumps and Geoff Gibbs was carrying the school bat and some old motorcycle gloves we used for wicket keeping. Drip stuck the stumps in and paced out eighteen steps.

'Make it full length, Drip.'

'You gonna bowl fast, Nipper?'

I paced out a fourteen-yard run and marked the place with my bloody hanky.

Geoff Gibbs took centre and stepped back to leg. 'You ain't gonna take it out on us are you, Nipper?'

I gripped my fingers round the ball and lay my index finger along the seam.

'Nipper?'

'Play!'

I loped a few strides and then speeded up. Geoff was hunched up over his bat as if he was riding a pogo stick. The stumps stood unprotected and Geoff stood unprotected. I aimed towards him but then veered to the left. The ball pitched at Geoff's toes and hit middle and leg stumps and left them sagging.

'Well, that's me out.' Geoff dropped the bat.

'Get back in, Gibbs.'

'But I'm out.'

'Get in.'

Geoff picked up the bat and stood up closer to the wicket. 'You ain't body-linin', are ya, Nipper?'

I fitted the ball into my hand. My fingers were going stiff. The wicket came closer as I raced up to the bowling stump. I hurled the ball short and it sent the middle stump cartwheeling and Paul Craven dived two ways at once to miss it and the ball.

'Careful, Simon. That's dangerous.'

'I'm out now, Simon.'

'No you're not, Gibbs.'

I stood at the end of my run as the ball came back from Jimmy Phillips to Maurice Geer and Colin Gander. My hand was stiffer and my wrist was feeling cold and my right arm was long and heavy. I ran up to the stump and lay back and hurled the ball loose-armed. It was a full-toss and Geoff fell back out of the way and the ball snapped the leg stump.

'Watch it, Nipper. You'll bloody kill me.'

Colin Gander and Maurice Geer were whispering and the other fielders had sat down together.

'Here, stick this one in.' I slung the bowling stump down to Paul and put my pullover down to bowl from.

Geoff stood back by the wicket but he was only standing there and he just watched as the next two flattened his stumps. The Guv trod the holes back firm and stuck the stumps in by tapping them with the handle of the bat and he stood them up again when I knocked them down.

'I think that's enough, Simon.' He walked up the pitch towards me holding the ball between his finger and thumb. 'Satisfied?'

He rubbed one finger on the ball and looked at the blood and took my right hand and turned it over.

'Sure you're satisfied?'

'Yeah.' I splayed my fingers so that dried blood cracked. 'I've finished this over.'

'Go and wash your hands in cold water and then I think you'd better go home, don't you?'

'Yes, sir.'

We were leaving the school for the last time. The boys were saying 'goodbye' to Milly and Miss Anderson and they were joking with the Guv about next term but I went on ahead. I knew it was the last time I'd walk out past Miss Anderson's green door, that still smelt of paint, and dodge the line in the tarmac between the playground and the pavement and leave the gate open behind me. But this time I slammed it and I didn't run my fingers along the black railings. I let my head and neck and shoulders roll loose and my shadow walked ahead of me as if I was a giant and I strode out long strides and got from the end of Nurse McLaine's to Grandad's gate in twenty steps. Grandad was in the front garden and I waited for the boys to catch up with me.

Grandad was straining to fix a plank of wood under the main bough of the apple tree that was half eaten through at the base. He heaved up with his shoulder but the bough dropped as he slid the plank under and it wouldn't fit. He stood back and his shoulders sagged.

'You comin' out tonight, Nipper.'

'Dunno, Geoff.' Grandad's heavy boots sank into the soft soil as he turned round. 'I'll have to see.'

'What you waitin' for, Simon?'

'Nothin'.'

'Well, let's get goin'.'

'In a minute.'

Grandad was standing against the background of the raspberry bushes next to where we used to have bonfires and a tugging feeling like a hand gripping the insides of my stomach drew me towards the gate. My hand was on the latch and I looked for him to see me but he'd turned and was straining at the bough again. His back was bent and his cap was crooked and his jacket was hanging loose and he looked as if I'd never known him.

The boys were watching. My stomach seemed to fill until it felt as if it was seeping out of my eyes. I willed him to turn round and call to me but he didn't so I slapped Geoff Gibbs on the back. 'C'mon then. Let's go.'

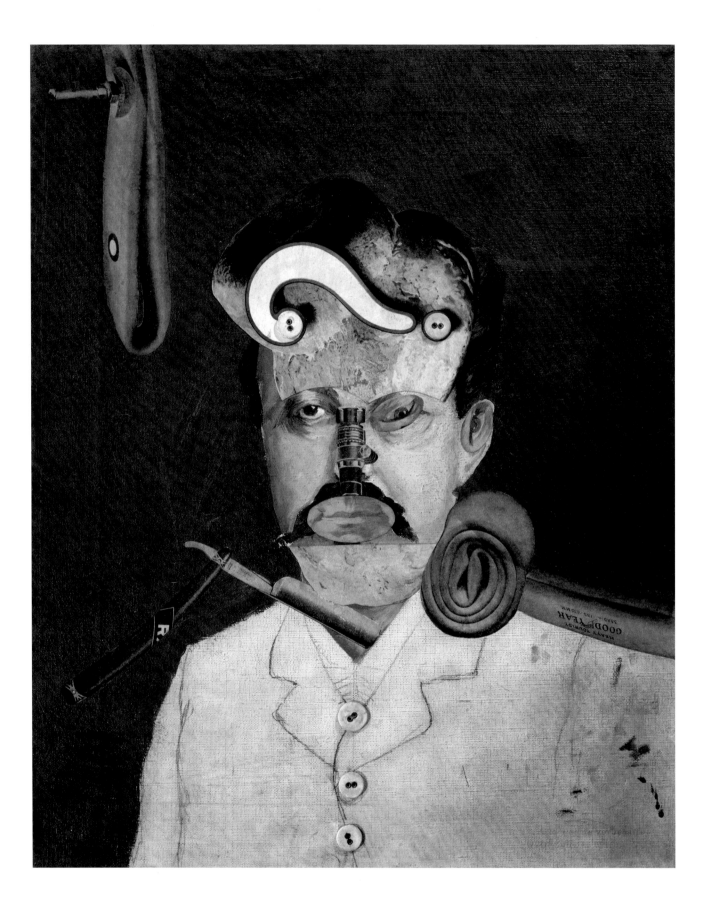

Dietmar Elger
Uta Grosenick (Ed.)

Dadaism

TASCHEN

Contents

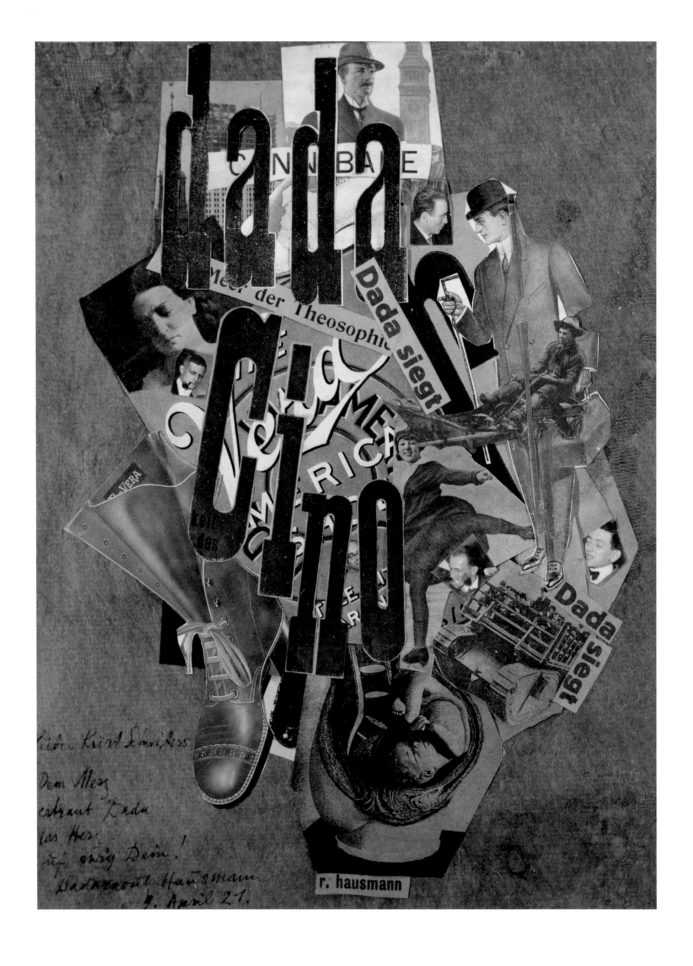

"Before Dada was there, there was Dada"

In its second issue, which appeared in December 1919, the Berlin magazine *Der Dada* asked its readers the question "What is Dada?" and at the same time suggested a series of possible and impossible answers, ranging from "an art" to "a fire insurance". And the questioner finished by asking another question: "Or is it nothing at all, in other words everything?" It was precisely this assessment, one that refused to tie itself down in the slightest, that came closest to the aims and the spirit of Dada. The formulation hints above all at the contradictions which the Dadaists were only too happy to promote. Dadaism was not exclusively an artistic, literary, musical, political or philosophical movement. Indeed it was all of these, and at the same time the opposite: anti-artistic, provocatively literary, playfully musical, radically political but anti-parliamentary, and sometimes simply childish. Many of the Dadaists nurtured their double talents accordingly. As performing artists they were no less committed or inventive than they were with visual techniques.

In spite of the numerous manifestos composed by the Dadaists, there was no tight-knit group behind the movement. Nonetheless, there were those in every town or city who acted as their spokesmen. They provided a focus for their many sympathizers, of whom some in turn took part in Dadaist activities only briefly or occasionally. The period during which the Dada movement was active can be dated approximately to the years between the founding of the Cabaret Voltaire in Zurich in 1916 and the early 1920s in Paris, where the movement came to an end.

The literati and artists involved were themselves not agreed on when precisely Dadaism ended. Thus the Zurich Dadaist and initiator of the Cabaret Voltaire, Hugo Ball, placed its finale just a few months after its inauguration. However that may be, the movement's appearance and disappearance were above all a reaction to the political situation at the time, to a Europe of hostile nation states, which in 1916 were in the middle of waging a frightful war on each other, and after 1918 created a new political and social order.

Dadaism differed from the various artistic and literary trends in the years immediately preceding – Futurism in Italy, Cubism in Paris and Expressionism in Germany – if in no other way than because it enjoyed broad international support. Artists and men of letters in Zurich, Berlin, Hanover, Cologne, New York, Paris and many other cities were in direct contact with each other, taking part in Dadaist activities and making their own contributions to the movement's numerous publications.

Hugo Ball in Cubist costume
from Marcel Janco
At Cabaret Voltaire, Zurich, 1916
Photograph, 71.5 x 40 cm (28¼ x 15¾ in.)
Zurich, Kunsthaus Zürich

PAGE 6
Raoul Hausmann
Dada-Cino, 1920
Collage, no dimensions available
Private collection

In Zurich, the city of Dada's birth, its exponents presented themselves to the public chiefly with literary programmes on the stage. In Berlin, Dadaism also saw itself as a political protest. Cologne's Dadaists by contrast concentrated on the development of new artistic techniques of image creation. Numerous magazines, most of them short-lived, served not only the purposes of internal communication, circulating between the international Dadaist centres, but also reached a broader public. Thus the *Ventilator* in Cologne had a circulation of 40,000. While the Zurich Dadaists could attract audiences of several hundred – a respectable enough figure – to their literary evenings in 1916, their counterparts in Berlin three years later were filling halls of up to 2,000. And Kurt Schwitters' slim volume of poems *Anna Blume* went through several editions within a few months in 1919.

"It's not Dada that is nonsense – but the essence of our age that is nonsense."
— THE DADAISTS

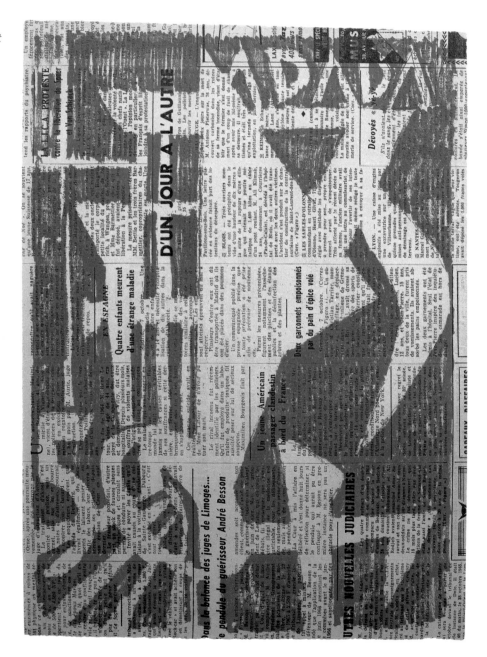

Marcel Janco
50-DADA, 1966
Woodcut, 32 x 24 cm (12½ x 9½ in.)
Private collection

Dada Meeting, 11 January 1921
Paris, Bibliothèque litteraire Jacques
Doucet, Archives Charmet

The Dadaists were skilled self-publicists. They knew precisely how to keep the expectations of their public on the boil, but it was precisely because these expectations were so high that they eventually failed. Surprise, shock and scandal were deliberately calculated, and the public and the authorities reacted as expected. The Dadaist events provoked the hoped-for protests in the audience, and frequently ended in uproar and tumult. Numerous Dadaist magazines were banned, exhibitions closed, exhibits confiscated, and the artists occasionally arrested. But the more the public came to events with the expectation of being entertained by Dadaist provocation, the more these provocations lost their effect and ran into the ground. Dada's sarcastic laugh, of which the Dadaists liked to speak, was reversed: it was the audience that laughed with pleasure. Dada was ultimately the victim of its own success.

Dadaism was above all the expression of the particular attitude of mind with which international youth reacted to the social and political upheavals of the time. They formulated their opposition in anarchical, irrational, contradictory and literally "senseless" actions, recitations and visual artworks. On the occasion of the movement's golden jubilee, Hans Arp congratulated it thus: "Bevor Dada da war, war Dada da" (Before Dada was there, there was Dada), thus pointing to two different aspects. Firstly, literati and artists had in earlier comparable situations already had recourse to Dada-like forms of expression. And secondly, every definition of Dada was so vague that it could be stretched to include distant sympathizers and many a fringe figure too, including for example the Dutch De Stijl artist Theo van Doesburg, whose Dadaist manifestation went by the name of I. K. Bonset, or the mysterious and equally pseudonymous Arthur Craven, who published the magazine *Maintenant* in Paris and also made a name for himself as a boxer.

The Dadaists wanted to have an effect in their own time, which was why they emphasized above all the "active" element in their activities. It was for this reason that Tristan Tzara said that Dada demonstrated its truth by its actions. Even so, Dada's spontaneous literary and artistic formulations (and in those days, they were spontaneous) came to occupy a firm historical position and became an important landmark for a younger generation of artists to orient themselves by. If Dadaism today is mentioned in the same breath as other stylistic developments of the first half of the 20th century,

"Dada for me was a new beginning and a closure. In free Zurich where the newspapers can say what they want, where magazines were founded and poems against the war read out, here where there were no ration-cards and no 'ersatz', here we had the possibility of shouting out everything that was filling us fit to burst."
— RICHARD HUELSENBECK

such as Expressionism and Surrealism, it is first and foremost because the Dadaist artists and literary figures succeeded in finding pioneering creative processes or further developing existing ones.

Zurich – A Hobby Horse Enters the Stage

In 1916 Switzerland was an island of peace in the midst of the bloody battlefield of the Great War. Young artists, pacifists and revolutionaries from all over Europe found refuge here. It was from his base in Zurich that Lenin laid the groundwork for the Russian Revolution; until April 1917 he lived in the immediate vicinity of the Dadaists' Cabaret Voltaire.

In May 1915, Hugo Ball (1886–1927) and his lover Emmy Hennings arrived in the city. He studied philosophy and German literature in Munich, where he had worked at the "chamber theatre" alongside the dramatist Frank Wedekind. In February 1916 Hugo Ball founded the Cabaret Voltaire in Zurich. Those who came to be his most important colleagues in this enterprise were also émigrés, among them Tristan Tzara, Hans Richter, Marcel Janco and Hans Arp. Not long afterwards, Ball also welcomed Richard Huelsenbeck to the group; the two knew each other from time spent together in Berlin. They all had the same reasons for seeking refuge in Switzerland, which Huelsenbeck expressed in the following drastic terms: "None of us had any understanding for the courage that is needed to allow oneself to be shot dead for the idea of the nation, which is at best an interest group of fur-dealers and leather-merchants, at worst an interest group of psychopaths, who, from the German 'fatherland', set out with their volumes of Goethe in their kitbags to stick their bayonets into French and Russian bellies."

It was in fact no coincidence that the young literati and artists who started the Dadaist movement in Zurich in 1916 included not a single native-born Swiss. They were brought together here by their detestation of war and their fear of being conscripted to serve at the front. Unlike the Italian Futurist Umberto Boccioni and the German Expressionists Max Beckmann, August Macke and Erich Heckel, they never fell for the naive temptation to transfigure the War into some kind of heroic community experience for the youth of Europe. Franz Marc was another who, to start with, saw the War as the great event that would renew society: "That Augean stable, old Europe, could not be cleansed in any other way," he wrote to his friend Wassily Kandinsky on 26 September 1914, "or is there a single person who wishes this war had never started?" From the very outset, Hugo Ball was much more critical of this blind enthusiasm. "What has now broken out is the total machinery and the Devil himself. The ideals are mere fig-leaves," he noted in his diary in November 1914. Six months later he fled to Switzerland. When he opened his Cabaret Voltaire in February 1916, Boccioni, Macke and the Expressionist poet August Stramm had already been killed in action. The Western Front had got bogged down into unrelenting trench warfare. Not long afterwards, on 4 March 1916, Franz Marc was killed at the Battle of Verdun, which claimed the lives of more than 700,000 French and German soldiers.

The Dadaists reacted with horror and disgust to the brutality of the war, to the mechanical anonymous killing, and to the cynical justifications put forward by the powers-that-be on both sides, who sought to use the seeming logic of their arguments to legitimize their war policy. The Dadaists accused the public in the belligerent nations of a deferential, nationalist attitude. They formulated their own position with corresponding self-confidence. "Dada wanted to destroy the deceptions of reason and discover an irrational order," was how Hans Arp characterized their goal. To achieve it, however, the Dadaists used very different methods. While the Berlin group also took part in political debate in an attempt to activate their public to think and act for themselves, the Zurich Dadaists relied solely on irony, irrationality and the shock effect of their literary provocations.

Hugo Ball himself had lively memories of the foundation of the Cabaret Voltaire: "I went to Mister Ephraim, the owner of the 'Meierei' and said: 'Please, Mister Ephraim,

George Grosz
Republican Automatons, 1920
Watercolor and pencil on paper,
60 x 47.3 cm (23½ x 18½ in.)
New York, The Museum of Modern Art

August Sander
The Dadaist Raoul Hausmann, 1928
Photograph, 25.1 x 17.6 cm (10 x 7 in.)
Zurich, Kunsthaus Zürich

can I have your hall?' And I went to various friends and said: 'Please, can I have a drawing or a print? I'd like to combine my cabaret with a little exhibition.' I went to the friendly Zurich press and asked them: 'Write a few notices. It's planned to be an international cabaret. We're planning to do some nice things.' I got the pictures and the notices. And so on 5 February we had a cabaret." The modest hall at no. 1 Spiegelgasse had enough room for a little stage and about fifty guests. The walls were decorated with works by Max Oppenheimer and Hans Arp and masks by Marcel Janco. Every evening, Ball and his friends staged a varied programme of songs, readings, music and dances. The opening was accompanied by pieces he had written himself, along with texts by Frank Wedekind, Alfred Jarry, Guillaume Apollinaire, and not least, by the club's "patron saint", the French Enlightenment philosopher Voltaire. The musical accompaniment consisted of pieces by Debussy and Ravel. The dance numbers were performed by members of the Laban School, directed by the choreographer Rudolf von Laban, which had been evacuated from Munich, and the dancers included Mary Wigman, Sophie Taeuber and Ball's partner Emmy Hennings. The masks and costumes for the exotic dances were designed by Marcel Janco and Hans Arp respectively.

For Zurich, the programme for the first few months was something new, though it was by no means unusual by international standards. Hugo Ball had already organized similar soirées in Berlin together with Richard Huelsenbeck. Nor can it be said that the first events were typically Dadaist in character. The poems and texts were still geared to the familiar pathos and power of language of Expressionism. Only gradually, and driven by the heightened expectations of the audiences, did the organizers grow more courageous, venturing to do new things. The news that filtered from the fronts across the borders to peaceful Zurich could only encourage them in their enterprise: there was method in the madness. The total rejection of all rules and the breach of all existing barriers seemed now to be the only appropriate response to this war. Hugo Ball described this radicalization of the programme as follows: "Our attempt to entertain the public with artistic things pushes us, in a manner which is as instructive as it is stimulating, towards the uninterruptedly lively, new and naive. It is a race with the public's expectations, which demands all our powers of invention and argument." The "performers" found new forms of literary expression in meaningless phonetic sound-poems and the so-called simultaneous poems, where all the performers on the stage read their texts at the same time. The artists appropriated the collage technique invented by the Cubists Pablo Picasso and Georges Braque in France. All they needed was a correspondingly forceful name: DADA!

Few if any other names of movements have generated so many myths. Several Dadaists claim to have discovered or invented it. Friends supported now one version, now the other. In the battle of priorities – and not just in the disputes concerning the origin of the word Dada – most Dadaists suddenly became deadly serious. Among the Parisian group in the early 1920s, the honours were accorded to Tristan Tzara. Following his return from Zurich in January 1920, he had claimed to have found the term Dada in the Larousse Dictionary. When rumours suddenly sprang up that Hans Arp was the only begetter, however, Tzara is even said to have forced a denial out of him, which then appeared in 1921 in the magazine *DADA*: "I hereby declare that the word Dada was discovered by Tristan Tzara at six o'clock in the afternoon of 8 February 1916; I was present with my twelve children when Tzara first pronounced the word, which naturally filled us all with enthusiasm." Later Hans Arp was moved to deny the suggestion that his very choice of words was enough to reveal the ironic nature of this statement. In fact, many Dadaists seem to have believed that his declaration did indeed constitute a confirmation of Tzara's claim. In 1921 the future Neue Sachlichkeit painter Christian Schad, who worked with the Dadaists for a short time, became another who felt obliged to set the record straight concerning the chronology of events. In a letter to Francis Picabia in Paris he wrote: "So here is what I have found out and what every German or Swiss writer will tell you if you ask him. The word Dada was found by Mr Hülsenbeck and

Raoul Hausmann
P, 1921
Collage, 31.2 x 22 cm (12¼ x 8¾ in.)
Hamburger Kunsthalle

Mr Ball. There are numerous witnesses who will testify that Mr Tzara was somewhere completely different at the time."

The most credible version is indeed the one which Richard Huelsenbeck himself put about in his book of memoirs *En avant Dada*: "The word Dada was discovered by chance by Hugo Ball and me in a French-German dictionary while we were looking for a name for Madame le Roy, the singer at our cabaret. Dada means hobby-horse in French. We were impressed by its brevity and suggestivity, and in a short time dada became the label for all the artistic activities we were engaging in at the Cabaret Voltaire." The term is first publicly documented in the preface to the first edition of the magazine *Cabaret Voltaire*, which appeared at the end of May 1916, in which Ball reports on the foundation of the Cabaret, and goes on to announce: "The next goal of the artists

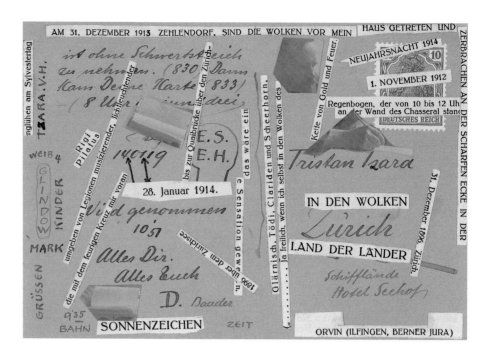

Johannes Baader
Postcard to Tristan Tzara
Collage
Paris, Bibliothèque litteraire Jacques
Doucet, Archives Charmet

assembled here is the publication of a Revue Internationale. La revue paraîtra à Zurich et portera le nom *Dada*. ('Dada') Dada Dada Dada Dada." He had already used the word a couple of times in private diary entries the previous month.

In this naive babytalk, the Dadaists found an appropriate expression for their nihilism, their disgust at all bourgeois convention and at the warmongering of the politicians. In its combination of onomatopœic conciseness on the one hand and freedom from interpretable meaning on the other, the term seemed to be a good war cry in their assault on the traditions of literature and art, as well as on the harmonious order of composition, colour theory and prosody. While the Dadaists could not abolish war, the political power structures, or the class system in society, they could make their point by smashing the formal structure of pictures and poems. It was only in Berlin that the Dadaists, under the leadership of Richard Huelsenbeck, George Grosz and John Heartfield, turned this literary and artistic proxy war into an active political struggle.

A typical appearance by Hugo Ball on the stage of the Cabaret Voltaire at no. 1 Spiegelgasse in Zurich is indicative of what the audience had to prepare themselves for. In his own words: "I wore a costume specially designed by Janco. My legs were covered in tubes of luminous blue cardboard which reached to my hips." Round his shoulders, Ball wore a broad collar, on his head a stovepipe hat. Marcel Janco had made the costume from cardboard. The collar and hat were gold and shiny, making him look rather like a Cubist sculpture. In this get-up, Hugo Ball presented himself to his audience as a high priest of Dadaism, and when after a short pause he embarked on his recitation, the amazement of the visitors in the hall developed into a raging storm of protest. He began his performance with the following lines, spoken in a loud voice: "gadji beri bimba glandridi laula lonni cadori / gadjama gramma berida bimbala glandri galassassa laulitalomini / gadji beri bin blassa glassala laula…"

Hugo Ball was the inventor of these sound poems, which became the preferred form for Dadaist stage artists. In the sound poem, traditional order, the interplay of sound and meaning, is abolished. The words are dissected into individual phonetic syllables, thus emptying the language of any meaning. Finally, the sounds are recombined into a new sound picture. This process robs language of its function. Because, in the view of the Dadaists, instructions, commands and the conveyance of information had deprived language of its dignity. "With these sound poems," said Hugo Ball in justification of their intentions, "we wanted to dispense with a language which journalism had made desolate and impossible." Instead, the Dadaists sought to restore words to their pristine innocence and purity. Other Dadaists sought to aestheticize their text material by arranging the syllables in such a way as to produce music-like sound-picture verse-compositions through repetition and rhythm. And in fact the Hanover Dadaist Kurt Schwitters did succeed, over a period of ten years, in advancing from such modest beginnings to compose a forty-minute sound picture "Sonate in Urlauten" (Sonata in Elemental Sounds), which was structured in a number of movements to which classical tempo indications such as rondo, scherzo and presto were assigned.

These literary and musical experiments culminated in the so-called simultaneous poems, which were recited by several people at once, the various contributions producing a frenetic confusion of voices which could be interpreted as symbolic of the deafening background of noise in the trenches and of the dynamics of modern urban society. The simultaneity of these impressions, the large-format advertising hoardings, the speed and noise of technological forms of transport: these were already the themes of the Italian Futurists. In 1911, their spokesman Umberto Boccioni painted the movement's programmatic picture *The Noise of the Street Invades the House*. However, the Dadaists were disgusted by the Italian Futurists' enthusiasm for technology when applied to modern war machines. Mechanical Dadaist constructions, as designed by, among others, Raoul Hausmann, Max Ernst, Francis Picabia and Kurt Schwitters, were never anything but functionless, ironic or erotic.

Another literary technique widely employed by the Zurich Dadaists at the Cabaret Voltaire was the "random poem". As the name suggests, the random principle plays a decisive role in the production of such a poem. It allowed the Dadaists to reduce their creative influence to just a few predefined inputs. In 1916, Tristan Tzara came up with a graphic instruction for the production of such poems: "In order to make a Dadaist poem, take a newspaper. Take a pair of scissors. Choose an article of the length of the intended poem. Cut the article out. Then cut out each of the words which comprise the article, and put them in a bag. Give the bag a light shake. Then take out one snippet after another, just as they come. Write everything down conscientiously. The poem will be similar to you."

The example which Tzara then quotes as a result of such a process, however, cannot have arisen randomly in this way. It begins with the words: "Wenn die Hunde die Luft kreuzen in einem Diamanten wie die Ideen und der Fortsatz der Hirnhaut die Stunde des Erwachens eines Programms zeigt…" (When the dogs cross the air in a diamond like the ideas and the appendix of the meninx shows the hour of the awakening of a programme…). What makes his instructions so exciting, nevertheless, is the fact that here for the first time a procedure is being described which was to leave its mark on the artistic process in the coming decades. The Dadaists were not so much the inventors as the recyclers of existing (everyday) materials, to which they then gave aesthetic form. In the techniques of collage and photomontage, the visual artists of the 20th century had recourse time and again to similar techniques of picture production.

In Zurich, the dynamics of the Dadaist movement soon began to display symptoms of dissolution. While all the Dadaists had still taken part in the 1st Dada Soirée on 14 July 1916, the event did not take place in the Cabaret Voltaire, but in the Zur Waag guildhall. Just two weeks later, Hugo Ball left the city and withdrew temporarily to Ticino. In his diary he noted at the time, in respect of the event of 14 July: "My manifesto for the first soirée was a barely concealed rejection of my friends. That's how they received it, too. Have you ever known a new cause's first manifesto to rebut that cause in the presence of its adherents? And yet that's how it was. When things are exhausted, I cannot stay with them any longer." However the other Zurich Dadaists continued their activities and events with unbroken energy under the leadership of Richard Huelsenbeck and Tristan Tzara.

***Richard Huelsenbeck and Raoul Hausmann in Prague**, 1920*
Photograph from the *Dada Almanac*
Zurich, Kunsthaus Zürich

"First International Dada Fair"
Opening, 1920
Berlin, Berlinische Galerie,
Landesmuseum für Moderne Kunst,
Fotografie und Architektur

<small>FROM LEFT TO RIGHT</small>
Hannah Höch, Otto Schmalhausen, Raoul
Hausmann, John Heartfield (hidden) with
son Tom, Otto Burchard, John Heartfield's
wife Lena, Wieland Herzfelde, Rudolf
Schlichter, the architect Mies van der
Rohe, unknown, Johannes Baader;
<small>ON THE LARGE PHOTOGRAPH</small>
George Grosz

Nonetheless, when the Galerie Dada was set up in March 1917, Hugo Ball was involved once more. Albeit belatedly, the Dadaists thus seemed to concede that the visual arts should at last be accorded more importance in their movement. The programmatic orientation of the inaugural exhibition sought above all, however, to link up with the roots of literary Dadaism. On view were works by Expressionist artists associated with the gallery Der Sturm, which were accompanied by a Sturm soirée with literature and music by Alban Berg, Wassily Kandinsky, Arnold Schönberg and Paul Scheerbart.

In spite of the participation of Hans Arp and Marcel Janco in the Zurich Dada movement, the mood among the literati involved was basically anti-artistic. They were prepared to allow the visual arts some entitlement to a place in the Dadaist movement, if at all, only if they proved themselves radically anti-aesthetic and ahistorical, and liberated from all art-historical role models. A renunciation of traditional work in oils on canvas on the part of the visual artists was one of the consequences of satisfying such demands by their fellow Dadaists. If the Dadaist artists did re-work familiar motifs from art history and integrate them into their own works, then it was always with a disrespectful undertone.

1917 was not out before Hugo Ball withdrew to Ticino once more. Hans Arp left Zurich in 1919. He went first to Cologne, where he met up with Max Ernst again, and together with him and Johannes Theodor Baargeld established the Cologne Dadaist group. Richard Huelsenbeck had already returned to Germany in January 1917 in order, together with like-minded persons in Berlin, to breathe new life into the Dadaist idea. After his friends had left, it was Tristan Tzara who became the sole spokesman of the movement in Zurich. In the next two years, he organized further evenings and published among other things the magazine *Der Zeltweg*. The young author Walter Serner was his most important colleague at this time. Dadaism came to an end in Zurich at the latest with Tzara's departure for Paris in January 1920. By this time Dadaism had only just reached the climax of its international triumphal march through Berlin, Paris and New York, as well as less metropolitan locations such as Hanover and Cologne.

Berlin – "Dada is: a flourishing business"

As a medical student in Berlin, Richard Huelsenbeck (1892–1974) had made contact with the local literary Expressionist scene before the First World War. His later Dadaist appearances were once described by Hans Richter in the following terms: "He is regarded as arrogant, and that's also how he looks. His nostrils vibrate, his eyebrows are arched." At the start of 1917, Huelsenbeck returned from neutral Switzerland to Berlin, where at first he joined the literary circle centred on the magazine *Neue Jugend* (New Youth). In May that year he published his text "Der neue Mensch" (The New Man). The magazine's title and his own contribution are still characterized by the verbal exuberance of the Expressionists: "The new man must spread wide the wings of his soul, his inner ears must be aimed at things to come and his knees must invent an altar before which they can bend," is just one pathos-filled example. There is suddenly no sign here of the ironic playing with words that was so characteristic of Zurich Dadaism. Huelsenbeck had, as he later himself confessed, temporarily parted company with Dadaism. Indeed, it took a whole year for him to renew his public commitment to the movement with an appearance at the Graphisches Kabinett I. B. Neumann on 22 January 1918. That evening he ignited the spirit of Dada in Berlin with a fire-raising speech. His ideas were spontaneously and enthusiastically taken up in the Reich capital by numerous young literati and artists. "He carried the Dada bacillus to Berlin, where Raoul Hausmann, already infected from birth, was so receptive to the infection that came from Zurich that the bacilli themselves didn't know whether they descended from R. H. or R. H. on their father's side," was how Hans Richter appraised Huelsenbeck's importance as the midwife of Berlin Dadaism.

The difficult living conditions and the chaotic political situation in Germany had deteriorated still further by the beginning of 1918. In the cities, the people were starving, and following the end of the battles in Flanders in November the previous year, the whole extent of the slaughter in the trenches, which had claimed hundreds of thousands of lives, was slowly becoming obvious. There was very little left of the initial enthusiasm for the war in the population at large. Gradually, Germany began to see the

"What we call Dada is a piece of tomfoolery from the void, in which all the lofty questions have become involved …"
— HUGO BALL

"First International Dada Fair",
Catalogue, 1920
With texts by Wieland Herzfelde
and Raoul Hausmann
Berlin, Berlinische Galerie,
Landesmuseum für Moderne Kunst,
Fotografie und Architektur

first signs of protest against the official admonishments to hold out. The so-called "January strike" in Berlin in 1918, in which more than 400,000 workers had taken part, finally triggered demonstrations throughout Germany. The atmosphere intensified with the armed naval mutiny in Kiel in November. Berlin and other major cities saw the formation of workers' and soldiers' councils on the Soviet model, their example being followed by committed artists who formed a "working council of art", whose members included the Expressionist painters Otto Mueller, Emil Nolde and Karl Schmidt-Rottluff, along with the architects Bruno Taut and Walter Gropius, the founder of the Bauhaus in Weimar. The Berlin Dadaists by contrast formed their own movement.

"This evening," confidently proclaimed Richard Huelsenbeck in January 1918 in the Kunstkabinett I. B. Neumann, "is intended as a demonstration of sympathy for Dadaism, a new international 'artistic trend', which was founded two years ago in Zurich." In the following months, he was joined by, among others, Johannes Baader, George Grosz, Raoul Hausmann, Hannah Höch and John Heartfield. The onomatopœic term Dada seemed to give expression to their unease at the social situation in Germany, and in the activities of the Zurich group they found pre-formed possibilities of giving artistic form to their protest. For 12 April 1918 Huelsenbeck and Raoul Hausmann organized a recitation evening at the Berlin Sezession, where Richard Huelsenbeck intended to proclaim the first manifesto of the Berlin movement and announce the establishment of the Club Dada. His address, entitled "Dadaism in life and art", took the form, to start with, of a polemic directed against German Expressionism, before going on to emphasize the special features of Dada: "By shredding all the slogans of ethics, culture and inwardness, which are only cloaks for weak muscles, Dadaism is for the first time not confronting life aesthetically." As examples of the creative means it used, Huelsenbeck adduced the bruitist, simultanistic and static poem, as well as "the use of new material in painting", in other words the deployment of collage and photomontage for artistic purposes. The "Dadaist Manifesto" ends by noting: "Being against this Manifesto means being a Dadaist!" As with the Zurich Dadaists, contradiction and illogicality were to be among the hallmarks of Berlin Dadaism too. The same evening saw the recitation of the first examples of Dadaist verse – or would have done, had they not been drowned in the tumult of the outraged public. The event had to be brought to a premature end.

The printed copies of the Manifesto, which the businesslike Huelsenbeck had signed with the intention of selling them for five marks each, were confiscated by the police. Three days after the event, Raoul Hausmann was taken temporarily into custody. The Dadaist onslaught in Berlin thus received a major setback right at the outset, from which the group was not to recover until the end of the year. Even so, Hausmann judged the evening to have been a success. He reported proudly to his lover Hannah Höch: "For 22 marks in cash, until 27 April we kept the newspapers in such suspense that they provided our publicity." Following Huelsenbeck's first appearance in Berlin, two years passed before the Dadaists finally formed a closer association in early 1919 and began to turn to a broader public with numerous activities and publications. The trigger, according to Raoul Hausmann, was the murder of the leading Communists Karl Liebknecht and Rosa Luxemburg on 15 January 1919. "The proletariat was paralyzed and could not be shaken out of its narcosis. So we had to intensify the DADA actions: against a world which could not even react manfully to unpardonable horrors," he recalled in his book *Am Anfang war Dada* (In the Beginning was Dada).

Richard Huelsenbeck could still describe Dada in April 1918 as a club which anyone could join without obligation, but the choice of words now became more aggressive and the club more exclusive. No way were they going to continue to accept any applicant as member, least of all Kurt Schwitters from Hanover. The rivalries between existing Dadaists also intensified, and the name they chose for themselves now, borrowed from the revolutionary political soviets, had more than just a satirical function. The Berlin Dadaists now met under the institutional title "The Dadaist Central Council of the World Revolution". Huelsenbeck's letterhead identified him as "Central Councillor

*"Art is dead.
Long live Dada!"*
— WALTER SERNER

of the Dadaist Movement in Germany", while Johannes Baader had himself addressed as "President of the Globe", and Raoul Hausmann's visiting card suggested that he was the "President of the Sun, the Moon and the Little Earth (Inner Surface)". In addition they bestowed so-called titles of honour upon each other, which they all bore with a certain pride: Richard Huelsenbeck who had arrived from Zurich was respectfully referred to as "Weltdada" (World Dada), while Hausmann was the "Dadasopher" and his lover Hannah Höch the "Dadasophess".

Even though all the manifestos and proclamations were signed jointly by all the Dadaists, most of the projects continued to be individual activities. The members of the Club Dada, who urged the leading representatives of politics and society in the German Reich to embrace anarchy, themselves embraced its practice enthusiastically within their own group. Egomania and petty jealousies among its members led to constant disputes. Fifty years later, Raoul Hausmann could still vividly recall these ideological battles: "Heartfield-Herzfelde and Mehring worshipped George Grosz, that pseudo-revolutionary, Huelsenbeck worshipped only Huelsenbeck; although he had produced most of our twelve events together with me, he was always ready to incline towards the Groszists. Conversely I tended to side with Baader, who unfortunately was too often obsessed with his paranoid religious ideas."

Dada Berlin evinced a more aggressive expression than its exemplar in Zurich. While the Swiss model was basically a literary cabaret, with a few anarchist features, the Club Dada adopted explicitly political attitudes. The Zurich people expressed their disgust with political events by radically rejecting any attitude of their own and retreating to a nihilist position. By contrast, the Berlin Dadaists formulated opposition to the war, the Weimar Republic, the Prussian bureaucracy, and the conservative bourgeoisie in numerous polemical proclamations, manifestos and public events.

Their most important communication organs were the numerous little Dadaist magazines which admittedly vanished after just a few numbers. These included *Der Dada*, edited by Raoul Hausmann, *Die freie Strasse* (The Open Street), which he edited

Hannah Höch
High Finance, 1923
Collage, 36 x 31 cm (14¼ x 12¼ in.)
Private collection

jointly with Johannes Baader, and *Der blutige Ernst* (Deadly Serious) and *Die Pleite* (Bankrupt). In addition, the Berlin Dadaists repeatedly succeeded in interesting the major daily newspapers in their activities, and in getting them to support their goals. Huelsenbeck, Hausmann, Baader, Grosz and Heartfield proved to be skilful publicity strategists, past masters in the art of drumming up support. "Dada conquers" and "Join Dada" were just two of the pithy slogans which they repeatedly employed in a variety of contexts. In 1920, the five protagonists of the movement even formed a Dada Advertising Company, which doubtless never won any commercial contracts. The Berlin Dadaists had an eye for business in other respects too. They had Dada Tours, which they used to take their ideas and activities to other cities, organized by large event agencies. Tristan Tzara could thus say in 1920 without a trace of irony: "Dada is: a flourishing business."

The attacks of the Berlin Dadaists on the political system were often acerbic in the extreme. They even threatened the destruction of the Weimar Republic: "We will put a bomb under Weimar. Berlin is the Dada Place. No one and nothing will be spared." Or they offered their services to revolutionary and separatist groups: "The Club Dada has set up a bureau for separating states. Fixed price-list for state-formation according to scale of operation." In impressive fashion, a large-format collage by Hannah Höch dating from 1920 describes better than any other work the mood of the times and the political direction Berlin Dadaism was taking. Its telling title: *Incision with the Dada kitchen knife through Germany's last Weimar beer-belly cultural epoch.*

The Berlin group extended Dadaist imagery by taking up the photomontage technique, which, though unknown in Zurich, had important precursors among the Russian Constructivists and Italian Futurists. This technique extended the familiar collage by including photographic fragments, the realism of which imported a new degree of provocation into the genre. Compared with drawings and paintings, however realistic, a photograph is always more credible. In combination with other typographical design elements, such as newspaper cuttings and printed headlines, photomontage conveys a dynamism, immediacy and actuality impossible in all other means of artistic expression. The rapidity made possible by the use of scissors and paste was just what the Berlin Dadaists were looking for. After all, most of their photomontages were not designed as autonomous works of art, but as posters, book covers, or as illustrations to accompany newspaper articles or advertising copy.

In view of the Dadaists' numerous spectacular actions and manifestos, it seems all the more surprising that it was precisely a somewhat traditional exhibition in the premises of an established art dealer that both marked the culmination of the movement in Berlin and at the same time ushered in its end. The "First International Dada Fair", which was held in the rooms of the art dealer Dr Otto Burchard from 30 June to 25 August 1920, remains the only attempt ever undertaken by the Dadaists to document the global character of their movement by means of an exhibition. The catalogue published to accompany it listed 174 works created by the widest possible variety of techniques. The organizers of the "Dada Fair" were the Propagandada Marshal George Grosz, the Dadasopher Raoul Hausmann and the "Monteurdada" (Mechanic Dada) John Heartfield. The gallery owner Otto Burchard not only made his rooms available, but also gave financial support to the enterprise, a gesture which moved Richard Huelsenbeck to bestow on him the honorary title of "Finance Dada".

On the surviving photographs of the exhibition it is possible to discern, among other things, posters with various Dadaist slogans: "Dilettantes! Rise up against art!", "Take Dada seriously, it's worth it", and "Dada is political". The photographs capture very well the atmosphere of the exhibition. The walls of both rooms in the gallery and in the connecting corridor are hung with every kind of exhibit cheek-by-jowl. In the middle of one room stands the splendid construction by Johannes Baader *The Great Plasto-Dio-Dada-Drama*, described in the catalogue as "Dadaist Monumental Architecture". From the ceiling of the other hall, John Heartfield and Rudolf Schlichter have

Für Moholy-Nagy von Hannah Höch.   Hochfinanz   1923

*"gadji beri bimba
glandridi laula lonni cadori/
gadjama gramma berida
bimbala glandri galassassa
laulitalomini/
gadji beri bin blassa
glassala laula lonni cadorsu
sassala bim/
gadjama tuffm i zimzalla
binban gligla wowolimai bin
beri ban/
o katalominai rhinozerossola
hopsamen laulitalomini hoooo
gadjama rhinozerossola
hopsamen/
bluku terullala blaulala
loooo"*

— HUGO BALL,
"GADJI BERI BIMBA", FIRST VERSE

Dada Almanac, 1920
18.3 x 13.3 cm (7¼ x 5¼ in.), 160 pages,
"commissioned by the Central Office of
the German Dada Movement, edited by
Richard Huelsenbeck"

suspended a tailor's dummy in officer's uniform and a pig mask. This exhibit later resulted in prosecution on a charge of "insulting the German army".

While the exhibition focused on Dada Berlin, many others also took part, including Hans Arp from Zurich, Otto Dix from Dresden, Francis Picabia from Paris, Max Ernst from Cologne, and Otto Schmalhausen from Antwerp. One man conspicuous by his absence was Kurt Schwitters from Hanover. But the "Dada Fair" did include a contribution by Rudolf Schlichter, which bore the title *The Death of Anna Blume*, a malicious allusion to Schwitters' popular poem "An Anna Blume". The "Dada Fair" had plenty of other provocative material on offer besides. But the public showed little interest, and there was no scandal. "They exhibited every possible boldness in respect of material, opinion, invention – unparalleled even by today's Neo-DADA or Pop Art – but the public wouldn't play along, no one wanted to see Dada any more," was Raoul Hausmann's sober résumé of the event many decades later.

Notwithstanding, Hausmann believed even before the exhibition opened that he could predict the press criticism, and thus published a parody of the expected reviews in the accompanying catalogue. Under the title "What the art critics will, in the opinion of the Dadasopher, say about the Dada exhibition", he wrote: "Let us establish at the outset that this Dada exhibition is a perfectly ordinary bluff, an unworthy speculation on the curiosity of the public – it is not worth coming to see it." A few lines later, he enlarges on the matter as follows: "Nothing they do can surprise us any more; everything is submerged in spasms of originality, which, devoid of any creativity, simply lets off steam in absurd antics."

And indeed, the review penned by the publicist and satirist Kurt Tucholsky for the *Berliner Tageblatt* newspaper read as follows: "If we discount that part of the club's activities which are pure bluff, there is not so awfully much left… It is pretty quiet in this little exhibition, and no one actually gets worked up any more." And he ends with the telling word-play: "Dada – na ja." (Dada, oh well…) So the charge of insulting the German army became the Berlin Dadaists' final triumph and a confirmation that they still had the capacity at least to annoy and provoke the authorities.

The result of the subsequent trial in April 1921 was, however, sobering. The charge against Hausmann was dropped completely. Baader, Burchard and Schlichter were acquitted. Only George Grosz and Wieland Herzfelde were convicted, and given trivial fines. The court judged the figure entitled *Prussian Archangel* hanging from the ceiling and Grosz' folder of prints entitled *God With Us* as nothing more than bad jokes in poor taste. The artists' defending counsel had argued thus himself – with devastating consequences, as Raoul Hausmann noted in retrospect: "His closing address saved Grosz' skin, but demolished him and his friends. Is this what your defence looks like: You didn't really mean it?" At the very moment Dada was really taken seriously by the powers that be, and was hauled up before the law to answer for its actions, the Dadaists got cold feet.

However, by this time the Berlin Dadaist movement was already in a state of dissolution. Heartfield, Hausmann, Baader and Grosz were beginning to go their own separate ways. As late as 1920, Richard Huelsenbeck had published a number of tracts which already sought to draw up a balance-sheet regarding the achievements of the Dada movement: "Germany must sink. Memoirs of an old Dadaist revolutionary" was the title of one of these books, and it was not intended ironically. "The victory of Dada. A balance-sheet of Dadaism" was another. In fact, the anti-art of Dadaism had already become part of art history. A few years later, it was simply being seen as yet another artistic trend among many others in the first half of the 20th century, and appraised for its historical significance. Even Raoul Hausmann chose this moment to seek a new way ahead: "Dada was dead, without glory and without a state funeral. Simply dead. The DADAists returned to private life. I declared myself as Anti-DADA and a PREsentist, and took up the fight on another level together with Schwitters."

Hanover – Kernel- and Husk-Dadaists

Raoul Hausmann had met Kurt Schwitters at the end of 1918 in the Café des Westens, when the latter introduced himself with the words: "I am a painter and nail my pictures." The two became friends at once. However, when Hausmann presented Schwitters' request for membership of the Club Dada the next day, he was forced to accept that "we knew next to nothing of this Schwitters". But an even more decisive factor was that "Huelsenbeck didn't like him". Like many others, Kurt Schwitters was denounced by Huelsenbeck as imitative, as well as for having an allegedly immoral eye for business. "In recent times, Dadaism has been embraced by many publishers on business grounds and by many poets on the make," he warned in the *Dada Almanac*, published in 1920. The surprising commercial success of Schwitters' verse collection *Anna Blume* only seemed to confirm these fears. Supported by a skilful advertising campaign, the slim volume sold more than ten thousand copies within a few months. In terms which could not be misunderstood, Richard Huelsenbeck therefore noted: "Dada vigorously and categorically rejects works such as the famous 'Anna Blume' by Mister Kurt Schwitters." His dismissive attitude was finally confirmed, however, by a visit to Schwitters in Hanover: "He lived like a Victorian petit bourgeois – we called him the abstract Spitzweg, the Caspar David Friedrich of the Dadaist revolution," Huelsenbeck later recalled, and added aghast: "I have never been able to come to terms with the similarity of Schwitters' bourgeois and revolutionary worlds."

Schwitters himself reacted to his rejection by the Berlin Dadaists in general and to Huelsenbeck's attacks in particular with a self-assured polemic of his own. In a magazine article in December 1920, he counter-attacked, wickedly distinguishing between what he called the kernel-Dadaists and the husk-Dadaists. This was a play on Huelsenbeck's name, "Huelse" being the German for "husk". "In the beginning there were only kernel-Dadaists," declared Schwitters in the article. "The husk-Dadaists peeled off from this original kernel under their leader Huelsenbeck, taking parts of the kernel with them." And Schwitters added, in a burlesque of Huelsenbeck's formulation in the *Dada Almanac*: "Merz vigorously and categorically rejects the illogical and dilettante views of art held by Mister Huelsenbeck." At the same time, Schwitters proclaimed his artistic and personal sympathy with some of the artists whom he called kernel-Dadaists, such as Hans Arp, Tristan Tzara and Francis Picabia. But above all, he enjoyed an intense friendship with Raoul Hausmann and Hannah Höch, with whom he frequently undertook joint activities.

As early as the summer of 1918, Kurt Schwitters had joined the circle centring on Herwarth Walden's gallery Der Sturm in Berlin. From now on, Der Sturm provided him the artistic home in the capital which the Club Dada would not. Schwitters exhibited a number of times in the Der Sturm gallery, and published regularly in the magazine of the same name. Particularly important was his first solo exhibition, which Der Sturm staged in July 1919, and in which Kurt Schwitters first presented his works under the term "Merz". He had used the word "Merz" (which has no meaning in German) as a fragment in one of his first assemblages, having cut it out of the name "Kommerz- und Privatbank" (Commercial and Private Bank) and introduced it into one of his works.

The assemblage was then given the title *Merz picture* on the basis of this snippet of text. Unable to use the term Dada for his art, he called all his art after this work "Merz": "Having exhibited these works for the first time at Der Sturm in Berlin, I now sought a collective name for this genre, as I was unable to classify my pictures according to old categories such as Expressionism, Cubism, Futurism or whatever. I now called all my pictures generically Merz pictures, after the characteristic picture."

For Schwitters, the Merz principle was superior to pure oil-painting if for no other reason than that it did not just use paint, but any artistic or everyday material whatever. In the process, all the materials used are subsumed into an abstract pictorial composition. He once summarized the creation of these early *Merz pictures* as follows: "At first I constructed pictures from the material which I happened to have conveniently to hand, such as tram tickets, cloakroom tickets, bits of wood, wire, string, twisted wheels, tissue paper, cans, glass splinters etc. These objects are integrated into the picture either as they are, or altered, according to the demands of the picture. By mutual comparison

Dada conquers!, 1920
Exhibition poster for the re-opening of the "Dada Pre-Spring" exhibition at Schildergasse 37 in Cologne, after it was closed by the police, 28.7 x 40 cm (11¼ x 15¾ in.)
Zurich, Kunsthaus Zürich

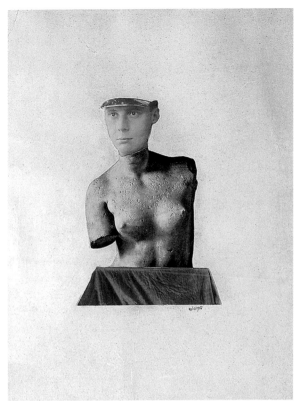

they lose their individual character, their individual poison. They are dematerialized, and are the material of the picture." Schwitters always went out of his way to stress the aesthetic quality of his works of art, thus emphasizing once more the difference between them and the Dadaist objects: "The pure Merz is art, pure Dadaism is non-art; both deliberately." With their political anarchism and their anti-art gesture, the Berlin Dadaists must naturally have felt this, if anything conservative, view of art on Schwitters' part to be a provocation.

Schwitters' Merz art is in no way limited to collages, which he called *Merz drawings*, or to the larger-format assemblages, the so-called *Merz pictures*. The term quickly became, for him, synonymous with all his artistic activities. Thus he produced a number of *Merz sculptures* and an extensive body of Merz poetry. Kurt Schwitters designed models for a Merz stage, and several pieces of Merz architecture. He founded the Merz advertising centre, which, in contrast to the Dada Advertising Company of the Berlin Dadaists, actually took on and carried out numerous contracts, and in the late 1920s, even undertook the revamping of all the written material produced by Hanover City Council. Finally, Schwitters had the vision of all his activities being subsumed in a utopian Merz total world picture. "Merz means creating relationships, preferably between all the things in the world," he proclaimed as early as 1924 in one of his theoretical manifestos, and three years later was able to assert: "Now I can call myself Merz."

Cologne – Dada as a burgeois art business?

Unlike Kurt Schwitters, the Cologne Dadaists were represented at the "First International Dada Fair" in Berlin. Even before it opened in June 1920, Max Ernst, known as the "Dadamax", Johannes Theodor Baargeld, whose real name was Alfred F. Gruenwald, and Hans Arp, who had arrived from Zurich at the beginning of 1919, had organized the "Dada Pre-spring" at the Winter tavern in Cologne, with works by – apart from the organizers themselves – Francis Picabia, Heinrich Hoerle and Louise Straus-

LEFT
Max Ernst and Hans Arp
Physiomythological Diluvial Picture (Fatagaga), 1920
Collage and mixed technique,
11.2 x 10 cm (4½ x 4 in.)
Hanover, Sprengel Museum Hannover

RIGHT
Johannes Theodor Baargeld
Typical Vertical Misrepresentation as a Depiction of the Dada Baargeld, 1920
Photomontage, 37.1 x 31 cm (14½ x 12¼ in.)
Zurich, Kunsthaus Zürich

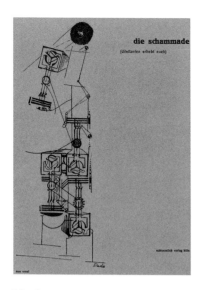

Max Ernst
Die Schammade
Title page of the periodical, 1920
Edited by Max Ernst and Johannes
Baargeld

Ernst. Some of the exhibits which survived the aggression of the public were subsequently sent to the "Dada Fair" in Berlin.

Cologne was not the centre of a broad Dada movement. The group's activities were focused primarily on the trio of Ernst, Baargeld and Arp. They not only organized the "Dada Pre-spring", but published such magazines as *Die Schammade* and *Der Ventilator*, the latter having a print run of 40,000 copies. *Die Schammade* was subtitled "Dilettantes arise" and on its cover page presented an absurd, Dadaist machine construction by Max Ernst. Although it never got past its first number of February 1920, *Die Schammade* was of decisive importance for the Cologne Dadaists. Via the international authors who had been invited to contribute, they were able to make numerous contacts in the Dadaist centres of Zurich and Berlin. For Max Ernst, the magazine also marked the interface between his activities as a Dadaist in Cologne and his approach to French Surrealism, whose future spokesman André Breton, along with Louis Aragon, Paul Éluard and Tristan Tzara, sent detailed articles to *Die Schammade*. For Hans Arp, Cologne was no more than a brief stopover on his way to Paris. In 1922 he was eventually followed there by Max Ernst.

As early as March 1919 Max Ernst, together with his wife Louise Straus-Ernst and the artist Willy Fick had taken part in a disruptive Dada action on the occasion of the premiere of the play *Der junge König* (The Young King) by Raoul Konen in Cologne's playhouse. Heckling loudly ("Throw the author out, this is not watchable!") they interrupted the performance until the police came to take them away. They saw their protest both in political and artistic terms, as they were as opposed to established Expressionism as they were to political conservatism. "For us in Cologne in 1919, Dada was primarily a mental attitude. We set out to prevent the performances of the 'Young King', a monarchist and patriotic play of provocative stupidity," was how Ernst described their motives. But just six months later, with the founding and first exhibition of Gruppe D, the Dadaist movement in Cologne also got some organizational structure.

Illustrations from the catalogue of the
Kölner Lehrmittel-Anstalt (page 142).
Max Ernst turned to drawings like these
for inspiration for his work *the master's
bedroom it's worth spending a night in it.*

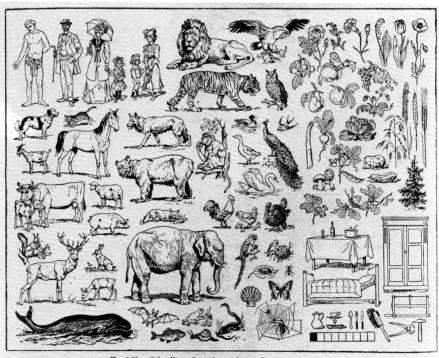

Max Ernst
the master's bedroom it's worth spending a night in it, 1920
Collage, gouache and pencil
on paper, 16.3 x 22 cm (6½ x 8¾ in.)
Private collection

So many artists were involved in the exhibition, however, among them Heinrich Hoerle, Otto Freundlich and Paul Klee, that others, such as Franz Wilhelm Seiwert, withdrew their participation on the grounds that Dada had become a bourgeois art business. Although this judgement seems too harsh, the only event in Cologne to uphold the anti-art impulse of Dadaism was the event in the Winter tavern. Opened in April 1920, the "Dada Pre-spring" was closed by the police after just a few days on the grounds that it was disseminating pornography. The only piece of evidence, however, was the reproduction of a classical nude by Albrecht Dürer which Max Ernst had incorporated into one of his collages. The organizers Ernst and Baargeld celebrated the official re-opening as a personal triumph. "DADA conquers" they printed in large letters on the new exhibition poster, and ironically emphasized their pro-state attitude: "DADA stands for law and orders!" (using the German word "Orden", which means "orders of chivalry, medals", in place of the usual "Ordnung").

In his autobiography Max Ernst listed the historical high points of this exhibition individually: "Baargeld's *Antropophiler Bandwurm* and *Fluidoskeptrik der Rotswita von Gandersheim*, Dadamax's *Unerhörte Drohung aus den Lüften* and *Original-Laufrelief aus der Lunge eines 17jährigen Rauchers*. The works destroyed by the public in fits of rage were regularly replaced by new ones." According to other sources, the organizers explicitly urged visitors to smash a sculpture by Max Ernst with a hammer they made available for the purpose.

Within such prescribed limits, Max Ernst too accepted the anti-art attitude of Dadaism. Otherwise he proved to be a brilliant creator of pictures who, like no other artist, knew how to exploit all the possibilities of collage, and in the decades to come, how to try out a succession of new pictorial techniques. "What is collage?" he asked in his "Biographical Notes", and answered in the third person: "Max Ernst for example has defined it thus: the collage technique is the systematic exploitation of the chance or artificially provoked confrontation of two or more mutually alien realities on an obviously inappropriate level – and the poetic spark which jumps across when these realities approach each other." Max Ernst's description of the collage principle is indeed closer to the Surrealist approach to picture creation than to the ironic or aggressively political montages of the Berlin Dadaists. The true spirit of Dada emanates above all from his collage drawings of senseless mechanical constructions and biological structures.

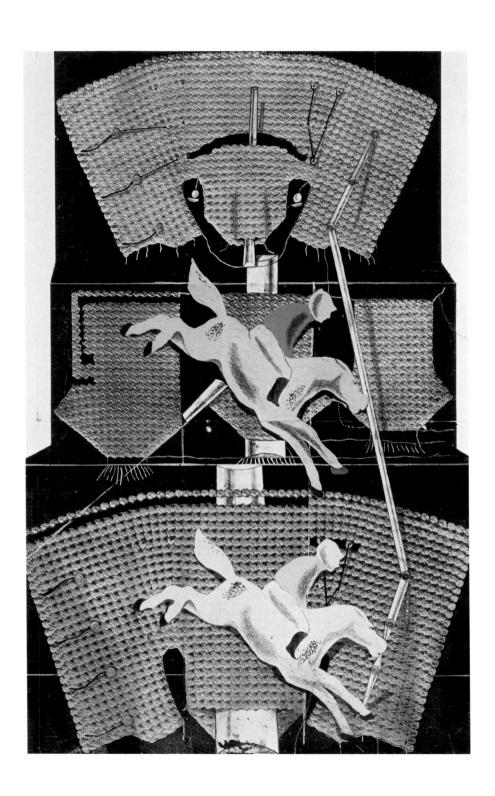

Max Ernst
Dada-Degas, c. 1920/21
Collage, 48 x 31 cm (19 x 12¼ in.)
Munich, Pinakothek der Moderne

New York – "Dada is American"

In New York it was likewise chiefly the émigré European artists who brought the anarchic Dada impulse to the city. The two Frenchmen Marcel Duchamp and Francis Picabia met here in 1919 and got together with Man Ray from Philadelphia, the gallery owner and photographer Alfred Stieglitz, and the poet and patron of the arts Walter Arensberg. Cheaply produced magazines were, for the New York Dadaists too, an important means of communication with the other international centres of the movement. In 1915, Stieglitz had started publishing the series *291*, whose title was derived from the address of his gallery. Two years later it was superseded by Picabia's *391*, which appeared until the end of 1924. Whatever the title might otherwise suggest, in his pamphlet "Dada is American" Walter Arensberg emphasized above all the international character of the movement: "Dada is American, Dada is Russian, Dada is Spanish, Dada is Swiss, Dada is German, Dada is French…" And he closed with a typical Dada contradiction: "I, Walter Conrad Arensberg, American poet, declare that I am against Dada, because it is only thus that I can be for Dada."

New York also had its share of typical Dada scandals. Thus at a performance organized by Marcel Duchamp, the boxer and man of letters Arthur Cravan shocked the respectable citizenry by presenting them with a suitcase full of dirty underwear. In contrast to their counterparts in Berlin, however, the New York Dadaists were not interested in anarcho-political spectacle for their own sake. The city on the other side of the Atlantic was too far from the battlefields of Europe for their horrors to need to be discharged in provocative, oppositional and anti-rationalist gestures.

In contrast to Zurich or Paris, here it was not the literary members who claimed to be the spokesmen of the Dadaist movement. Rather, in the persons of Picabia, Man Ray and Duchamp, it was the visual artists who made the most important contributions to New York Dada, introducing developments that paved the way for much of subsequent 20th-century art. At the same time, their works too came under the heading of "anti-art". Francis Picabia drew absurd mechanical constructions which parodied the prevailing enthusiasm for technology and the modern faith in progress. Man Ray used everyday utilitarian objects and pictorial motifs which he alienated by combining them with other materials and less-than-obvious titles.

For Marcel Duchamp's ready-mades, not even the Dadaist idea of anti-art is adequate. When in 1917 he presented a signed urinal under the title *Fountain* to the jury-less exhibition of the New York Society of Independent Artists, his intention went beyond a mere salutary provocation of the academic art business. Ready-mades are selected utilitarian objects which are raised to the status of works of art simply by dint of being defined as such by the artist and being put on display in an exhibition. Duchamp was not concerned with the Dadaist rejection and destruction of the existing concepts of art, but with removing boundaries and taking this process to its logical conclusion. His ready-mades stand above all for a radical redefinition of what can constitute a work of art, how we can perceive it, and how we deal with it. For the first time, the ready-mades drew the attention of the beholder to the importance of the context for the definition and evaluation of a work of art. This redefinition and the so-called "context debate" which it initiated made Marcel Duchamp the most influential artist of the 20th century.

Paris – "It is our differences which unite us"

The international Dada movement was born in Zurich in 1916 and buried just six years later in Paris. But it was in the French capital that it experienced a final and belated heyday. During the war, the young generation of artists had either served at the front, or else fled abroad in time to avoid military service. Only after the Armistice of 11 November 1918 did Louis Aragon, André Breton, Philippe Soupault and Tristan Tzara gradually return to Paris. In 1919, Francis Picabia and Marcel Duchamp returned from New York. Their colleague from there, Man Ray, followed two years later. After a stop-off in Cologne, Hans Arp arrived in Paris in 1920, where he was visited that same year by Max

Max Ernst
The Punching Ball or Buonarotti's Immortality or Max Ernst and Caesar Buonarotti, 1920
Collage, photograph and gouache on paper, 17.6 x 11.5 cm (7 x 4½ in.)
Private collection

Ernst, who himself moved to the French capital in 1922. Major impetus was given to the Dadaist movement by the arrival of Tristan Tzara in January 1920. Breton had urged him several times to come back from Zurich, writing for example at the end of 1919: "You'll be coming at just the right moment. Life here has become more active." Just six days after his arrival, Tristan Tzara proclaimed the birth of Parisian Dadaism at the first Friday soirée of the magazine *Littérature*. Tzara enjoyed his role of revolutionary spokesman, and here in Paris he could speak with the authority which derived from the aura associated with being one of the founding fathers of the movement in Zurich. The other leading figure in the French group was the likewise 24-year-old poet André Breton.

In Paris too, Dada was first and foremost a literary movement, but in contrast to the Cabaret Voltaire in Zurich, where the Dadaists performed a lively programme of short recitations, poems, musical numbers and dances, their French counterparts expressed themselves chiefly through their numerous publications. It seemed almost as if each of the Paris Dadaists had founded his own mouthpiece in which to publish his own manifestos, essays and poems and those of his friends. Arthur Cravan's magazine *Maintenant*, which appeared from 1912 to 1915, became the role model for many of the later publications. In 1919, Breton founded the magazine *Littérature*, while Francis Picabia continued to publish his own *391*. Tzara published the series *Dada*, and the Belgian Paul Dermée added to this flood of magazines at the end of 1920 with his *L'Esprit Nouveau*. Paul Éluard called his publication *Proverbe*. One rendezvous for the French Dadaists was the Au Sans Pareil bookshop and gallery, founded in 1919, which staged Max Ernst's first Paris exhibition in May 1921.

André Breton found a metaphor for the Paris group which encapsulated the typical Dadaist oxymoron: "It is above all our differences which unite us," he observed. Thus it is hardly surprising that his alliance with Tristan Tzara, whose arrival on the scene he

"Dada Max Ernst"
Opening of the exhibition at Galerie
Au Sans Pareil, Paris, 2 May 1921
Paris, Musée national d'art moderne,
Centre Pompidou

FROM LEFT TO RIGHT
René Hilsum, Benjamin Péret, Serge
Charchoune, Philippe Soupault, Jacques
Rigaut (with his head lowered), André
Breton

The Rope Dancer Accompanies Herself With Her Shadows

had awaited with such yearning, broke up again as early as 1921. As the Paris Dadaists had only come together after the war had ended, they lacked any common aim on which to concentrate their rage and their actions.

André Breton had discovered the technique of automatic writing as early as 1920. The following year he went to Vienna to see Sigmund Freud, who had founded a theory of the interpretation of dreams linking them to the subconscious. Breton went on to replace the aggressive, provocative and satirical contributions of Dadaism with a literature which excluded any rational control of the creative process by employing techniques of automatism and chance, and drawing on the subconscious. In 1924 he published his new insights in the first *Surrealist Manifesto*, in which he demanded "a 'think-diktat' free of any control by reason, beyond all considerations of ethics and aesthetics." Breton's methodology filled a vacuum which for many artists and writers had arisen now that, following the end of the war, Dadaism was increasingly losing its influence and raison d'être. Enthusiastically, Paul Éluard, Philippe Soupault, Francis Picabia, Hans Arp, Man Ray and Max Ernst joined with him to form the Paris Surrealist group. After initial doubts, even the arch-Dadaist Tristan Tzara took an active part in the new movement from 1929 on.

Man Ray
The Rope Dancer Accompanies Herself with Her Shadows, 1916
Oil on canvas, 132.1 x 186.4 cm
(52 x 73½ in.)
New York, The Museum of Modern Art, Gift of David Thompson

Hans Arp
Relief Dada, 1916

b. 1887 in Strasbourg
d. 1966 in Basle

"We do not wish to imitate nature, we do not wish to reproduce. We want to produce. We want to produce the way a plant produces its fruit, not depict. We want to produce directly, not indirectly. Since there is not a trace of abstraction in this art we call it concrete art."

— HANS ARP

Relief Dada, 1916
Wood, painted,
24 x 17.5 x 8.9 cm (9½ x 7 x 3½ in.)
Basle, Kunstmuseum Basel,
Gift of Marguerite Arp-Hagenbach

Like many of his fellow Dadaists, Hans Arp was an acknowledged talent in both literature and the visual arts. His first poem was published as early as 1903, while his academic training as an artist had led him between 1901 and 1907 from Strasbourg, the capital of Alsace, which at that time belonged to Germany, to Weimar and then to Paris, where he attended the renowned Académie Julian, at which Marcel Duchamp also took painting lessons in 1904. Arp was caught out in Paris by the outbreak of the Great War. Classified as an enemy alien, he managed to take refuge in Switzerland in 1915.

The *Relief Dada* dates from 1916, the year the movement was founded in Zurich. The object is part of a series named *Earthly Forms (Irdische Formen)*. Following a group of works he had executed jointly with his lover Sophie Taeuber, which consist of austerely geometric additions of forms, what we have here is a surprising new beginning within his visual œuvre. The *Earthly Forms* are reliefs in wood which Hans Arp has screwed together one on top of the other, and then painted. Compared with earlier works, their vocabulary of organic and biomorphic forms is conspicuous. In these constructions, he banned the right angle from his repertoire, and gave the individual pieces of wood curved, wave-like outlines.

Another noteworthy feature is that the elements are not fastened to a neutral rear wall. Instead, their external contours grope irregularly into the surrounding space. For art, this was a new experience and an important formal insight. By dispensing with a frame or a base, the gulf between the beholder's actual space and the artwork's own space was abolished. In respect of fitting and painting, too, Hans Arp has attempted to avoid any illusionism. Not only does the material structure of the wood retain its visible identity in spite of the coat of paint, but the surface also still shows traces of the brushstrokes and casual craftsmanship. Arp explicitly reveals the five screws which hold the individual parts of *Relief Dada* together. The aesthetic issues which concern Hans Arp here already confirm that he was keeping a certain distance from the anti-art assertions of the other Zurich Dadaists.

The term *Earthly Forms* hints at Arp's confrontation with nature, whose formal language provides the exemplar for his own artistic creativity. The poetic titles of some of the reliefs in this series, such as the 1916/17 *Interment of the Birds and the Butterflies (Die Grablegung der Vögel und Schmetterlinge)*, or *Plant Hammer (Pflanzenhammer)*, dating from 1917, along with their abbreviated forms, still hint at the landscapes which provided their inspiration. In the case of *Relief Dada*, there is no longer any sign of a figurative representation of nature. The work's formal vocabulary is abstract, but is still oriented towards organic structures. The contours are surprising, irregular and slightly curved. They follow no pre-formulated principle. In the wood reliefs, the individual coloured elements come together to form a "harmony in parallel with nature", as the Impressionist Paul Cézanne described his own painting. Arp's other artistic relationships were with the Blauer Reiter painters Wassily Kandinsky and Franz Marc. As the latter had already done with his animal motifs, in the midst of war Arp sought in nature a peaceful and ethical counter-image to the de-humanized killing on Europe's battlefields. To this extent, Arp's attitude was in accord with that of his fellow Dadaists in Zurich and Berlin, even though he found a quite different pictorial language to express his revulsion.

Hans Arp
Untitled (Squares Arranged According to the Laws of Chance), 1917

Two features were of decisive importance for Hans Arp's Dadaist work: cooperation with other artists and the principle of chance. Both served to enable him to subvert the myth of the individual artistic genius. Instead, he sought to give his works an impersonal character. For his reliefs, he usually sketched out the shapes of the wood elements before having them cut out by a joiner. In this way, he could make multiple copies of the individual motifs, or create different variations for different works. In his collages, a random structure often forms the starting situation for his artistic design. 1917 or thereabouts saw the appearance of a whole collection of such collages, which he entitled *Untitled (Squares Arranged According to the Laws of Chance) (Ohne Titel [Quadrate nach den Gesetzen des Zufalls geordnet])*. This claim notwithstanding, it takes no more than a cursory glance at the work illustrated here to see that the arrangement of the papers is by no means so random as the title would have us believe. In his memoirs *Dada Profile*, the Zurich fellow Dadaist and future chronicler of the Dadaist movement, Hans Richter, commented as follows on Arp's use of the random element: "A torn corner became the starting point for new compositions, a chance rain-blot the centre of an explosion, which then spread across further areas of the picture. The recognition of chance as the actual centre of Dada vitalized him and became in his hands the magic which imbued not only his work but his whole existence."

The chance principle however is only ever the basis of the design. Hans Arp cut the twelve coloured papers for the collage into approximate squares, albeit invariably avoiding actual right angles. These snippets of paper were then allowed to fall onto the cardboard. The resulting configuration served to inspire the next "ordering" intervention. As is known, Tristan Tzara also suggested the same technique for creating Dadaist poetry. Arp pushed his bits of paper around on the cardboard until he had found a definitive composition. In the example illustrated here, the dark papers group in dance-like fashion around a pale quadrilateral in the centre. The paper surfaces do not overlap, but merely touch at their vertices. Two pieces of paper extend beyond the edge of the cardboard, or rather would have, had not Arp cut them off at this point. The final result evinces a balance between compositional order and the principle of chance. The chance configurations, which are manifested in the details, are so to speak cancelled out in the total composition. Thus the motif is in a constant state of tension. The shaping hand of the artist is apparent to the beholder, but at the same time there is no dominant order.

The technique used here by Hans Arp, namely to allow his picture construction to be guided by chance structures, was also being used at the same time by Max Ernst. But it was above all the Surrealists, who, in the 1920s, were to make random and uncontrollable techniques the principles of their artistic and literary creativity. Hans Arp never allowed himself to be totally absorbed into the Dadaist movement, always maintaining a critical aloofness. This was also true of his later cooperation with the Paris Surrealists and of his membership of the international art association Abstraction-Création. Surprisingly, his independent work allowed links with all these very different artistic movements.

Untitled (Squares Arranged According to the Laws of Chance), 1917
Collage, 33.2 x 25.9 cm (13 x 10¼ in.)
New York, The Museum of Modern Art,
Gift of Philip Johnson

Hans Arp
i-picture, c. 1920

Hans Arp first met Hugo Ball as early as 1915 at the Hack bookshop in Zurich. When Ball opened his Cabaret Voltaire in February 1916, Arp was responsible for the decor. He chose the colours for the walls and used them to exhibit works by himself and by other artist friends. Later Hans Arp took part in the cabaret programme by reading his own poems. Nevertheless, he kept aloof from certain Dadaist actions, and in a letter to a girl-friend complained about the anti-German attitudes of his fellow artists. After the end of the movement in Zurich, Hans Arp stayed for a time in Cologne, where he created collages together with Max Ernst, for which they invented the term "Fatagaga" pictures. The word was an acronym based on fabrication de tableaux garantis gazométriques (production of guaranteed gasometric pictures).

Arp was always particularly interested in cooperation with other artists. This was because, like the principle of chance, it allowed him to hive off a part of the creative process. He also produced many works in collaboration with Sophie Taeuber, his future wife, whom he had met in November 1915 at an exhibition at the Galerie Tanner in Zurich. The repertoire of austere geometric forms in the *i-picture* illustrated here (dating from c. 1920) is ultimately due to her influence. As an artist and above all as a designer, Sophie Taeuber preferred a vocabulary of reduced, geometric and blocklike forms.

This small-format collage is composed of various pieces of paper cut into rectangular shapes. Their austere arrangement alone (the elements are all positioned parallel to the sides of the picture) distinguishes the work from the earlier *Untitled (Squares Arranged According to the Laws of Chance)* (1917). The base at the bottom of the picture occupies some two-thirds of the total height, and is dominated by a solid dark area. This is balanced at the top by a second rectangle cut from the same piece of paper.

The most striking detail of the work is, however, the powerful representation of the letter "i". Arp did not cut it out of a printed text and stick it into the composition, but drew it using a stencil. Fragments of text do occasionally crop up as graphic design elements in other collages by this artist, but here the motif could go back to two other sources. Time and again, Hans Arp invented figurative "abbreviations" which can be seen as either iconic in character or as abstract shapes. In this sense, it would be possible to recognize in the letter the abstract representation of a human figure with a stylized head and body.

The letter "i" also plays an important role in the work of Kurt Schwitters. From 1920, he gave the name *i-drawings (i-Zeichnungen)* to those of his collages which were created not through the composition of individual elements, but by defining a detail of a larger motif. Hans Arp, who at this time had been friends with Schwitters for two years, could have appropriated this method for the work illustrated here, having cut the composition out of a larger collage. The final addition of the letter "i" might then serve as a somewhat unsubtle clue to the way the work was created.

Hans Arp always accorded his work an ethical component. As early as 1915, on the occasion of his exhibition at the Galerie Tanner, he introduced his works in the catalogue with the words: "These works are buildings constructed of lines, surfaces, shapes, colours. They seek to approach what is inexpressible about man and eternity. They represent a turning away from the self-seeking aspect of mankind."

i-picture, c. 1920
Collage, 20.6 x 16.6 cm (8 x 6½ in.)
Zurich, Kunsthaus Zürich

Johannes Baader
The Author of the Book
"Fourteen Letters of Christ" in His Home, c. 1920

b. 1875 in Stuttgart
d. 1955 in Adldorf

Double portrait of Johannes Baader
and Raoul Hausmann, c. 1919/20
Photoprint of a montage on
newsprint, 25.4 x 15.8 cm (10 x 6¼ in.)
Zurich, Kunsthaus Zürich

Johannes Baader studied architecture and is said to have designed, among other things, the rocks for the polar-bear enclosure in Hagenbeck's Zoological Garden. It was more by chance than anything else that he joined the Berlin Dada group. In 1918 John Heartfield and his brother Wieland Herzfelde discovered in him the born Dadaist, and introduced him to their friends. Herzfelde later reported: "Anyone could call themselves a Dadaist; they had to see to it that they did so. Some we discovered, for example a man certified as having diminished responsibility and was thus not culpable for his actions. We met him at our printer's during the first days of November 1918, where he was collecting the book he had written, *Vierzehn Briefe Christi*. He introduced himself as the 'President of the Universe'. Immediately we took him to Grosz' studio, declared him to be the 'Oberdada' (Supreme Dada) and treated him in a correspondingly reverential fashion…"

The 1920 photomontage, stuck on to the page of a book, of Johannes Baader *The Author of the Book "Fourteen Letters of Christ" in His Home (Der Verfasser des Buches "Vierzehn Briefe Christi" in seinem Heim)* is designed as a self-portrait. In spite of this, there is no recognizable similarity between the figure portrayed and Baader's public image. The Dadaists honoured him as their Supreme Dada, as a figure who personified Dada in his lifestyle. Baader for his part used Dadaism and the publicity value of its actions in order to propagate his own extreme views. This is why he was controversial even within the movement – and quite definitely so when during the Dada tour of Prague in the spring of 1920 he suddenly disappeared with the day's takings.

Raoul Hausmann however always stuck by him, and photographs exist in which their heads seem almost symbiotically fused. But their relationship was not without its tensions, as Hannah Höch reported: "From an early stage a friend – an enemy – a friend of Hausmann's. To start with, it was impossible to understand the associations in this man's essence, or his manifestations." Indeed, he took perfectly seriously the boastful title of "President of the Universe", with which he adorned himself even before being accepted by the Club Dada in Berlin. With his dense, dark beard, he came across as an obscure wandering preacher. He was an egomaniac and a self-appointed prophet who formulated his claim to rule the world with unshakable conviction. In 1917 in Saarbrücken he stood unsuccessfully for the Reichstag. A year later, he even claimed to be above the National Assembly and declared: "Those who will not follow me as 'Christ', are welcome as friends of the 'Supreme Dada.'" The period of the war and the subsequent revolutionary unrest was one in which old traditions collapsed to leave a political vacuum. It was a climate in which a number of self-styled saviours and Führer-figures could flourish, Johannes Baader among them.

Baader had published his *Fourteen Letters of Christ* in 1914, styling himself as the reborn Christ. In this collage he presents himself through Dadaist role play, as proclaimed by the stuck-on text "dada". However, he has substituted an advertising figure for his self-portrait. On its forehead it has an indecipherable sticker. It is a photograph of the figure which Baader that same year had created in his *Great Plasto-Dio-Dada-Drama*. In the clutter of his home, this well-dressed "author" seems, however, somewhat out of place. With his austerely parted hair, the twisted moustache and the uniform-like suit, he represents precisely that conservative middle class which the Dadaists otherwise held in such contempt.

The Author of the Book "Fourteen Letters of Christ" in His Home, c. 1920
Photomontage, 21.6 x 14.6 cm
(8½ x 5¾ in.)
New York, The Museum of Modern Art

Johannes Baader
The Great Plasto-Dio-Dada-Drama, 1920

Most of the Dadaists never appreciated the work of art as traditionally understood. Numerous pictures, collages and photomontages were created for particular occasions as poster designs, book illustrations or exhibition pieces, and subsequently ended up unceremoniously in the waste-paper basket. Accordingly, the artists attached no importance either to precise dating or to titles. As a result, in the case of numerous surviving works, uncertainty exists as to when they were created, and sometimes there is more than one title. Indeed, titles are sometimes contradictory. This is true of Johannes Baader's most important work: *The Great Plasto-Dio-Dada-Drama: GERMANY'S GREATNESS AND DECLINE by Teacher Hagendorf or The Fantastical Life-Story of the Supreme Dada (Das große Plasto-Dio-Dada-Drama: DEUTSCHLANDS GROESSE UND UNTERGANG durch Lehrer Hagendorf oder Die phantastische Lebensgeschichte des Oberdada)*. The assemblage was created in 1920 for the "First International Dada Fair" at Dr Otto Burchard's gallery. After the exhibition had ended, the work was destroyed.

All that has been preserved is a single photograph of the assemblage, along with a detailed description of the work by Baader himself in the *Dada Almanac* published a few months later. There, the various storeys of the tower are commented on as follows: "The cylinder soars into the sky and extols the glories of teacher Hagendorf's reading desk." In the exhibition leaflet, Baader was somewhat more ironic: "The cylinder screws itself into the sky and proclaims the resurrection of Germany through teacher Hagendorf and his reading desk." In fact, this "reading desk" is no more than a reading aid for bedridden patients: Johannes Baader had worked briefly for the manufacturer.

The *Great Plasto-Dio-Dada-Drama* is a looming tower, a wood and cardboard-box construction, to which Baader has attached numerous posters, whole newspapers, among them the popular *BZ am Mittag* and the Dadaist *Die Pleite*, a mousetrap, a woven basket, a section of stovepipe, a toy train carriage, and the advertising figure familiar from the photomontage *The Author of the Book "Fourteen Letters of Christ" in His Home*. As in the collage, it represents here too the self-portrait of the artist. Baader has divided the tower into five storeys, which are designated by large-format panels. On the photograph the figures 2 and 5 can be made out clearly. Each storey has a particular theme assigned to it. "1st storey: the Preparation of the Supreme Dada; 2nd storey: the Metaphysical test; 3rd storey: the Inauguration; 4th storey: the World War; 5th storey: World Revolution." The text written by Johannes Baader to accompany the work turns out to be a model of explanation of the world, which goes somewhat over the top in its oscillation between irony and pathos, combining fragments of Baader's own biography, political splinters of the age and all kinds of culture-historical references. Thus on the assemblage in the second storey of the structure he says: "A museum of the masterworks of every century opens up under the twitching of the 'old Germanic' mousetrap. Burst in two in the middle is the church, the third part having been demolished in accordance with its purpose and standing as a prison on Alexanderplatz (comfortable sojourns possible on all weekdays, Sundays, holidays, and putsch days)."

During the "Dada Fair", Kurt Schwitters came to Berlin and visited the exhibition. Baader's *Great Plasto-Dio-Dada-Drama* must have exerted a particular fascination on him, for – as evidenced by a photograph – he was already working at the same time on a similar, so-called *Merz Column* on which were stuck newspaper cuttings, posters, and fragments of objects, the whole being crowned with a doll's head. Following the example of the "Dada Fair" in Berlin, Kurt Schwitters also papered the walls of his Hanover studio with numerous poster texts and pictures, as well as pieces of newspaper.

The Great Plasto-Dio-Dada-Drama, 1920
Assemblage, no dimensions available (destroyed)
Photograph of the "First International Dada Fair"

Johannes Theodor Baargeld
The Red King, 1920

b. 1892 in Stettin (Sczcecin)
d. 1927 at Mont Blanc

*"I have no pillow
for my urn."*

— JOHANNES THEODOR BAARGELD

Dada in Cologne was always a two-man band, which grew into a triumvirate during the occasional visits of Hans Arp to the city. They worked together on various projects. Max Ernst and Johannes Theodor Baargeld were represented at the "First International Dada Fair" in Berlin in June 1920 among other work with the so-called *Simultantriptychon*. As early as February 1919 they had, according to Ernst's reminiscence, co-authored a number of contributions for *Ventilator*. However, neither their names nor the term Dada appear in the magazine. Even so, the six issues which appeared in February and March 1919 are regarded as the first publication of the Dada movement in Cologne. It has since transpired that Baargeld financed the magazine, which attained a print run of up to 40,000 copies.

Johannes Theodor Baargeld's real name was Alfred F. Gruenwald. In 1914 he had, like many of his generation, volunteered for military service, a decision he very soon bitterly regretted. The experience of war in the trenches formed the basis of his later political commitment. In 1918 he joined the left-wing worker's party, the U. S. D. P. (Independent Social Democratic Party of Germany), the next year the Dadaist movement.

Politics and art were for him the same thing. He hoped that his Dadaist protest against bourgeois society would further the movement for political renewal in Germany, a hope shared by some of the Berlin group. In fact, he came from an upper-middle-class background himself. His father was managing director of a re-insurance firm based in Cologne, the Kölnische Rückversicherungsgesellschaft. His parents were culturally open-minded, but politically conservative. It was because of his prosperous background that his friends called him Baargeld ("cash"). As a Dadaist he also bore the title "Zentrodada".

The Red King (Le roi rouge/Der rote König), dating from 1920, is one of the few pictorial works of Johannes Theodor Baargeld to have survived. It is a piece of wallpaper with a decorative pattern, drawn over in Indian ink. Baargeld employs the same pictorial principle as his fellow Dadaist Max Ernst. An arbitrary starting material is treated, re-shaped and manipulated in such a way as to create a new reality. Here, the pen-stroke follows a few lines of the original structure, adds a few details in other places, and thus creates new links between the individual elements.

The result is a mechanical construction. Numerous screws can be discerned; from a flywheel in the middle, which Baargeld described as "Le curé" (the priest), the energy is transferred with the help of a rod to a further wheel. The neat inscriptions produce in the beholder a first impression that he is looking at the design for a piece of technical apparatus. To this extent it is a typical Dadaist theme, as pursued also by Max Ernst, George Grosz, Francis Picabia and Marcel Duchamp. It was also a gesture directed at the Expressionists, who in 1914 had, with such fateful enthusiasm, allowed themselves to be drawn into the alleged "communal experience" of the war.

The Red King, 1920
Pen and Indian ink on wallpaper,
49.2 x 38.7 cm (19¼ x 15¼ in.)
New York, The Museum of Modern Art

Johannes Theodor Baargeld
Venus at the Game of the Kings, 1920

Max Ernst in later years recalled Johannes Theodor Baargeld – who as so often was creating a certain alienation by talking of himself in the third person – as saying: "When Max met him, they were both dada-ready, still numbed by the howl of war and sickened by its causes. Baargeld had a clear head and an ice-cold intellect, a fiery heart full of curiosity, impatience and lust for life. A solid education (Oxford), all-round knowledge. Outraged at the status quo, the root of all evil, enthusiastic for what is appearing, the source of all joys. Thus twofold action: political (although he is doubtless aware of the madness of such an enterprise) and poetical, in the only way possible at the time, namely desperate affirmation of life in work and behaviour."

Poetic qualities are evident above all in his artistic works; here he was in no way a provocative activist against the conservative bourgeoisie from which he came. After the politically combative *Ventilator* was banned in March 1919, the movement's subsequent publications were marked very much more by Dadaist irony, nonsense and playfulness.

His 1920 collages are larded with erotic allusions. In the picture *Vulgar misrepresentation: Cubic transvestite comes to an alleged parting of the ways (Ordinäre Klitterung: Kubischer Transvestit vor einem vermeintlichen Scheideweg)* (whereby the German expression *Scheideweg* "parting of the ways" or "crossroads" could also be interpreted as "vaginal path") he places two of the cubic bodies in front of the seated figure in such a way that they form a monstrous phallus. The same is true of *Venus at the Game of the Kings (Venus beim Spiel der Könige)* which dates from the same year. In this work, Johannes Theodor Baargeld has taken various pictorial sources and put them together in such a way as to derive three altogether peculiar bodies. The centre of the picture is taken up by a black rectangle with amorphous white shapes in which various kinds of fruit are arranged. Baargeld has taken a picture of a much bemedalled officer, cut it apart in the face and stuck it over, and under, the black area. Next to it is the head of a young woman. The amorphous shapes adjoin the three figures exactly, producing the impression that these bodies are growing directly from the heads. Baargeld has in addition emphasized the fruits with Indian ink and placed them in the white shapes in such a way as to make them look like female genitalia. He had already carried out this kind of re-interpretation by cutting out or retouching in his work *The Red King*; later Max Ernst in particular raised the technique to the status of the design principle for his Surrealist works.

The *Venus at the Game of the Kings* attempts to cover her pudenda. The man by contrast, and this impression veritably forces itself on the beholder, seems to have nothing in his head apart from the distorted image of a naked female body. The depiction of the officer and the allusion in the title to war ("the game of kings") cryptically formulate a theme which was to be of central importance for art in the young Weimar Republic. In many artistic depictions, violence and sexuality became the symbol of a society that had lost all inhibitions, a society seeking to repress the early warning signs of the next catastrophe.

Following the scandal-laden exhibition at the Winter tavern in Cologne, Johannes Theodor Baargeld gradually withdrew from the Dadaist movement. As early as autumn 1920 he resumed his law studies at Cologne University, and by the time he came to write a short *curriculum vitae* in 1923, he was denying any association with the Dada movement, listing the years in question as devoted to "private study".

Venus at the Game of the Kings, 1920
Collage, 37 x 27.5 cm (14½ x 11 in.)
Zurich, Kunsthaus Zürich

Marcel Duchamp
Fountain, 1917/1963

b. 1887 in Blainville
d. 1968 in Neuilly-sur-Seine

"I tell them that the tricks of today are the truths of tomorrow."

— MARCEL DUCHAMP

This work by Marcel Duchamp revolutionized art like almost no other. He was indisputably the most influential artist of the 20th century. Through the invention of the ready-made, Duchamp succeeded in demolishing the dominance of painting over sculpture. Whole generations of young artists, above all in the 1960s and 1980s, would swear by him, basing their own work on his fundamental concept.

Marcel Duchamp studied at the renowned Académie Julian and developed into a highly successful painter. Even so, he always remained sceptical where the potential of painting was concerned. It did not satisfy his demands regarding the objectivity and scientific character of art. Thus, for Duchamp, painting could be "only one means of expression among others", as he himself once put it.

Finally in 1915 Duchamp gave up painting almost entirely. Two years earlier, his first ready-made had already made its appearance. It was a stool on which a bicycle wheel had been mounted. In 1915 Marcel Duchamp left France for New York. Here he entered his most provocative object, to which he had given the quite neutral title *Fountain*, for the annual exhibition of the Society of Independent Artists.

Ready-mades are a new autonomous artistic genre invented by Marcel Duchamp. They are industrially produced utilitarian objects which achieve the status of art merely through the process of selection and presentation. Duchamp did not design these works, but designated objects he had found as works of art by definition. In so doing, he poured a bucket of cold water on the traditional myth of the artist as a creator of genius. He was interested instead in a rupture with conventional public expectations of art, in the limits of what constitutes a work of art, and in their radical extension. All his ready-mades pose a fundamental question: what are the characteristics and conditions that define an object as a work of art? Marcel Duchamp tried to answer this question for himself in as exact terms as possible. *Fountain* is an industrially produced urinal, to which the artist has made three changes in order to raise it to the status of a work of art: 1. he has placed it on a base or plinth; 2. he has signed and dated it; and 3. he has entered it for an exhibition of contemporary art. There was supposed to have been no jury for this exhibition, but the work was rejected nonetheless: this rejection confirmed the aesthetic explosiveness of his concept.

Duchamp's approach assumes that any object whatever can be declared to be art by being equipped with the characteristic attributes of a work of art. In our example, the first of these was the plinth, which treats the urinal as though it were a sculpture, makes it stand out from its surroundings and ennobles it. The inscription "R. Mutt 1917" designates the object as a work of art, because it now has a signature. Marcel Duchamp deliberately did not use his own name, but rather a pseudonym, because for him the signature was an artistic gesture: he was interested in the resulting claim of the object to be a work of art. Finally the object was to be presented to the public at an established art exhibition.

Duchamp recognized that an object is defined first and foremost by its context and is perceived differently in different environments. His pioneering achievement for art was to point to the importance of this context for the evaluation of a work of art.

Fountain, 1917/1963
Porcelain urinal, 33 x 42 x 52 cm
(13 x 16½ x 20½ in.)
Stockholm, Moderna Museet

Marcel Duchamp
L. H. O. O. Q., 1919/1930

The Dadaists recognized their own concept of anti-art in Marcel Duchamp's ready-mades. But unlike the movement in Zurich, Duchamp was not rebelling against art as such. He was not concerned to destroy art or to make it ridiculous. Instead, he wanted to pose new, previously unasked questions about art. For him, the possibilities of traditional painting had been exhausted, while the border regions of art had not been explored.

At the moment when Marcel Duchamp opened up the art business to utilitarian objects such as a bottle-rack or his *Fountain* urinal as ready-mades, the aesthetic standards, judgements and mechanisms of the business came under the spotlight. At the same time, he broke with the romantic creator-myth by demonstrating that *objets trouvés* and mass-produced everyday functional objects could also be raised to the status of works of art simply by definition as such. On the other hand, precisely in so doing, Marcel Duchamp once again confirmed the artist myth, because it was for himself as artist that he claimed this extraordinary ability and authority. For the banal object only became a work of art because it was an artist who said so. Ten years later Kurt Schwitters made the same point even more exclusively: "Everything an artist spits out, is art."

Marcel Duchamp's presentation of everyday objects as works of art provoked New York exhibition-goers, who were accustomed to traditional paintings and sculptures. The art scandal was a typical Dadaist strategy. His disrespectful treatment of one of the icons of painting, Leonardo da Vinci's *Mona Lisa* (c. 1503–1506), also moved Duchamp closer to the European Dada camp. The picture dates from 1919 and consists of a postcard-size colour reproduction of Leonardo's painting on which Duchamp has made some pencil alterations. Thus he has provided her with moustache and goatee beard, and below the picture itself added the mysterious sequence of letters "L. H. O. O. Q.". For Marcel Duchamp, such works also confirm his concept of the ready-made, even when the material – as here – is interpreted by him in the form of tendentious interventions. Duchamp treated the sublime values of art history with the same sort of disrespect as other Dadaists. Thus Kurt Schwitters stuck ironic quotes over a reproduction of the *Sistine Madonna* by Raffael (c. 1513/14) in 1921. The year before, Grosz and Heartfield had mounted the face of Raoul Hausmann onto a photo of the painter Henri Rousseau. And the Cologne Dadaist Johannes Theodor Baargeld likewise put his own head on a picture of the marble bust of a Classical female nude.

Marcel Duchamp was pursuing the same sort of humorous gender-bending as Baargeld by giving his Mona Lisa a beard. In the art literature, this gesture is continually interpreted as a hint by the Dadaists at speculations regarding Leonardo's (homo-)sexuality. Marcel Duchamp's work of this period is indeed full of sexual allusions, both open and concealed. These include the seemingly nonsensical letters "L. H. O. O. Q." If they are read quickly and in French, they produce the phonetic equivalent of the sentence: "Elle a chaud au cul", in other words, literally, "She has a hot arse" or figuratively, "She's a scorcher". A cryptic and at the same time somewhat coarse joke on Duchamp's part at the expense of the woman on Leonardo's untouchable masterpiece.

L. H. O. O. Q., 1919/1930
Pencil on a reproduction of the *Mona Lisa*, 19.7 x 12.4 cm (7¾ x 5 in.)
Private collection

L. H. O. O. Q.

Marcel Duchamp (réplique 1930)

Marcel Duchamp
Marcel Duchamp as Rrose Sélavy,
c. 1920/21

Marcel Duchamp as Rrose Sélavy, 1920
Photograph by Man Ray,
13.8 x 9.9 cm (5½ x 4 in.)
Paris, Musée national d'art moderne,
Centre Pompidou

Like the reproduction of the *Mona Lisa* with its pencil additions, the photograph *Rrose Sélavy*, dating from 1920/21, also plays with gender roles. And once again, the title conceals an erotic word-play. The photograph shows Marcel Duchamp disguised as a woman. In a fashionable hat, elegant fur stole, eyes and lips conspicuously made up, and a ring on his left hand, he presents himself here as a lady from New York's high society. His artist friend Man Ray photographed Duchamp in the role of "Rrose Sélavy" in 1920/21.

Duchamp adopted this female identity on a number of occasions, including another photograph portrait by Man Ray. If we compare the two pictures, the earlier one, dating from 1920, comes across as a still imperfect preliminary draft or sketch for the later. With a hat drawn down over his face, a conspicuous wig and shawl pulled around him, the artist comes across here more as an actor in some amateur costume drama. This pose and the elegant appearance in the 1920/21 photograph are indeed worlds apart.

In Marcel Duchamp's self-portrait as "Rrose Sélavy" there are no longer any clear boundaries between the sexes. The male artist is not only slipping into an alien role, but is adopting a female identity. The name of his female *alter ego* is at the same time a cryptic commentary on his total artistic œuvre, laden with numerous sexual motifs. If we give the name "Rrose Sélavy" its French pronunciation, we can also interpret it as "Eros, c'est la vie" (Eros, that's life). In an interview in 1966, Marcel Duchamp openly admitted: "I believe very strongly in eroticism, because that's really a pretty universal thing the world over, something that people understand."

Duchamp's game with his own sexual identity reflects the uncertainty of an unambiguous position, as we see in many of his artistic works. Above all his ready-mades focus on this sudden change from one context to a very different one, in that they can be either utilitarian objects or works of art. Without themselves changing, they are assessed in different ways, depending on where they are and with what expectations the beholder perceives them. The earlier "Rrose Sélavy" motif was used by Marcel Duchamp in 1921 as a sticker for a perfume bottle he had designed, which he called *Belle Haleine. Eau de Voilette.*

As a company logo, the label bears the inscription "RS, New York – Paris", the Rrose Sélavy monogram. Duchamp packed the glass bottle in an elegant box. With this home-produced ready-made, Marcel Duchamp – presumably unwittingly – was reforging a link with the origins of Dada in Zurich. Alongside the well-known legends surrounding the vehemently defended claims of individual Dadaists to have invented the term Dada, there is one more possible source for the word. Since as early as 1906, the Zurich firm of Bergmann & Co. had been manufacturing a toilet water advertised as strengthening the hair. The name of this miracle product was simple and pithy: DADA.

Marcel Duchamp as Rrose Sélavy, c. 1920/21
Photograph by Man Ray,
21.6 x 17.3 cm (8½ x 6¾ in.)
Philadelphia Museum of Art,
The Samuel S. White 3rd and
Vera White Collection

lovingly
Rrose Sélavy.

alias Marcel Duchamp

Max Ernst
Fruit of Long Experience, 1919

b. 1891 in Brühl
d. 1976 in Paris

*"Art has nothing
to do with taste. Art is
not there to be tasted."*

— MAX ERNST

Fruit of Long Experience, 1919
Relief, wood and wire, painted,
45.7 x 38 cm (18 x 15 in.)
Private collection

As an artist Max Ernst was self-taught. He had studied art history, philosophy and psychology in Bonn. In 1919 Max Ernst, together with Johannes Theodor Baargeld founded the Cologne offshoot of the international Dada movement under the title "Dada Conspiracy of the Rhineland". After the dissolution of the Zurich group, they were joined by Hans Arp. In his "Biographical Notes", Max Ernst reports enthusiastically of his arrival: "Joy in the Dada house. A few days later it spreads like wildfire through holy Cologne: Arp is here! Conspiracy in the Dada house on Kaiser-Wilhelm-Ring, foundation of the W/3 Centre. W for West-stupidities, 3 for the three conspirators: Hans Arp, J. T. Baargeld and M. E." Max Ernst had met Arp back in 1914 at the Feldmann gallery in Cologne.

Fruit of Long Experience (*Frucht einer langen Erfahrung*) dates from 1919. The title is an ironic allusion to the labour of the creative process. The wood relief is reminiscent of Kurt Schwitters' *Merz pictures* of the same period, although Ernst cannot have known of them at the time. In his œuvre, these montages form a small group of objects which were made in the same year. A second construction with the same title carries by way of explanation the inscription "Sculpto-Peinture".

For Max Ernst, then, these works are hybrids between sculptures and paintings. As in the case of Schwitters, the wood assemblage, while it has figurative qualities, can also be regarded as a purely abstract composition. Max Ernst has taken various wooden elements, all of which previously fulfilled some other function, painted them and mounted them on a rear wall. On the left- and right-hand edges of the picture, the vertical wooden elements stand out like buildings. In the centre, there looms a kind of chimney against a pale, yellowish sky. Max Ernst has joined up a number of white dots on this surface with lines, so that they come across as conventional representations of the constellations. At the bottom right plus and minus signs and a rising mesh of wire mark the energy exchange between the two opposite poles. Max Ernst's wood relief, screwed together as it is, represents an anonymous industrial landscape which has been reconstructed in makeshift fashion from the ruins of the war.

As a result of the identical painting, the frame of the wood construction here is more than just a frame for the picture, forming as it does a thematic unit with it. In this way the relief can be recognized as a work which deals with the artistic process itself. The *Fruit of Long Experience* marks for Max Ernst the climax of the centuries-long artistic development of the traditional panel picture, and yet at the same time stands for the fact that it has now at last been outgrown. Ernst ignores the functional associations of his starting materials, and gives the wood fragments in his sculpture-painting a new identity within the depiction.

Although he uses the lofty title to create an ironic aloofness from the wood construction, *Fruit of Long Experience* stands among other things for an artistic paradigm shift. The collage principle, which also characterizes this work, would indeed become the new driving aesthetic design concept which would give a decisive impetus to the art of the 20th century.

Max Ernst
little machine constructed by minimax dadamax in person, c. 1919/20

Together with Hans Arp and Johannes Theodor Baargeld, in 1919 and 1920 Max Ernst published a number of Dadaist magazines, most of them short-lived. All the publications in Cologne were subject to censorship by the occupying British forces, and although the Dadaists here, unlike those in Berlin, were not conducting any explicitly political agitation, they nevertheless had to struggle with the censorship authority, albeit cunningly reacting to its prohibitions by continually founding new journals. After *Der Ventilator* was closed down, the Cologne Dadaists founded the magazines *Bulletin D*, *Die Schammade* and later *Querschnitt*. All these publications were produced at the Max Hertz art printing works. It was here too that Max Ernst found the originals for his collages and frottages. The magazine titles and his own contributions he illustrated for preference with technical drawings he had simply picked up, or else with printed letters assembled into pictures.

In the picture *little machine constructed by minimax dadamax in person (von minimax dadamax selbst konstruiertes maschinchen)*, which dates from 1919/1920, Max Ernst combines various artistic techniques and colour materials, which provide convincing evidence of his creative inventivity. For this, he used existing printing blocks of individual letters which he found in the printing works. He either pressed them against the sheet of paper, or transferred them to the paper on the frottage or brass-rubbing principle: placing the paper over the contoured object, and creating the image by rubbing the paper with a soft pencil.

In the case of the work *little machine constructed by minimax dadamax in person* the bars and letters were combined, and coloured with Indian ink and water-colour, in such a way as to produce in the eye of the beholder the impression of a rickety technical structure. The most striking detail is a protruding phallic tap halfway up the picture, from which a red drop with the greeting "bonjour" is emerging. The surprising function of this construction was revealed by Max Ernst in a detailed description at the bottom edge: "little machine constructed by minimax dadamax in person for fearless pollination of female suckers at the start of the menopause and similar fearless tasks". The artist has signed the work with his Dadaist pseudonym "dadamax ernst".

As already in the *master's bedroom* (ill. p. 27), the choice of title is not without sexual allusions. In this respect, many of his works resemble those of Marcel Duchamp. Even though the two artists did not yet know each other personally in 1920, works such as Duchamp's alienated Mona Lisa *L. H. O. O. Q.* dating from 1919 or *The Large Glass (The Bride Stripped Bare by her Bachelors, Even)*, on which he had worked since as far back as 1915, must have been familiar to Max Ernst.

In 1920 Max Ernst was represented with several works at the "First International Dada Fair" in Berlin. Together with numerous other exhibits, his contributions were due to be exhibited subsequently at the Société Anonyme in New York. Allegedly however the ship with all the works on board sank on the crossing. Whether there is any truth in the story or whether it is merely a Dadaist legend, remains uncertain to this day.

little machine constructed by minimax dadamax in person, c. 1919/20
Pencil and ink frottage, watercolour, and gouache on paper, 49.4 x 31.5 cm (19½ x 12½ in.)
Venice, Peggy Guggenheim Collection – The Solomon R. Guggenheim Foundation, New York

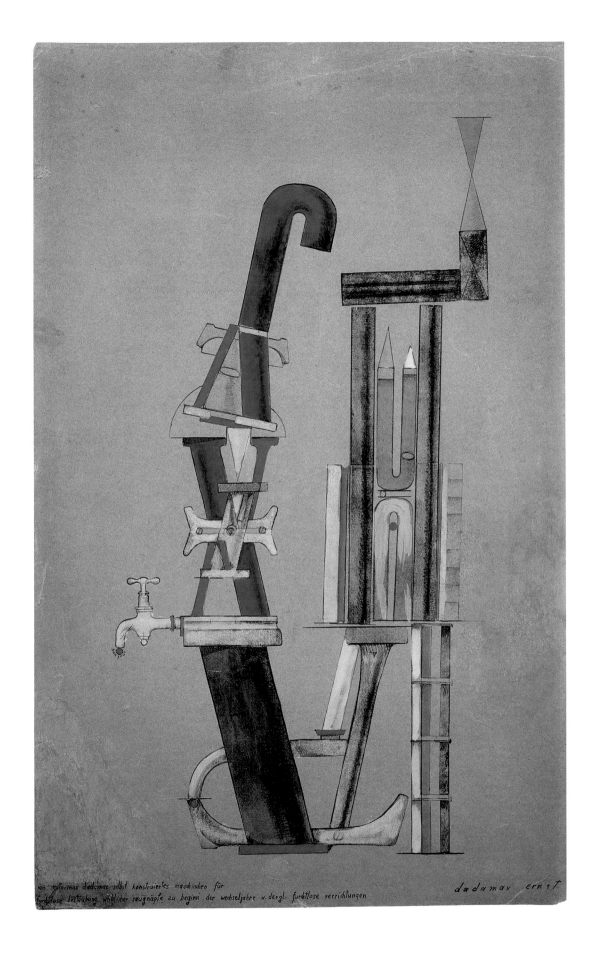

von minimax dadamax selbst konstruiertes maschinchen für
furchtlose bestäubung weiblicher saugnäpfe zu beginn der wechseljahre u. dergl. furchtlose verrichtungen

dadamax ernst

Max Ernst
the chinese nightingale, 1920

In his autobiography, Max Ernst noted under the year 1919 a definition of the collage which differed in major respects from that of the Berlin Dadaists: "Collage technique is the systematic exploitation of the chance or artificially provoked confrontation of two or more mutually alien realities on an obviously inappropriate level – and the poetic spark which jumps across when these realities approach each other." Ernst only wrote this definition some years later, for it places his collage technique very close to Surrealism, which defined itself, on the basis of a text by Lautréamont, as "the chance encounter of an umbrella with a sewing-machine on a dissecting table". Nor would any other Dadaist, let alone one from Berlin, have dared to use a term like "poetic" in order to describe the effect of his photomontages.

1920 and 1921 saw the appearance of a small group of photomontages whose starting material, at least, possessed no such poetic qualities. For these works, Max Ernst used photographic reproductions from popular scientific books on the recently ended war, which were largely concerned with military technology.

Ernst's motif *the chinese nightingale (die chinesische nachtigall)* is based on one such illustration of a bomb. He himself had served in the field artillery throughout the war. "Howling, cursing, puking are no help," he later wrote of his experiences at the front. He therefore could only react with disgust or Dadaist irony to the books that appeared immediately at the end of these terrors praising the technical achievement and progress in weapons technology and air power.

After Max Ernst's treatment of the original, the bomb lying in the grass is hardly any longer recognizable as such, all the more so as he has rotated the depiction through 90°. The attachment for the bomb can thus easily be re-interpreted by the beholder as the beak of a nightingale. It presents itself as a chimera of man and beast with human arms and eye, a fan as decorative head-dress and an elegant white scarf.

Max Ernst is here applying the same principle that was to be characteristic of his later Surrealist works. A hint discovered in the starting material (here it is the attachment, which, when he rotates the picture, protrudes from the object like a beak) is further developed and clarified. Finally, Ernst photographs and enlarges the photomontage. This evens out the different tones of the papers used and the interfaces between the various pictorial sources. The total impression is more homogeneous and the collaged motif gains in photographic realism.

Max Ernst borrowed the title of the work from the fairy tale of the same name by Hans Christian Andersen. The theme of the story is a competition between a mechanical and a real nightingale as to which of them should rescue the life of the king with its song; in Max Ernst's picture, we have a war machine which is deprived of its lethal effect by being transformed into a peaceful "Chinese nightingale".

the chinese nightingale, 1920
Photomontage, 12.2 x 8.8 cm (4¾ x 3½ in.)
Musée de Grenoble

George Grosz
The Guilty One Remains Unknown, 1919

b. 1893 in Berlin
d. 1959 in Berlin

George Grosz was born as Georg Ehrenfried Groß in Berlin. Like John Heartfield, he anglicized his name in 1916 (the characteristic double-s or ß sign in German being technically "sz"), deliberately provoking those around him by speaking the language of the enemy. In 1914 he was one of the few artists who immediately recognized the madness of the war. Grosz had studied at the Kunstakademie in Dresden since 1909, at the same time observing the activities of the local Brücke group and those of the Blauer Reiter in Munich. From 1912, back in Berlin, while adopting the repertoire of forms and the colour dynamics of the Expressionists, he did not use them as the expression of an individual state of mind. This is why his actual medium was the drawing. By increasingly eliminating the expressive gesture from his depictions, and making his drawings more and more impersonal and unemotional, he hoped to arrive at an objectivization of the artistic statement.

The persons who appear in his works therefore never evince portrait-like features, but are only recognizable as representatives of their social class. George Grosz drew both the victims of the war and those who gained from it. He realized that the line between these two groups ran straight through the middle of the German people. On the streets of Berlin those crippled in action, along with beggars and prostitutes would encounter the well-fed middle-class who continued to pursue their pleasures, and the industrialists whose profits the war had only increased. Grosz understood his artistic work as a political struggle designed to arouse the beholder. "I drew and painted in a spirit of contrariness and tried to use my work to convince the world that it was ugly, sick and hypocritical."

George Grosz maintained a somewhat critical distance towards the first Dadaist activities in Berlin in 1918. Together with John Heartfield, he took up a radical political position, which he could not find in the Dadaist programmes that Richard Huelsenbeck had brought with him from Zurich. That he joined the German Communist Party at the same time as he joined the Club Dada, therefore, was doubtless no coincidence, but rather the logical consequence of this attitude. The other Dadaists nicknamed him "Propagandada".

This work, *The Guilty One Remains Unknown (Der Schuldige bleibt unerkannt)*, dates from 1919 and was exhibited at the "First International Dada Fair" held the following year. George Grosz here combines his sharp penstroke with the typical Dada collage elements, fragments of text commenting on the picture. The "guilty" perpetrator mentioned in the title dominates the foreground. A small printed figure is screaming "Treh-teh-teh! The Guilty One Remains Unknown" in his left ear. Grosz caricatures the perpetrator figure by giving him a broad, coarse face portrayed both frontally and in profile. With both hands and a greedy gesture, the "guilty man" grabs all the money he can and seems to be walking over corpses, as the word "Muerte" stuck over his left hand seems to indicate. The word "capitalist" is written obliquely over his almost bald scalp. In the townscape, partly drawn and partly composed of photomontage, we find the names of several international cities: Hamburg, Antwerp, Newcastle. On all sides in the conflict, Grosz believed, there were those who had done well out of the war. In the background of the picture a prostitute strides through the city streets. Her world is marked out by the two words "pimp" and "mission hotel". For Grosz, she is not only a victim of the emergency, but also a perpetrator, wielding power over her clients in her turn.

The Guilty One Remains Unknown, 1919
Pen and Indian ink drawing, collage on cardboard, 53.8 x 35.9 cm (21¼ x 14¼ in.)
The Art Institute of Chicago, Gift of Mr. and Mrs. Stanley M. Freehling

George Grosz

"Daum" Marries Her Pedantic Automaton "George" in May 1920, John Heartfield Is Very Glad of It (Meta-mech. Construction after Prof. R. Hausmann), 1920

George Grosz met the brothers Wieland Herzfelde and John Heartfield (*né* Helmut Herzfelde) in 1915. Grosz' drawings later appeared in the magazines *Neue Jugend* and *Die Pleite*, which were published by Wieland's Malik-Verlag. Grosz was not much interested in the traditional art market, and therefore sought to reach his public by alternative routes. He judged his drawings less by aesthetic criteria than by their political force. The publications of the Malik-Verlag provided him with the ideal platform for escaping from the limited circle of gallery visitors and addressing a broader public with his drawings. In addition he was fascinated by the credence accorded, immediately and without any apparent doubt, not only to the printed word, but also to the printed picture. "It said so in the newspapers, in other words, it must be true. I had respect for what was printed, and as I was printed too, I had respect for myself."

The watercolour with the original English title *"Daum" Marries Her Pedantic Automaton "George" in May 1920, John Heartfield Is Very Glad of It (Meta-mech. Construction after Prof. R. Hausmann)* dates from 1920. The work was put on display under the same title shortly afterwards at the "First International Dada Fair". In the leaflet accompanying the exhibition, Grosz' publisher Wieland Herzfelde described the work in unusual detail. In the introduction he says: "The title is in English, because the work deals with intimate things that not everyone is intended to understand. Grosz is getting married! For him, though, marriage is not just a personal, but primarily a social event." Herzfelde also speaks of marriage as a "concession to society". The work shows Grosz' lover Eva Louise Peter, whom he married that year, as well as the artist himself as an anonymous mechanical puppet. "Daum" is an anagram of "Maud", his pet-name for his wife. In the top left-hand corner of the picture he has added her photograph. Grosz presents the two lovers in totally contrasting fashion: the female figure in realistic style, her genitalia drastically emphasized. The collaged man's hand gropes quite openly at her bared right breast. She casts her gaze seductively at the partner beside her. George Grosz depicts himself as a mechanical figurine, devoid of any human features. Its body consists of mechanical gears which can be set in motion by means of a crank, and whose workings can be monitored by a number of gauges. In his description, Wieland Herzfelde also provided an explanation for the differential depiction of the bridal couple: "The symbol of the maiden is the naked figure covering her pudenda with her hand or the corner of some garment, but in marriage, there is no place for this denial of sexual need; on the contrary, it is emphasized. But it falls like a shadow between man and wife from the first hour of their nuptials: they see that at the very moment the woman can air her body and give free rein to her secret desire, the man turns his attention to other sober, and pedantic tasks. She is taken aback, and only shyly does she touch her husband's head as though it were some dangerous apparatus."

The male figurine points already to the influence of the Italian Pittura metafisica of Giorgio de Chirico and Carlo Carrà. Their *manichini* figures appeared, also for the first time in 1920, as anonymous jointed puppets in the works of Raoul Hausmann. The austerely perspective view of the architecture in the background of Grosz' picture is in addition reminiscent of the deserted Italian townscapes in de Chirico's paintings. For the French Dadaists, the example of Pittura metafisica had opened the way to their Surrealist pictorial worlds. In the case of Grosz and Hausmann, these influences were limited to a brief episode, without any lasting effect on their later artistic work.

"Daum" Marries Her Pedantic Automaton "George" in May 1920, John Heartfield Is Very Glad of It (Meta-mech. Construction after Prof. R. Hausmann), 1920
Watercolour over pen and pencil, Indian ink, collage, 42 x 30.2 cm (16½ x 12 in.)
Berlin, Berlinische Galerie, Landesmuseum für Moderne Kunst, Fotografie und Architektur

Raoul Hausmann
The Art Critic, 1919/20

b. 1886 in Vienna
d. 1971 in Limoges

In 1918 Raoul Hausmann published his manifesto, the "Synthetic Cino of Painting", in which he attacked Expressionism and proposed the use of new materials in art. Dadaism, according to Hausmann, transcended the state-of-the-emotions art of the Expressionists and their "exploitation of so-called echoes of the soul" in painting. Dada, he said, was using an un-hackneyed pictorial vocabulary to provide new artistic impulses, and, he claimed, created a radical reality of expression by its use of fragments of the real world. "The painter paints as the ox bellows: this solemn insolence of bogged-down impostors, with an infusion of profundity, has provided happy hunting-grounds for German art historians in particular. A child's discarded doll or a brightly coloured rag are more necessary expressions than those of some ass who seeks to immortalize himself in oils in finite parlours." Thus did Hausmann give free rein to his rage against established Expressionist painting and the art critics who were promoting it. About a year later, he took up this theme once more in his photomontage *The Art Critic (Der Kunstreporter [Der Kunstkritiker])*, which dates from 1919/20.

In his collage *The Art Critic*, Raoul Hausmann has created the "sitter" from a number of pictorial sources and given the reporter the face of his fellow Dadaist George Grosz. He has stamped the bust of the figure in duplicate with the words "Constructed Portrait George Grosz/1920", but this text has been crossed out. For what Hausmann shows here is not a portrait. Grosz merely appears in the role of the art reporter. The two Dadaists had met in the spring of 1917. Hausmann spontaneously related his first impressions of George Grosz to Hannah Höch: "This is someone who does not wear his heart on his tongue, fabulously ironic, he seems to be just chattering, but makes revealing fools of others. He is calm, confident and knows when to keep quiet. We'll be hearing more of him."

The picture is dominated by the three-quarter-length portrait of the "art reporter", which occupies a central position. He is dressed in an elegant three-piece suit and in his right hand holds an excessively large pencil, which he wields like a sword. His eyes are stuck over with pieces of paper, on which are drawn two casually sketched eyes. As a result, his vision comes across as impaired: the "art reporter" can no longer properly perceive art, the object of his criticism. His judgement is therefore correspondingly impaired. His mouth too is stuck over and replaced with teeth drawn in by Hausmann with a coloured pencil, and a collage tongue. At the back of the figure's head a banknote can be discerned: it has been cut to a sharp point. Someone seems to have shoved it down his collar: as a bribe, perhaps?

The utterances of the art critic are not comprehensible. Like two huge banners they run across the background of the picture. Only individual letters and syllables, devoid of any meaning, can be deciphered. Raoul Hausmann has stuck his portrait of the "art reporter" over one of his phonetic poster-poems. The young woman on the right-hand edge of the picture presents the object of his criticism on a board, on which a schematic male figure in a hat can be made out. As the heading, an extract from Hausmann's visiting-card, suggests, female beauty here stands for the "President of the Sun" and Dadasopher, Raoul Hausmann himself. And even the shadowy figure on the board can be identified. Hausmann has cut its outline from the business section of a daily newspaper, for we can recognize a number of relevant words such as "banks", "liquidation", "discount" and "shareholders". Above all, though, the beholder can read the word-fragment "merz", printed clearly in bold type, cut out from the word "Kommerz" (commerce). This is a clear allusion to his friend, the "Merz" artist from Hanover Kurt Schwitters, whom he is here portraying as the victim of uncomprehending and arrogant art critics.

The Art Critic, 1919/20
Collage, 31.8 x 25.4 cm (12½ x 10 in.)
London, Tate

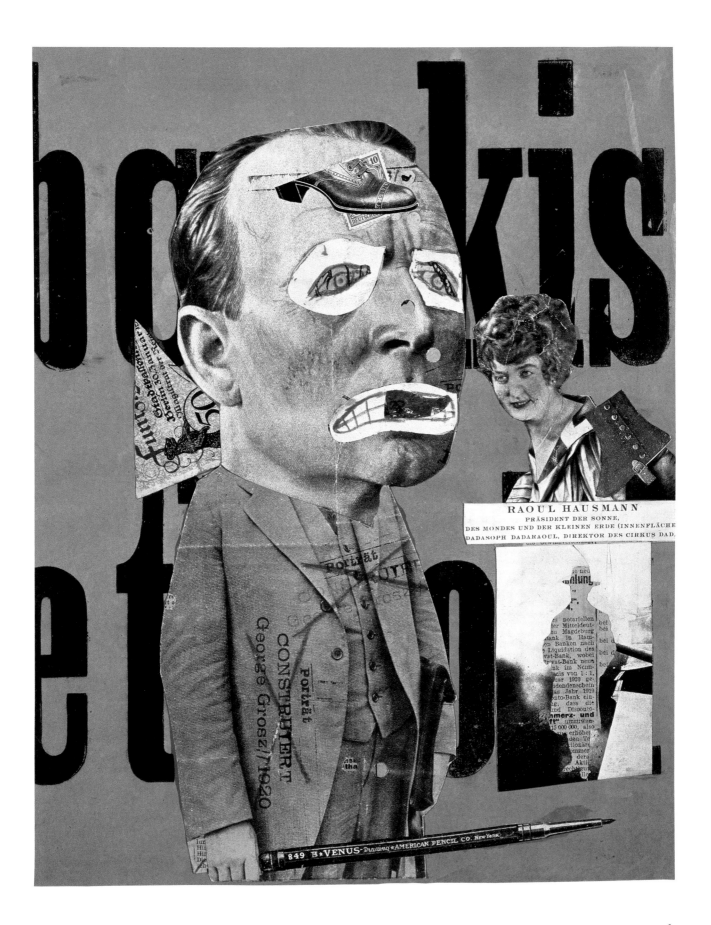

Raoul Hausmann
Tatlin Lives at Home, 1920

"Dada … wants over and over again movement: it sees peace only in dynamism."

— RAOUL HAUSMANN

Raoul Hausmann was fourteen years old in 1900 when he moved with his family from Vienna to Berlin. Taking instruction from his father, an artist, it was here that he made his first attempts at painting. Stylistically, Hausmann took his bearings at first from Expressionism and Futurism. As early as 1905 he is said to have made the acquaintance in Berlin of the older Johannes Baader. Later he made friends with Erich Heckel and joined the circle which centred on Herwarth Walden's gallery Der Sturm. His friendship with the writer Franz Jung and his meeting with the Zurich Dadaists Richard Huelsenbeck and Hans Arp made Hausmann one of the leading figures in the Dadaist movement in Berlin. His visiting-card in 1919 identified him grandiloquently as the "President of the Sun, the Moon, and the little Earth (inner surface), Dadasopher, Dadaraoul, Ringmaster of the Dada Circus". His title of "Dadasopher" was bestowed by fellow-members of the Dada group in Berlin.

As with the name "Dada" itself, whose parentage was claimed by, among others, Hugo Ball, Richard Huelsenbeck and Tristan Tzara, the paternity of the photomontage technique was also disputed. Raoul Hausmann claimed to have discovered it in 1918 while on holiday on the Baltic with Hannah Höch. In a photographer's shop-window they chanced upon pictures in which the faces of the persons photographed had been replaced by different heads.

The photomontage technique was characteristic of Berlin Dada, where it was a further development of Cubist collage, from which it differed primarily by the use of printed text elements and photographic images. The use of the term "montage" was chosen deliberately in order to deprive these works of any "artistic" character. After all, there was no way the Berlin Dadaists wanted to be seen as artists in the traditional sense. By describing themselves as photomonteurs (photo-fitters) instead, they took up a position in the, to them, far more congenial vicinity of the proletarian industrial workers and fitters.

The photomontage *Tatlin Lives at Home (Tatlin lebt zu Hause)* dates from 1920. For years the work, like Hausmann's other important montage *Dada Conquers (Dada siegt)*, was thought to be lost. The two pictures hung side by side at the "First International Dada Fair", held in Dr Otto Burchard's art gallery in Berlin, and can be made out in the background of a photograph showing Raoul Hausmann and Hannah Höch at the exhibition. Another photograph taken at the exhibition shows George Grosz and Richard Huelsenbeck holding up a sign with the words "Art is dead. Long live TATLIN'S new machine art". Hausmann's photomontage *Tatlin Lives at Home* takes up the theme of this exhortation, by presenting a portrait of the Russian Constructivist and having a complicated mechanism of pistons, wheels, gauges, gears and screws growing out of the crown of his skull. Behind Tatlin's head, the beholder can see a wooden stand supporting a kind of vessel in which there is an organic structure. The numeric inscriptions point to a biology textbook as source. The organic and mechanical worlds are the two opposite poles in Hausmann's photomontage.

According to the title, the subject of the picture is Tatlin's home. And indeed, Hausmann has assembled his pictorial fragments in such a way that the result is a closed room with floorboards. On the left-hand wall there hangs a map. In the background to the right our gaze falls upon the hull of a ship with its propeller. The motifs suggest that Tatlin has put his brain on the stand and exchanged it for a piece of machinery. Thus the picture illustrates a Dadaist utopia in which emotional thought is replaced by mechanical thought. Only thus, according to the Dadaists, could a new (machine) art appear, which would stand up for a mechanical, rational and ultimately peaceful world.

Tatlin Lives at Home, 1920
Collage and gouache,
40.9 x 27.9 cm (16 x 11 in.)
Stockholm, Moderna Museet

Raoul Hausmann
Mechanical Head (The Spirit of Our Age), c. 1920

In the many-faceted Dadaist œuvre of Raoul Hausmann, the *Mechanical Head (The Spirit of Our Age)/Mechanischer Kopf (Der Geist unserer Zeit)* occupies a central position. This unique assemblage was created around 1920, though Hausmann had already formulated the theoretical basis of the work two years earlier, when in his "Synthetic Cino of Painting" he demanded: "Dada: this is the perfect, valid malice, alongside exact photography the only justified pictorial form of information and balance in common experience. Anyone who takes his own most personal tendency to the point of release is a Dadaist. In Dada you will recognize your own personal state: wonderful configurations in real material, wire, glass, cardboard, cloth, organic in accordance with your own altogether perfect fragility, your battered state."

With sentences like this, Raoul Hausmann compared Dadaist artworks to photography. He wanted to transfer the latter's characteristics, its unemotional, precise and objective documentation of reality, to his own works, by using materials taken from the immediate surroundings of human beings. As a result, he hoped that the Dadaist works would be superior, in their authenticity and reality, to Expressionist painting in oil on canvas.

Accordingly, the *Mechanical Head* is an assemblage of real *objets trouvés*. First of all we have the wooden head of a dummy that would normally be used by a hairdresser to display wigs. It has been alienated by Hausmann by having various materials attached to it. In the middle of its forehead is a tape measure. Balanced on its crown is a telescopic beaker of the sort issued to German soldiers at the front. Also on the forehead is a sign with the number 22 printed on it. Next to this, fastened to the right temple, is the mechanical movement of a clock. As a substitute for an ear, Hausmann has attached to the head a jewellery box containing a printing roller. On the other side are a wooden ruler and a number of screws, which originally belonged to a camera. Finally, at the back of the head, the artist has nailed an old, worn-out leather purse.

In a text written many years later, in April 1966, Raoul Hausmann recalled the motivation behind this work at the time: "I created my sculpture, the 'Mechanical Head', in 1919, and gave it the alternative title 'The Spirit of the Age', in order to show that human consciousness consists only of insignificant appurtenances stuck to it on the outside. It is actually only like a hairdresser's dummy head with attractively arranged locks of hair." For various reasons, doubt has since been cast on this early date of 1919. As the head was not exhibited at the "First International Dada Fair" held at Dr Otto Burchard's gallery in July 1920, scholars assume that it dates from later than this. Another circumstance which speaks in favour of this hypothesis is its affinity to the art of Italian Pittura metafisica, by which Hausmann was not inspired until the second half of 1920 at the earliest.

According to its creator, this work represents the "spirit of our age", in other words the atmosphere of the immediate post-war years. All the significant attributes of the object have been mounted by Hausmann on the outside of the head. The artist is introducing us to someone who only trusts in what he can measurably experience using objective equipment. In place of being felt expressively, the world is encompassed in precise fashion by means of the ruler, the mechanical clock and the camera. No credence is placed in anything but the printed word. All the information it might need is funnelled into the head through the beaker. By contrast, the head's own eyes remain vacant.

*Mechanical Head
(The Spirit of Our Age)*, c. 1920
Assemblage, 32.5 x 21 x 20 cm
(12¾ x 8¼ x 8 in.)
Paris, Musée national d'art
moderne, Centre Pompidou

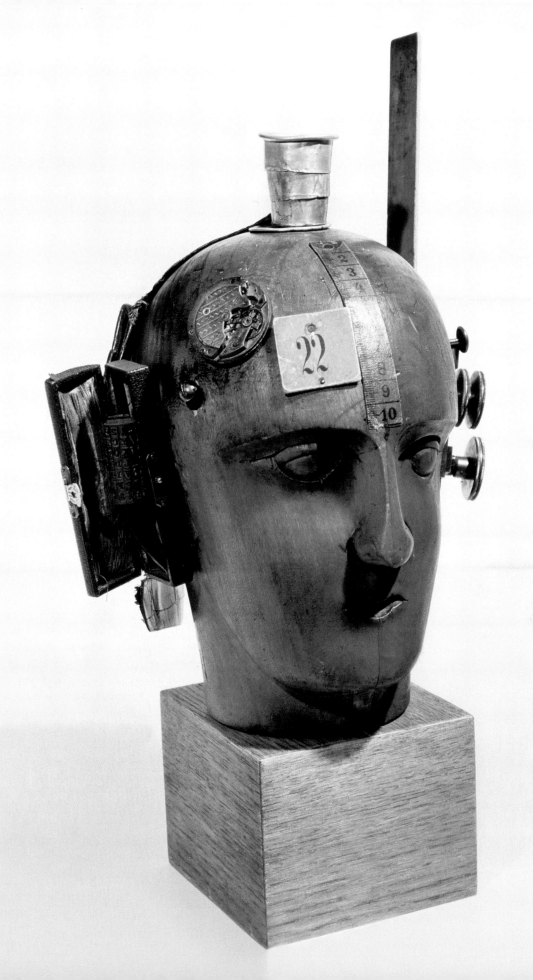

Raoul Hausmann
ABCD, c. 1923

In the middle of the second decade of the 20th century, while Raoul Hausmann was still moving in the circle associated with the Der Sturm gallery in Berlin, he attended a recitation evening given by the poet August Stramm, the power of whose Expressionist language he still remembered with fascination years later. The gallery also gave him an early opportunity to get to know Futurist poetry. The sound poems of the Zurich Dadaists, by contrast, were unknown to him, or at least so he said, when he started making his own experiments in this direction in 1918. In his own sound poems, Hausmann smashed the language up, isolated individual syllables, broke meaningful elements into pieces and re-assembled the scraps in a different order. Language was robbed of its communicative function; the sounds took on a life of their own; they had nothing more to say. The resulting sequences of sounds created for listeners a new, unfamiliar, acoustic experience. In his "opto-phonetic" poster poems, Raoul Hausmann linked this linguistic expression with a pictorial one. By printing the texts of his sound poems on large pieces of wrapping paper, he gave the sounds visual form. These works were designed to overwhelm the beholder-cum-listener visually and acoustically.

One of his best-known poster poems is the two-line *fmsbwtözäupggiv-..?mü*, which he recited at a joint Dada soirée with Kurt Schwitters in Prague in 1921. While returning from their appearance, Schwitters repeated Hausmann's short sequence of sounds, varying it and constantly extending it. In the following ten years, he developed out of it a more than forty-minute-long "Sonata in Elemental Sounds". Hausmann's original line is hardly identifiable in it, but nonetheless, he accused Schwitters of plagiarism. What annoyed Raoul Hausmann all the more, however, was that Schwitters had used his "language-busting" sound-poem on which to compose a traditional sonata in three movements, albeit with the "sound-painting" element retained.

The photomontage *ABCD*, dating from around 1923 differs conspicuously from Raoul Hausmann's earlier collages. Here, he has not designed a uniform, perspective space for his depicted figures to move in. Instead, he presents the picture as a collage of different fragments of reality, different pictorial planes and perspectives. The central motif is a self-portrait of the artist as a photographic representation. Hausmann shows himself with wide-open mouth reciting his sound-poem *ABCD*. The four letters are veritably flung at the beholder. Hausmann's head is surrounded by isolated sequences of letters and figures. Each fragment is typographically different from the others.

The beholder can take in the picture without deriving any coherent sense from it. In one place only, on the right next to the artist, do four letters produce a coherent term, namely "VOCE", the Italian for voice. This foreign word can be seen as a hidden clue to the influence of the Italian Futurists on his sound-poems and his visual works. His friend Kurt Schwitters is also present in the work once more: "Raoul Hausmann as Emotional Margarine" and the word "MERZ" can be discerned on a stuck-on announcement. The description "emotional margarine" is to be understood as an ironic allusion to the art of the Expressionists. The announcement itself refers to the "First Great Merz Matinée" which Kurt Schwitters held jointly with Hausmann at the Tivoli-Theater in Hanover on 30 December 1923. The typography of the announcement was designed by the Russian Constructivist El Lissitzky, who was living in Hanover at the time. In the immediate vicinity of this announcement, Hausmann has stuck a Czech banknote as a souvenir of their appearance in Prague and also as an allusion to the origin of Schwitters' "Elemental Sonata" in Hausmann's *fmsbwtözäupggiv-..?mü*.

ABCD, c. 1923
Collage, 40.4 x 28.2 cm (16 x 11 in.)
Paris, Musée national d'art moderne,
Centre Pompidou

John Heartfield
(in collaboration with George Grosz)
Sunny Land, 1919

b. 1891 in Schmargendorf
d. 1968 in Berlin

"War can only be combatted with the language of war."
— JOHN HEARTFIELD

John Heartfield (*né* Helmut Herzfelde) moved to the capital in 1913, together with his brother Wieland, who was five years younger. Hans Richter later recalled the brothers: "Wieland was as methodical, businesslike, more-brain-than-heart, as John was erratic, unpredictable and emotional." John anglicized his name after meeting George Grosz in 1915. Together they wanted to make a personal gesture against what they regarded as intolerable German jingoism. Thus Helmut Herzfelde became John Heartfield and Georg Groß became George Grosz.

Heartfield first wanted to become a painter. Landscapes were his preferred subject at that time. His meeting with Grosz changed his artistic outlook radically. They formed the "Grosz-Heartfield-Corporation" and together began to work on photomontages. They later quarrelled with Raoul Hausmann about who had first used the technique; Grosz dated their own invention of it to 1916: "In 1916, when Jonny Heartfield and I invented photomontage in my South End studio one May morning at five o'clock, neither of us had any inkling either of its great potential or of the thorny but successful path that this invention was to take." Certainly they took the technique further to its logical conclusion than did Hausmann, for they not only accorded the work itself a greater importance by replacing the painted depiction by a stuck-on fragment of a picture, but also redefined the artistic work process.

John Heartfield appeared exclusively in blue overalls, so that he was given the honorary title of "Monteurdada" (Mechanic-Dada) by his Dada friends. Joint photomontages such as the 1919 *Sunny Land (Sonniges Land)* were signed by Grosz and Heartfield not in handwriting, but with the printed text line "Grosz – Heartfield – mont." added to the collage. "mont." here is an abbreviation of "montiert", which means "fitted", "installed" or "assembled", a formulation which points to the fact that they took industrial production processes as their exemplar. They quite expressly departed from traditional artistic techniques, and claimed that their activity was in character equivalent to the technical and mechanical production process. *Sunny Land* was "assembled" by them in the way that factory workers screwed together components. This photomontage is known today only in the form of a reproduction; the whereabouts of the original, if it still exists, are unknown. This is entirely in the spirit of Heartfield's work-principle: even in his later years, his motifs only attained their valid formulation by being mechanically reproduced.

The title *Sunny Land* is an almost cynical description of the motif. The two authors John Heartfield and George Grosz have created a confrontational dialogue between sentimental picture-postcard motifs and family photographs on the one hand, and contemporary (1919) newspaper cuttings on the other. "U-boat – England's death!", "Away with these workers' soviets!" and "Hunger! Civil War!" are interspersed between images of the Virgin and pictures of Sunday excursions. Against the dark background, the collage elements form only a loose structure. The artists have concentrated not on the total structure, but on individual details of the picture. Thus in the sentence "Nur am Rhein da will ich leben" (Only on the Rhine – there's where I want to live) they playfully change the word "da" (there) to "dadada". Or else they dress up a guardian angel in a top-hat and give him the face of Gustav Stresemann, the future foreign minister and chancellor, and leader of the conservative political party, the Deutsche Volkspartei.

Sunny Land, 1919
Reproduction, original lost
Berlin, Akademie der Künste,
John-Heartfield-Archiv

Grosz-Heartfield mont.   Sonniges Land

John Heartfield
Title Picture Der Dada 3, 1920

R. Sennecke
"First International Dada Fair", 1920
Photograph
Berlin, Berlinische Galerie,
Landesmuseum für Moderne Kunst,
Fotografie und Architektur

At the "First International Dada Fair", held in Berlin in 1920, there hung on the wall of Dr Otto Burchard's art gallery a large poster with the photograph portrait of John Heartfield. He has cupped his hands around his mouth in order to amplify his message, namely: "Dada is great…". The sentence continues: "…and John Heartfield is its Prophet." On the white bar above and below the photograph, beholders were treated to further sayings of the "Monteurdada". "Down with art" and "Down with bourgeois mentality!" A further exhibit at the "Dada Fair", the ceiling sculpture *Prussian Archangel*, created jointly by him and Rudolf Schlichter, actually resulted in his prosecution for "insulting the German army".

Together with his brother Wieland Herzfelde and his friend George Grosz, John Heartfield represented the radical political wing of the Berlin Dadaist group. As Hans Richter put it, they stood "somewhat to the left of left". As early as 1918 Heartfield also joined the German Communist Party. The political nature of Berlin Dadaism was largely due to his initiative.

As a do-it-yourself publisher, Raoul Hausmann had already brought out two issues of the magazine *Der Dada*. The third and final number, however, was published by the Malik-Verlag owned by Wieland Herzfelde, whom the other Dadaists called the "Progress Dada". The issue named its responsible editors as Groszfield, Hearthaus and Georgemann. It was John Heartfield who put together the cover picture. Here too, the collage which he created as a basis for the work was, for him, not an autonomous work of art, but merely the basis for a printed cover. For Heartfield, the valid version consisted only in the mechanically duplicated reproduction of the work on the magazine cover. The stuck-together original was therefore disposed of without a thought once it had fulfilled its purpose. Like many Dadaists, Heartfield was concerned to break with the traditional claims of the artistic "original" and the "aura" of the work of art connected with it. Contemporary forms of artistic expression should, in their view, be geared to modern materials and the latest production techniques. Accordingly, for his collages, Heartfield had recourse to photographic sources and duplicated their motifs using industrial rotation-printing methods, with the result that there was no longer any unique original: in fact, the cheap reproduction was the original. For his Surrealist collage novels after 1929, Max Ernst used the same reproduction technique.

Heartfield's cover montage is less a composition than a powerful combination of overlaid fragments of texts and pictures. There is no ordering principle. The cut-out pieces of paper push into one another and thus formulate a number of obvious commentaries on Berlin Dadaism. The centre of the montage is formed by a large portrait of a screaming Raoul Hausmann, who founded the magazine in 1919. At the top centre there are four individual fragments of text placed close together. If they are read as a single sentence, they produce the statement "Hausmann dada Brüder Baader". "Brüder" means "brothers", and hence the text is an allusion to the close friendship and joint activities of the two Berlin Dadaists Hausmann and Baader. Elsewhere one can identify the word combination "Circus Grosz". Small, but centrally placed, the beholder can see a formulation of one of the central Dada themes: "den Siegeszug über veraltete Anschauungen" (the triumph over obsolete views). In the spirit of a Dadaist panorama, the cover page provides an introduction to the personalities and world of motifs awaiting the reader of the following pages, only sixteen in number, of *Der Dada 3*.

Title Picture ***Der Dada 3***, 1920
Magazine, 23 x 15.7 cm (9 x 6¼ in.)
Berlin, Handschriftenabteilung,
Staatsbibliothek zu Berlin - Preußischer
Kulturbesitz

DER dAdA 3

John Heartfield mont.

Hannah Höch
Da Dandy, 1919

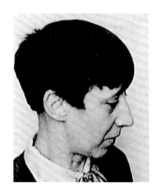

b. 1889 in Gotha
d. 1978 in Berlin

"I wish to blur the firm boundaries which we self-certain people tend to delineate around all we can achieve."

— HANNAH HÖCH

In 1912, Hannah Höch began to study at the Kunstgewerbeschule in Berlin. Later she transferred to the Staatliche Lehranstalt des Kunstgewerbemuseums. In 1915, during this period, she met Raoul Hausmann. Both were at that time associated with the circle centring on Herwarth Walden's gallery Der Sturm. Through Hausmann, she subsequently made the acquaintance of the Berlin Dadaists. Johannes Baader gave her the title "Dadasophess", a friendly allusion to her lover, the "Dadasopher" Raoul Hausmann. The "h" at the end of her first name was added by Kurt Schwitters in 1921, on the grounds that it made her name palindromic, like the Anna in his Merz poem "An Anna Blume".

At the Kunstgewerbeschule Hannah Höch had taken lessons chiefly in interior decorative design; consequently her earliest artistic works included abstract motifs with ornamental forms and repetitive patterns. By contrast, she had difficulty coming to terms with the anarchic actions and political demonstrations of the Dadaists. And while Hausmann constantly sought to give his artistic work some theoretical legitimacy, the Dadasophess for her part evolved a spontaneous, playful and elegant irony in her work.

The photomontage *Da Dandy* was created in 1919, and depicts a complex, many-layered arrangement of pictorial motifs. Like many of Hannah Höch's works, this one too deals with the theme of gender relationships and the role of women in modern society. The artist's day job at the time was as an archivist at the Ullstein publishing house in Berlin, which gave her unrestricted access to all the magazines, including some illustrated periodicals which were already propagating a new, modern feminine image. *Da Dandy* also alludes to her stormy relationship with Hausmann, which is also the subject of other works. The eponymous motif is of course Hausmann himself, whose appearance she was later to describe as follows: "The mere sight of a monocle in those days hurt the feelings of the petty bourgeoisie, who regarded themselves as progressive. But particular outrage ensued when a dandy from the Dadaist group, armed with a monocle, took the rostrum at a communist meeting."

Hannah Höch incorporated the title of her photomontage as a graphic element in the design. The work, however, centres on the silhouette of a head in profile, though at first sight it is difficult to recognize as such, since the artist has hidden it in the manner of children's puzzle pictures. This area is filled out with several motifs of young fashionable women in elegant clothing and extravagant hats. They smile seductively at the beholder. Höch has covered, and thus emphasized, this eye-catching motif with other people's eyes. The "Da Dandy" thus appears here to have his head full of nothing but women. In this sense, the work is key to an understanding of her relationship to Raoul Hausmann, who at the time was living both with his wife Elfriede and with Hannah Höch. As he had no intention of choosing between the two women, there was constant tension between him and Hannah. The work *Da Dandy* is an aloof but ironic reflection of this complicated relationship. The portrait of her lover is merely schematic, and is covered by depictions of the artist's numerous young rivals.

Da Dandy, 1919
Photomontage, 30 x 23 cm
(11¾ x 9 in.)
Private collection

Hannah Höch

Incision with the Dada Kitchen Knife through Germany's Last Weimar Beer-Belly Cultural Epoch, 1920

As the only woman in the Berlin Dada movement, Hannah Höch had no easy time of it. For all the proclamations of her male fellow Dadaists in favour of emancipation, and their political support for equal rights and opportunities for the sexes, as an artist she was not taken seriously by most of the other Dadaists. A telling example of this attitude is the back-handed compliment paid her by Hans Richter in his book of memoirs *Dada Profile*, in which he praises her talent in particular as the "hostess of the Hausmanns' studio evenings", at which she made herself indispensable by "managing somehow, in spite of the lack of money, to conjure up buttered rolls plus beer and coffee". George Grosz and John Heartfield only consented to her participation at the "First International Dada Fair" in 1920 after massive intervention by Raoul Hausmann. Hannah Höch took her revenge for this mistrust on the part of some of the male Dadaists by producing one of the most impressive exhibits on display. In the catalogue, her unusually large collage is entitled *Incision with the Dada Pastry Knife through Germany's Last Beer-Belly Cultural Epoch (Schnitt mit dem Kuchenmesser Dada durch die letzte Bierbauchkulturepoche Deutschlands)*, but the artist herself is listed as Hannchen Höch (a diminutive form). On a photograph which shows her together with Raoul Hausmann at the exhibition, the collage can be seen in the background.

The work is a splendid snapshot of the year 1920. Hannah Höch has interwoven countless details, figures, portraits, mechanical elements, cityscapes and textual exhortations into her collage. It depicts a situation of upheaval, chaos and contradiction. Thanks to the pictorial fragments' being arranged additively rather than compositionally, the work does particular justice to this prevailing atmosphere. Here we see the representatives of the old, toppled order: Kaiser Wilhelm II, who had abdicated, the crown prince, and Field Marshal Hindenburg. They are confronted by the representatives of the new order: Friedrich Ebert, the first president of the Weimar Republic, and Hjalmar Schacht, banker and later on president of the Reichsbank. Between we see sports personalities, actors, dancers and acrobats. Hannah Höch has in most cases taken the bodies of her "sitters" from a variety of pictorial sources. The result is a picture populated by clownlike, in some cases disfigured individuals. At the same time the work is a huge panopticon, in the middle of which some of the Berlin Dadaists can be seen at their anarchic tricks. Johannes Baader, Raoul Hausmann and Hannah Höch herself are not difficult to identify. Well-known Dadaist sayings, cut out by the artist from various publications, comment on the political chaos. At the bottom left-hand edge of the picture we can read the exhortation "Tretet Dada bei!" (Join Dada!), while elsewhere we see slogans such as "Invest your money in Dada!" or "Dada conquers!"

Alongside the personalities familiar from politics, the arts, sport and Dadaism, this collage also shows the image, characteristic of Dada, of a modern machine world. Diesel locomotives, a carriage of the Orient Express, automobiles and turbines, ball-races and gear-wheels are distributed over the entire surface of the picture, combining the individual scenes. At the same time, they set the entire tableau in motion. Among other details, we can recognize New York skyscrapers. With these motifs, Hannah Höch has composed a prophetic picture of a future Berlin, somewhere between a metropolis and a Moloch. The present title of the work, *Incision with the Dada Kitchen Knife [Küchenmesser] through Germany's Last Weimar Beer-Belly Cultural Epoch*, has a double meaning which is more obvious in German, where the word "Schnitt" (incision) can more easily also be related to the scissor cut-out by which the picture was created, as well as to the artist's incisive view: she is applying a surgical scalpel to the political events and upheavals of the time.

Incision with the Dada Kitchen Knife through Germany's Last Weimar Beer-Belly Cultural Epoch, 1920
Collage, 114 x 90 cm (45 x 35½ in.)
Berlin, Staatliche Museen zu Berlin, Nationalgalerie

Hannah Höch
My Domestic Mottoes, 1922

Hannah Höch was a collector. In her hidden-away summerhouse in her garden in the Heiligensee district of Berlin, she assembled numerous documents, materials, and records of Dadaism, arranged them according to a system comprehensible only to her, and thus preserved many ephemeral witnesses to the movement over the decades. After her death in 1978, the Berlinische Galerie acquired the archive and arranged it on more scholarly principles.

This 1922 collage *My Domestic Mottoes (Meine Haussprüche)* is also a collection of Dadaist souvenirs. The Dadasophess Hannah Höch was never a theoretician. She preferred to leave definitions of position to others, first and foremost her lover Raoul Hausmann. The collage also has room, however, for many other of her friends and fellow Dadaists. *My Domestic Mottoes* is Hannah Höch's little ironic self-portrait as reflected in quotations from Kurt Schwitters, Hans Arp and Johannes Baader. The collage comes across as a sort of pin-board, on which the background is formed by various papers with decorative patterns, photographic depictions, scientific illustrations and a detail of a map. The mechanical motif of the ball-race appears here too. And once again she has not so much composed her materials as simply added them one after the other. As already in the *Incision with the Dada Kitchen Knife through Germany's Last Weimar Beer-Belly Cultural Epoch*, the beholder can find her self-portrait here too, hidden between the other elements of the collage.

On top of the papers stuck to the cardboard, Hannah Höch has written some pithy Dadaist slogans and signed them with the names of their authors. "Only an undecided mixture is dangerous" derives from Raoul Hausmann; "Let them say they don't know where the church tower stands" is a quotation from Kurt Schwitters' poem "An Anna Blume". And the insight "Dada polices the police" is due to Richard Huelsenbeck. It is through these slogans, carefully written out in neat handwriting, that the work gets its vitality.

By 1922 the Berlin Dadaist movement had already broken up. Its individual members had begun to go their own ways or to forge new coalitions. One such project in September of that year was the "International Congress for Constructivists and Dadaists", held at the Bauhaus in Weimar. Hannah Höch's personal relationship with Raoul Hausmann also broke up. In her *Domestic Mottoes* she had united all the Dadaists once more: Hans Arp from Zurich, the Hanover Merz artist Kurt Schwitters, and the Berliners Richard Huelsenbeck, Walter Serner and Raoul Hausmann. She herself is looking somewhat shyly from behind a pale grid. The collage preserves those Dadaist mottoes which were to accompany her artistic work in the subsequent decades of her life. Even though in the future Hannah Höch was to devote much more of her time to painting once more, the principle of photomontage and collage continued to characterize her artistic output.

My Domestic Mottoes, 1922
Collage on cardboard,
32 x 41 cm (12½ x 16¼ in.)
Berlin, Berlinische Galerie,
Landesmuseum für Moderne Kunst,
Fotografie und Architektur

Francis Picabia
Love Parade, 1917

b. 1879 in Paris
d. 1953 in Paris

*"DADA talks with you,
it is everything,
it includes everything,
it belongs to all religions,
can be neither victory
nor defeat, it lives in space
and not in time."*

— FRANCIS PICABIA

Francis Picabia was the scion of a prosperous family from Cuba. Financially independent, he was an amateur painter in the true sense of the word, that is to say, he painted out of a love for painting. His second great passion was for fast cars. In 1913 he was the only French artist to be able to afford the expensive trip to New York for the opening of the "Armory Show". He himself was represented at the exhibition with three works. It was in New York in June 1915 that Francis Picabia began to compose the first symbolic machine pictures. The theoretical concept behind these works was formulated by Paul Haviland in the September issue of the magazine *291*, in which he wrote: "We are living in the age of the machine. Man made the machine in his own image. She has limbs which act; lungs which breathe; a heart which beats; a nervous system through which runs electricity. The phonograph is the image of his voice; the camera the image of the eye. The machine is his 'daughter born without a mother.'" That same year, Francis Picabia dedicated one of his machine portraits to the poet in the form of an electric table-lamp, to which he had added the inscription: "La poésie est comme lui."

The format, the complex execution and the use of colour make the *Love Parade (Parade amoureuse)*, which dates from 1917, the central work in this series of machine motifs. As with many other Dadaist works, here too the artist has integrated the title into the picture. This creates a certain distance between the beholder and the work, thus preventing any emotional approach to the motif. The same purpose is fulfilled by the artless execution, which dispenses with any painterly gesture and instead prefers purely objective, technical and anonymous brushwork. The title of the work, however, suggests an erotic motif, which seems, then, to irredeemably contradict the constructivist depiction. For surely a "love parade" has different associations for most beholders. However, and this is true also of this work by Francis Picabia, many Dadaist works have similar subliminal erotic components, which, often articulated precisely in such mechanical depictions, suppress any subjective element.

In this large-format work, Francis Picabia has placed the apparatus of the *Love Parade* in a closed space. On closer inspection, the machine turns out to be composed of two elements, one grey and one coloured, which are connected by rods. The two parts can be identified as the male and female elements in this "love parade". The grey structure consists of two upright cylinders, in which a thin rod, divided at its lower end, moves rhythmically up and down. This construction can be interpreted as the male sexual organ. Its strength and dynamism are transferred via a complicated system of rods with a number of screw-threads to the coloured apparatus on the right. This is the female counterpart to the grey shape. The central element in this machine is the vertical brown piston, which rhythmically penetrates the green (female) vessel. Picabia's machine image is in fact an ironic commentary on and a symbol of the role of the sexes in a modern industrial society.

Love Parade, 1917
Oil on cardboard,
96.5 x 73.7 cm (38 x 29 in.)
Private collection

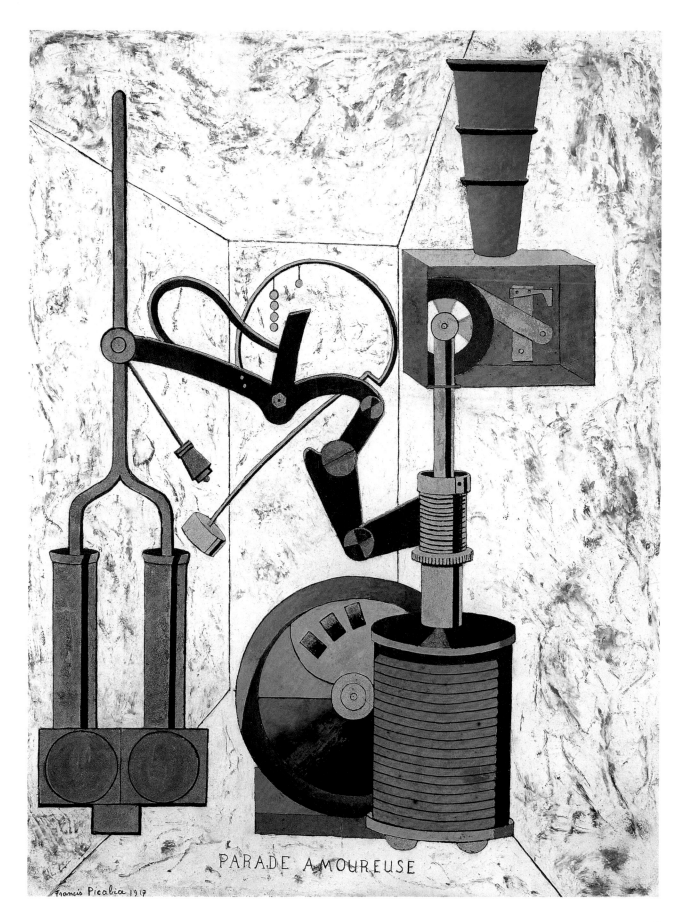

PARADE AMOUREUSE

Francis Picabia 1917

Francis Picabia
Dada Movement, 1919

The "Armory Show" 1913 in New York became a huge *succès de scandale* largely thanks to the presentation of Marcel Duchamp's large-format painting *Nude Descending a Staircase*.

Duchamp and Francis Picabia had been linked by a close artistic friendship since their first meeting in Paris in 1910. It was through Duchamp that Picabia made the acquaintance in 1913 of the New York photographer and gallery owner Alfred Stieglitz. Picabia's art derived decisive impetus during this sojourn. He was fascinated by the achievements of American engineering. He admired the city's architecture and bridges. This fascination, together with his enthusiasm for the latest and increasingly fast automobiles, provided him with the impulse to develop his so-called machine pictures.

One of the first of these was *Here, This Is Stieglitz/Faith and Love,* which dates from 1915, during his second trip to New York. Already on his first trip two years earlier, Stieglitz had devoted an exhibition to him in his Little Gallery of the Photo-Secession. Now Francis Picabia was able to repay him in the form of a portrait, albeit one lacking in any individual features; the sitter is identified only symbolically, by means of a folding camera. Picabia is here adapting the style of technical drawings. His picture evinces the same reduced, precise and anonymous character, without however fulfilling their function as a blueprint for some construction or other.

Francis Picabia's drawing *Dada Movement (Mouvement Dada)* dates from 1919 and shows in schematic form the artistic energy supply for the magazine *391*, represented by the numerals at the bottom right-hand edge of the picture. Picabia had published the first issues in Barcelona in 1917 and continued the magazine later in New York. Its title is an allusion to Stieglitz' own magazine *291*, which in turn took its name from the address of the gallery in New York: 291, Fifth Avenue. In the drawing, two batteries supply power to a machine with a time-switch. To them are assigned the names of artists like Cézanne, Matisse, Braque, Picasso, and Picabia himself, as well as the inscription "Mouvement Dada". Alongside, arranged as though on a clock-face we see among others the names of the Dadaists H. Arp, Stieglitz, Tr. Tzara and M. Duchamp. At a particular point in time, suggests the drawing, the time-switch will release a stream of energy and channel it to the element with the inscription *391*. This latter object is a bell. The magazine "391", in the view of Picabia as expressed in the idea of the "Dada Movement" depicted in this drawing, was to act as an alarm-bell to awaken the people of Paris and New York to Dadaism.

Dada Movement, 1919
Pen and Indian ink on paper,
51.1 x 36.2 cm (20 x 14¼ in.)
New York, The Museum of Modern Art

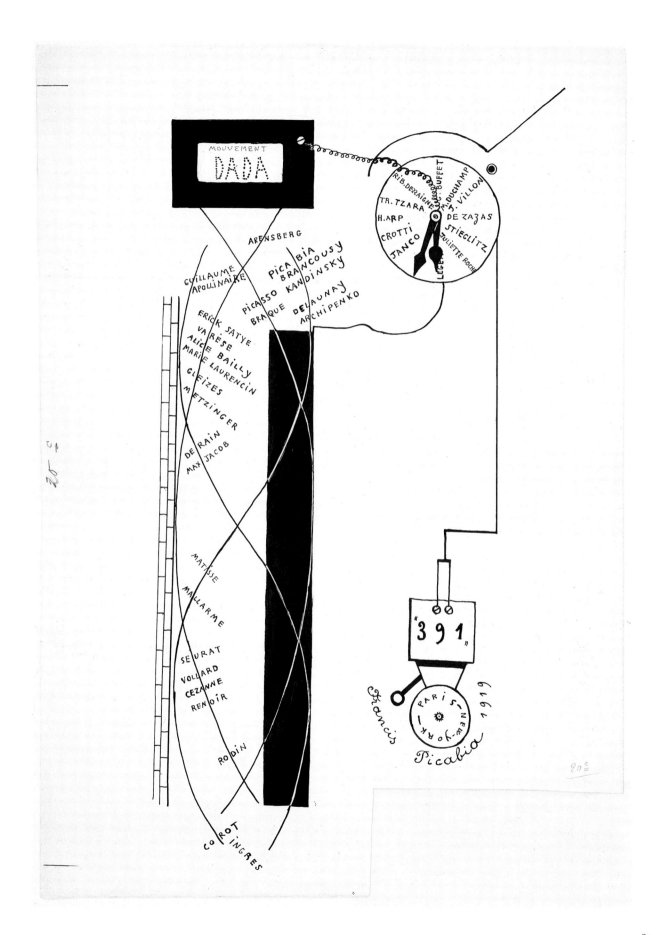

Francis Picabia
Beware: Painting, 1919

Francis Picabia's magazine *391* carried the message of Dada New York across the Atlantic and the front-lines of the belligerent powers all the way to neutral Switzerland. In his literary collection published in 1961, *Dada Profile*, Hans Richter recalled: "With *391* our panorama extended by as many degrees. The magazine of that name was for us in Zurich like a mirror, in which the extent of the transformation in art that we were seeking was reflected. The New Yorkers felt and thought like us, or even more so, as we realized. The new lack of preconditions was therefore general." Alongside this magazine, Francis Picabia's machine pictures made the central contribution to the international Dada movement.

The first examples of these machine pictures appeared as early as 1915, in other words a few months before the actual foundation and naming of the movement in Zurich. And if these works are anti-art, then it was in a quite different sense from that employed by the Zurich and Berlin Dadaists in respect of their own work. Picabia's machine pictures are a statement against traditional painting and derived from a desire to find an aesthetic expression in painting for the modern age of the engineer. The fact that he gave his friendship portraits the outward form of technical drawings seemed in accord with the typically nihilist or satirical attitude of the Dadaists. His works of this period, like those of Man Ray and Marcel Duchamp, are nevertheless proof of the international integrative force which the Dadaist movement, in spite of internal power struggles, was able to unleash.

Beware: Painting (Prenez garde à la peinture) dates from 1919 and is an ironic commentary on traditional established painting. Francis Picabia was setting up an alternative model to the standard idea of the creative process, according to which a work of art materializes by dint of the creative power of its creator. His picture centres on a cylinder shown in cross-section, so that the beholder is permitted to see into its interior. The lower part of the object bears the inscription "Dieu brouillon", as though the apparatus served to produce divine inspiration. On the right, two thin lines connect the cylinder with a circular area, in which there is nothing but the two words "Domino" and "Celeste". On the left, a line runs across a number of wheels back to the cylinder. Each of these little wheels carries an inscription: "Lyrisme", "Folle" and "Biscotte". It is the lyrical and carnival element, even the fragment of rusk, therefore, that according to Francis Picabia constitute the power of artistic inspiration. They drive the piston in whose interior an initial ignition is triggered. The energy released at this moment is transferred to the disk at the right, where painting has a great deal of space to develop.

At the same time, Picabia's title for the picture *Prenez garde à la peinture*, in other words "Beware: Painting", is a warning in respect of this work, and could also be understood as an ironic commentary on the anti-art demands of his Dadaist friends in Zurich. Immediately before the picture was painted, in the winter of 1918/19, he had spent a while in Switzerland, where he had taken part in a Dada exhibition at the Kunsthaus Zürich.

Beware: Painting, 1919
Oil, enamel and gloss-paint on
canvas, 91 x 73 cm (36 x 28¾ in.)
Stockholm, Moderna Museet

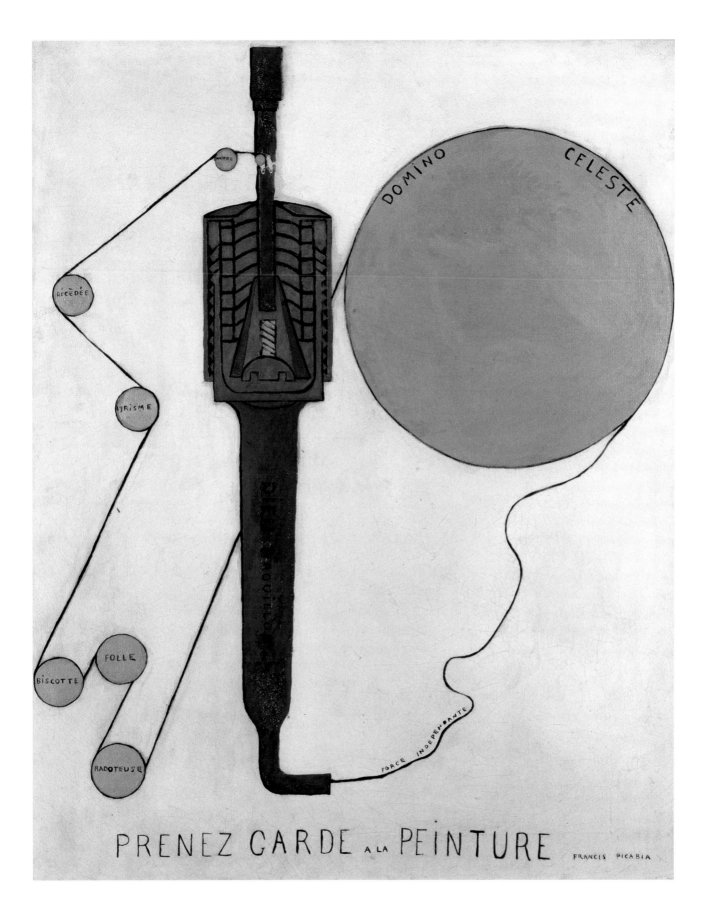

PRENEZ GARDE A LA PEINTURE   FRANCIS PICABIA

Man Ray
Clothes Stand, 1920

b. 1890 in Philadelphia
d. 1976 in Paris

"I photograph the things that I do not wish to paint, the things which already have an existence."

— MAN RAY

Man Ray was born Emmanuel Radnitzky in Philadelphia and grew up in New York. At the age of 24 he assumed his pseudonym. The surname, with its allusion to light, seemed to be a prophetic reference to his future career as a photographer. At this time, however, Man Ray was still devoting himself exclusively to painting. He was a regular guest at Alfred Stieglitz' gallery 291, had visited the "Armory Show" in 1913 and in 1915 had become friends with Marcel Duchamp. Together with the art-collector Katherine S. Dreier, they initiated the Société Anonyme in 1920, New York's first museum of contemporary art. The famous Museum of Modern Art in New York was similarly founded on private initiative, albeit nine years later.

Marcel Duchamp's works were an important source of inspiration for Man Ray. The decisive artistic step came in 1916, when he liberated his art from the traditional form of painting with a paintbrush. With the airbrush, Man Ray adopted a creative technique with which he was able to achieve a more technical and more anonymous expression of his motifs than was possible with traditional painting in oil on canvas. The resulting technique he called "aerography": "I was looking for something quite new, something for which neither easel nor brush nor any of the equipment of a traditional painter was needed."

Man Ray used stencils and applied the paint with a spray-gun. He was fascinated by the mechanical character of the work-process, which left no individual or gestural brush-stroke on the picture surface. In this sense, his interest in the more technical process of photography, which he took up professionally at the latest on his arrival in Paris in 1921, was only logical. In this genre too, Man Ray enjoyed experimentation. He worked with the solarization technique and re-discovered how to create photographs without a camera, by laying various objects direct on light-sensitive paper and exposing them to light. With great self-assurance, he called the results "rayographs".

The *Clothes Stand* of 1920 is an early work, unusual for Man Ray, but perhaps precisely for that reason one of his typical Dadaist works. At first sight it seems to be a collage. In fact he staged the motif and then photographed it. A nude female model is hiding behind a kind of clothes stand, which consists of an open base and a vertical metal rod, to which, cut out of cardboard, the outlines of head, shoulders and arms have been attached. The hair, eyes, and mouth are drawn on the cardboard. Man Ray has left the surroundings entirely black, so that the beholder has no spatial orientation.

As a result there is close fusion between the female body and the doll-like construction. The two unite to form a new being. Similar *manichino*-figures in the Italian Pittura metafisica paintings of Giorgio de Chirico had been models not only for Man Ray, but also for the Dadaists in Berlin and Cologne. The hybrid of human being and machine was a topos in the 1920s when modern was the thing to be and everyone believed in progress, and it was present in one form or another in every artistic genre. It is no coincidence that the artificially created woman in Fritz Lang's 1927 masterpiece *Metropolis* resembles the female figure staged and photographed by Man Ray in 1920.

Clothes Stand, 1920
Photograph of a sculptural
collage, 25 x 16.5 cm (10 x 6½ in.)
Zurich, Kunsthaus Zürich

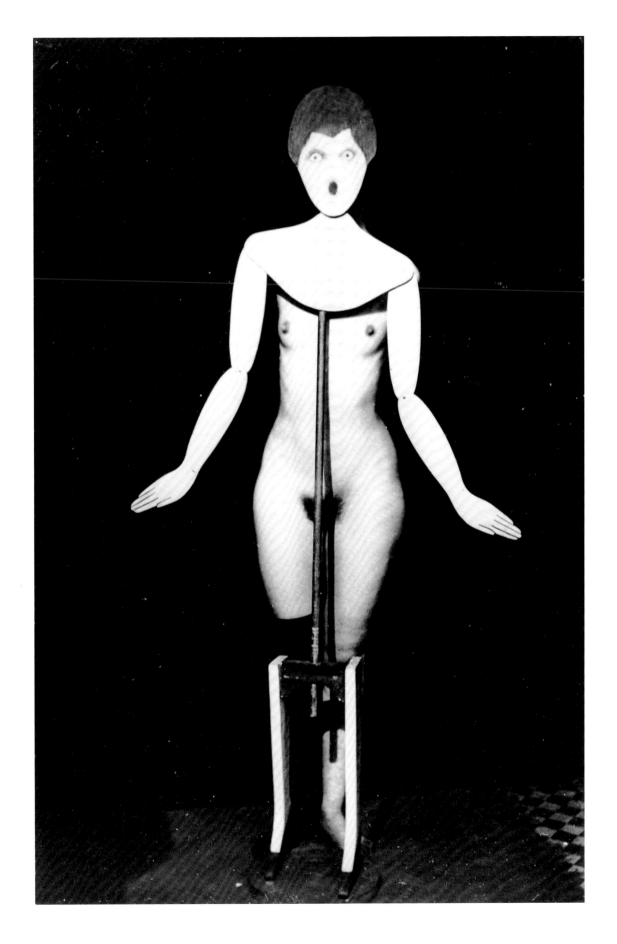

Man Ray
Gift, 1921/1940

Gift (Cadeau) is Man Ray's best-known object. It dates from 1921 and timewise stands on the cusp of his artistic development from New York Dadaism to being one of the central figures in Parisian Surrealism. The work has, however, often been described as an altogether typical object in the spirit of Lautréamont's definition of Surrealism.

For this assemblage, Man Ray took an iron and stuck fourteen copper nails to its underside. Following Lautréamont's description of the chance confrontation of a number of objects from different areas of life in an alien situation, for which he adduced the example of an umbrella and a sewing-machine on a dissecting table, we could here speak of the encounter between flatiron and nails, which must surely appear to the beholder as equally nonsensical, illogical, in fact surreal.

However, what we have here is not the confrontation of two mutually alien objects. Man Ray does not allow the materials to retain their own identity, but uses the combination to create an entirely new object, unknown in this form, a mutation of the familiar and useful flatiron. Precisely because the object loses its practical purpose, we have an irredeemable conflict between the functionality of the object and the failure of its function. It is at this point that the attention of the beholder comes to focus on the ironic and Dadaist potential of the work *Gift*.

Man Ray had already related another object to the poet Lautréamont, whose real name was Isidore Lucien Ducasse. In 1920 he had created *The Enigma of Isidore Ducasse*, a mysterious object which Man Ray had tied up in a thick sackcloth blanket. It was irregular in shape, with a number of bulges, which however did not permit the enclosed object to be identified. In fact Man Ray had packed Lautréamont's famous sewing-machine together with an umbrella and thus alienated both.

The two objects, incidentally, were soon destroyed, and have only survived in the form of Man Ray's own photographs. Later the artist made several replicas of *Gift* and produced a limited edition (1940), albeit of 5,000, an unusually large number (with thirteen nails). This *Gift* however is a deceptive one, disappointing its recipient because it does not fulfil its domestic purpose. The pointed nails would tear the material if ever an attempt was made to use the iron for its usual purpose. In fact however it is worth very much more, because it has a playful value and a value between friends. Marcel Duchamp "defined" Man Ray that same year, 1921, in this spirit as though he were a dictionary entry: "Man Ray, masculine, noun, synonymous with: pleasure in play, enjoyment."

Gift, 1921/1940
Flatiron, nails, 15.3 x 9 x 11.4 cm
(6 x 3½ x 4½ in.)
New York, The Museum of Modern
Art, James Thrall Soby Fund

Kurt Schwitters
The Pig Sneezes to the Heart, 1919

b. 1887 in Hanover
d. 1948 in Ambleside

*"You know exactly as
I do what art is: it is nothing
more than a rhythm. But
if that is so, I shan't
bother myself with imitation
or the soul, but purely and
simply produce rhythms with
whatever takes my fancy:
tramways, oil paints, wooden
block – yes, now you're
gawping like a blockhead!"*

— KURT SCHWITTERS

In 1909, Kurt Schwitters left his native city of Hanover to study at the Königlich Sächsische Akademie der Künste in Dresden. But instead of using the course as a springboard into one of Germany's art centres, say Berlin or Munich, he returned to his provincial home city in 1915. Here in the post-war years he led the life of an avant-garde artist who camouflaged himself as a petty bourgeois. During his student years in Dresden, Schwitters seems to have taken no notice of the local group of Expressionist artists known as Die Brücke. Instead, he tried his hand at academic landscapes and portraits. Throughout his life, Kurt Schwitters never gave up this traditional form of painting, not only for commercial reasons but also seeing them as a necessary counterweight to his abstract collages and assemblages. He was indeed that "Caspar David Friedrich of the Dadaist Revolution" about whom Richard Huelsenbeck got so worked up. Schwitters however succeeded in balancing out all these contradictions in his life and work.

In 1918 Kurt Schwitters began to draw closer to contemporary developments in art. At first Expressionist and Futurist elements started to appear in his works. In 1919 he produced a small group of so-called Dadaist drawings painted over in water-colour. These included this work, *The Pig Sneezes to the Heart (Das Schwein niest zum Herzen)*, whose title takes up the absurd word-games played by the Dadaists. Schwitters was inspired to produce these works by Paul Klee, with whom he had exhibited in January of the same year at Berlin's Der Sturm gallery. On a spatially undefined surface, Kurt Schwitters here combines various motifs which have no logical connexion: a funnel, a hilltop, a pig, a bottle, an old man with a walking-stick, a male profile and a stylized heart. Schwitters once described his artistic technique at the time by saying that he was balancing sense against nonsense.

The individual motifs are items of a repertoire which crop up time and again in other water-colours in this group of works. Schwitters' drawing has been executed in fine pen-strokes and coloured in tender hues. The combination of motifs comes across as all the more absurd in view of this restrained presentation. Between the individual details there is no obvious association; the proportions are seemingly arbitrary. Schwitters uses his motifs as props which he places on the picture in unexpected juxtaposition. In the process, a poetic atmosphere is developed, which we also find in his poems written at this time. For the beholder, these works set in motion an associative process that follows no logical theme. The combinatorial technique works in a similar way to Schwitters' collages, which he developed the same year. And indeed, we see the same motifs once again in these works. Only the absurd title of the work has any justification in the picture itself, for the beholder does indeed see a pig sneezing to a heart. A pencil-drawn arc leads from the pig's right nostril through a funnel and a bottle direct to a red heart.

The Pig Sneezes to the Heart, 1919
Pencil and watercolour on paper,
25.9 x 20.5 cm (10¼ x 8 in.)
Hanover, Sprengel Museum Hannover,
Kurt und Ernst Schwitters Stiftung

Das Schwein niest zum Herzen. 25. Schwitters 1919
Olg. 6

Kurt Schwitters
Untitled (May 191), c. 1919

In November 1918 Kurt Schwitters resigned from his job at the Wülfel ironworks in Hanover. The revolutionary workers' insurrections had by now reached even that provincial city, and for Schwitters, they primed the pump of his new art. "I felt myself to be free and had to shout my joy to the world. On grounds of thrift I took for the purpose only what I found, for we were an impoverished country. One can shout with bits of garbage too, and that's what I did when I glued and nailed them together. I called it MERZ, it was my prayer following the Victorious Outcome of the war, for peace had conquered yet again." That was how Kurt Schwitters assessed the dramatic situation later. In the autumn of 1918 he had just made the acquaintance of Raoul Hausmann, Hannah Höch and Hans Arp in Berlin. It was first and foremost Arp who inducted him in the pictorial technique of collage and it was doubtless for this reason that Kurt Schwitters presumably dedicated to him his first known collage *Drawing A2 Hans (Hansi)* in 1918. Among the materials used was the wrapping paper employed by the Dresden chocolate company Hansi-Schokolade. In other respects too, Schwitters preferred to use found materials for his collages, for example used tickets, advertising leaflets, old bits of cloth and details from newspaper headlines. Since 1919 he called all his collages *Merz drawings,* thereby setting them apart from his larger-format assemblages, the so-called *Merz pictures.*

Untitled (May 191) was probably created in 1919. It is a particularly good example of Schwitters' aesthetic way with his material and of his allusions to current political affairs. For the collage, he has used primarily pieces of paper with fragments of text, along with a few pieces of unprinted paper. The text fragments probably all derive from posters which Schwitters had removed from the advertising columns in the streets, something he liked doing. Unlike some Dadaists, Kurt Schwitters was an artist to the core, and good composition of his works was always important to him. This is true of this work with its rather modest format. The text serves first of all as a constructive element. The black bars and shapes structure the area of the picture. In the lower third they form a powerful base or plinth, while ascending vertically upwards in parallel lines in the middle of the picture.

It is always surprising to observe how Schwitters forever succeeds in fusing the manifold sources of his motifs and the disparate materials into a unity. In the collage *Untitled (May 191)* the individual pieces of paper were still being torn into irregular shapes by hand. Two years later, he came to prefer scissors and clean-cut edges. This was partly a consequence of his drawing closer to the international Constructivist movement. In this 1919 work, the individual snippets of paper are so closely interlocked that the result is a uniform surface in earthy beige and faded red. Only the powerful black printed letters are in hard collision.

Unlike the Dadaists in Berlin, Kurt Schwitters never saw himself as a political artist. But he did not exclude politics from his work. As an acute observer of his age from the perspective of Hanover, a provincial capital, he incorporated the current revolutionary events into his œuvre. These political tensions are visible in the way the scraps of text are juxtaposed. The clearly legible "Mai 191" fixes the events to a precise date. From the remaining identifiable text fragments, a number of key concepts emerge, which describe the revolutionary atmosphere in that May of 1919. We read of strikes of metalworkers, of electricity workers and businessmen, as well as of food, which was rationed in postwar Germany. This, too, distinguishes the Merz artist Kurt Schwitters from the Dadaists in Berlin. He was never an aggressive agitator, but always the silent, but all the more emphatic chronicler of his age.

Untitled (May 191), c. 1919
Collage, 21.6 x 17.3 cm (8½ x 6¾ in.)
Hanover, Sprengel Museum Hannover,
Kurt und Ernst Schwitters Stiftung

Kurt Schwitters

Kurt Schwitters
Merz Picture 29A. Picture with Flywheel, 1920/1940

Since the summer of 1917, Kurt Schwitters had worked for more than a year for the Wülfel ironworks as a technical draughtsman. In the first few years after the end of the war, he produced numerous works in which fragments of machines, wheels and discs occupy a central position in the composition. One of the most important examples of this group of works is the 1920 *Merz Picture 29A. Picture with Flywheel (Merzbild 29A. Bild mit Drehrad)*, which the artist revised slightly twenty years later. Unlike the more modest *Merz drawings,* for which he primarily used snippets of paper, in the *Merz pictures,* as he called his larger-format assemblages, he also employed three-dimensional materials. In *Merz Picture 29A* these include a lid, a piece of cotton-wool, a broken spoked wheel and an iron chain. Two parallel fragments of toothed wheels, extending from the left into the area of the picture, define the composition. All the other elements of the picture are oriented to them.

Unlike those in the *Merz drawings* dating from the same period, the *objets trouvés* used here have been painted over. The coloured setting of the objects often forms larger units and thus composes a number of elements into a single form, as can be seen particularly graphically in the large light triangle in the middle of the picture. The overpainting serves, first and foremost, the purposes of the total composition and stops the work becoming a mere addition of many small objects on a large surface.

Merz art has always allowed observation and interpretation on a number of levels. As early as 1919, Kurt Schwitters realized that it could be taken as purely abstract art, whose materials possess nothing more than their own values in respect of shape and colour. In the programmatic text on *Merz painting*, he says accordingly: "The Merz paintings are abstract works of art. The word Merz means essentially the summarization of all conceivable materials for artistic purposes, and technically the – on principle – equal valuation of the individual materials… In Merz painting the box-lid, the playing-card or the newspaper cutting becomes the surface, the string, the brush-stroke or pencil-stroke becomes the line, the wire-net, the overpainting, or the stuck-on greaseproof paper becomes the varnish, and cotton-wool becomes the softness."

Schwitters not only dissolves his alien materials in abstract shapes, however, but at the same time allows his *objets trouvés* an illustrative function. The *Merz Picture 29A* thus also presents itself to the beholder as the depiction of a monumental factory hall, in which huge cog-wheels and pulleys drive the machines. The quartered rectangular shape, in the top centre of the picture, comes across as the window of a building, graphically illustrating the proportions of the huge machines. However, there is no sign of the enthusiasm for technology which characterized the Italian Futurists. Schwitters' machine-park comes across, if anything, as out-of-date, partly defective, and seems to be producing nothing. It is his ironic response to the mood of the times, whose enthusiasm for modern technology was in stark contradiction to the prevailing political chaos. With a scrap of paper on which is written his address in Hanover, Kurt Schwitters has introduced himself into the composition. Hemmed in by cog-wheels and pulleys, the artist seems to be in the process of being ground between the wheels of a gigantic machine.

In addition, Kurt Schwitters has also given this mechanical construction a political interpretation. Not, it is true, explicitly and openly, but hidden in a clue which he notes on the reverse of the work: "Instructions for use. From the position where the centre points vertically downwards, the wheel must only be turned to the right, until the right-hand spoke is pointing vertically upwards. It is forbidden to turn the wheel to the left. Kurt Schwitters. 5. 8. 1920." Thus his ironic commentary on the political struggles between the conservative parties and the socialists.

Merz Picture 29A.
Picture with Flywheel, 1920/1940
Assemblage, picture: 85.8 x 106.8 cm (33¾ x 42 in.); including the box frame added by Schwitters in 1940: 93 x 113.5 x 17 cm (36½ x 44¾ x 6¾ in.) Hanover, Sprengel Museum Hannover, Kurt und Ernst Schwitters Stiftung

Photo Credits

The publishers would like to express their thanks to the archives, museums, private collections, galleries and photographers for their kind support in the production of this book and for making their pictures available. If not stated otherwise, the reproductions were made from material in the archive of the publishers. In addition to the institutions and collections named in the picture captions, special mention is made here of the following:

© Archiv für Kunst und Geschichte, Berlin: pp. 1, 8, 26 (top), 47, 49, 61, 91
Art Institute of Chicago: p. 59
Berlinische Galerie, Landesmuseum für Moderne Kunst, Fotografie und Architektur: pp. 16, 72
© Blauel/Gnamm - Artothek: p. 28
bpk: pp. 17, 19
bpk | Staatsbibliothek zu Berlin | Ruth Schacht: p. 73
Bridgeman Images: pp. 2, 9, 11, 13, 14, 67

Centre Georges Pompidou – MNAM-CCI, Paris © Photo CNAC/MNAM Dist. RMN: pp. 50, 69
© 2004 Kunsthaus Zürich: pp. 7, 12, 15, 22, 24, 25 (right), 37, 45, 87
Photography © Musée de Grenoble: p. 57
Öffentliche Kunstsammlung Basel. Photo: Martin Bühler: p. 33
© Philadelphia Museum of Art: p. 51
© Photo Scala, Florence/The Museum of Modern Art, New York 2016: pp. 35, 39, 43, 83, 89
Kurt Schwitters Archiv im Sprengel Museum Hannover. Photo: Michael Herling/Aline Gwose: pp. 23 (left and right), 93, 95
© The Solomon R. Guggenheim Foundation, New York: pp. 55
Sprengel Museum Hannover: p. 25 (left)
Stiftung Archiv der Akademie der Künste, Berlin: pp. 71
© Tate, London 2016: p. 63

Imprint

EACH AND EVERY TASCHEN BOOK PLANTS A SEED!
TASCHEN is a carbon neutral publisher. Each year, we offset our annual carbon emissions with carbon credits at the Instituto Terra, a reforestation program in Minas Gerais, Brazil, founded by Lélia and Sebastião Salgado. To find out more about this ecological partnership, please check: www.taschen.com/zerocarbon
Inspiration: unlimited.
Carbon footprint: zero.

To stay informed about TASCHEN and our upcoming titles, please subscribe to our free magazine at www.taschen.com/magazine, follow us on Twitter, Instagram, and Facebook, or e-mail your questions to contact@taschen.com.

© 2016 TASCHEN GmbH
Hohenzollernring 53, D–50672 Köln
www.taschen.com

Original edition: © 2004 TASCHEN GmbH

Design: Birgit Eichwede, Cologne
Editorial coordination: Inka Lohrmann, Cologne
English translation: Michael Scuffil, Leverkusen
Production: Thomas Grell, Cologne

Printed in Slovakia
ISBN 978–3–8365–0562–8

PAGE 1
Max Jacob and Hans Arp
Dada 3 and **Der Zeltweg**
Title page *Dada 3*, 1918, edited by Tristan Tzara and title page *Der Zeltweg*, 1919, edited by Otto Flake, Walter Serner and Tristan Tzara

PAGE 2
George Grosz
A Victim of Society (Remember Uncle August, the Unhappy Inventor), 1919
Oil, pencil and collage on canvas, 49 x 39.5 cm (19¼ x 15½ in.)
Paris, Musée national d'art moderne, Centre Pompidou

PAGE 4
Marcel Duchamp
Bottle Rack (Égouttoir or **Porte-bouteilles** or **Hérisson)**, 1914/1964
Ready-made, galvanised iron, 64,2 cm (25¼ in.)
Numbered edition, catalogue raisonné no. 306